Burn it All Down

ERIN CB

*Dedicated to anyone who is struggling to find
themselves again after a period of darkness.
It's never too late to start again.
Your story is so very important.
Stay.*

Hannah could feel the arms of hundreds of old friends embracing her as she walked in the front door of Stonebridge Books. She relished being among stacks of books she visited time and again. As she stepped through the vestibule and onto the main sales floor, she breathed in deeply the scent of decaying paper and ink. If heaven smelled like anything, she was sure it would be just like this.

Hannah brushed aside a wisp of chestnut brown hair that slipped out of the ponytail at the base of her skull. Her black Converse sneakers sank into the plush royal blue carpeting while her gaze followed foot trails weaving in and out of each aisle. Planks of dark walnut delicately held books of all kinds that had been passed between generations of town bibliophiles. To the left side of the store sat a small cafe with tables lined up in a single row along the wall of windows. The scent of coffee and sweets lingered throughout parts of the store. Pendant lights with dimmed bulbs hung from wooden beams providing a moody atmosphere; it was especially perfect for quiet, rainy days. Some of Hannah's favorite moments were spent sitting cross-legged in the middle of an aisle, engulfed in a new story with rain tapping gently against the glass. On hot, sticky summer days, she found refuge in the iciness of the industrial air conditioners working overtime. Those days were only made better by the presence of Jimmy, her new boyfriend, who loved books nearly as much as she did.

On that day, though, she was not looking to get lost in the pages of a new tale. Instead, she was meeting up with her best friend, Amanda, who was finally home from college for the summer. Hannah had been smiling for days, thinking of all the fun they would get up to in the summer sunshine of the Jersey Shore. They had just finished their first year of college, with only about a week to go until Memorial Day weekend, marking the unofficial start of summer. Amanda attended a private university at the opposite end of the state, while Hannah stayed home and commuted to Safe Harbor University, also known as "SHU" or "shoe" among the locals. The girls had made a long distance friendship work during their senior year of high school when Amanda's family moved away because of her dad's job, but something between them changed with their transition to college. Maybe it was the greater physical distance that created the bigger emotional rift, or maybe it was just the natural evolution of two individuals growing apart.

Regardless of the reason, she felt it on an excruciating level; she missed her best friend, her soul sister. When Hannah broke up with Manny, her boyfriend of one year, she wished she had Amanda's ear to listen as she cursed his name. She wanted to gush about the deep dive into love she took with Jimmy, whom she met through a student newspaper at SHU; it was a love Hannah never thought could be real. When her grandmother died that year, she just wanted to cry on her best friend's shoulder. Instead, she found herself crying alone. Hannah couldn't even find an opportunity to gossip with Amanda about people they knew from Harborvale, or to complain about the endless piles of homework.

She and Amanda had inevitably become more like strangers than best friends that year. Hannah tried to repair the bridge between them, replacing rotted wood planks and crumbling bricks with calls, texts, and instant messages. Amanda seemed to be following behind, tearing out all of her hard work, always meeting Hannah with some version of: "I'm too busy doing [fill in the blank]." Usually, she was in the library studying or heading out to yet another fraternity party.

Hannah did her best to take it all in stride by keeping herself busy with work, her friends from SHU, and Jimmy. In some ways, she felt guilty for having new friends and a new life. Like she was moving on from her best friend. If anyone had bothered to ask, Hannah would have admitted that she felt broken by Amanda's distance. She just didn't understand why she couldn't have both her new life and her old one. Why did it feel like she had to choose?

So when Amanda sent a text message asking to meet at the bookstore, Hannah felt their friendship ignite again. She saw it as a reconciliation of sorts, that Amanda had finally come to her senses and realized how much she missed having her in her life. It was the reunion Hannah had so patiently spent a whole year waiting for, and she could not wait to spend the next few hours catching up. She imagined what it would be like to introduce Amanda to Jimmy, having her two favorite people in the same place at the same time, and spending the summer with them both.

Still standing in front of the entry display table, Hannah looked to her left and was surprised to find Amanda sitting in the cafe with a coffee. She had cut her hair shorter than Hannah could ever remember, with her brown curls falling in line with her chin. She tucked it behind her right ear, showing off the large pearl earrings she had worn. Amanda hadn't noticed her enter the store, or walk right up to her, too caught up in the book she was reading.

With a big smile, Hannah excitedly said, "Hey, Murphy!" They had taken to calling each other by their last names in high school, but Hannah had forgotten why.

Amanda's stunning blue eyes lifted from the pages of her paperback, while her lips formed a tight smile. "Hey, O'Malley," she said flatly.

Hannah pulled the heavy wooden chair out from the table and sat down, talking so quickly that she stumbled over her words. "I'm so happy to see you! I can't tell you how excited I was that you wanted to meet up! So what's going on?" Hannah asked, eager to hear Amanda's stories from school. "Oh, wait! Maybe I should grab a coffee first," she suggested as she moved to get up from the table, but was stopped by Amanda, who put a hand out flat in front of her. Hannah took note of the subtle pink polish on her nails, removing her own hands from the table to hide her uneven nails and jagged cuticles.

Amanda exhaled forcefully through her nose and shook her head, maintaining that tight smile. She bent down to pick up her purse from the floor, placing her book inside its large compartment and pulling an envelope from the smaller pocket at the front. "I didn't come here to chit chat, O'Malley. I just wanted to give you this," she told Hannah as she slid the envelope across the table. Amanda stood, grabbed her coffee, and slung her pocketbook over her shoulder. "It was good to see you."

She brushed past Hannah quickly and marched out the front door of the bookstore without looking back. Hannah sat frozen in her seat, her green eyes wide, and a hand resting on the envelope bearing her name. Through the large window, she watched Amanda cross through the parking lot to the sleek black

Mercedes-Benz her parents had bought for her last Christmas. She hurriedly pulled out of the parking lot, never once hitting the brakes in reconsideration.

Hannah blinked hard as the car drove out of sight. The bookstore, her safe place, went out of focus like she was viewing it through heat waves off hot pavement after a summer thunderstorm. She put a hand to her chest, feeling it tighten, and a churn in her stomach. As she took a deep, steadying breath, Hannah glanced around at the other bookstore patrons, waiting to see them react to the nuclear bomb that had just exploded in the middle of the cafe. Yet everyone just went about their business as if nothing had happened. She stared at the envelope that her hands were cradling, unsure what to do with it for fear of what it contained.

Scraping the chair against the tan tiled floor, Hannah stood from the table and wandered out to her car. After gently placing the envelope on the passenger seat beside her, she drove straight home, ready to dissect its contents. She knew it was best to be alone when she read that letter, sensing something more powerful inside of it, waiting to finally blow her to smithereens.

When she walked into the back door of her home a few minutes later, Hannah was met by her mother, who was making a cup of coffee in the kitchen. With a grumpy look, she told Hannah, "I wasn't expecting you home anytime soon."

"Me either, but Amanda didn't want to hang out. She just handed me this," Hannah held up the envelope, "and left."

Looking from the letter to Hannah, her mother snickered and asked, "Well, what the hell is it?"

Hannah shrugged. "No idea. I haven't opened it yet," she said, swiftly jogging up the stairs to her bedroom in the attic.

Kicking off her sneakers and sitting in the middle of her bedroom floor, Hannah placed the envelope in front of her. She considered calling Jimmy for moral support, but ultimately decided against it. She had a hard enough time letting people in, and their relationship was still so new that she didn't want to burden him with whatever this was.

Trying to find her courage, Hannah took a deep breath and ripped into the envelope's seal. Amanda had written her a letter on a single piece of college-ruled notebook paper. She could tell it had been hastily torn from its spiral binding, with a jagged edge left behind. It was so unlike Amanda, who preferred everything to be so neat and orderly. Hannah unfolded the paper and read:

Dearest Hannah,

Writing this is one of the hardest things I've ever had to do because you've been such an important part of my life all these years. Our memories together, the laughter, the support, and the adventures are all things I will cherish forever. You have been more than a friend to me; you've been like family to me—my soul sister, like we always used to say. It's clear to me now that we aren't that anymore. We haven't been for a long time, and it's imperative that we both come to accept that fact.

As time has passed, I've realized that our paths are diverging. Our friendship has changed in ways that I can't seem to reconcile. I've felt a growing sense of strain in our interactions. It has left my heart battered and bleeding, because I have been trying to hold onto something that no longer fits. I've spent countless nights thinking about this, and I believe it's time for us to part ways so we can find happiness and fulfillment on our own.

I will always wish you the best,

Amanda

Hannah exhaled the breath she had been holding in without even noticing, and fixed her ponytail into a loose bun. Immediately, tears flooded her eyes as her mind turned over the words she had just read. She wiped her cheeks with the back of her hand, rereading the letter several times. She must have misread it or overlooked one crucial word that could turn the whole message around, but she didn't. Amanda had ended their friendship so easily for reasons she didn't fully address in the letter. After seven years as best friends, and a year of trying endlessly to resurrect their friendship, Hannah felt like she deserved more than that. She was owed some real answers.

She felt her anger surge as she picked up her cell phone and navigated to Amanda's name in her contacts list. She was fully prepared to call and talk this through. She couldn't lose her best friend like this. Not with a letter. She would demand an explanation and a second chance to make right whatever wrong she had committed. Hannah's thumb lingered over the "call" button, but she knew Amanda wouldn't answer.

Amanda hadn't answered one of Hannah's calls in the last six months, so why would today be any different? Flipping closed her cell phone; Hannah lobbed it absentmindedly from her hand to the floor. She let out a long sigh and lay down, spreading her arms and legs out like a starfish, letting her bun act as a sort of pillow to comfort her head. She stared at the ceiling above her, tears streaming from the corners of her eyes and into her ears, as she replayed dozens of her favorite memories with Amanda. She walked through each one like the well-worn paths on the carpet at Stonebridge Books, retracing each step to find where their sisterhood had gotten lost.

"Ms. DeLuca?" A quiet voice emerged from the space between her daydream and the present moment. "Um, Ms. DeLuca?"

Hannah shook with a start and cleared her throat. "Yes?"

Lucy crossed her arms and asked, "Were you even listening?"

"Yes, of course I was. I just like to make sure you have a moment to finish your thought before I jump in," she said as sincerely as possible, adjusting the notepad in her lap.

Hannah had gotten lost in her thoughts again, completely tuning out her new client, who had been discussing the universal struggle of making and maintaining friendships in this new chapter of adulthood. Lucy sat across the room from Hannah, her right foot nervously shaking as she fiddled with the ends of her long black hair. Lucy was in her mid-twenties and newly married with a flashy diamond on her left hand. After her wedding, she had seen the ending of several friendships, including one that had spanned nearly her entire lifetime. Hearing her story had caused Hannah to lose herself in the memory of her old friend, Amanda, and how they had lost one another nearly twenty years ago.

Lucy's big brown eyes leered at Hannah suspiciously and said, "Well, I was done with my thought. I guess I'm not sure what else to say."

Hannah glanced at the clock on the wall over Lucy's head, tucking her silver-threaded brown hair behind her right ear. "All right. Well, unfortunately, we are out of time for this week. Before we see each other again, I want you to consider writing down your feelings in a journal, a Word document, or even using the note-taking app on your phone. I know it can feel intimidating, but I find it helpful for many people, including myself, to put their feelings down on paper rather than expressing them aloud. This would be just for you, but you're free to bring it here to share if you'd be comfortable with that."

"I saw someone on TikTok talking about journaling, but it kind of seems childish to me. I had a diary when I was, like, eight. One with a little gold lock and a flimsy key." Lucy giggled at the memory. "I don't know that it's for me."

"Well, it's something to think about. I would encourage it. I've been an avid journaler since I was a kid," Hannah told her, even though it wasn't entirely true. She had kept a journal in her youth and early twenties, but not recently. At one time in her life, an empty notebook had been her only friend. Her one lifeline that kept her heart beating when all she wanted to do was curl up and die.

In some ways, she felt like a fraud because it was what she had built her practice on; she had, for years, given journals and writing assignments to her clients as part of their therapy with her. It was what she was known for, yet Hannah couldn't even recall the last time she picked up a pen and notebook for something other than work. "If a journal feels like too much, you might consider just writing a letter to your friend, Veronica. You can discuss how this has made you feel and share anything with her that you wish you could in real life. Again, it would be just for you. What do you think about that?"

Lucy nodded and gave a non-committal, "I guess."

Hannah got up from her chair with a polite smile and crossed the room to a storage cabinet. When she opened it, she frowned as her eyes fell on the last two journals in her collection. These had once been part of her personal collection of empty journals that lined the shelf above her desk at home, just waiting for her to spill her guts into. "Great. Well, I've got a journal here that you can have," she said, pulling the light pink notebook from the shelf and passing it to Lucy. "I'll walk you back out to the lobby, okay?"

Lucy stood from her chair and walked with Hannah down the long hall that exited into the small foyer of the office building. After promising to see her again next week, she walked back toward the white door with a black and gold plaque on it bearing her name: *Hannah DeLuca, LPC.* Even though she had been married for ten years now, it was still weird not to see her name displayed as Hannah O'Malley anymore.

She shut the door quietly behind her and plopped into the desk chair at her computer, swiveling it around to stare out the ground-floor window. Pulling her chilly hands into the sleeves of her sweater, she let a long breath sputter from her lips.

I can't believe I almost blew it back there. What am I even doing? she asked herself.

Hannah had been an emotional wreck since finding out six months ago that her first love, Jimmy Taylor, had died by suicide. They had dated for about five years while they finished college and started their lives as full-fledged adults. She had even moved twelve hours away from home to be with him in that last year together. While their romance had been a whirlwind fraught with issues, it was one that left a lasting mark on her life; Jimmy would always hold a special place in her heart, unlike other guys she had dated.

The grief still felt overwhelming most days, but it had also opened Hannah's eyes to the fact that she had spent the last several years of her life on autopilot. She often joked that she felt like some sleeper cell agent who had been woken up with the push of a button. Life somehow seemed so much clearer to Hannah. Yet, when she looked in the mirror, it felt like a stranger was staring back at her. There were the same green eyes she had looked into her whole life—the ones with a ring of yellow around the pupil that made them look like miniature sunflowers. Sure, wrinkles were forming in the corners of her eyes and mouth, but it was still the same face. Her once chestnut brown hair was now streaked with gray, not that she'd been bothered to do anything about it, though. Something within her had forced her to look into every dark corner of her life, making her mind spiral out of control. More often than not, she found herself asking, "What happened to me?"

One morning, she woke up with more than just a case of the Sunday Scaries. This deep dread over her current life and career situation felt like a heavy blanket she couldn't shake off her shoulders. She had become nothing more than a servant to paperwork and numbers at the county clinic where she worked, the same one she had interned at during her graduate studies. Hannah couldn't ignore the utter lack of fulfillment she felt in her job, and how vastly different that was from when she first started working there, with a head full of ambition and a heart ready to change the world.

The hours had only become longer, and each new case she took was more demanding and complex than the last. She found herself having to collaborate with the judicial system over divorce settlements, custody battles, and increasingly more substance abuse cases. Hannah had always tried to avoid bringing her work home, but it was hard not to when she always had paperwork for lawyers and the courts to complete, usually on a last-minute basis. Some nights, she stayed in the office late into the night, but on other occasions, she brought it home to be in the comfort of her office there and a cozy pair of pajamas.

As if learning of Jimmy's fate hadn't been devastating enough, just a few short weeks later, Hannah's father unexpectedly passed away. The pain of her losses had become so immense, and Hannah had not been an effective therapist, wife, or friend since. She was surprised that none of her clients had asked to see someone new.

When she quit her job at the clinic, Hannah was set on starting her a private therapy practice. She had left the clinic more or less on a whim and didn't have a plan on how she would build a therapy practice. It had also been a good excuse to take some time away from the hefty responsibilities of the job. So she thought. Hannah spent countless days trying to figure out a budget for rent on an office and then actually finding a suitable office space. Her eyes were often sore from staring at a computer screen and filling out forms for various licensing boards and state offices. All of it had done nothing to lessen her stress levels or dull the tremendous aching in her heart, but she eventually found a therapist for herself and began trying to untangle everything that held her in a chokehold.

The losses only served to remind Hannah how alone she felt. There was no one she had to talk to anymore about the things that weighed heavily on her. She did try to bring up these feelings to her friends and old coworkers, though, but they would only joke that she was simply having a midlife crisis. When Hannah tried to explain that it was so much more than that, they would laugh it off some more and tell her to just "relax." Oh, how she loathed that word.

That loneliness consumed her now as she watched the last leaves on the small oak tree outside her office window dance in the November breeze. She wondered when the feeling had settled into her bones, thinking it must have slipped in so quietly that day at the bookstore with Amanda; watching her walk out the door that day had been the first real heartbreak Hannah had ever experienced. Not even the ending of her relationship with Manny (the cheating, lies, and accusations) had been enough to break her the way Amanda did. There was something about childhood best friends that made them something more like the love of your life, and their leaving always felt so unusually cruel.

She had found a genuine connection in an online community of female therapists who specialized in art and expressive writing therapy. Hannah gleaned so many prompts and ideas for her clients to use in their sessions and at home on their own time. Without a place to go every day, Hannah found herself yearning for a sisterhood more than she had before, and she found it in that group of women from all over the world. She loved their bi-monthly meetings on Zoom and the active chat forums. They didn't just talk about work, though. They made space for each other to talk about their personal lives, and Hannah felt compelled to open up about her life; it was the most honest she had probably been in years. It was easy to do when they were all, essentially, strangers to each other. There, she found a place to talk about Jimmy, her dad, and the grief that followed her through every day. They had championed her decision to leave her dead-end job and cheered her on as she checked off each step of the plan to open her practice. It felt good to have that.

There was one person in the group, Willow, with whom she had initially formed a strong bond. She also lived in the United States, but was thousands of miles from Hannah, who was located in Bay Point, New Jersey. Willow encouraged Hannah to talk more about Jimmy, their relationship, and her grief. At first, it felt comforting to have that outlet, but it became apparent rather quickly that Willow didn't quite understand her grief either when she'd asked Hannah why she felt so heartbroken with all the years between them and how he had treated her. That if he had really loved her, he would've never left her like he did. That he would've fought for her, and tried to fix himself to be with her.

That conversation had been enough for Hannah to distance herself from Willow; she knew it would never make a difference, no matter how much she tried to explain and argue. After all, people could only comprehend the situation from the depth of their own experiences; she knew they would never understand their soul-level connection unless they had felt something like that themselves. Hannah also knew the truth: Jimmy had loved her beyond measure. He had fought for her, for both of them, by trying to fix himself for so long. Even if he lost the battle in the end. Even if there was no way to fix him. Not really.

Hannah pivoted back to her computer screen, noticing she still had nearly two hours left of her work day. With no other clients on her schedule, she decided to pack up her belongings and leave early. She couldn't wait to get home and sit down at the kitchen table with her husband, Jake, to bemoan the fact that she felt like the world's worst therapist. Before going home, though, Hannah decided to drive over to Stonebridge Books. She figured there was no time like the present to get herself back into the habit of writing, to start practicing what she preached, and to replenish the stock she kept for her clients.

When she arrived home, Hannah found Jake playing a video game on the couch with a mix of beer and soda bottles strewn on the floor before him. His thick, black hair was a mess, long overdue for a haircut, and he was still wearing the same plaid pajama pants and a long-sleeved shirt with stains down the front that he had worn to bed the night before. He didn't react to the sound of the front door opening, or her shoes on the hardwood floor as she walked into the living room. Diesel pranced around her feet, lifting himself several times on his back legs, his front legs outstretched toward her. His tail wagged wildly, excited for her to be home finally.

Jake merely moved his head to see the television around her as she passed through his line of sight and sauntered into the kitchen. She sighed at the sight of the sink, still full of dishes from the night before, and moved them into the dishwasher with a loud clattering. She looked around both rooms, noting that the house was still as unorganized as it had been when she left for work that morning.

She poked around the corner into the living room and asked Jake, "Hey, did you not clean the house like you promised?"

Without looking away from the game, Jake simply said, "Oh, no. I didn't."

"So, what have you been doing all day?"

"I've been playing this game—just released yesterday," he told her, bobbing his head in time with the robotic music playing through the television.

Hannah rolled her eyes and crossed her arms over her chest, and reminded him, "You promised you would take care of the cleaning for me. It would have taken maybe an hour of your day."

"Hannah, I took the day off to relax. I deserve to have some time just to chill."

"You're right, you do. So do I, though. My days off are always spent on chores and errands while you just sit here and play video games all day," she said with a scowl.

"All three days you have off?" Jake questioned, screwing his face up in disbelief. When she went to work for herself, Hannah decided to work only four days a week to make time for her therapy appointments with Linda and to allow more time to just decompress.

"Yes, Jake!" Hannah shrieked. "How do you think your laundry gets done and folded? *And* put away for you? Or how food gets into your fridge? Or how appointments get scheduled, the yard work gets done, gifts bought and sent, bills paid—should I go on?" Hannah stared at Jake, waiting for him to respond, but his eyes remained fixed on the television screen, his face blank; she knew he had just tuned her out. Frustrated, she stepped into his line of vision. "You could have at least said 'hi' when I walked in the door, you know."

Jake had no choice but to look at her again. "Hi," he said, obviously annoyed. "Do you mind? I think I'm almost at the boss for this level."

"I do mind, actually." Diesel ran for the back door, pawing at it. "When was the last time you let Diesel out, anyway?"

"Uh," he said before pausing for several seconds. "Not sure." She rolled her eyes again and slid open the door to let him into the yard. "Did you even start dinner?" she asked, turning to see that the oven had not been turned on.

"Shit. I'm sorry. I lost track of time," Jake admitted.

"C'mon, Jake," Hannah grumbled. She thought there was still time to throw everything into one pot, and they would just eat a little later than usual. She opened the door to the refrigerator, looking for the roast that should have been defrosting, but it wasn't there. Hannah opened the freezer with a low growl to find it on the top shelf. "You didn't even take it out to defrost!"

Jake sucked in a breath. "Nope. I guess I forgot that, too, like an idiot."

"Fine," she said. "Figure it out yourself, then. I'm just going to heat some canned soup." Hannah let Diesel back inside the house before stomping back through the house to their bedroom so she could change out of her work clothes.

She took a moment for herself, sitting on the edge of their bed, waiting to hear Jake say something. An apology would have been nice, but she would have even accepted some sort of acknowledgment that she had even been talking. The silence echoed in her ears as she sat beside Diesel, her shoulders slumped and her knees bouncing wildly with bitterness.

"At least *you're* happy to see me," she whispered as she stroked his head.

Hannah changed into an oversized hooded sweatshirt and sweatpants, throwing her hair into a messy bun, before stomping back into the kitchen to make dinner for herself. She sat at the kitchen table with a bowl of soup, scrolling Instagram on her cell phone for nearly ten minutes before Jake entered the room. He opened the refrigerator and stared into it for a while, hoping a meal would magically appear before his eyes.

"My day was just peachy, thanks for asking," Hannah said sarcastically.

Jake peered around the refrigerator door, its light illuminating his face. "Huh?"

"You didn't ask how my day was," she repeated.

Jake sighed and looked back at the food in front of him. "How was your day?" he asked with a syrupy smile.

She exhaled a deep breath. "I had a new client today, and I totally zoned out while she was talking. She noticed, too, which was even worse."

Jake chuckled. "She was that boring, huh?"

"No, it was just what she was talking about. She's losing friends left and right and has trouble meeting new people. I related so much to what she was saying that I got lost in my mind for a while."

Jake grunted in reply, pulling leftovers from the fridge before returning for another beer.

Hannah continued. "It just made me think, like—when did my circle get so small, you know?"

He busied himself preparing a plate and putting it into the microwave to reheat. "It's not that bad. I mean, it's not like you don't have *any* friends."

"I have more acquaintances than actual friends," she corrected him. "I don't have anyone to go out with, and who do I have to call when shit hits the fan?"

"Shannon? She's your best friend," Jake suggested.

"I love her. I do, but she's so draining. She turns any conversation into a two-hour monologue about everything going wrong with her," Hannah said.

"Okay, fine. Then, Nicole?"

"Nicole has Teddy now, and she's literally across the country. It's been nearly three months since we had a decent conversation on the phone. The time difference makes it complicated. Besides, everything is always about Teddy. It's all she ever wants to talk about. I know she has a lot going on right now, too, so I don't want to dump all my heavy stuff on her," Hannah explained.

Jake drew his eyebrows together. "What do you have that's so heavy?"

Hannah dropped her spoon into the bowl, which made a

loud clunking noise that startled him. "You're not serious," she said.

"What?" he asked.

"I swear it's like I talk to a brick wall some days," Hannah said with a sigh, placing her head in her hands. "I've only been drowning in grief over here for the last—how many months? My work is suffering. My friendships are suffering. *We're* suffering."

He pulled his plate from the microwave. "Grief? What do you mean?"

Hannah swallowed a spoonful of soup and looked at him disbelievingly. "Jake—really? My dad? Jimmy?"

"Oh, right. Jimmy. I guess I didn't realize you were still upset about that," he said coldly, sitting across from her at the kitchen table. "We're hardly suffering, though."

Hannah snorted, letting a spoonful of soup drain back into the bowl. "You barely even acknowledge my existence in this house, Jake. Never mind *wanting* to hang out with me. You could give two shits about what's happening in my day-to-day life, and you don't seem to care to help me around here."

Jake balled his free hand into a fist. "That's not true," he snapped.

"All of that has literally happened since I got home from work today. Don't tell me that it's not true. It's been my life for *months* now," she screeched.

Jake rolled his eyes and took a couple of swallows of beer. "It has not, Hannah. You're being dramatic."

"It has, too!" she shouted. "Don't you dare sit there and tell me I'm making it all up!"

Quickly standing up from the table, Jake angrily grabbed his plate and beer bottle. "I'm gonna take this into the other room and watch some TV," he said as he left the kitchen.

With her hands raised in question, facing the empty doorway, she loudly asked, "Are you serious right now?"

"Yeah, I am. I don't need to take this from you," he called out. Hannah looked at the empty doorway with her mouth hanging open. She huffed and turned back to her dinner. Blinking back tears, she shoveled another spoonful into her mouth, grimacing at how cold it was becoming.

Her mind churned with memories of this same fight she had with Jake at least once a week for the last several months. He was so distant these days, yet always denied anything was wrong. She could see how the long hours at work were wearing on him, though. Jake had always been a fan of video games, but they had just become a distraction rather than something he actually enjoyed; she often found him in front of the television, completely dissociated from the world around him and the world inside of him. Hannah usually felt like a stranger to most people, but Jake had always been an exception. She could be herself with him, and he had always been so loving and supportive of her. These days, though, they felt like mere acquaintances, or roommates, rather than husband and wife. While he had once been her best friend, these days, Jake was the last person who she would go to for a shoulder to cry on.

Hannah looked down at her phone on the table, wishing there was someone she could call to talk about all of this with. She scrolled through her short list of text messages with friends and former colleagues, but made excuses for why they wouldn't have the time for her. Alan Reed's name appeared below Nicole's, giving her pause. Hannah had met Alan when she was living in Riverside Springs with Jimmy. Alan had been his best friend, and during that time, he had quickly become Hannah's best friend, too. That was true until the night she left unannounced, when her relationship with Jimmy had ended for good. She and

Alan started talking again this past spring after he found Hannah on social media to deliver the news to her that Jimmy had died.

Jimmy. He had always been someone Hannah could talk to about anything, and now she wished she could just pick up the phone to call him, to hear his gravelly voice tell her everything would be okay. She would believe him, too, because that's just who he was; she used to joke that he could sell sand to someone sitting on the beach. What she wouldn't give for one of Jimmy's hugs, too. She used to love how he'd lean his head against hers, as her chin rested so perfectly in the curve of his neck. There wasn't anything romantic in her longing now. Not anymore. Hannah just wanted someone who could understand her, and she knew Jimmy would without question.

Part of her debated calling Alan or texting him, but she felt weird reaching out to talk about her crumbling marriage. He had been happily married to his wife, Phoebe, for a few years, and she doubted he could relate to her marital problems. Alan and Hannah's friendship was as good as brand new, too, and she didn't feel right to burden him with her troubles. She thought about sending him a message to say 'hi', but even dismissed that idea. Despite texting each other regularly, Hannah still felt hesitant about opening herself up to Alan again. Or maybe it was just that their collective past was so heavily tied to Jimmy. Even now, he was still the thing that connected them, even though they had avoided talking about him and the years after Hannah left South Carolina; Alan had said a little too much about Jimmy in those years the first time they reconnected, and it had made Hannah skitter back into her shell.

Hannah stood up from the kitchen table, bringing her dishes to the sink where she left them for Jake to do in the morning. If he thought to, anyway. She headed for her home office, closed the door harder than necessary, and turned on a random soft and slow folk song playlist. Sitting at her desk, Hannah reached for the journal she had bought that afternoon and found a pen in the desk drawer. She wrote the date "11.01.23 to _______"on the inside cover. She left the last half empty, waiting to fill it in until the journal was full with her thoughts.

Hannah's Journal
Wednesday, November 1, 2023

i'm a little rusty at this, putting my thoughts down on paper, but here it goes. i guess i'll backtrack a little to get the history down first...

i feel like my life has been just a giant mess lately. since i found out that jimmy died back in may, really. he actually died at the end of february, but i didn't find out until may. i was on my way to work and stuck in traffic when the thought of him crossed my mind like it did from time to time. that would happen sometimes, at these really random moments, and i used to wonder if he was somehow thinking of me at that exact moment, too. i googled his name and the first thing that appeared was his obituary. suicide. i think of piece of me died in the driver's seat on route 626. if i close my eyes, i can feel the gut punch all over again. i still can't believe he's gone. not that we were in touch or anything. hadn't been for years and years. i still cared for him, though. still wished him well and thought of him fondly. i still loved him, honestly. not in a way that i'm not "over" our relationship, but just in the way that he was such an important influence on my life. he changed me in ways that i'm still discovering. it's the way that what we had mattered so much. that it meant something. i guess that's the beautiful thing about love: it may change and take new shape, but it's always there. it never <u>really</u> dies. i can't help but think of everyone else who loved him, how his absence is surely affecting them if i am left this heartbroken over it.

i do my best to just think about the good memories i have, rather than the end of his life. i try to focus on how goofy he was, always trying to make me smile or laugh. he used to play this game where he'd try to aim a pencil through the loop my hair would make when i wore it in a bun. or how he knew i hated to be bothered by strangers when i was trying to read or study out in public, so he'd sneak up behind me, trying to disguise his voice and start a conversation with me about slugs or something. sometimes i think about the more quiet, tender moments together. all the nights we spent stargazing at the beach, and all the deep conversations we had about life. the things we never told anyone else. it helps to ease the grief and regrets.

one good thing out of all of this, though, is it brought alan back to me. he found me on facebook back in may to let me know about jimmy. he'd apparently been trying like hell to find me in the three months after it happened, but couldn't find a trace of me until then. of course, i had already found out on my own by then. something about that conversation with alan made me feel a little more whole again. i could talk about jimmy with my friends and jake, but they never met him. they didn't know him. talking to alan, though, someone who knew and loved jimmy, felt so good. i needed that and, in some ways, i think he did too. even if he does still talk to our old friends from riverside springs.

alan and i have kept in touch, which is nice. even if it does still feel weird for me. i've been so closed up for so long about my past, and now in walks alan who knows those pieces of my story. it's scary to reconnect with that, having to face it myself and for the potential of other people seeing that part of me. i've worked really hard to curate this palatable version of myself. i feel sort of like a fire pit doused in lighter fluid with alan holding the one match that could burn down that whole image.

life hit me upside the head again when my dad died in june. it all happened so fast. he woke up feeling unwell one morning, and by the afternoon, he was gone. just like that. it fucking kills me that i never got to say goodbye to him. i wasn't able to get there in time and i can't seem to get over it. i just can't seem to find a way to move on. i just wanted to be there to hold his hand while he died. to tell him i loved him. there was so much left unsaid that i wish now i had the chance to say. that's the funny thing, right? we always think we have time when we really don't, and there are no redos. my dad was the stoic type of man who never expressed his love. i always knew there was a soft spot for me in his heart. i could see glimpses of it from time to time, even if i always yearned to be loved out loud. i eventually learned to settle for the scraps.

losing these two men broke something in me. jimmy's death made me face the many sides of myself, and my past, that i had locked up for a long time. it made me rethink everything about my life. losing my dad, though, was like losing a piece of myself, my entire childhood. the more i think about it, i don't need to worry about alan burning anything down because the fire has already been burning. everything is already crumbling to ash amongst the embers. if jimmy's death ignited the fire, my dad's death, was the can of gas that was dumped over top of it.

so basically i've been consumed by grief and anger for the last six months. it's eating me alive. i know it is, but i can't stop it. i wake up every day with this literal pain in my stomach. it's a burning ache. like how an arthritic knee would twinge with the first sign of rain, except that it's always raining it seems. i imagine it like some cavernous pit opened up in me. it's dark and deep, with no beginning and no end. how can you possibly fill something like that? you can't. it has to just exist, and you have to find some way to live with it. somehow, some way. i used to be so good at hiding things, at pretending everything was okay. the thing with this cavernous pit is that it's too big to hide, no matter what i do. most people don't seem to notice, though. if they do, they don't mention it. the only one who has is my best friend, shannon. i just brush off her comments about how i'm not myself or something, and then we move on. not that it takes much for her because realistically, her favorite subject to talk about is herself. her problems, her marriage, her family squabbles. so as long as i can turn the conversation back to her, i'm in the clear. it's been my go-to tactic for a while now.

my anger has thrown me into this existential crisis. or maybe it's more of a spiritual one. not that i was ever one to spend a lot of time thinking about god or the universe or whatever it is. now, though, i think about it a lot. i think about what happens when we die. where we go and all of that. and i think a lot about how unfair life is. it's unfair that jimmy is dead. that someone with so much to give the world had to suffer with a damaged brain. it's unfair that my dad died so young. that i was so young, too, to have to live without him. it's unfair that i didn't get my 'goodbyes' and that we all left so much unsaid. it's unfair that good people have to die young, before their time, and the worst kind of people get to live. not just live, but seemingly thrive.

all of that anger and grief has culminated into a bigger beast - depression. despite knowing all the things i should be doing to help myself, and despite all of my education and experience, i can't seem to manage it. i'm at least going to therapy, but it just doesn't feel like it's enough. not that i have the motivation to work on myself outside of linda's office, though. i wake up, go to work (where i can barely function), come home and do nothing until i put myself to bed. most nights i go to bed so ridiculously early. not necessarily because i'm tired, but just to cry. to lie in the dark alone and just let myself cry in peace. i can't cry in front of jake - he doesn't understand and i don't think he cares to. i cry a lot of the time because i feel so fucking lonely. i cry because i miss my dad. i cry for jimmy, for a lot of reasons. i even find myself talking to jimmy, too, like he is actually there with me. i tell him about everything that's going on in my life, how hurt and broken i feel. if anything, it helps me to just get some of that out of my head. i guess i have this journal for that now, but i think it also helps me still feel connected to him in some way. i find that i miss him most then, in the quiet. when my mind is free to drift off on the soft breeze outside my window. when my heart finally lets its guard down.

one thing that has been making me feel better has been going through some of my old memories. pictures and journals and things. i was motivated after finding out jimmy was gone. like i had this need to <u>prove</u> he existed in this world and in my life. that what we had was real and it meant something. it sounds silly now, but it really has felt more like an escape; my late teens and early twenties just felt like it held so much possibility. i guess most people would say the same. the nostalgia sinks in eventually, though, and then i just feel kind of sad and empty. i realize just how many people have come and gone from my life, and i can't help but relive the hurt. like today - my client was detailing the loss of her own childhood friend and all i could think about was my old best friend, amanda. i mean, i completely spaced out in this vivid memory of the day she walked out of my life forever. like i was really 18 again, sitting in that bookstore. for as much as it feels like an escape, it's also become a distraction to the here and now. which is sometimes nice, but not when your new client is baring their soul to you. sometimes i just think it's a way to leave the door cracked open for the old stuff to come back to me. not the people, necessarily. except maybe just myself. i miss her.

anyway, getting back to jake - things between us haven't been great, either. i know it's largely because of me. i can't imagine it's easy to live with someone who is so completely incapable of feeling any level of happiness. i mean, i break down into tears over everything and nothing all at once. i know it's hard for him to deal with, which is why i don't let myself do it in front of him anymore. jake is a fixer, but he just can't fix me and i can see it slowly eating away at him. work has been hard for him lately, too. he's been trying to get this promotion that never seems like it's going to come. i see that gnawing at him, and it's even affecting his health now; he's been getting these bouts of stomach sickness and heartburn lately. he won't talk to me about any of the stress he is carrying around no matter how hard i push. i wish he'd open up to me, but all he does is get angry and accuse me of trying to be his therapist, or he says that i just wouldn't understand. i listen to people talk all day about things i don't understand, that i've never lived with or experienced. it's what i do.

i think he's getting to point of just being over it.

over me. i don't blame him. i'm over it, but i can't exactly walk away from myself. i've been trying so hard to get through this, to overcome this heaviness. i've been trying to return to normal, to make an effort of connecting with him again on every level possible. some days it works, but other days he feels as far away from me as ever. and then i question what normal even is, and if i ever could get back there. i'm beginning to think more and more that i can't. that _this_ is my new normal. but still i try. i make suggestions of things for us to do, or places for us to go, but he's not really interested most of the time. i think he's just not interested in spending the time with me.

if i can get real and candid here for a minute - it feels like forever since we were even intimate. i miss him in all the ways i possibly could. i just don't know if he feels the same way. if he misses me, i mean. he's barely even tried to kiss or touch me lately. i worry that he no longer finds me attractive, but i don't know if it's me or because of jimmy. jake really struggled with learning more about my relationship with jimmy. i had only come clean about _all_ of it after he died. jake knew about him, of course, and he knew about my time in riverside springs. i just don't think he had a grasp on all that jimmy meant to me, but why would he? i never talked about it, so that's on me. now that he does know, i still don't think he quite understands. or maybe it's that he just doesn't want to. anyway, i just worry that jake looks at me and sees jimmy's hands on my body. like i'm tainted or something.

what's funny is that jake was the one who called jimmy my soulmate. i didn't deny it because, well, i think he was right. he also called himself my soulmate, which i think is equally as true. i know that's confusing. we're always told we have one soulmate in life, but i believe we can have more than one. and that they come in all different forms: lovers, friends, pets. when i met jake, i felt that same stirring in my heart that i felt the day i met jimmy. if i close my eyes tight enough, i can imagine i'm right there again, in classroom 202 in the student center at SHU. i can feel every missing piece fall into place watching jimmy walk so casually and cool into the door, the way the smell of patchouli incense and tobacco made me feel so at home. so i knew that when i met jake and felt all of it all over again, in this new way, that i couldn't possibly walk away from it again.

jake, i think, had a hard time with learning he wasn't my only love, even though he knew i had other relationships before him. i do feel bad about that, but i've never talked to anyone about jimmy. i might mention his name here and there, usually when the fact that i used to live in south carolina comes up in conversation. "oh, yeah, i moved down there to be with my boyfriend at the time, jimmy." that's about it. i guess it just wasn't something i felt was necessary to dive into with him. or anyone else. i just think some people have a hard time wrapping their heads around fate and soulmates, strong connections that go beyond anything we've ever felt with someone before. that's what jimmy and i had, and bonds like that never die. not really. unless you've been there, though, you wouldn't get it. and in today's world, i think it's harder and harder for people to comprehend something like that.

if i'm being honest, i've refrained from talking about him for fear it would drown me, like a tsunami wave or something. i put everything about jimmy into this imaginary box, sealed it tight, and stuffed it down so far for the simple reason of moving on. so i could have the chance to fall in love again. if i didn't hide it all away, i knew i'd always be stuck on jimmy taylor.

November 4, 2023

A few days later, on a quiet Saturday morning, Hannah awoke to a strange sound coming from across the hall. She rolled over toward Jake's side of the bed and put a hand out for him, but all her fingers found were empty sheets. Her eyes shot open as her brain processed that it was retching she was hearing. She got up and cautiously approached the bathroom door, as her own stomach turned at the mere thought of what was happening in there.

She leaned near the door and asked, "Jake? You okay?"

Jake sniffled and coughed. "No," he responded with a hoarse voice.

"Did you get sick?"

"Yeah."

Hannah frowned. "Do you need anything?"

There was a pause. "No, I'm okay. I know this makes you squeamish."

As if on cue, her stomach backflipped. Hesitantly, she asked, "Are you sure?"

"Yeah," Jake told her. "I think it's over, anyway."

A sigh of relief escaped her lips as she lingered in the hallway. The toilet flushed and the sink turned on for a few moments, then squeaked off. When Jake opened the door, she was visibly taken aback by his bloodshot eyes and puffy, red face.

Jake chuckled. "That good, huh?"

"You've looked better," Hannah said with a slight smile. "What happened?"

He wiped a drop of water from the corner of his mouth. "I woke up with all of this acid kicking up, and then I just felt it *all* coming up."

"Heartburn *again*?" Hannah questioned, her concern for him growing. Jake was experiencing stomach acid flare-ups at least a few times a week for the last several months, and it sometimes seemed to come out of nowhere.

Jake nodded. "I didn't even eat anything spicy or greasy, but it was bad this time. It felt hard to breathe, almost."

Hannah's eyes went wide. "That's not good."

"I know. That one was scary," Jake admitted.

She sighed, furrowing her brow in thought. "You should've woken me up. Did you drink last night? Maybe that was it? Were you super stressed yesterday?"

"No, I didn't even have a beer," he told her without addressing his stress levels. Jake groaned and continued, "I have to work today, too. Dammit."

She gently laid a hand on his arm. "Do you have to? Just tell them you can't make it because you're sick."

"I really need to be there," he insisted. "It's a big implementation day today."

Jake busied himself with a shower, then dressed to go into the office. He had been working as a Project Lead for a technology company for the last three years and was elbow-deep in the rollout of new software for a major client. As a result, he often worked late nights and weekends. Hannah wished he would slow down or take some time off, thinking the sickness would subside if the stress did, too. Not that the almost daily fast food, sugary snacks, and beers were helping either, though. Like everything else, Jake denied there was a problem with any of it. The stress was not just from the long hours, though, but from his boss, who seemed to always pick on him. He was by far the hardest-working person in the room, and he was also the most liked. However, she had a way of finding the smallest things to punish him over. Hannah knew that he was working so hard to secure an opportunity to get out from under her, but from her side of things, it looked like he was just spinning his wheels.

Once Jake was gone, she took a deep breath and made herself some coffee. Hannah put it down on the side table next to their bed, then climbed into the attic of their beach bungalow home. She spent the month of May going through some of her old journals from college and beyond, coming across two additional shoeboxes of mementos from her high school days. Today, she felt called to relive some of her memories with Amanda, who had been on her mind since Lucy's session. She gently brushed a thick layer of dust off each lid and peeked inside to find an unorganized mish-mash of photographs.

Hannah brought the boxes into her bedroom and sat in the middle of her bed. Opening the top box, she dumped the photographs into a singular mound. Faces of people she hadn't seen in nearly twenty years stared back at her, and a small smile crept across her face. She picked up a photograph from 2003, specifically a New Year's Eve sleepover hosted at Amanda's house. Hannah was striking a silly pose on the floor, wearing her favorite pajamas with gnomes all over them, a noise maker in her mouth, and a sparkly hat atop her head. She picked up the following photo from the same party, where Amanda and Melissa, their mutual friend, were making funny faces on the couch.

As she dug through the photos, Hannah decided to organize them as best she could and began creating individual piles around her. There were photos from random school days, field trips, various talent shows and theater productions she had assisted with, house parties, Senior Prom, and random summer shenanigans. These photos reminded Hannah of growing up in the small town of Harborvale and how out of place she felt among a large group of school acquaintances. They were all merely memories now, and everything suddenly felt so temporary and fleeting.

She tried to remember the first time she had met Amanda, or when their friendship had blossomed, but she couldn't recall the memory. She was sure it had been during their middle school years, recalling an English class where they sat at the same pod of desks. Although they had both grown up in the same town, Amanda lived on the wealthier side of town, which meant she attended a different elementary school than Hannah did. Their friendship blossomed quickly, as the two bonded over a deep connection they found in the books required for class. It was the first time Hannah felt like one of her peers saw inside her heart; it was scary, but exciting to be that vulnerable. Amanda drew her away from the clique of friends who had taken her in during gym class and lunch periods. That was fine, though, because those girls were just as bad as this one group of boys who relentlessly bullied Hannah for every little thing; her teeth, her hair, how skinny she was, how tall she was.

Amanda had been a much more polished version of Hannah, wearing all the latest preppy brand-name clothes, with perfectly straight teeth, and her curly hair done just so. Hannah always wore jeans and T-shirts, dirty sneakers, crooked glasses, and metal braces on her teeth. Her hair was always thrown up haphazardly in a messy bun or ponytail. They often joked they had been sisters, separated at birth and raised in two completely different worlds.

Still flipping through photographs, she came across one from the eighth-grade dance that Amanda had somehow convinced her to attend. Hannah softly giggled as she looked at the image of her younger, and much more awkward, self in a black and purple gown she had bought from dELiA*s with her babysitting money. It was a pretty dress, but she could remember feeling so uncomfortable in it. Something in her back then was so afraid to embrace any hint of femininity. Hannah had done her own makeup, which was hardly noticeable behind her big, round glasses; that was probably for the best, since it was her first time really putting on makeup, and it was likely not her finest moment.

The next picture made her cackle loudly, startling Diesel awake, who had curled up on the armchair nearby. There she was, in her gown and kitten heels with a full face of makeup and a curly updo, lining up her shot on the basketball court in the school gymnasium with her guy friends. Another photo showed her, red-faced and sweaty, post-game with her arms around the shoulders of her friend's brother. That same girl would have her first-ever slow dance with that same boy at the end of the night and know what it felt like to be held by another, no matter how awkward they had both been.

Hannah's smile turned into a frown then, as she turned to another photo that Amanda's mom had taken as they were all entering the dance that night. The snap had taken her by surprise, and it wasn't exactly her best angle; Hannah's hands were raised in front of her while her mouth gaped open. Nobody would've looked good in a position like that, but all she could remember about this picture was her mother's reaction. "Oof! Your arms look so… *fat!*" she had exclaimed in shock. Hannah tossed the photograph onto the middle school pile, upside down, not wanting the memory to linger any longer than necessary.

By the time they reached high school, Hannah and Amanda had become inseparable, spending nearly every weekend together. Hannah had even been invited for week-long trips to the Murphys' summer house, which she always looked forward to. They signed up for most of the same classes, often having lunch and gym together as well. Their favorite class was Creative Writing, which Hannah took every year of high school, and twice in her senior year. When it came to after-school activities, they signed up for the same clubs and participated in the same events that those clubs hosted.

Amanda generally made better grades than Hannah, putting her into more advanced classes, but she had also tried much harder. It's not that she didn't care about her grades, but Hannah never felt like studying worked for her; she knew what she knew. She was also just as happy with a 'B' as she was with an 'A,' but the same couldn't be said for her best friend.

Hannah grabbed another stack of photographs that were rubber-banded together. She instantly recognized that they were from a school-sponsored two-week trip throughout five European countries that she and Amanda had taken along with a dozen other students. The trip occurred at the end of their sophomore year in 2003. Hannah smiled widely as she flipped through the pictures; she always regarded that trip as the best experience of her teenage years. That was only because she chose to remember the best parts of it: the fantastic food, the culture, all the trouble they got into (but never got caught doing), the friendship she rekindled, and the connections she made with people she had never met before. The truth was that the trip had been a pivotal point in her friendship with Amanda; they had their first big fight that week, and their friendship never fully recovered from it.

As she flipped through the photographs and scraps of

memories from restaurants, stores, and hotels, Hannah couldn't help but laugh and shake her head. It was so obvious to see the envy that existed between them back then. How Hannah was jealous of Amanda for having this perfect family life, and the means to shop in the expensive stores or be involved in all kinds of extracurricular activities. Amanda, in hindsight, seemed to be equally jealous of Hannah for the ease she had with schoolwork and friends, as well as the freedom to express herself as she wanted through her clothes, music, and art. She could see it so plainly now in those snapshots from their trip where Hannah was in group photos with classmates, their arms around each other while Amanda stood off to the side with an awkward smile. Or how she seemed the most genuinely happen in photos where she was wearing a simple T-shirt and jeans, rather than a proper blouse or a dress with jewelry dripping from her neck and wrists; she looked utterly uncomfortable in clothes like that.

Envy was a poison that took its time to wind its way through their veins until it reached their hearts. Once it reached those pumping chambers, there was no escaping the inevitable death that would take place. It was only a matter of time.

She sighed and put the pictures back into the boxes, having had enough of reliving her first friend breakup for one day.

Hannah's Journal
Sunday, November 5, 2023

today i realized that i've been so stuck in the past lately. it's like the absence of jimmy's life in this world made me question my own existence. as if being so consumed by death has me obsessing about life. i dug out all of my old journals, scrapbooks, and pictures after he died. like i suddenly needed to do this post-mortem of my life, to find out where it all just went so wrong. i needed to feel it all again. the good and the bad. i think it just made me even more sad to face all that i've lost. even myself. if i'm honest, i feel like a shell of who i used to be. i barely recognize myself in the mirror, and so now i avoid them as much as i can. i look at the clothes hanging in my closet and wonder who they belong to. i feel so fake, like i'm wearing someone else's skin or something. i'm finally seeing that now, that i haven't really been <u>me</u> in a really long time. maybe <u>that</u> is the plus side of all of this pain? i'm not sure.

anyway, my newest client (i'll call her L) is having troubles in her social life, and it's bringing my own shit back into focus. i've lost so many friends over the years that i thought would be forever friends. the kind i could see myself having wheelchair races with in the nursing home. i laugh to myself thinking about it, how we'd be drunk on the pitcher of margaritas we downed while hiding out somewhere. we'd be giggling like a bunch of school girls afraid of getting caught, but excited at the prospect of it at the same time. i some how manage to attract clients with all kinds of relationship problems, but this one is really getting to me after just one session. something in my gut is telling me that L won't be the only one learning a thing or two from this therapeutic journey.

i remember jimmy always had this thing about his friends being "found family." he was never close to his actual family. except for his mom, but i think she kept him closer than was healthy. i could relate to his family stuff - feeling like you don't quite belong. i remember thinking the whole idea of being able to choose your family was really beautiful. that here are these people who <u>chose</u> me, that <u>wanted</u> to be that close to me. not because they felt obligated. that idea has driven me in my own quest for true friendship my whole life, but i never seem to pick the right people to call my home. not like jimmy. everyone who met him instantly loved him, while i've always just been tolerated.

now i'm going through some old photo boxes from high school that i found up in the attic when i was going through my SHU and riverside springs stuff. it brought so many memories back up. some good, and some of them i'd rather forget. it's crazy to admit, but i still miss amanda sometimes. it's been 20-something years? or close to? our friendship had been dead for a long time before she passed me that letter across the cafe table and walked out on me. i guess people grow apart, just the natural cycle of life. we change as individuals, and sometimes we just don't change in alignment with the people around us. i can't necessarily be mad about that. can you tell how many times i've rehearsed that? how many times over the years i told myself that in an effort to dumb down the hurt?

in some ways we were good for each other. i remember when we were in high school, we got to talking about some serious topics. both of us were only children, and we made this pact to be there for each other when our parents eventually died because there were no siblings to lean on. there would be no one else who could understand our loss, but we would. we talked about cleaning out their houses together. all of it. when dad died, i wished that she was there. even though i had jake, and he loved my dad like his own, he just didn't get it fully. i don't know that amanda would have either, though. both of her parents are still living as far as i know. it was the thought, though, of having experienced this loss of a parent and remembering the loss of that best friend, too. it felt like a double gut punch.

i also remember times just dreaming of what life would look like when we were grown. she always knew she'd have kids, and she'd refer to me as their "crazy aunt o'malley." it makes me smile even now, thinking about it. i wonder if she has kids now? i wonder if they've seen pictures of me and her when we were young? if she would even tell them my name? we used to talk about getting our own apartment in driftwood heights, right on the water, and how we'd have a constant flow of fresh flowers on the kitchen table. the walls would be decorated with posters from our trips to the met or the MOMA, and we'd have shelves overflowing with books. we weren't friends long enough to even consider it, though. besides, by then i had moved to south carolina with jimmy and was an entirely different person. it's funny when you look back on dreams like that to see just how differently life turned out.

but then the bad memories come flooding back and i'm reminded why we're no longer friends. all of the unanswered phone calls, text messages, and even instant messages. all of the excuses of why she couldn't find 5 minutes for me in the span of a week. how she left me sitting alone in a hallway when i went to visit her at school so she could attend a yoga class. i remember sitting there, practically in tears, on the phone with jimmy who insisted on driving all the way there to come pick me up. i refused, of course, because i didn't want to make things worse. even before college, there was a lot of red flags i chose to ignore for the sake of having someone i could call my best friend. it's sad to think about all of the bullshit we put up with when we're lonely.

during our junior year of high school, we went on this trip to europe with a dozen or so other classmates. it was probably the coolest experience of my life, but it nearly tore apart our friendship then. a couple of my old friends from grade school (brandon and jessica) were on the trip, too, which was really fun. jessica and i sat up all night in the hallway of some hotel just talking and catching up. we talked about all the days i'd go to her house after school, and all the food her grandmother would make for us. all the weird shit we used to do, like trying to make our own peanut butter or going through boxes of goods for the store her parents owned. we talked about all that we had missed in each others lives since we had drifted apart in middle school, like first kisses and slow dances with boys at co-ed parties. i remember feeling whole that night for the first time in a long time. amanda got so jealous that i was spending time with jessica. i tried to involve her, but she just wasn't having it. so i stopped, and figured out how to split my time between the two. it wasn't enough, though. one night i came into our hotel room from a gathering in jessica's room to find amanda asleep in her bed and a note on my pillow. in it, she told me how upset she was with me for not spending more time with her. she made some stupid "great gatsby" reference of how she'd always leave the light on for me. the next morning we had a big fight, and things were never really the same after that.

and brandon - we had always had some unspoken feelings for each other, i think. there were times of heavy flirting here and there, but neither of us ever crossed a line with the other. but on that trip, the flirting hit an all-time high. there was cuddling and stolen glances across the group and his head in my lap and my fingers running through his hair. we sat together during most meals, walked arm-in-arm through the cobblestoned streets of whatever country we were in that day. and then it culminated into this one night when he walked me back to my hotel room after a party in someone else's room. we were talking in front of the door and he leaned in to kiss me, but just before our lips met, the door to my room swung open. amanda was standing there in the threshold staring at us. we backed away from each other pretty quickly, and she stepped out and blatantly started flirting with him right in front of my face. i just said goodnight and walked into the room, leaving the two of them in the hall together. i knew she'd been watching from the peephole, and i was so angry with her for stopping what was about to happen. it was for the best, i guess. likely it would have ruined my friendship with brandon. not that we would be friends much past our high school graduation, though. anyway, amanda pursued him when we got home and eventually got what she wanted. i think they dated for the summer, and then it was over. the fun was in the chase for her, i guess. she won, and i lost. that was all that mattered. i found it hard to believe that any guy could possibly like me after that. i was always waiting for some girl to appear who was prettier or smarter or funnier than me. she would be chosen over me every single time.

and, yet, she blamed me for the downfall of our friendship. i know i said it's natural for people to grow apart, but i can't help feeling like it's always my fault. she's not the only one who has told me i fucked up in so many ways, never acknowledging how i put myself out for them or how they hurt me, too. i find my mind spiraling sometimes, thinking about all the ways i could've done better. that i take all of that crap to heart. i let it break me down over the years, feeling like i don't have anything to offer anyone. i just feel like a failure when it comes to my relationships, like something is broken inside of me. all i do is let people down. jake. my clients. most of all, myself. i do often wonder why i feel that way. i guess it's all the blame that's been laid at my feet over the years. from friends, my parents, ex-lovers. i've willingly picked it up and carried it for so long that i just eventually started to believe it. how do i unbelieve it, though?

why is it that it's always been so much easier for me to pick at my wounds rather than just leave them alone to heal? like i am glutton for the pain and punishment. sometimes i think about what life would look like if i didn't let the weight of it all drag me down. it's fleeting, though, because in some ways i feel like i _deserve_ to hurt this much for all of the fuck-ups i've committed in my life.

November 6, 2023

Hannah awoke on Monday morning, hours before the sun, tossing and turning in an attempt to convince her mind to quiet down. With the weight of grief looming over her at all hours of the day and night, she had not slept until her five o'clock alarm in months. She groaned, wanting nothing more than to go back to sleep for a couple more hours since it was her day off.

She got out of bed quietly so as not to wake Jake too early, which would only set him on a grumpy path for the rest of the day. Their dog, Diesel, followed her out of bed looking for breakfast. He watched Hannah from the doorway of the bathroom as she turned the faucet on and stared into the mirror. She looked away from her reflection and frowned at Diesel, who gazed at her as if she held the whole world in her hands.

"I wish I could look at myself the way you do, Diesel," she told him, letting the words fall out with a tired breath.

Out of nowhere, her throat tightened, and tears spilled from her eyes. Hannah gripped the sides of the sink, steadying herself against the shuddering wave of sadness pulling her under its tides. She cursed under her breath, hating how it usually came on so suddenly like this. It had been like this for the last six months, since she had lost Jimmy and her dad. There were days when she could look at their pictures, and even listen to Jimmy's music with a smile on her face. Other days were much like today.

When the water finally ran warm, Hannah washed her face and applied a myriad of creams to her skin. She dared to peer into the mirror again, noticing how red and puffy her eyes had become. She lowered them almost immediately and grabbed a towel off the hook next to the sink. A long breath left her lips as she sank her face into the soft terry cloth fabric, letting herself stay like that for longer than necessary to absorb the water from her skin.

Diesel pranced alongside Hannah as she entered the kitchen, now whining loudly for his breakfast. She watched the bounce in his ears and the way his tail curled into a hook when it was upright. She had seen his picture on the website of an out-of-state adoption agency and just knew he had to be her dog. Jake had disagreed, but Hannah pushed until Jake eventually just conceded. They met him at the airport, and Diesel bonded immediately with her, sitting in her lap the entire way home. He was a sweet little mutt of about five or six years old now, with an insatiable hunger. Diesel often got himself into trouble, trying to eat anything and everything. She and Jake had this joke that anything could be edible if only Diesel tried hard enough. A slight grin broke through her heartbreak at the thought.

"No way. It's too early for breakfast, Diesel," she whispered as she turned on the kitchen light. Regardless, he continued to dance around her as she made herself a cup of coffee. "Come on," she said to him. "Go outside and go potty." Hannah opened the sliding glass door leading to the back deck. Diesel hustled down the steps, getting lost in the darkness of the yard below.

Hannah made her coffee with extra milk and sugar, just as she had preferred it since her college days. She had Jimmy to thank for that. She loved her coffee this way in his absence during their first summer together, when a concussion had triggered a bout of depression so bad that he stayed in the hospital for a couple of weeks under supervision. Hannah was lost without him then, like a ship unmoored in a storm, and had clung to the one thing he loved the most: large light and sweet coffees from Dunkin' Donuts.

She cradled the warm mug and shuffled to the back door, staring into the darkness while waiting for Diesel to return. When he eventually did a few minutes later, they both made their way into the living room, where he snuggled up in her lap and fell promptly asleep. Hannah put on the newest true crime documentary from Netflix, ensuring the volume was low. She tried not to feel guilty over her relief of having some time alone like this, and not having to constantly tiptoe around whatever mood Jake would find himself in.

Later that morning, Hannah sat in a green armchair in the waiting room of her therapist's office. It was significantly larger than her own, and more professional, with a private lobby area and bathroom. The heavy wood door opened with a creak of the hinge, and Linda appeared in the doorway with a pleasant smile on her bright red lips. Hannah noted that she had recently cut her dyed blonde hair, as it now brushed the tops of her shoulders.

"Come in," Linda told her melodically.

She looked Linda up and down as she passed by, inhaling her sweet, floral perfume. She had always been envious of Linda's sleek wardrobe, which she undoubtedly had purchased at the Nordstrom in the high-end mall in Cedar Cove; Hannah had stuck to shopping at the more affordable mall by SHU, the one she had often gone to with her college friends.

"How are you doing?" Linda asked, shutting the door behind them.

Sitting in a plush black armchair, Hannah said, "I'm doing okay. How are you?"

"Just fine, thanks," Linda replied, sitting in a matching chair across from her. "How was your week? How are you sleeping?"

Hannah took a deep breath and exhaled loudly. "Pfft. It's still hard. I was up at a quarter to three this morning. I just couldn't sleep anymore." She looked down at the square black carpet beneath their feet, trying to think of what to say to summarize her week. "I had a new client start with me on Wednesday, but I already messed it up. I think it's gotta be a new record or something!" she joked.

Linda chuckled softly. "Tell me more about that. Why do you think you 'messed it up'?"

"So she's in her early twenties, newly married, and having difficulty in her social relationships. One of which recently ended after they had known each other since early childhood," Hannah explained. Linda nodded but remained silent, waiting for Hannah to continue. "It just—I don't know—I got so lost in this memory of one of my old friends. We met in school when we were around twelve. I was right back to the day when she ended our friendship, like I had time-traveled back to being eighteen in the old bookstore with her. I still felt the pain of it as fresh as I did then. Anyway, my client totally noticed how zoned out I was, and asked if I had been listening to her." Hannah looked up at Linda with a slight pout. "But, one good thing that came out of it was I picked up this after my session with her," she said, pulling the notebook from her bag.

Linda raised an eyebrow. "A journal?"

"Yeah, I mentioned it to my client that it might be a good idea for her to process some of her emotions. I've always felt like a hypocrite because I haven't done it for a long time. Writing used to be so therapeutic for me, until I let myself believe it was hurting more than helping because it just dug up all the ugly stuff in me."

"I think it's a great idea, Hannah," Linda said with a hopeful smile. "You mentioned your old friend. Was that Amanda that you were referring to?"

Hannah nodded. "Yep. Ever since my session with her, I've been thinking so much about my old friends and my old life. Just how lonely I feel."

"Lonely? What makes you feel lonely?"

"I've lost so many friends along the way," she uttered with resignation. "Listening to her talk brought all of that loss back to me. I know I'm better off with some of them being gone. Amanda, for one. I think about other people, though, and I'm not sure that I am better off for the distance between us."

"Does anyone come to mind?" Linda asked.

Hannah ran down a list of her old friends. "Katie. Jenny, maybe. I wonder what happened to her. Some of my friends from South Carolina, like Steph and Ali."

Linda jotted a few things down on the notepad balancing on her knee. "Have you thought about reaching out to any of them?"

A small chuckle escaped Hannah's lips. "No. Gosh, I wouldn't even know where to look for some of them. I think Alan might still talk to some of the Riverside Springs people, I'm not entirely sure."

"Alan?" Linda questioned. "I don't remember you mentioning him before."

"Oh, maybe I haven't," Hannah admitted. "He was Jimmy's best friend in Riverside Springs. They were really close, more like brothers, you know? We naturally got close, too, but we lost touch when I left. I just cut him off, I guess, like everyone else."

"But you're in contact now?"

Hannah nodded again. "Yeah, he reached out after Jimmy died, said he spent months searching online for me to tell me what had happened. We've stayed in touch since then. Just easy, surface-level conversation, you know?"

"He could maybe be a gateway to those people again. Would you want that?"

"I don't know. I doubt they'd welcome me back after how I left things. When I left town, I just cut everyone off. Never answered their calls or texts. It was too painful at the time."

"I'm seeing this pattern in your relationships, these abrupt endings. Regardless of fault. I'm curious if you've noticed the same?"

Hannah took a moment to contemplate this suggestion. "I guess I do," she finally replied. "I can't help but sometimes feel like I'm meant to love other people more than they are meant to love me. I mean, I haven't talked to some of these people in twenty-ish years, and I'm still sad just thinking about them. What sense does that make? It's like I exist only to *give* all of my love, but never to get it back."

"That's a heavy thought," Linda concluded.

"I guess there's just a part of me that's scared."

"Of what?"

Hannah took a deep breath. "Reconnecting with them, and things going well, just to lose them all over again. I think that's why I keep everyone at an arm's length, you know? I'm forever expecting people to leave. I've lived with enough goodbyes that it's just expected now. Or maybe it's just that they won't like this person I've become. Sure—we were damn near like family at one time, but I know I'm a different person now. Whoever that person is… ." Hannah let her voice trail off.

Linda cocked her head to one side. "What do you mean by that?"

With a shrug, she said, "I barely recognize myself anymore. I've shape-shifted so much over the past years to fit in as I needed to. I don't recognize myself anymore, not even the sound of my heartbeat or my breath. Just, again, giving and giving so much of myself away. At work, with friends, with Jake's family. There's this saying about setting yourself on fire to keep other people warm. Or it's something like that. That's how I feel, like I'm just ash. Does that make sense?"

"I think it does. You don't feel like you're expressing your genuine self?"

"Right!" Hannah declared. "The music I listen to, the clothes I wear. Even how I spend my time! I feel like I have no hobbies anymore. My body feels more like a skin suit I wear; it's not really me."

Linda took some more notes, a thoughtful look on her face. "Can you think of a time when you last felt genuinely yourself?"

A breath sputtered on Hannah's lips before she confidently answered, "When I lived in Riverside Springs."

"Have you thought about taking a trip back there? Just putting yourself back into that environment again?"

She laughed. "I'd love to, but it's not exactly around the corner. That, and I'd be so nervous about running into some of those old friends that I mentioned before."

Linda laughed with her. "Okay, that's fair, but can you think of someplace else then? That's closer to home?"

Hannah thought about her life before she moved to South Carolina. "When I was at SHU, I guess."

"Okay," Linda said with a more upbeat tone. "That's a lot closer than Riverside Springs. I'm wondering what you'd think of taking a drive over there and walking around campus to see some of your old stomping grounds? It may help you feel more grounded in who you are, the piece of yourself that you miss."

"That's not the worst idea."

"You mentioned clothes and music before. Hobbies, too. Those are easy things to work with. I would encourage you to maybe listen to some of your favorite songs or music groups from that time in your life. Go to the mall like you used to do with your girlfriends! Window shop or go with intent to buy something you wouldn't normally purchase for yourself now. Try out some of your old hobbies. You've mentioned writing and art before. *Explore* that. What are your thoughts?"

"It's something to try, I guess. I don't know where I'd really start, though."

Linda paused for just a beat before continuing, "I do want you to consider something, and you don't need to have an answer right now. You mentioned that your old friends from Riverside Springs might not like the current version of you, as it's so far removed from the Hannah they knew. While you've changed, yes, I'm sure it's not as drastic as it might feel. Your friends saw something in you that resonated with them. She's still in there. You've mentioned that you often felt unlovable. Yet, they found something in you to love. I wonder what that might have been?"

"I guess I always assumed they were my friends because they had to be. They were Jimmy's friends, and to stay friends with him, they had to accept me." Hannah shrugged again. "He made it so easy for me to be around other people. To have fun and open up. He was so naturally charismatic that it was contagious. So when I think about engaging with the mutual friends we had, it feels *impossible* to do without him."

"It might have started that way," Linda said, "but you grew

real bonds with them. That wasn't Jimmy's doing. It was yours."

Hannah only shrugged in response, now biting at her cuticles. Linda glanced at her watch. "We still have a little time. What else is on your mind?"

"Well, when my dad died, I was thinking of this promise Amanda and I made to each other when we were, like, sixteen or so. One day, we were talking about what would happen when our parents died, being that both of us were only children. Out of that was born this promise to be there to help each other through it," she told Linda as tears trickled out from the corners of her eyes.

"I can imagine how nice it would have been to have that support from her. Did you get that support from your current friends?" Linda asked.

Hannah shook her head. "Not really. The first week, yeah. I got all of the 'so sorry for your loss' stuff. After that, it felt like nothing ever happened, you know? Life moved on, but I didn't. I got stuck in this hellscape, and everyone around me was just too uncomfortable with it. The mention of death was like the worst curse word a person could say, and it just added to my loneliness. I think having the memory of that promise, and then falling behind everyone else in the midst of grief, just had me feeling like I've been stuck in the same place for months. Even before my dad died."

"When Jimmy died," Linda said.
Hannah nodded her head slowly as Linda passed her another tissue.

"We are at time for this week, but you are doing such a beautiful job navigating through all of these heavy, messy feelings. I just want to acknowledge that," Linda continued.

She nodded again, taking an extra moment to collect herself before being ushered out the door. Hannah took care to avoid eye contact with the next client waiting in the vestibule, ashamed of her red, watery eyes. As Hannah's car warmed up, The Tidewater Hellraisers began playing through the car's speakers. It was the final band that Jimmy had played with, lending his heavy punk guitar riffs and raspy voice to their sound. She sadly smiled, staring out at nothing in particular, her hands loosely gripping the steering wheel. This type of music always made her nostalgic for her college days, wishing she could somehow go back in time to those years when she had been so in love with life, and a boy who brought her so far out of her shell. When she used to smile a whole lot more than she cried. When she had wanted to set the world on fire, and believed she actually could.

Throughout the afternoon, Hannah managed to turn her mood around from the gloom she felt after her session with Linda. She had managed to finish her weekly to-do list and had made Jake one of his favorite dinners: meatloaf with baked potatoes and corn on the cob, which she had stowed away in the freezer during the summer. As soon as she heard the front door close behind him, Hannah glided into the living room with her arms open wide for a hug. She wrapped them around Jake from behind, leaning her cheek against his upper back, and felt his body tense as a sigh escaped his lips. He turned around to meet Hannah's gaze. She was oozing with desire, as the good mood she found herself in had spilled over into other areas of her mind. She leaned in and kissed him, but his lips felt cold on hers.

When she pulled away and opened her eyes, Hannah could immediately feel the energy of the house change. Trying to ignore it, she smiled wearily and said, "Hi."

Jake's voice was quiet as he responded, "Hey."

"How was your day?" she asked.

"Fine," Jake answered with a slight shrug of his left shoulder as he headed for the bedroom to change out of his work clothes.

Hannah stood there for a moment, arms hanging limp at her sides. She waited for him to ask about her day, but he didn't. She sighed and offered, "I had a good session with Linda this morning, and I got so much done in the afternoon."

Jake walked out of the bedroom in sweatpants and an old T-shirt from a trip to Virginia they had taken nearly four years ago. "Oh, yeah?" he said, walking into the bathroom and closing the door.

She rolled her eyes as she walked in that direction. "Yeah," Hannah told the front side of the door. "We talked a lot about my old friendships, and some of the loneliness I've felt."

"That's good," he replied through the door.

"I thought so. I was thinking about it while doing my errands and chores, how some of this stuff has bothered me for so long. Like with Amanda, you know, how it still kinda hurts even now," Hannah told him.

There was silence from the bathroom, except for the toilet flushing and sink faucet squeaking on and off. Before she knew it, Jake opened the door and was practically nose-to-nose with her.

"What?" she asked, wondering why he looked bewildered to see her standing there.

"You stopped talking," he explained. "I thought you left."

"I was waiting for you to respond," Hannah told him. "That's how conversations work."

"Oh, right," he said. "So what's for dinner?"

She followed Jake into the kitchen. "I made your favorite!" she told him with a sparkly in her eyes, motioning a hand toward their plates set out on the kitchen table. After an obviously long day, she hoped it would at least make him smile.

A slight grin did creep across his lips. "This looks so good," he murmured.

"So, yeah, anyway—" Hannah began as she sat at the table to eat.

"Hey, babe, do we have butter?" Jake asked.

Hannah nodded and stood again, getting the tub from the fridge across the room. "Sorry," she apologized. "I forgot to grab it." When she sat down, Hannah started again to say, "So it was an interesting conversation with Linda, to say the least."

Jake grunted in acknowledgment, focusing solely on the food before him. Hannah pushed around cut-up pieces of potato with her fork as she watched him eat. She knew it was no use trying to talk to him about anything that was on her mind; he clearly wasn't interested.

After a couple of minutes of quiet, Hannah cleared her throat and asked, "Rough day?"

Jake shoveled another large forkful of meatloaf into his mouth, followed by a long swallow of beer. "Rough is an understatement," he told her.

"What happened?"

"Gabrielle was riding my ass all day long. She called me into her office three different times today. Once because I was on my phone for all of two minutes while I was on a break. I don't think she realized I was, but she also didn't care when I tried to tell her that. She just talked over me the whole time about how unprofessional I was being in front of the client."

Hannah swallowed the food in her mouth quickly and asked, "What else was she uppity about?"

"Oh, just how I answered the phone on this conference call we had, and then how I was being distracting," he told her with a roll of his eyes.

"Wow," Hannah replied. "I guess she's pretty stressed about this project, too, huh?"

Jake chuckled. "I don't know what she has to be stressed about. I'm handling everything on our end. I'm the one taking the flack for all the shit that goes wrong."

Hannah looked at him with a long face. She hated to see him so upset over work, which was nearly every day now. "I'm sorry, honey."

"Nothing I ever do is good enough for her, but *her* boss always says what an asset I am to the team. He's always letting me know I'd be his first consideration for a promotion. She obviously just doesn't like me, and I don't know why," Jake told her.

"I'm sure it's more to do with her than you," Hannah suggested. "Maybe her boss isn't saying those things to her? Maybe she doesn't feel adequate enough to make that type of decision."

"Little Miss Golden Child, who can do no wrong? *Ever?* Please," he said sarcastically.

Hannah winced at his response. "I'm just saying—I know it's hard for you, but I'm sure it's pretty hard for her, too. You guys are on the same side of this thing."

"Yeah, but I just know she is *loving* watching me struggle through this project," Jake said with a snarky smile.

"Maybe it wouldn't hurt to ask her for some advice? She's been a director for a while now, right?"

"She has, yeah. She's not exactly the best boss, though. The other leads all say the same things—it's not just me. She'd be the last person I'd ask, honestly," he admitted.

Hannah took a long drink of water before asking, "So what are you planning to do? You can't keep going on like this."

Jake suddenly snapped at her, saying, "Hannah, I don't know. Okay? Do we have to keep talking about this?"

Caught by surprise at his sudden attitude shift, she lowered her eyes to her plate. Hannah felt her entire body shrivel up in the chair where she sat. "No, I just thought it might help."

Jake sighed, dropping his fork heavily onto the plate. "You don't have to therapize me—I'm not some freakin' client of yours."

"Maybe therapy wouldn't be the worst thing?" Hannah delicately proposed. "It would give you someone to talk to outside of me, since that doesn't seem to be very helpful."

"That's not gonna happen," he replied with a scowl. "I don't need it, and I don't even know when I'd find the time for it."

"You'd have to make the time for it," she said bluntly.

Jake glared at Hannah for a long moment before standing up from the table. "I'm going out to the shed for a while," he told as he grabbed another beer from the refrigerator and twisted off its cap.

Before Hannah could respond, he was out the door and walking down the stairs. Jake had a woodshed out back where he sometimes tinkered with various tools and scraps of wood, building knick-knacks and furniture. It was something he hadn't done for a while, though. Most of the time when he was out there now, Jake just sat scrolling through videos on YouTube or reading articles from "The Chive." Hannah hated it when she caught him scrolling past photos of big-busted women in bikinis that were splattered in the middle of every article, it seemed.

"Good talk," Hannah whispered to the empty room as she

fought back tears. She cleaned the kitchen up so that no evidence of their dinner could be seen, expertly maneuvering around Diesel who remained underfoot. She then busied herself preparing for bed. When she got under the covers, Diesel snuggled up close to her while she found a show to fall asleep to so the silence wouldn't swallow her whole.

Hannah's Journal
Monday, November 13, 2023

so i took some of linda's advice and i spent my day off diving back into all of this music i lived and died by in high school and college, and that i had completely forgotten about for years. i even remembered some old pictures i had of jimmy where he's wearing band t-shirts, and i got some ideas that way, too. honestly, the whole thing was kind of exciting. it felt like meeting old friends for the first time in a long time. i got lost in it for hours making a giant playlist to come back to. but then i feel that aching in my gut again as i thought about driving around aimlessly in my car with jimmy playing dj, or sitting on the trunk of his car in the parking lot of the thrift store i used to work at listening to music during my breaks. or how me, katie, whitney, and jenny (my old friends from SHU) used to dance around chris's basement apartment to songs by pop punk bands. we'd try to get the guys into it, but it never really worked. jimmy would sometimes play along, doing an awkward jig. i'm cracking up just thinking about it. that's just who he was, though. he was more free-spirited and silly than the other guys on the newspaper staff, and not so worried about keeping up appearances.

anyway, i weirdly feel like i am buzzing on the inside. it's like listening to all of that music flipped a switch and turned on this light inside of me that i thought had burned out a long time ago. i guess it never really did. i guess it's been there this whole time. i just couldn't remember how to turn it back on. or maybe it was just on a dimmer switch, and with every song it got a little brighter and a little brighter.

it also reminded me of this thing i used to do when i was younger: i would write down the things that made me feel something, no matter what it was. song lyrics, a movie quote, a line from a book. anything. when i would reread them, it would stir my own emotions and thoughts and give me this jumping off point for a new poem or story. sometimes i would even take a song and write a short story around the lyrics, working off the story the songwriter had laid the foundation of. i still had some of those notebooks in the attic, and i went up there and brought some of them downstairs. i just sat in the middle of the floor with the music blasting, flipping through pages and pages. it was like a diary in itself. i could kind of track how i was feeling through it because some stretches were really sad and others were about being in love and happy. it just felt really magical to listen to that music, and read through those words that, at one time, felt so important.

i haven't written shit in years, though. i don't know that i'd be any good at it now if i tried to come up with something original. while i was going through those notebooks, i did try to think of something i would write based on the words on the pages, but nothing came to me. that creative spark is dead. it is not a switch that needs to be flipped or a dimmer that needs a push in the right direction. it's just dead. it's like integrating writing into my therapy practice dampened my passion for it. i hear it from so many people, how they lose their creativity when it becomes something that makes them money. maybe that's what happened to me? that coupled with the busyness of life, who has the time? or maybe as life goes on, and the hurts feel heavier, it gets harder to face it all.

like everything else, i just stopped. i can't tell you exactly why i put the pen down, or why i never picked it up again. i wish i still had that ambition in me, though. that creative spark. the version of me sitting in that creative writing class in high school, dreaming of becoming an author someday. the one that believed i actually might do it.

i was reminiscing about all of the poetry festivals i'd go to in high school, and the open mic nights i would go to with jimmy at this coffee shop near SHU we frequented. i loved the singer/songwriters but there was something special about the slam poets that would get up and perform. i was even thinking about the teen arts festivals i was a finalist in over the years. i can't remember what grade i was in, but one year i had been selected to read my entry, a short story, to the crowd. i was <u>so</u> nervous that the papers were literally shaking in my hands as i stood there in front of all these other kids and teachers from all over the state. it felt so good when they clapped for me at the end. that was probably the first and last time that ever happened to me.

Hannah's Journal
Wednesday, November 22, 2023

i feel so angry and frustrated with myself today. i've never had problems focusing like this before, but lately i just feel like it's impossible for me to keep my brain on task. my thoughts are so scattered, and it feels like hundreds of them are swimming around up there. L was just here. i can't believe she's come back for 4 sessions with me so far. i felt myself slipping almost the entire time she was here. i've been on extra high alert about it since our first session, but i'm still messing up. at least she didn't seem to notice today.

don't get me started on this imposter syndrome. i feel like it's getting worse by the day. i question my career choice all the time. who am i to be giving people advice on sorting out their baggage, anyway, when i've haven't been able to do it myself? if i'm honest, i feel like i just pretended like i did because that's what everyone wanted from me, what they expected out of me. so i faked it. just like now. but all i've ever managed to do is bury it all under some dirt and plant pretty flowers on top of it. then i flaunt this flower bed around for everyone to see, but even the best dams and levees break. they wash away all the pretty gardens planted on top of all the shit, leaving it all exposed. in some ways, i feel like that's what is happening to me now. i've shapeshifted so much that i can't keep it all straight, and now it's all out in the open for all to see.

jake and i had yet another fight the other night. something about work upset him again. i tried my best talk to him and be helpful, but all it did was piss him off. i think he's told me twice in the last month or so that he feels like one of my clients more than my husband. but isn't that part of being married? or any relationship? talking and working out problems together? being there to support one another? i just wish he would open up and stop running from me. i made the stupid mistake of suggesting that he see a counselor, but that didn't go over so well. i don't know what i thought his reaction would be. he's in such denial that anything is wrong. with him or us. he always makes it out that i'm the one that has the problem. i'm too overbearing. i'm too emotional. i'm too pushy.

before that fight happened, i tried to get something started between us. physically, i mean. i turned my flirtatiousness on, touching and kissing him. how did he react? like a cold, dead fish. i try like hell to just tell myself that he's not in the mood because of work and stress and whatever. but there is this voice in my head that tells me it's my fault. and why wouldn't it be? everything else is. i'm a liar and a fraud. i've loved another man before him. i'm aging, and my body has changed. i'm just not what he wants anymore. and the look on his face when he pushed me away... .

i think the take away here is this: i'm a sham of a therapist, a wife, and a lover.

unrelated, i've been thinking of writing jimmy a letter. i told L to consider writing one to the friend she parted ways with, to find some kind of closure. there's a lot that i never got to tell jimmy, even if it's years overdue. like how sorry i am that i never reached out to him to at least try and make a friendship work between us, and that i have always regretted letting all of that time go by. that i never forgot him - how could i have? that he died without knowing how deeply he touched my life, and how i can still feel the place where his fingers once wrapped around my heart so tightly. i know it would probably do me some good to just get it all out but i don't even know where to start, and i don't know what i'd do with it.

some small part of me wants to take a trip to riverside springs. i guess linda planted the idea in my head a couple of weeks ago. it was the place i ran to years ago, following my heart to be with jimmy, and the last place i ever felt at home. truly at home. back then, i was desperate for change (not so unlike how i feel now) and it easily became one of the best years of my life. in some ways, i feel like there is something still there for me to discover or learn. i also think it would be nice to visit jimmy's grave, finally. it would be an opportunity for me to say goodbye to him. like i could find some closure if i could just see his grave, and really see that he's dead because it's still so hard to believe it's true. but what even is closure? you hear people all the time saying that closure doesn't really exist, that it's just something we say to make people feel better. to give them hope that their nightmare, their pain, could really be over. who knows? if i write this letter, maybe i can leave it at his grave. or somewhere else in town that meant something to us. under the porch at campbell street, or at that old pool they all used to skateboard at. what if someone found it, though? i literally feel myself slowly dying at the mere thought of that happening.

dear jimmy,

i never thought i'd be writing a letter like this. where do i even start? i used to be able to tell you anything, but i find myself at a loss for words. i just can't believe you're really gone.

Jake's cell phone jingled loudly, disturbing Hannah out of a surprisingly deep sleep. She groaned and rolled over toward him. "What time is it? Who's calling you this early?"

Jake shifted on his side of the bed, and Hannah could see the glow of the phone's screen moving in the dark. "It's six o'clock, and it's Gabrielle," he told her as he quickly got out of bed. "Hello?" she heard him say as he left the room, his voice groggy and sounding of forced cheer.

Hannah lay back on her pillow, staring at the ceiling in the darkness with her brow furrowed. *Why is his boss calling so early on Thanksgiving morning?* she wondered.

A few minutes later, Jake stalked back into the room, his fingertips rubbing his forehead. "I have to go in today," he stated as he opened the closet and began sorting through his shirts.

Hannah sat up fast. "What? Why? It's Thanksgiving Day!"
"I'm well aware, Hannah," he spat, tossing a polo shirt onto the bed.

"Well, what happened? I don't understand," she said.

With a heaving sigh, Jake explained, "Gabrielle said some alert came in early this morning. There's a glitch in the software, and I've gotta go in to fix it."

Hannah's voice rose with anger. "It can't wait a day?"

Jake shook his head, placing a pair of khakis and socks on top of the shirt.

"Well, why can't she go? Or someone else on the team? Why does it have to be you?"

Jake brushed past her and into the bathroom to run a comb through his hair. "She's apparently out of state visiting family for the holiday, and I'm not entirely sure where things went wrong, so I don't know who would be equipped enough to work on it. Plus, how do I look as a leader if I drop this big problem in someone else's lap on a holiday?"

Hannah put a hand to her cheek, rubbing the side of her face in frustration. "So you're not going to be there with me and Mom? Will you be back in time for dessert with your family?"

"I don't know. I'll try to make it to wherever you are once it's finished," he promised, even if it felt empty. "You'll be fine on your own. It's not like you don't know anyone."

"I just don't want to do this without you today," she told him.

"You can handle our families for one day without me," Jake sarcastically responded.

Hannah scoffed, "That's not what I mean. It's the first holiday without my dad—it's a big deal for me."

"What isn't a big deal to you these days?" he snapped. "Anyway, I'm getting double-time-and-a-half today for doing this. At least it will help us out."

Her mouth hung open as she watched Jake get dressed in a hurry before she said, "The money is nice, but it's fucking Thanksgiving, Jake!"

"This is the deal with this job. You know that. This is the way it's been for years. I thought you'd be happy about the holiday pay.It's kind of on you that we're having to pinch pennies anyway right now," he said, stunning her.

Hannah crossed her arms. "What do you mean? Where did that come from?"

Exhaling deeply, Jake stopped and looked at her. "I don't know. I've got a lot on my mind."

"We wouldn't be that bad off if you cooled it with the big purchases. All the video games? The new gaming computer? It adds up!"

Jake put his hands on his hips, turning his gaze from her to a spot on the floor a few inches from her toes. "I work hard for my money, Hannah. I deserve to spend it how I want to."

"You can, but after the bills are paid. That's how this works. You know—I also work hard for my money, but every dollar I could put toward something for myself has to go to pay the bills or to buy things for the house." Hannah laughed. "Hell, I *wish* I could spend money on myself like you do without feeling the guilt!"

Jake bent over to get his loafers from the bottom of the closet. "Oh, please. How many Amazon boxes come every week with your name on them?"

"It's stuff for the house!" Hannah picked up her cell phone from the nightstand, navigating to the orders page in the mobile app, and shoved the phone in his face. "Here! Look at my list of orders! Dog food, toothbrush head replacements, Diesel's supplements, heartburn relief for you—"

"Get your phone out of my face," he said, pushing Hannah's hand away from him. "I get your point."

"Do you? Because we've been through this a half dozen times in the last few months."

He walked into the living room, snatching his keys off the hook by the front door. "Yes!" he snapped. "I do! Anyway, you could at least say 'thanks' that I'm sacrificing my holiday so we can have some extra money coming into our account for once."

"We'd have extra money in the account if you hadn't

spent three grand on that new computer," she said, cracking up as the anger consumed her; she always had this weird habit of laughing when her anger reached a certain level. "I can't believe you'd talk to me like this today, of all days, then up and leave and expect a thank you from me?"

With his hand on the doorknob, Jake turned to her and said, "I'm doing this all for you. So, yes, a thanks would be nice."

Hannah hated that she could feel tears beginning to well up in her eyes as they just stared at each other in the entryway. Her thoughts swarmed with dozens of things she had done for him over the years, with no thanks at all, most of the time without even an acknowledgment. Not that Jake was the only one in her life like that. She would bend over backwards to make things just a little easier for someone else, and she would always do it willingly at the detriment of herself.

She blinked hard, causing a single tear to escape against her will. Hannah clenched her hands into fists and said through gritted teeth, "Maybe you're right. I should thank you—this day might actually be enjoyable without you there."

Jake turned the doorknob, flinging the front door open, and turned his back on her without another word. As he walked out of their house, Hannah slammed the inner door closed, spinning around to lean against it. She swallowed hard, bringing her hands to her eyes, forcing herself not to cry anymore.

Hannah spent the early afternoon at her mother's house with Diesel, trying to enjoy what she could of their Thanksgiving dinner. The scene was jarring when she arrived, seeing three places set at the table. The third was for Jake, obviously, but she couldn't help thinking of her dad and the many holidays they spent as just a family of three at this very kitchen table. It hurt just a little extra when her mom cleared the dishware from the table, packing it back into the hutch. She had gone with a rehearsed script of apologies for Jake's absence, but her mother was oddly sympathetic to his having to work. When she was done there, Hannah drove from Harborvale to Cedar Cove, the next town over, for dessert with Jake's large extended family. Again, she had come prepared with excuses for Jake's absenteeism, having to repeat it at least a dozen times over to each family member.

She checked her phone periodically throughout the day, but Jake had not messaged her with any updates on when she could expect him. Not that Hannah was waiting on bated breath for him to reach out after the fight they had this morning. She eventually sent him a text message to see if he would be making it to his parents' house, and he responded to say that whatever the initial problem was had spurred other offshoot issues that he was still working through.

When she arrived back home that evening, Jake's car was still missing from the driveway, and the house sat quiet and dark. She changed back into her pajamas, feeding Diesel his dinner earlierthan she should have. When he was done, he joined Hannah on the couch and curled up in her lap while she watched an episode of a new romantic drama. Only ten minutes into the episode, Hannah's cell phone rang. She checked to see who was calling, and a smile spread across her face when she saw Alan Reed scroll across the top of it.

Hannah's thumb swiped to answer. "Hey, stranger," she said, her voice bouncing.

"Happy Thanksgiving!" Alan roared on the other end.
She laughed. "Well, sounds like *someone* has been enjoying his holiday!"

"Yeah, might have let loose with an extra beer or two. Maybe three," Alan quipped. "Hey, you do know this thing works both ways, right? You can click my name on your phone sometimes, and it'll connect our two phones by magic."

Hannah laughed again. "Yeah, I know. I'm sorry about that, Alan. I've been so busy trying to get my practice off the ground."

"How's that going?" he asked.
"Good! Well, better," she admitted. "I had another new client start with me a couple of weeks ago, and a few others found me after I left the other place. I was surprised they wanted to keep seeing me."

"Why wouldn't they?"

"I haven't exactly been very good at my job lately," Hannah confessed. The familiar feeling of failure crept slowly along her spine, until it burrowed itself into the folds of her brain.

"Well, hey, I think it says a lot that they're still coming to see you. I'm sure you're doing a lot better than you think," he said.

Hannah shifted Diesel off her lap and stood up from the couch, walking into the kitchen to refill her wine glass. "Yeah, and it keeps my numbers up, which I need. I'd like to get a few moreclients on my roster to push me past what I was making at the last place."

"Got it," Alan said, as silence fell between them. Hannah could hear the laughter of children somewhere nearby.

"So how did you and the family spend the holiday?" she

asked.

He cleared his throat. "Oh, Phoebe's parents flew in from South Carolina a couple of days ago. We had dinner but," his voice lowered, "I needed a break, so I'm out supervising the girls on the swingset."

"I see," said Hannah with a giggle. "Trouble with the in-laws?"

"Listen—they've been so helpful with the girls while they're here. It'd be nice to have them here all the time for that, but there is only so much one man can listen to his mother-in-law whine about her hot flashes," Alan told her with a chuckle.

Hannah nearly spit out the sip of wine she had just taken. "Oh god!"

"Tell me something good. What did you and Jake do today? See your mom?"

Hannah leaned her back against the counter, hesitating to answer his question because she really didn't have anything good to say. She could just lie and tell him that they spent the day together, and that everything was wonderful. Or she could be honest and tell him that she spent her holiday holding back her rage and tears.

This is Alan, you're talking to. Of course, you can be truthful with him, she told herself.

"It's been a pretty crappy day over here," she confessed.

"Why's that?" Alan asked, his concern obvious.

"Jake went to work this morning, and we had a big fight before he left. I haven't seen or really talked to him since," she said.

"Work? It's a goddamn holiday, even the fishing boats stayed anchored today!"

Hannah turned around to face the oak cabinets, leaning her elbows on the tan laminate countertops. Her eyes flashed around the fixtures in front of her and frowned from the side of her mouth; she had always wanted to renovate this kitchen to upgrade its bland details, but Jake had always held up her plans with one excuse or another. "It wasn't anything scheduled. Something went wrong with whatever software rollout, and then it was like a domino effect after that, I guess."

"That's pretty lousy," Alan blurted out.
"Well, his boss didn't leave him much choice. Plus, he's been working toward this promotion and just wants so badly to prove to her that he's capable," she told him.

"Still, for you to go at it alone today. It's not like your dad has been gone that long," he recalled.

Hannah let out a small laugh. "You don't need to remind me." There was a pause before Alan asked, "So is that what your fight was about?"

"Yeah," she confirmed. Part of her wanted to say more, and felt like maybe she could since he had been receptive. "Well, that and he blames me for some financial stuff we're going through right now."

"Financial stuff?" Alan asked. Hannah heard rustling, as if he had moved the phone from his ear or covered the receiver with his hand. With his voice muffled, she could hear him say, "Girls. Girls! Get off of that! You'll bust your heads open!" In the next moment, Alan's voice was clear and calm. "Sorry about that."

"It's all right. I should let you go," she said hastily, knowing it was a mistake to try to have a serious conversation with him when he was watching two young kids.

"No, no. Don't," Alan insisted. "What were you saying?"

"Oh, nothing. Just that he blames me for some financial problems we're having," she said, trying to sound nonchalant about it now.

"What kind of problems?" When she didn't answer right away, Alan prodded, "Hannah, talk to me."

"Just a little hiccup. Nothing we can't come back from."

"Is there anything I can do?" he asked.

"No, I didn't say all of that so you would give me money or something," she told him, her voice rising just a little in defense.

"That's not—I didn't think you were," he said cautiously. "I just care about you, and if I can help—"

"We're fine. It's just growing pains," Hannah reconciled. "It was a big hit to our income when I left my job, and then having to pay all kinds of fees for everything, and then rent for my office. It added up. We could have afforded it if Jake had reined in his spending, but he's acting like we still have the same amount of money coming in. He says it's my fault, and I say it's his."

Alan grunted, taking his time to respond to her. "Well, maybe you could have waited to quit your job until you had everything squared away, but he could have also compromised on the spending until it all got figured out."

"Yeah," Hannah said. "So he has a hard time turning down the extra hours or delegating, even on holidays. All it does is make him cranky, though. He's unbearable some days, if I'm being honest."

"Yeah, I bet. I feel pretty testy, too, the weeks I gotta work overtime," Alan told her. "How are you doing, though? Really. I know this must've been a tough day for ya aside from this stuff with Jake."

Hannah exhaled. "I've been better. It was weird without my dad there. He always loved the holidays," she told him.

"I remember that from that year in Riverside Springs; he was so mad you weren't gonna be home for the holidays that year," Alan mentioned. "But the first one is always hard. Not that any of the others after that get any easier."

"Well, you would know about that," she said with a frown. Both of Alan's parents had died in a car accident just before he moved from Louisiana to South Carolina in his early twenties.

Changing the subject, she asked, "Hey, remember that Thanksgiving that Sven and Ali hosted the year that I was down there?"

Alan chuckled. "Yeah, I remember."

"That was the best," Hannah added. "I kept thinking about that all day today, how I wished I could just be back there instead of feeling like a ghost all day."

"Now I think about it, I wonder if they still host them."

Hannah stood up straight and put her free hand on her hip. "Are they even still together?"

"Oh, yeah. They got married, gosh, two years or so after you left. Must've been 'cause they just celebrated ten years last year, if I remember right. It was a helluva party. *That* I remember."

"I don't know why I'm surprised that they're married, but I am," she laughed, pacing the kitchen back and forth.

The front door suddenly swung open, and a haggard looking Jake walked into the house. He kicked off his shoes and hung his coat on the hanger by the front door. When he turned to walk into the living room, his eyes immediately met Hannah's. She could feel the tension in her face and made a conscious effort to relax it, even if she was still seething mad at him.

"Hannah, are you still there?" Alan asked.

"Oh, yeah. Sorry. Jake just got home," she told him. "Should I let you go?"

"Yeah, let me go. I'll talk to you again soon—promise," she said.

"You better keep that promise! Call me if you need anything, all right?"

"Yep, thanks," Hannah said quickly before hanging up the phone.

She stepped into the living room, attempting a smile. "Hey," she said in a hushed tone.

"Who was that?" Jake asked, walking past her and into the bedroom to change.

Hannah followed him. "Oh, that was just Alan. He called to say 'Happy Thanksgiving.'"

Jake eyed her from around the closet door. "Alan? Jimmy's friend?"

She nodded. "Yep."

"That's random."

She pinched her face in confusion. "Not really," she said. "He's my friend, too. We've been talking here and there since he called me about—"

"Jimmy?" Jake assumed, finishing her sentence. Hannah could hear the aggravation in his voice, which had become the typical response any time their conversation turned to him. "I guess I didn't know you were still talking to him. How often does he call you?"

"It's not a regular thing. We text mostly," she replied with a shrug.

Jake eyed her suspiciously, but changed the subject. "Are there any leftovers for me?"

"In the fridge," Hannah told him, leading the way into the kitchen to start making him a plate. "Did everything get fixed today?"

"Oh, yeah. It was a pain in the ass, but it's all working as it should be now. We're back on target again," Jake told her as he retrieved a beer from the fridge. "Honestly, I should work on my off days more often. It was so nice and peaceful without anyone up my ass all day."

Hannah turned to smile at him as he moved near her and leaned against the counter as she put his plate in the microwave. "That's great."

For the next twenty minutes, Hannah obediently listened as Jake rambled on about each step of the software fix process. She didn't understand half of what he was talking about, though; the world of technology was so out of her realm of interest. As she watched him speak and eat, Hannah couldn't help but feel utterly annoyed at him still. She had been enjoying her conversation with Alan, reconnecting with her old friend who had been the only person to show her genuine care today.

When Jake's dishes had been cleared from the table, he grabbed Hannah's hand suddenly as she tried to pass by him and forcefully pulled her into him. Jake sank into his knees so that he and Hannah were face-to-face, wrapping his arms around her lower waist, his fingers resting just inside the back waistband of her pants. His lips landed on hers firmly, but she did not reciprocate the sudden show of affection. She shimmied her arms free, putting her hands on his shoulders to gently push him away from her.

Jake relented. "What's the matter?"

"What do you *mean* 'what's the matter?'" Hannah crossed her arms hastily in front of her.

"What? I want my wife," he said playfully, again leaning in to kiss her.

Hannah pivoted her face away from him. "Not tonight, Jake. After everything today, do you really think I want this?"

He pulled his hands back, his whole body going stiff. "Fine," he mumbled as he left the room.

The next morning, Hannah awoke to find only Diesel in bed with her, laid out on Jake's unmade side of the bed. She guessed Jake had left for the office already, surprised that she hadn't heard him leave. Diesel stretched and pivoted himself toward her as she stirred, nuzzling his head underneath her chin and giving her cheek a couple of licks. Hannah kissed the curve of his forehead, the spot between his eyes, and rubbed his belly.

"Good morning, my favorite boy," she whispered to him. Hannah yawned big and thought she smelled coffee brewing. She sniffed the air again. "Is your dad home still?" she asked Diesel, who only looked back at her with wide brown eyes.

Hannah sat up, which prompted Diesel to jump down from the bed and trot out of the room. Peeling back the covers, she swung her feet to the floor, scowling at how cold it was that morning. She stumbled sleepily into the kitchen to find Jake wiping down the countertops with a dustpan and rags at his feet. He looked up when he heard her shuffling feet approaching, and met her eyes when she turned the corner into the kitchen.

Jake hesitantly smiled at her. "Hey," he said sheepishly.

Hannah froze on the spot; she hadn't expected to see Jake home still. "Shouldn't you be at work?" she asked, looking at the time on the microwave. It was after eight o'clock.

"I decided not to go in today," Jake told her.

She motioned with a hand toward him. "What are you doing?"

"Cleaning," Jake said, holding up the dirty Clorox wipe in his hand. "Is that all right?"

"No, yeah. Yeah! I'm just surprised."

Jake shrugged and looked down at the tub of wipes in front of him. "I know I can do better around here, and that I've been pretty absent lately. I fucked up yesterday. I was angry at Gabrielle, and I took it out on you. I'm sorry."

Hannah felt like the wind had been knocked out of her. After their fight the day before, and Jake's indifference to her struggles over the last several months, this had been the last thing she expected from him. She bobbed her mouth open and closed a few times, unsure of what to say.

Jake suddenly crossed the kitchen toward the coffee pot, still full and warm. As he reached for one of her mugs on the shelf, he paused to turn toward her. "I'm assuming you want coffee, right?" he asked.

Hannah nodded. "Please," she said as she walked to the table and sat down in her usual place.

Jake made her coffee and slid the mug across the table to her. Hannah looked down at it and frowned a little to see that its color was still relatively dark. With a reluctant sip, she winced hard at the bitterness of the drink.

"What's wrong?" Jake asked.

"Are you sure you put milk and sugar in this?" she asked, pointing to her coffee.

"Yeah," he responded.

Hannah stood up from the table to add more of each into her mug. "It doesn't taste like it," she said flatly.

"Yeah, I made it like usual," Jake insisted.

"Pfft. This is not the usual," Hannah told him.

"Well, you're always changing how you like it," he explained.

With her back to Jake, Hannah rolled her eyes. She was getting tired of him conveniently forgetting nearly every nugget of information he'd ever learned, and it being his excuse for everything he seemed to overlook. "What are you talking about? I've taken my coffee light and sweet since before I ever met you," she reminded him. With the coffee more to her liking, Hannah returned to her seat at the table.

"Sorry," Jake said again as he resumed his chores. "That's not how I wanted the morning to start."

"It's fine," Hannah told him quickly, letting tense silence fall between them; she hadn't wanted to start her morning off with yet another argument, either. She slowly sipped her coffee, looking out the sliding doors at nothing in particular.

"Hannah," Jake said, turning to face her again. "I'm sorry for yesterday. If I could have been there, I would have. You know that."

"I don't, though. You keep backing out of things all the time lately. I just can't believe someone else couldn't go in your place," Hannah suggested.

With a sigh, he told her, "I'm sure I could have leaned on someone on my team, but it was a massive lift. It wouldn't have been fair."

"I know this is how things are with your job. I get that, but I was hurt. It's just, like—of all the days of the year for something like that to happen, to pull you away from us, it had to be the first holiday without Dad. Maybe it sounds melodramatic, but I felt like you abandoned me yesterday."

His eyes fell to his hands resting on the tabletop. "It's not melodramatic. I didn't want to make you feel that way. I thought I was doing the right thing by sacrificing time with my family so my team could be with theirs."

"I understand what you're saying, but I was without my husband, my best friend, at a time when I needed him," Hannah told him, her voice shaking. Despite her anger and the letdowns, she still wanted to consider Jake her best friend. Perhaps that was why it hurt so much when he disregarded her or got mean.

"I know," he said with a hint of anger in his voice. "I made the wrong choice, and I'm sorry. I'm sorry for what I said to you, too, about all of this money stuff being your fault."

Hannah puckered her lips. "Yeah, especially because we made the decision together about me quitting and striking out on my own."

"You're right," Jake admitted easily. "I just didn't think you'd do it so quickly, and then figure things out from there. That's not like you to not have a plan. You always have a plan, and then a backup plan. Then a backup for the backup!"

She let out a low laugh and looked up at him to see him smiling at her, too. With a shrug, she suggested, "Maybe it is now. I've just come to realize how short life is, and it's not worth being so unhappy."

"I mean, I get that. It still wasn't like you, though," he told her. Hannah sighed. "These last six months have changed me, Jake."

"No kidding," he said with a roll of his eyes. "It's changed me on a lot of levels," she continued to explain, choosing to ignore his attitude. "I realized that all of the bullshit of the job wasn't worth it anymore. It was too expensive, but not in the monetary sense."

"It was," he agreed, which took Hannah by surprise. "But, anyway, I think we both could have done things differently. I know I can curb my spending more to help us out, and I will be more conscious about that. I promise."

Hannah tried hard not to roll her eyes at him again, knowing he was trying to be sincere. She believed him to an extent, knowing he'd likely make an effort for a week or two before giving up altogether again. That had been the pattern now for the better part of the year. "I hope so," was all she said.

"I will," Jake repeated, looking at her earnestly. "I was thinking—when I finish up here, do you want to go out for breakfast? Maybe the diner?"

Hannah shook her head. "I don't know, Jake. It'll probably be crowded with Black Friday shoppers. Weren't we also just talking about curbing our spending?"

"It's still early enough. They're probably still in the stores," Jake said. "I know about the money, but we don't get to do things like this often. Plus, I worked all of that overtime yesterday. Please? We can come home after, and do whatever you want today."

The thought was tempting. She had to admit that she did miss spending time with Jake, even if she was more than a little irritated with him. She looked up at him, noting the expectant grin on his face.

Hannah mustered up all the good feelings inside herself and smiled back at him, hoping that her weariness didn't show. "Yeah, okay," she told him. "Let's go."

what. a. shitshow. that pretty much sums up thanksgiving. jake had to go into work to fix something, and he never made it to either my mom's or to his parents' house. i know he can't help when these things happen but... really? i was exhausted from trying not to cry all day. i kept excusing myself to the bathroom, or to take diesel outside whenever it felt like it was just going to pour out of me. i managed to hold my composure enough, i think. i just didn't want to cry in front of any of them. especially my mom. i'd never hear the end of it, i'm sure.

i looked back at my last entry. at the unfinished (barely started) letter to jimmy. for some reason i just wanted to throw this journal out the window or in the trash. maybe just shove it down deep into my laptop bag for a while. it's not that i don't know what to say. it's that i have <u>everything</u> to say. when i sat down to write it all out, every single thought and emotion and regret all came rushing forward at once. like the words were shoulder-to-shoulder at the tip of my pen, elbowing each other for a way out of the tip, to have their turn on the page.

i guess i'm just not ready for that kind of goodbye yet.

it was nice to hear from alan yesterday, even if it got a little weird. but now that i'm thinking back on it, i think i made it weird. yeah. i definitely read too much into his offer of help. like i was some little girl being told she should've known better, a wagging finger in my face. that was the one thing my dad used to tell me: never talk money with <u>anyone</u>. i guess that's where that feeling came from. i instantly regretted opening up to him about all of this money stuff. i felt like such a burden in that moment, like he needed to try to save me. maybe that's why the offer felt so icky.

as if the phone call wasn't awkward enough, jake got all uptight about it. he came home in such a shitty mood (what else is new?). i guess he was mad because he didn't know we were talking, but i swear i told him a couple of times that i'd heard from alan since the spring. just another example of him not listening to me, i guess. that, and he's been so forgetful lately. not sure which one it is, but does it really matter? jake dropped it quick, but i can't help but wonder what the issue was.

i just have to get this off my chest, because i can't stop thinking about it. jake made me coffee this morning, and it was terrible. he didn't make it like normal, how i've had it since i was, like, 18! he said he didn't remember how to make it, but then blamed me and said i keep changing how i like it, but i've never once changed that. i keep telling myself it's stupid, and to just forget about it. i can't, though. i just keep obsessing about what it could mean. we've been together for so long, and these are just things you know about your partner. especially when you've lived together as long as we have.

i fear that things between us are worse than i thought. i'm really worried, and the aching in my stomach is worse because of it. maybe it's just that this coffee thing made me realize how far apart we are from one another. it's like i'm on my own lonely island, and he's on his, and there are hundreds of miles of ocean between us. have we really just become strangers overnight? have i really just become someone he doesn't know or recognize anymore?

what have i done? i can't help but feel like this is my fault. i let myself drown in my grief. in my depression. i've changed so much that, not only do i have a hard time recognizing myself, but my husband does, too. my best friend, and my biggest cheerleader. if i knew hiding jimmy away would destroy my marriage, i would have been more open about it. though, if i were more open about it, would we have ever gotten down the aisle? i feel like i was damned if i did, and damned if i didn't. no one wins, especially me.

November 27, 2023

As Hannah drove to her next appointment with Linda, she sang happily along with the music streaming through her car speakers. Jake had not only called out on the Friday after Thanksgiving, but he also stepped away from work all weekend to spend time with her. He seemed back to his usual self again, and she couldn't help but feel happy to have had that time with him. They had simply lounged around the house, watching movies and cuddling close to one another. It was almost easy to forget the catastrophe of their Thanksgiving.

Once settled into the office, Hannah's smile beamed as she told Linda, "It's been a bit of a rollercoaster week, but I've been on a high note the last few days." She went on to tell Linda about how she spent her Thanksgiving tackling both family obligations solo, the fight with Jake that resulted from it, and then the long weekend together to make up for it. "In some ways, it feels like I am starting to get the old Jake back again."

"Well—"

"But—" Hannah interrupted, "there is something that I can't seem to get past." Hannah took a breath as Linda leaned forward slightly. "The day after Thanksgiving, actually," Hannah said before becoming quiet again; her mind had been stuck on this one thing since it happened. "Jake forgot how I take my coffee. He made me a cup during his apology speech, and it was all wrong. He said he didn't know how I took it, but that's complete bullshit! I know it probably sounds so stupid," Hannah added quickly.

"It doesn't actually," Linda told her as she narrowed her eyes. "What feelings does it bring up for you?"

Hannah's shoulders slumped. "It made me feel invisible, or like a stranger in my own life."

"That's a word you've used before when we've talked about your relationship with Jake and some of your friends," Lisa stated. "I wonder where that pattern comes from?"

Her mind swirled with memories, but she only shrugged in response.

"If I can be blunt for a moment, it feels like you hold some blame over Jake for how your holiday turned out."

Hannah sighed from the gut punch of guilt Linda just socked her with. "I do, yeah. I mean, know that it's the nature of his job, but it was the worst year for something like that to happen. If it were last year, or even next year, it would've felt a lot different."

"How so?"

"Well, it was the first year without my dad. He *loved* the holiday season and always made such a big deal about celebrating the 'right' way. Although we never had big family get-togethers or anything, it still isn't the same now. They don't feel as special."

"What were your holidays like growing up?"

Hannah let out a deep breath and said, "Quiet. It was always just the three of us—my parents and I, I mean. The last time we did a holiday with *any* extended family was probably Easter at my grandmother's house. I must have been eight or nine at the time, so it's been a while."

"Why did that stop?"

"No one could get along!" she said through laughter. "There were so many stupid, petty fights that always turned so nasty. I could never understand it, but after some space apart, they would all act like nothing happened. No apologies, no talking it through. Just bury it and move on. I think that should've been the family motto. Eventually, it was obvious that it was better for everyone to be apart." Hannah shrugged again. "I just always wanted that big, happy family, you know? That was my idea of the American dream—the perfect family. I thought I'd be able to make one, but here we are."

Linda nodded. "What about the other side of your family?"

"Less drama, but equally as splintered. I can't even tell you the last time I saw any of them," she said. "I was definitely in high school." Before Linda could say anything, Hannah laughed again and told her, "I remember making up these stupid stories when I was a teenager. I'd tell these white lies, about how I spent time with this cousin or that one. I would recall a memory from when I was much younger and twist it to make it sound like it had just happened. All of my friends would come back to school after breaks and talk about the fun family time they had, and I had nothing to share. I just wanted to be a normal kid, so I created that narrative in my mind."

"Did you ever come clean about it?"

"No way," she said with a shake of her head. "I mean, I never got the chance to, but I don't know that I would have if I did. I know it's wrong to lie, obviously, but it didn't hurt anyone at the time."

Linda narrowed her gaze at Hannah again. "Was there anything else you lied to your friends about?"

Hannah took a few beats to think about it. "I mean—yeah. I lied mostly about myself. I hid so much of myself away for fear of being bullied again or being ostracized from the group. At the same time, though, I would share some secrets with certain friends. Amanda, mostly. Like, when I had this secret fling with a boy from our school this one year."

"You've told me Amanda was like a sister to you back then. How did she treat your secrets? Did she keep them? Did you feel safe with her?"

"Eh, not always. She told her mom *everything*, and then her mom would interrogate me about it sometime later. I always wondered if her parents ever really liked me or not. I'm pretty sure she also told some of our other friends things about me, but I don't know that I ever *really* felt safe with anyone back then."

Linda smiled sadly. "I am sorry that you didn't have that at such a tender time in your life." Hannah's eyes filled with tears again; Linda seemed to always have a way of saying the exact things she needed to hear, things that no one else would tell her. Linda hesitated before saying more. "I want to ask, to bring it back around again—was there ever a time you lied like that after high school? In your relationship with Jimmy? Or Jake?"

"No, I never had to with either of them. I could always just be myself and be completely accepted. Well, I don't know about Jake anymore. That's how it used to be. Other friends, though? I just don't tell them a whole lot. No lies, just omission."

Lisa nodded in understanding, then looked down at her wristwatch. "It's that time again but, before I let you go, I just want to recognize the progress you're making here. I hope you see it, too."

Hannah nodded and lied, "I do."

As she walked to her car, she couldn't help but think how she still felt as stuck as ever. Maybe Linda could see the progress she was making but, to her, she was still in the same place she was months ago when she first started coming to therapy. Some days, her depression felt worse than ever. This conversation about the family and friends she didn't have only made it worse.

Every shadow only proves that the light is near, Hannah reminded herself. She had said it to so many clients over the years, yet here she was, unable to believe it for herself. It didn't feel like things would ever get better.

Hannah's Journal
Monday, November 27, 2023

after my session with linda today, i'm thinking a lot about family. i guess it also being the holiday season has me thinking about it a lot, too. i've wished my whole life for a more connected family structure. one where my aunts, uncles, and cousins don't feel like total strangers. i think my neighbors are closer to me than my extended family. which sounds really sad. i wasn't raised having connections to them, so i don't know where this deep desire came from. i just know that it never felt normal to not go to some relative's house for thanksgiving or christmas dinner. or to not have people to celebrate birthdays with. i know that families aren't perfect, though. i'm not that naive to think everyone else is living some perfect "leave it to beaver" kind of life.

when i look back at my earlier years, i can see just how jealous of amanda i was about her family. she was so close with her extended family, even her cousins who were so much older than her. they took her under their wing and gave her that first sip of alcohol as a pre-teen, showed up to her awards ceremonies and graduations, and helped her blow out her candles on her birthday every year. i envied how close she was to her mom, like they were best friends. i'm pretty sure her parents never liked me, probably because of how much more a free spirit i was. like that was some kind of threat to their perfectly precious princess, like i would badly influence her fashion choices and musical tastes. i swore like a sailor (still do around the right people), but never in front of them. i wonder what they thought i was up to all those hours i spent riding my bike around town, completely unsupervised.

i just know i wanted that. i wanted my mom to be my best friend. i wanted to be able to tell her everything. i wanted cool older cousins who wanted to get me into the safe kind of trouble, the kind that doesn't have any real consequences, and that you laugh about later in life.

my mind keeps coming back to jimmy's idea of chosen family. i guess that's why it always meant so much to me to build those close friendships. i just wanted to feel like i had been chosen in return, even if it wasn't by my own flesh and blood. i had that chosen family for a while, when i was enrolled at SHU and then later on in riverside springs. and i walked away from them all. i've been trying tirelessly to build a family again, but it's never been the same since riverside springs. there's no one i could really call at 2am in tears to just talk to, or someone who would drop everything to sit by my side. it's hard enough to get together for a drink these days.

shannon is maybe the closest thing i have to that chosen family right now. but even that is questionable because i can't really talk to her about much of anything. not that she would rat me out or anything, but she doesn't have the time or the emotional capacity for me. i thought by this point in my life i would have a whole group of girlfriends who were ride-or-die for each other. instead, i have a couple of friends i barely see or talk to, who don't hold space for me, yet expect me to always be there to drop everything for them. to be on the phone talking or texting for hours, pouring everything i've got into them. frankly, i'm exhausted.

December 6, 2023

Hannah is standing on the bottom step of the stairs that lead up to her old bedroom in her childhood home. She stands there, watching her dad as he sits in his usual chair in the living room. Except, even in the cosmic space of this dream, she knows he has been dead for the last several months. She watches him for a few minutes. He seems to be watching her, yet his eyes are so distant. Like he is looking through her, not at her. Out of nowhere, he starts to giggle and give a hi-sign in her direction; he and Hannah had loved to watch old episodes of "The Little Rascals" when she was small, and it had always been their special thing. With his hand positioned under his chin and his fingers wiggling, he's acting like he is alone. Except he isn't. Hannah is there, and she can see him so clearly.

Finding her voice, she says, "Dad, I can see you."

Her father stops moving, completely stunned by what he has just heard. The look on his face is one of confusion, but also surprise. His lips move, but no sound comes out.

She nods and repeats with a chuckle, "Yeah, I can see you! You're so weird!"

Hannah's eyes flew open to find she was not in her childhood home, but lying in her bed in Bay Point. The room came more into focus as she shifted her eyes around wildly: the familiar blue walls, the early morning sun trying to creep through the navy blue curtains in the window, and a sleeping Jake next to her. Diesel startled her as he shifted into a tighter ball and sighed heavily, falling back to sleep nearly instantly.

Climbing out of bed as quietly as possible, she replayed the moment of recognition between herself and her father. It was almost like they had really been there in that room together, which completely bewildered her. A slight tremble took hold in her limbs as she traipsed delicately into the kitchen.

It was just a dream. It was only a dream, she told herself repeatedly as she scooped coffee grounds into the pot. *It wasn't real.*

Alone in her office, Hannah sat at her desk, completely zoned out and clicking the top of a pen at a fast pace. Her eyes were glazed over from lack of sleep, the adrenaline rush of her dream having dissipated. Lucy would be coming for her next appointment in about an hour, and Hannah was unsure of the direction she should guide her. She could barely remember their conversation from last week; Hannah's brain just would not let her think about anything other than the dream she'd woken up from. She sighed and let her face fall into her hands.

There was an unexpected knock on her office door, which caused Hannah to jump out of her chair. When she opened it, she was met with the glowing smile of a man who appeared to be in his early thirties. His face was flushed from the cold outside, while his short auburn hair was mostly covered in a brown knit hat with the UPS logo on it. It was Drew, the usual delivery driver for the building.

"Hey there, Hannah. Good to see you, as always," the man said with a playful smirk.

"Drew! Hey!" Hannah replied, noticing her voice sounded more excited to see him than she had intended.

Even though she had only been in her office for a couple of months, Hannah had several run-ins with Drew due to the numerous office supplies and furniture she had ordered to get set up. He was especially helpful when her office furniture had been delivered, assisting her with moving the boxes exactly where she needed them. On one occasion, he'd even gone as far as to help her unpack a couple of them because of the large, sharp staples used to hold the cardboard together; he'd been concerned she would hurt herself on them, like he had done so many times in the past.

"And how are you doing on this beautiful Wednesday?" he asked.

Hannah could feel her cheeks blush just a little. "Exhausted, but good," she said. "How 'bout you?"

"Just over here livin' the dream," he told her with a laugh. "I got a couple of things for you today. May I?" he asked, motioning toward the door with the handtruck piled high with boxes.

"Must be my stuff from Staples," she said out loud and backed into the office to give him enough space to pass by her. "C'mon in."

He wheeled the stack of boxes into her office and bent down on one knee to shuffle some of them around to get to hers. "You watch the game last night?" he asked, referring to the hockey game between the New Jersey Devils and the Vancouver Canucks.

"I did! Ugh, what a game!" Hannah told him, watching him work. They chatted enthusiastically about the match-up long after Drew had put the two boxes on her desk, and leaned an elbow against the handtruck's handle to talk to her a little longer.

"Well," Drew said as he stood more upright. "I'd love to stay and chat, but I should probably get these other deliveries done." He smiled big again before passing her the handheld scanner. "Just sign there for me."

Hannah took the device from him and signed her name before passing it back to him. When Drew reached out to take it from her, she couldn't help but notice how his fingers brushed hers ever so slightly. Since they had met, she often wondered if his actions were more than just a friendly or helpful gesture, a subtle indication that he found her attractive. She usually disregarded those thoughts, though, thinking she was just too deprived of that kind of attention.

He held her gaze and said, "Hope to see you again soon."

"Yeah, thanks," she said in a low voice as she watched him leave down the long hallway.

She closed the door and returned to her desk, where her thoughts lingered on Drew's sweet disposition. Hannah couldn't help but think of the way their friendship had blossomed in the short time she'd been renting her office, or how he seemed to always be flirting with her. His eyes gave him away most of all, taking her in the same way Diesel stares at any morsel of food. She shouldn't like the attention he gave her, but she did. She loved it and looked forward to running into him in the building. Hannah knew it was wrong, but it had been so long since a man had looked at her that way. Especially Jake. With a slight shake of her head, she forced her thoughts back to the upcoming session with Lucy.

Hannah glanced down at her cellphone and completely lost track of her mind again as she suddenly realized she hadn't spoken to her friend Shannon in a couple of weeks; that was unusual for them. They first met during Hannah's final internship rotation in graduate school at the county clinic, where Shannon was already an established therapist. The two found they had a lot in common, and their friendship eventually extended far beyond the office.

Despite their closeness, there was a lot that Hannah withheld from her. Not that it was something unique to Shannon, though; Hannah was always reserved with everyone in her life, only giving just enough of herself. Every person in her life had only small tidbits of facts, not all of them the same, and not one person with all of them. She often wondered if she hadn't subconsciously crafted a splintered group of friends on purpose, keeping them apart so they wouldn't ever be able to put their puzzle pieces together to create the full image of who she was. Not even Jake had the whole picture, though, he was the one person who probably had most of it now. The only person who had ever held all the pieces, who saw the bigger picture, was now dead. It was better that way, though. At least, according to Hannah. The less someone knew about her, the less ammunition they had to use against her.

With Shannon, she also had to consider that she would likely only get about five minutes to talk about what was on her mind before Shannon took control of the conversation. That usually meant having to hear about every little thing going on in her life, walking her through it all, and providing her with the comfort and attention she needed. No matter how much Hannah told herself that it was just her friend's way of trying to relate to her, it did nothing to quell the feeling that Hannah's woes weren't important or big enough. She'd tell herself that it was fine, that she was used to being the quiet friend. The one who listened and supported without judgment. She knew her role, and she played it well.

Hannah briefly thought about telling Shannon about her dream, wanting to get someone else's take on it, but she quickly reconsidered because her friend would only call her crazy and laugh. Maybe she was. She debated telling her about how unstable her marriage had become with all the fighting, the loneliness, and the ever-building resentments. Hannah shook her head, knowing there was no way she could be that honest about it. She was barely even able to admit it to herself most days. Besides, there was so much uncertainty about how Shannon would react to the news. If she would even believe her, since she and Jake always managed to hold it together around their loved ones. Again, Hannah knew her part, and she played it well. Too well, probably.

That's if she had to deal with all of this for much longer anyway, since Shannon was due with her first child in the spring. Over the last few years, her social circle had become increasingly crowded with more children than adults. Hannah had never been sure if she wanted kids, having never really felt that maternal drive that most women talk about. Growing up, she had never imagined herself as a mother, even while she rocked a baby doll in the cradle her grandfather had made for her. Back when she and Jimmy thought they'd be together forever, he had made it known that he never wanted children because of the poor paternal role model he had grown up with. It made no difference to Hannah, and Jake had been just as unsure about what he wanted when they got married. Sometimes their feelings would change as they watched their nieces and nephews grow up but, in the end, they kept their family as a party of two. Three, if you counted Diesel.

Being a childfree couple had certainly driven a lot of their friends away, as if they turned into some monsters who hated kids. Or maybe they thought that Hannah and Jake could no longer relate to them, and vice versa. It happened time and time again, and she was afraid the same would happen with Shannon eventually, too.

She tapped Shannon's name on her contacts list, listening to the line trilling in her ear as panic suddenly rose in her because she hadn't thought of a single topic to talk with her friend about. This call would at least earn her some friendship points, which might help to stave off the ending of their sisterhood.

She picked up on the third ring. "Hey, lady!" Shannon squealed into the phone.

"Shannon, hey! How are you?" Hannah asked.

"Oh, just between clients," she breathed into the phone. "What's up with you? I feel like it's been forever."

Hannah laughed, shaking a pen between her thumb and pointer finger wildly. "I was actually thinking the same thing, and I was also between clients, so I thought I'd call you to see how you've been."

"I miss you. It hasn't been the same since you left," Shannon admitted sadly. Hannah could picture the exaggerated pout on her face.

"It's only been a few months, Shan."

"And?" Shannon questioned. "Is my mourning period over or something?"

Hannah laughed again. "No, you're still allowed to be sad. So, how is everything over there anyway?"

With a loud sigh, Shannon told her, "Oh, you know—the usual. Interns running amok, and everyone trying to fight against the new regulations they're rolling out here. It's a losing battle. When are you going to recruit me to come work with you?"

Hannah snorted. "When I can get a full caseload for myself! The grass isn't exactly greener, you know."

"How so?" Shannon asked.

Wondering how much she should say, Hannah kept it simple. "Just that it's so much work to do it all myself, and I'm not exactly reaping the financial rewards quite yet. Besides, I'll be lucky if I can keep the clients I currently have."

"Oh, please. Why wouldn't you?"

"Because I'm not even a decent therapist, Shan. It's very obvious to me now that I'm barely mediocre."

"Hannah Elizabeth, where is this coming from?"

With a scoff, she asked, "Did you just drop my middle name on me?"

"I did. What of it?"

"Okay, Mom. Sheesh," Hannah teased.

With a serious tone, Shannon prodded her friend some more. "What's going on, though?"

"Oh, I don't know." She waved the hand holding the pen in front of her, knowing she'd said too much. "I've got this new client I'm just struggling with, I guess. I see myself in her, and I'm having a hard time separating that. We've clashed a couple of times. Nothing big but, you know."

"Aah," Shannon moaned. "Been there. You just need to remind yourself of it in the moment that you're two different people. It's not about what you would do or what you would want to hear."

"Yeah, and I know that," Hannah replied defensively.

"See? You're not as hopeless as you make it sound," Shannon told her with a chuckle. "If you ask me, it sounds like you're overthinking it."

"Me? Overthink it? What?" Hannah joked to lighten the mood.

"I know, right? Not you!" Shannon chirped. "What else is going on? You sound tired or something."

"Eh, I didn't sleep well last night. I feel so exhausted, and my client is going to be here in a few minutes. I'm fucked."

"Why didn't you sleep well?"

Hannah glanced at the clock, knowing she didn't have enough time to unpack everything with Shannon. Not that she knew if she should given her track record with trying to have serious conversations with her friend about life's disappointments. "I just had a weird dream, is all. There's a lot on my mind these days."

Shannon pushed. "Like what?"

"Just grief, I guess. My dad, Jimmy. Things with Jake have been a little off." Hannah shuddered after the words had spilled from her mouth unwillingly.

"Still? It's been a few months now, and Hannah, you weren't even *talking* to Jimmy," Shannon reminded her.

"Are you questioning the length of *my* mourning now?" Hannah questioned, only half joking.

There was a period of silence before her friend finally spoke again, and Hannah found herself obsessing on how Shannon was judging her silently now. "You know, I didn't sleep well, either," she admitted. "I feel so sick at night. Like, the opposite of morning sickness. Ugh, it's the worst. At least you're not dealing with *that!*"

Hannah grunted and bit her tongue to stop from saying something she would regret later on. "Well, let me go. My client is going to be here any second." It was a partial lie; Lucy wouldn't be arriving for another ten or fifteen minutes.

"Hey—let's set a time to get together for Christmas, okay? Let me know what you and Jake have going on in December," Shannon said quickly.

"Sure. Will do," Hannah said in a rush, ending their conversation. She had no idea what they were doing tomorrow, never mind in a couple of weeks from now. It was becoming increasingly difficult to make plans with him nowadays, as she never knew if he would keep them or not, and she was growing tired of having to make excuses for him.

Hannah dried her hands with a paper towel as she absentmindedly walked back to her office from the communal restroom down the hall. The last bits of her talk with Shannon lingered on her mind, and she couldn't help but feel misunderstood and angry with her friend for trying to push her grief to the background.

A voice called out from behind her, "Ms. DeLuca!"

Hannah screamed and spun around to see Lucy jogging toward her. For a split second, she swore she saw Jimmy running toward her with a skateboard in his hand, and a cigarette hanging from his lips, calling to her from the other end of some walkway at SHU. Almost instantly, Hannah could feel her heartbeat quicken and something catch in her throat.

Oh no, she thought, immediately worried that an anxiety attack was growing inside her.

As a reflex, Hannah coughed to try to clear the feeling, something she had started doing subconsciously in her teens. She forced her thoughts back into the present moment, here in this hallway with her client.

Lucy's expression changed from a happy smile to one of regret at Hannah's reaction. "I'm so sorry! I didn't mean to startle you!"

Hannah's palms became slick with sweat as she tried to collect herself and did her best to reassure Lucy that she was fine. She placed a hand over her heart as if to steady its beat and walked in the direction of her office with Lucy beside her. "I just startle easily. Always have. Anyway—how are you doing?"

"Doing okay. I'd ask how you are, but I guess not great right this second," Lucy said with a hesitant laugh.

Hannah chuckled, too. "Well, I'm glad one of us is doing okay then." She opened the door, motioning Lucy to enter. "Shall we? Make yourself comfortable, and I'll be right with you."

"Thanks," Lucy replied bashfully, walking quickly through the threshold and taking her spot on the loveseat.

Hannah walked around her desk, throwing the paper towel into the garbage can underneath the window. With her back to her client, she pretended to look over a piece of paper on her desk, needing the extra time to gather herself. Her heart was pounding now, while her breathing became more labored. Hannah's eyes shifted between each of the items on her desk, and she noticed the woozy, out-of-body feeling taking hold, like she was somehow seeing through someone else's eyes. She gripped the top of her desk tightly, trying to steady herself against the lightheadedness.

It was true what she had said to Lucy, about being easy to scare. It was something she had dealt with for as long as she could remember. That's not what this was, though. This was more than that; it was the first full-blown panic attack she'd had in years.

Why now? she asked herself. *You can't do this in front of her. How is it going to look to your clients that their own therapist can't even keep it together?*

She had to keep pushing forward. Hannah knew that leaving too much silence hanging in the room would only cue Lucy into the fact that something was wrong. She picked up her notepad and pen, took a deep breath, and turned around with her best fake smile plastered across her lips.

"So—how was your Thanksgiving? Do anything fun?" she asked as cheerfully as she could.

Just make it to your chair, she coached herself, *only a few more steps to go.*

Hannah dropped heavily into her armchair, practically collapsing into it, because her knees had given out under the weight of her body. Instinctively, she began wringing her hands in her lap, trying to find something in the room she could mentally anchor herself to. Nothing seemed to be working.

Lucy rolled her eyes and groaned. "The holidays are always chaos, honestly. Both of us come from such big families, and it's always this loud, overwhelming experience being with them all. I think we spend more time driving between houses than sitting down with everyone. How was yours?"

"Oh, mine was quiet," Hannah told her with a tight smile, still kneading her fingers together in her lap. "Yeah, my husband had to work, but I still visited with our families."

Lucy nodded. "Sounds a whole lot nicer than mine! Maybe we can trade next year!"

Hannah forced herself to laugh at the joke, wincing at how inauthentic she sounded. "Well, is there anything on your mind you'd like to discuss?" she asked as she shifted around in her seat, trying to get comfortable. All her body wanted to do, though, was to bolt from the room and never look back.

Lucy shrugged. "I'm not sure. I just felt frustrated this week because I felt like I had a good couple of days, and then just felt so sad and angry all over again. When does it get better?" she asked sincerely.

"That's the million-dollar question, isn't it? If there were a timeline for this stuff, we wouldn't need therapy. I wouldn't have a job!" she said with a smile that she could feel still echoed a certain fakeness.

"I guess," said Lucy. "It just sucks to feel so good, and then feel so low again."

Hannah knew exactly what she meant. "It's like I told you in our very first meeting: healing isn't a linear path." Trying to dislodge the hold her anxiety had on her body, she cleared her throat again. Lucy looked at her for a moment with concern. "Excuse me for just a second," Hannah said. "I'm just gonna grab my water bottle. I've got this little tickle or something."

She delicately stood from her chair, making sure her legs were properly under her before crossing the room to her desk. Hannah gulped down the cold water, not having noticed until right now how dry her mouth had become. Something in the coldness of it brought her back down, and she felt her heart rate steadying along with the pacing of her thoughts.

As she sat back down, Hannah asked, "So how can I help you through these highs and lows? What do you need from me during this time?"

Lucy made eye contact with Hannah again. "I'm not really sure," she told her with a shrug.

"Is it all right if I come up with some ideas? Just to brainstorm, not to set anything in stone just yet," Hannah proposed. They collaborated on ideas for the rest of the session, bouncing them off one another and discussing Lucy's goals for her future sessions. By the time she left, Lucy was smiling and feeling more optimistic than she had in months, and Hannah felt like she had actually made a difference.

Hannah's Journal
Tuesday, December 12, 2023

something in me changed this week. at least it was for the better. i just feel a little lighter. the imposter syndrome voice has grown quieter. i think seeing L leave my office last week with a smile on her face was exactly what i needed. for the first time in a long time, i felt like had actually done something right. that i left someone better than i had found them.

even with that win, i've still had some trouble concentrating on work today. i dragged my feet all afternoon to get some paperwork done. for as good as i feel, for as much as the imposter syndrome has quieted down, my mind is still wandering elsewhere. i'm lacking the motivation to do <u>anything.</u> more often than not, i find myself staring blankly out the window of my office, focused on nothing in particular, wishing i was anywhere else, doing anything else. wishing i could <u>be</u> someone else. sometimes i wonder if i'm over this job. i guess it's just burn out. i wish i could take some meaningful time off from everything, to really disconnect and just be with myself. like, turn my phone off and sit in a cabin in the woods completely alone. that kind of disconnection. in reality, it would probably look more like sitting around the house, tense and riddled with anxiety, walking on eggshells, and thinking endlessly about all the shit that's been weighing heavy on my shoulders. i would just be miserable because, really, that's all home is these days. maybe i <u>could</u> take a trip somewhere. maybe to see alan in louisiana? are we that close, though? or maybe out to oregon to see nicole? eh, i don't know.

speaking of nicole, i reached out to her today. i was really just looking for something else to do other than the paperwork, but it <u>had</u> been a while since we last talked. almost 2 months. i don't know why, but i suggested we meet on zoom or something for a breakfast/lunch date. the thing with nicole is this: she's my friend, sure, but she's really just a "reply only" friend. the kind of friend who will never reach out to me first, but she'll respond if i reach out to her. usually it's after a period of time. sometimes a few days. more often than not i just feel like some task for her to cross off her to-do list. she's also the kind of person who seems to always be in a crisis. i wonder if that's why she barely responds to my messages of good news, or even mediocre news, but rapidly responds if i tell her something bad has happened? i remember telling her i quit my job and planned to open my own practice, and all she did was "like" the text message. no congrats. no questioning my sanity. just a thumbs up. i've made excuses for her for so long. that she's busy with teddy, her 2 year old son. the time difference between the east coast and the west coast. all of her crises. we used to talk about everything, but that's changed a lot. honestly, i've sometimes thought about ending our friendship. i know she's not the kind of friend i need in my life, and it <u>would</u> be easy. all i would need to do is not reach out to her anymore. done. even still, i thought she might be a good person for me to talk to about all of this stuff with jake. in a roundabout way, she is a safe friend. she's safe because she lives across the country and is no longer friends with anyone here in nj, so who would she blab to? anyway, she surprisingly answered my text quickly and she agreed to a zoom breakfast/lunch with me on friday. and then she sent me no less than a dozen pictures of teddy. i'm rolling my eyes, if you couldn't tell. i like the pictures, but maybe just one at a time? he's gotten so big. i remember meeting him in the hospital just after he was born. time flies.

all of that being said, i've been thinking a lot about friends and family. i thought i could build a family with the man i married. i mean, we are a family. though, i guess it also depends on who you ask. i've been told a time or two that you're not a <u>real</u> family if you don't have kids. rolling my eyes again. i'm not unhappy at all that jake and i don't have kids. it wasn't in the cards for us, and i do very much enjoy the freedom i have. besides, i couldn't imagine trying to juggle parenting on top of all of this shit i'm slogging through. on top of trying to rediscover myself, and figure out what the fuck i'm doing with my life. frankly, our little family unit is starting to feel more and more like the extended family relationships i grew up with: distant and cold. full of underlying resentment. somedays it feels like only a matter of time until we walk away from each other and never look back, like my aunts and uncles and cousins and i have done.

Hannah's Journal
Friday, December 15, 2023

i'm having anxiety attacks again, and i fear they are going to keep coming. the last couple of weeks have just sucked because of it. i feel so mad at everything and everyone all the time, like there's this seething anger sitting right under my skin at all times, and it takes everything in me not to lash out. maybe i'm still dealing with the fallout of the dream i had about dad a week or two ago. it messed me up, and i wonder if that's where all of this anxiety and anger is coming from. not that the conversation i had with nicole the other day made me feel any better. i'll make note of that later, though. that dream felt so real, but how could it be? he's dead. turned to ash and set out to sea in time for my birthday last summer. i've just been trying to push it down, pretending it's not there. i should know by now that it doesn't work, but i'm too stupid to learn from my mistakes.

one good thing did happen in the time since i last wrote here. i went out to sunset cove, the mall by SHU, and bought myself some new clothes. it felt weird at first because for years i've really only bought clothes i could wear to work, not for the fun side of life. not that i've done much fun stuff in a while. when i got to the mall, though, i really leaned into my younger self. i bought a new pair of converse sneakers. the classic chuck taylors, like i always used to wear. it sounds stupid, but it felt _so_ good to put them on. it felt like coming home to myself or something. i picked up some raglan baseball tees and a sex pistols t-shirt. it has a photo of sid vicious on it, and i never realized until now how much jimmy looked like him when we were younger. it was all in the clothes and hair, how he used to spike it out in every direction. i know the clothes made young adult hannah happy because i could feel her smiling somewhere inside me, clapping her hands gleefully.

so, i had a virtual breakfast/lunch date with nicole this week. she surprised me with how hard-lined she was about everything going on with me and jake. she was surprised to hear what i had to say, but then told me she never really thought jake was good enough for me. it totally threw me off. i felt really annoyed that she had this secret dislike for him, and never said anything about it. would i have if the roles were reversed, though? no, i wouldn't have. i know this because i am living it. i don't really like her husband, but i also don't really know him. he just gives me a weird vibe. i was glad when they moved away because it meant i wouldn't have to pretend to be fine around him when we all got together. the whole meetup was just weird, but i think i'm more mad at myself for thinking it would be different somehow. that she could give me the space to just talk without judgment or her opinions.

i wish i could talk to shannon. i've been thinking about it, but i just remember what she said to me a couple of weeks ago when i mentioned i was struggling with grief still. she made it sound like i shouldn't be hurting so much since it's been a few months since my dad's death. and jimmy's, though, i am pretty sure she doesn't think i should be mourning him at all. she never even touched on the bit i dropped about jake and i. honestly, i'm not sure what she'd say if i spilled everything like i did with nicole. i'm sure she'd just blow me off to tell me all about her own problems instead, which would just piss me off. i don't think anything makes me feel more lonely than being in a position where i just need a friend, and no one is there for me.

i do have alan, but i haven't talked to him about all of this stuff yet. it's like, i know i can trust him yet i'm still hesitant. our bond is really just because of jimmy at this point. it's our shared grief that is holding us together. our friendship used to be more than that before everything fell apart. but could our relationship still be like it used to? could it get back there, if not? maybe the only way to find out is to test it, but my circle is so small as it is. what if it ruins what's left of what we have?

the loneliness is just eating away at me tonight. i guess it's the weight of everything these last couple of weeks with jake, my friends, and now this dream i had about dad. it made me miss him even more. life has just felt so heavy and i just want to put it down for a while, but i have nowhere to do that. i feel like i am repeatedly being reminded of everyone i've ever lost.

i tried to hang out with jake tonight, but he was so engrossed in yet another new video game he bought. he did finally put it down to watch tv with me, but i could tell he was just annoyed about it. i tried to snuggle up next to him, just to feel some sort of connection to him, even if it was just his arm around me or my head in his lap. i think it lasted all of 5 minutes before he got "too hot" and asked me to get off. i just wanted to be held tonight. to feel like <u>someone</u> loves me.

Hannah took deep and steady breaths to quell her quickened heartbeat as she picked at her cuticles, hands lying in her lap, as she tried to ignore that it felt like an alien was trying to burrow out from the center of her chest. Seeing a small bead of blood form at the base of her nail bed, she separated her hands, letting one grip the arm of the plush chair she sat in while she pushed the other into the leg of her dark denim jeans to stop the bleeding.

"I can see that something's weighing heavily on your heart," Linda observed with her head tilted to one side.

Hannah swallowed hard and looked down at her chewed-up cuticle, noticing a small bubble of blood beginning to form again. "I just—I have some doubts."

"What kind of doubts?"

She could feel her eyes fill with tears, and shut them tight to stop the flow. "I talked to one of my friends the other day, and I told her about me and Jake. Ever since then, it's all I can think about. If he still loves me. Hell, if he even still *likes* me."

"What makes you think he doesn't?"

Hannah shrugged. "It's in how he talks to me, and how he acts around me. There have been so many days where I just feel like I don't exist, you know? He doesn't look at me when I'm talking, or even just when I walk past him in the house. I can't remember the last time he touched me either, or tried to initiate anything with me. He barely even kisses me anymore. I just don't know what to do, and my friend was the first to say that maybe I should leave him. I can't stop thinking about it."

"When did all of this start? Can you pinpoint when the shift happened?"

Hannah sputtered her lips. "A few months ago, but the more I think about it, there were signs before then, too. It's a lot of things, honestly. It all came to a head when everything with Jimmy came to light, but he denies it. It's his job, but he won't admit it. It's—a lot, and it's created this complacency in him about *everything*."

Linda grunted softly. "What was the tipping point for you? Because up until now, you haven't mentioned wanting to leave him," she pointed out.

"It's something I've passively thought about. Nothing serious, until the whole coffee incident the morning after Thanksgiving. It just really hit me that Jake doesn't even know who I am anymore, and that he doesn't seem to care either. I feel like a stranger in my own life."

"What are your feelings toward him?"

"I still love him," she said with a nod, sure of that still despite everything. "I just don't know if I like him very much right now. If that makes sense?" Hannah looked at Lisa, who nodded in understanding. "It sounds crazy because things seem to be on the upswing. Like, he's been in a better mood lately, but I can't help but wait for the other shoe to drop. I can't help but still walk on eggshells, just waiting to do or say the wrong thing that will ruin his mood all over again. It's so frustrating because even when I'm trying to help or trying to do better, I'm not. Everything I do pisses him off."

Linda's expression turned to one of concern. "What happens when he gets mad?"

"He becomes distant and usually leaves the room to go off and be by himself. I get the need for space; I don't want to make it sound like that's a bad thing or something. I just wish we could talk things out, but he'll either give me the silent treatment or start making snide, sarcastic comments. It's all under the guise of 'playing around' or ' just joking,' but it's never funny. Then it just snowballs into a fight," Hannah told her.

Linda smiled softly. "I know you know this, but it's worth saying to you now: you don't deserve to be treated that way. I'm worried you feel like you do, because it sounds like you blame yourself for 'ruining' his mood."

"I've spent the last few months feeling like I do deserve it, but I am starting to see that maybe I don't. At least not all of it. I know I haven't been the happy, present partner that Jake's needed," she said, before adding in a faint whisper, "And I know he thinks I've lied to him about my feelings for him."

"That may be so," Linda said as she leaned forward toward Hannah, "but you've needed him equally as much this year. If not more. Have you considered marriage counseling?" Linda asked.

"Jake would never go for it," Hannah choked out.

"Have you asked?"

She shook her head. "No, but I've tried to talk to him about going to therapy just for himself, and I got an earful about that."

Linda nodded deliberately. "Who do you have in your life that you can trust? That you can really talk to about these things? Other than me, that is."

Unable to meet Linda's gaze, Hannah stared back down at her fingers and once again picked at her skin. "All of my friends tell me they're too busy to talk, or I just know from prior history that they're not the right person for that kind of conversation, you know?"

"So you talked to your one friend, and she was suggesting you leave Jake. There's no one else you've tried talking to?" Linda said.

"Well," she said quietly. "I mentioned something to Alan, and I did *try* to talk to my best friend, Shannon, about it. She just glommed onto something else I said and then started talking about herself. As usual."

"And what happened when you talked to Alan?" Linda asked.

"Well, for one thing, he was kind of distracted because he was watching his kids at the time. I only mentioned some financial stress we've been under, and he immediately jumped to wanting to send me money or something."

"How did that make you feel?" Linda questioned, pinching her eyebrows together.

Hannah nodded emphatically. "Annoyed, honestly. I could never accept financial help like that, and it annoyed me that he thought I was asking to begin with."

Linda bobbed her chin slightly. "Would you be open to approaching the conversation with him again? Perhaps you could lay a foundation ahead of time by telling him that you're just looking for a space to talk, not necessarily for anything else. That may give you some runway to be able to talk about more of the issues."

"I don't know. Maybe," Hannah said with an edge of uncertainty in her voice. She could immediately feel the walls of her heart closing in tighter, shutting her in and preventing her from reaching out again. She had been in this position with friends of the past before, trying so hard to be heard. Hannah's thoughts brought her back to her younger self and how the world had turned her so inward. How so much of her had changed, and how she'd given up on herself so easily. She had always been an anxious and introverted person, but also knew when enough was enough. She used to stick up for herself, but now she just took it.

"What are you thinking?" Linda asked suddenly, tearing Hannah off the hamster wheel in her mind.

With a slight shake of her head, she admitted, "That I'm not sure when I became this person."

"What person is that?" Linda questioned. "How is she different from the person you were a year ago? Or five, ten, years ago? What's changed?"

A fresh stream of blood flowed like a tiny river along the edge of Hannah's nail bed as she picked some more at her fingers. "I'm not a black and white thinker, but I've always felt like I was a black and white person. A walking dichotomy. Hard, but soft. Someone who was often a doormat, but then also someone who took no shit. But now? I'm just soft. I'm just a dirty, sun-faded doormat. A pushover."

"Have you ever pointed out to Jake when his jokes are mean, or when he is being particularly cold and distant?"

"I've tried to," she said with a nod. "He just tells me I'm being dramatic, and that he's just 'joking around.' Conversation over. I guess I've just gotten to the point where I wonder what's the use in even saying anything anymore?"

"It seems like the apathy hasn't only affected Jake," Linda observed. She watched Hannah for a few beats, whose eyes were beginning to overflow with tears. "Are you happy, Hannah? I don't mean here, now, in this moment. In general. Are you happy?"

Hannah knew the answer immediately, and supposed Linda did, too. She wasn't happy, and she hadn't been for a long time. The sadness she felt was more profound than just grief. It was like she had been lost in the undercurrent of the last year or so. Hannah had always been an expert at burying her feelings, able to pretend like things were okay, but it was becoming harder to do so. The only time she had ever known the freedom to drop the mask was when she was with Jimmy and, later, Jake. Now, even that had changed.

Linda cleared her throat, bringing Hannah's attention back to their conversation, still waiting for a response.

"No," she said flatly.

Linda leaned forward again, this time resting her elbows on her thighs. As she clasped her hands together, she said, "It's okay, and perfectly reasonable, that you feel that way. We need to find a way for you to feel that happiness again. I know you've got your journal to let some of this out, and that's great. I do, however, think you should consider figuring out who in your circle is a trusted friend to lean on, and then lean on them. If you only ask, I'm sure they will show up for you in unexpected ways. Those who *really* know us can still hear the unspoken words in our hearts."

Hannah dabbed at her eyes with a fresh tissue. It was a simple suggestion on the surface, but she thought scaling Mount Everest might be an easier feat to accomplish. She would need to push back against every brick in the walls surrounding her heart, and the subliminal messages she'd taken as gospel over the years, and all of the rigorous training she'd put herself through to not ever rely on anyone else. Ever.

Hannah's Journal
Wednesday, December 20, 2023

i'm playing a dangerous game. i know i am, but i can't stop. there's this UPS driver at work, drew, who i've become friends with since i started renting my office in the business complex here in bay point. we have a lot in common, and he's so easy to talk to. he's not terrible on the eyes, either, i guess. but we're friends. just. friends.

i ran into him in the hallway today. he was making his usual deliveries, and i was coming back from the bathroom. we stopped to chit chat for a minute, and then went on our separate ways. but, then, he stopped by my office about 10/15 minutes later. he didn't have a package for me. not that i was expecting one. he said he was giving candy canes out to his "best" customers, and just wanted to drop one off for me even if he wasn't delivering to me today. we talked some more in my office mostly about the hockey game last night. when that got stale, we started talking about other things, which was out of the ordinary. he told me about his divorce, and how he's back living at home with his mom until he can get on his feet again. they've apparently always been close, so it's not the worst thing. people always like to divulge things to me. i guess it's the therapist in me. but with him, it feels like more than that.

sometimes it's like he finds reasons to talk to me or ways to touch me, even if it's just his hand when he's passing me a box or that handheld thing to sign on. i'm probably just overthinking it, though. it's hard to believe i am when i think about the ways his eyes trace the edges of my body, up and down every inch of me.

therein lies the danger: it's the way he looks at me as if i'm the most beautiful thing he's ever seen. i know i'm not nearly that attractive, but then i see his cheeks flush a little when i open the door to my office, and i feel like maybe i could be. i know he has gone above and beyond his job responsibilities to help me out, like breaking down big boxes for me or moving things around my office to make space for the new stuff he delivered. and it's obvious that he finds ways to just stay a little longer to talk to me some more. like today.

i've seen him sometimes in the parking lot loading boxes onto the dolly and looking in the direction of my window, like he's trying to see if my light is on or something. it's crazy, but i find it... nice? flattering, for sure. just to have a man pay attention to me like that. to look at me with those wanting eyes, like he wants me in every way possible. i wonder if drew has noticed my wedding ring, or if he just pretends not to. maybe he can just tell how lonely and desperate i am, and he's taking pity on me. throwing me a bone. the sad, old hag that i am.

if i'm being honest, i find myself looking for his truck in the parking lot some days. when i go to the bathroom, or out to my car around the time he usually comes, i tell myself that there is a purpose, but it's really just to see if he's there. to feed this hunger for his attention. for his eyes to be on me, filling me up with this false confidence. i notice some days when i feel the worst about myself, or my marriage even, that i'm craving that attention more. like it could fix me.

i hate to even admit this part, but i've been dressing a little nicer and wearing more makeup. it's purely to get the side glances when he thinks i'm not looking. jake hasn't even noticed that i've been going to work more dolled-up than usual, not that he's home much in the mornings, anyway, since he keeps having to go in early for one reason or another. even if he were home, though, i don't think he'd notice. when i was at the mall a few weeks ago, i bought this dress with flowers on it. it's so pretty but when i put it on at home, it was much shorter and low-cut than i thought. i was going to just return it, but i then didn't because i thought of drew. i've worn it to work a couple of times, and his cheeks flushed each time he has seen me in it. so the dress did what i wanted it to do, and i felt better about myself. if only for a short while.

i've never been the type of woman to consider an affair, but i see now what could lead someone to that. i'm trying hard to stick to my moral code, but somedays it feels impossible. i have these thoughts sometimes of the two of us on the couch in my office, or in the back of his delivery truck.

i'm so ashamed about it, even if it doesn't sound like i am. i feel sick just thinking about the hands of another man on my body. but i know in a day or two i'll be glancing out the window looking for his truck again. i keep reminding myself that this isn't who i am. that i'm better than that. that i wouldn't ever cave to the temptation, but the more time goes on, the more i'm not entirely sure.

Hannah sat anchored in the driver's seat, her knuckles turning white from the death grip she held on the steering wheel. She and Jake had just pulled into the Gallos' driveway for their annual Christmas dinner, as per tradition, on the Friday before Christmas Day. Hannah, Jake, Shannon, and her husband, Rob, had gotten together for the holiday like this every year since they had known one another.

The sound of the passenger side door suddenly closing caused her to jump, shaking her hands loose from the steering wheel. With a deep breath, Hannah unbuckled herself and stepped out of the car as Jake was already walking up the driveway toward the front door of the house. She could feel an anxiety attack lingering beneath her skin, with its familiar tendrils causing jittery twitches in her fingers and sweat pooling under the surface, waiting to start leaking from every pore.

The car ride had been tense with silence. When Jake had come home from work in a bad mood about something, not that he would say what, Hannah knew she would be in for a fight to get him back out the door. She was right, of course. The whole conversation quickly devolved into another argument, but Jake eventually got into the car unwillingly. Hannah tried to talk to him on the drive, telling him this funny story from her day to get him to loosen up a little, but it only seemed to anger him more. Now they stood on Shannon and Rob's front porch, barely able to look at each other.

"Can you just *try* to act normal?" Hannah quietly pleaded while her finger mashed the doorbell.

Before Jake could make some snappy comment back, Shannon swung open the door, her pregnant belly barely showing under the loose knit sweater she wore. Hannah was surprised to see her in glasses instead of contacts, and her mousy brown hair up in a messy bun. Despite her unusually disheveled appearance, Shannon's smile beamed. "Hi, you guys! I know I look like a hot mess," she said to them as she waved them inside. "Come in!"

Hannah immediately felt queasy as she entered the house, the smells of dinner wafting in from the kitchen, and the warmth from the oven wrapping around her like a noose. She reminded herself it was just nerves, that she was safe in her best friend's home. She smiled tightly, looking at the impeccable Christmas decorations on display throughout the living room and dining room. "Smells good in here!" Hannah declared with a nervous laugh.

Shannon's husband, Rob, came around the corner from the kitchen. "Hey, buddy," he said to Jake as he shook his hand. "Can I get you a beer?"

"That'd be great," Jake replied, his tone still dismal. Hannah winced at Rob's offer to Jake, afraid he'd let himself get as sloppy as he'd been at home lately. It was essential to her that they maintain the facade of being the perfectly happy couple tonight.

Rob leaned in to give Hannah a hug and a kiss on the cheek. "Glass of wine?" he asked her, pulling his face back from hers, the stubble of his dark five o'clock shadow scratching her face.

"Sure, thanks." Fighting the urge to fidget, Hannah rubbed her hands in front of her and followed their hosts into the kitchen. "Anything I can do to help?" she asked.

Shannon rubbed her stomach and chuckled. "Drink enough wine for both of us, will you?"

Hannah forced herself to laugh in response, cringing at the nervous edge behind it. She whispered a thanks to Rob as he handed her a glass of red wine before shuffling Jake off to the living room, where a college football game was playing on the television. Their voices carried over the announcer's, but she couldn't quite make out the exact words they were saying, and it made her nerves spike again. Hannah silently pleaded with Jake to behave, hoping that he would somehow pick up the frequency of her telepathic message.

Meanwhile, Shannon talked incessantly about work and her pregnancy. Their conversation flowed easily, mainly because Shannon was the one who did all the talking. Hannah listened with one ear while the other was still trying to make out the conversation in the next room. Not that her friend noticed at all.

"Hey, Rob?" Shannon shouted into the next room. "Can you take Archie out to pee before we eat? Food'll be ready in a couple of minutes!"

Rob and Jake both appeared in the doorway as Archie, the Gallos' Boston Terrier, followed behind at a slow trot. Rob clipped the leash on him while Hannah took his face in her hands and crooned about what a handsome little pup he was. Jake stood in the doorway that separated the two rooms, leaning against its frame, as Rob disappeared through the back door with Archie. His gaze met Hannah's, who managed a rigid smile. Jake's face remained flat as he chugged the last of his beer.

Shannon happened to look up as the exchange was happening, catching Hannah's eye briefly when she turned away from her husband. She glanced over at Jake, who was crossing the kitchen to throw the bottle in the recycling bin before helping himself to another. When Shannon turned back to her, she raised an eyebrow in question, but Hannah only responded with a quick shrug.

"Jake, it's been forever since we've seen you," Shannon started. "How're things? How's work? Seems like you're always at the office these days."

Jake turned to her, taking two big gulps as if getting his thoughts straight before answering. "Yeah, it's all right. Busy," he told her simply.

"Hannah said something about a promotion?" Shannon asked in an attempt to keep him engaged.

Hannah's heart sank. She was for sure going to hear about this when they got back into the car later. Jake had a peculiar habit of keeping any good news locked away until it was a sure thing. She guessed it was to avoid feeling embarrassed if things didn't work out. Hannah anxiously glanced in Jake's direction, noticing his eyes had gone wide.

"Oh, uh, yeah," he stuttered. "Yeah, maybe. We'll see." He was doing his best to sound nonchalant about the whole thing, like he didn't care if he got it or not. He did care about it, though. He cared about it so much that he was allowing it to make the acid in his stomach churn day and night.

Shannon handed Hannah a handful of silverware to set on the table, following behind her to put the plates out. She looked up at Jake, smiling sweetly before saying, "Well, I hope you get it. You deserve it with how much time you're spending over there!"

Jake nodded and opened his mouth to say something, but the moment was thankfully interrupted as Rob and Archie reappeared.

"All right! Everyone, grab a seat. Let's eat!" Shannon announced.

The four of them sat at the table, doling out food to one another and exchanging pleasantries. As everything settled down, Hannah noticed that the atmosphere had become awkward and uncomfortable. Sitting next to Jake, she could feel the annoyance coming off him, as if it were something palpable she could reach out and pet with her fingertips. Glancing around the table, Hannah wondered if anyone else could feel it, too. Just then, her eyes met Shannon's, who had been shifting her gaze between the two of them.

I guess it's not just me, Hannah thought.

Her mind raced with something to say to fill the silence, to cover up the truth of what was happening between her and Jake. "So, how excited are your moms about the baby?" Hannah asked, adjusting her tone to attempt excitement. A new baby was always the perfect distraction.

Shannon and Rob talked excitedly about the reactions of both sides of their family, how they were all anticipating the arrival of the first grandchild. Hannah felt her shoulders instinctively relax, now that the focus had shifted back onto them. Jake didn't contribute much to the conversation, except for a few grunts and a well-placed smile.

While they talked on and on about their birthing plan, Hannah glanced at the clock every few minutes, anxious to see the minutes ticking down until it was an acceptable time for them to leave. This was something she often did when she found herself in a situation she wanted to escape. If she could see the next marker on the journey, and estimate a time frame for how long it would take to reach it, she could feel like some progress was being made toward her goal of getting home. Hannah checked dinner off the mental to-do list of this evening's activities.

Just coffee and dessert left. Another hour, she assured herself. Just the mere thought brought her comfort.

After dinner, Hannah helped Shannon clear the table as another silence fell over the four friends. It was the natural ebb and flow of a conversation, but Hannah could feel the panic in her building all over again. Shannon broke the tension by talking about this new bakery that had opened up in Cedar Cove, and how she nearly bought one of everything for their dinner tonight. Hannah shoveled heaps of sugar into her mug, followed by a generous pour of milk, and topped it off with a bit of coffee. Shannon made a choking sound from across the table.

"What's so funny?" Hannah asked with a confused grin, looking at the three faces around the table.

"Do you want some coffee with your sugar milk?" Shannon quipped. Hannah heard Jake snort beside her, peering at him from the corner of her eye. "I swear I put that much sugar in my coffee when I was a kid trying to convince myself I actually liked it!" Shannon howled.

"What? I do like it this way! You know I've always done it like this!" Hannah said with a laugh, but her tone was slowly turning defensive.

Jake, staring at his plate, chimed in to add, "Well, most people move past the things they were into in college. They move on." His icy gaze slid sideways to Hannah.

Dazed, she looked at him as redness appeared in her cheeks. She knew he wasn't talking about coffee anymore, and she hated him in that moment for bringing Jimmy into this, for letting his jealousy shine through in front of their friends. She opened her mouth to say something, but no words came out. What could she even say, anyway?

Shannon let out a short breath, an attempt to laugh at a joke that Jake was clearly not making. Rob cleared his throat and commented on the Italian pastry in his hand. Jake merely snickered and diverted his focus back to his own dessert. Hannah just sat in her seat, staring at the table but seeing nothing at the same time. It felt like her stomach had fallen right out of the bottom of her body, and she had died right there without anyone even noticing.

When the clock finally hit 9:00 P.M., Hannah delicately suggested to Jake that they head home to get Diesel outside for the night. As they said their goodbyes, Shannon held her tightly in a hug for just a little longer than usual.

In the car, Jake asked sarcastically, "So did my performance meet your expectations?"

As she turned to back out onto the street, Hannah paused long enough to shoot him a stony look. "I just wanted things to go smoothly tonight. I didn't want to make our friends uncomfortable because we can't get along."

Jake scoffed, "We're getting along just fine."

Hannah snorted. "Right."

"Fine," Jake started. "Then let's do this. I can't even believe you told her about the promotion. I haven't told anyone, Hannah."

"I can't believe you brought up Jimmy," she shot back.

"I did not!"

Hannah's lips sputtered. "Please! We both know you weren't just talking about coffee back there!"

Jake smirked before turning away from her to stare out the window for the remainder of the ride home. Hannah turned up the music and quietly sang along until a song by The Tidewater Hellraisers played. The opening guitar riffs thrummed heavily as the hazy, jagged vocals of Jimmy Taylor shouted about the state of corporate America. Hannah's body stiffened for a brief moment before she hastily reached for her phone to change the song.

With a confused look on his face, Jake turned to Hannah and asked, "What the hell is this?"

She didn't know what to say, knowing he would be beyond angry if he knew he was listening to Jimmy's music. "Oh, I, uh—I found them on Instagram the other day."

"Really?" Jake looked at her as if she had suddenly turned an ugly shade of puke green. "This is nothing like the music you listen to."

"I used to listen to music like this all the time," she told him guardedly. Her taste in music had mellowed out some around the time she and Jake had begun dating, so she wasn't entirely surprised he didn't remember.

"What's the name of this band?" he asked, craning his neck to get a look at the phone in her hand.

Hannah turned it over in her lap before he could, not that he would have recognized Jimmy's face in the band photograph that appeared on the screen. "They're called The Tidewater Hellraisers. Or something like that. I'll change it," she said quickly, remembering she could change the track from the buttons on the back of the steering wheel.

"Never heard of them. You said you came across them on Instagram?"

"Yeah. Well, rediscovered them is more accurate, I guess," she said, stumbling over her words. "They were a band I knew from back in the day, but they never got big."

"Interesting," Jake said simply as he turned his attention back to the world passing outside the passenger window.

December 23, 2023

Hannah is again standing on the bottom stair that leads up to the second floor where her childhood bedroom is located. Her father is sitting in his usual spot in the armchair, and she is watching him act all weird and goofy again. Their eyes meet, and they both instinctively know that they can see each other. Her father's lips start to move, and some sound is coming out, but she can't make out the words he is saying. The sound is disturbing, like the death rattle of someone at the very end of their life. It is breathy, low, and shaky.

"Dad, I can't hear you," she tells him, stepping down from the stairs and taking small, calculated steps in his direction.

He tries to speak again, but the same gargling noise is all that can be heard. His face tenses with panic. He is looking at her wild-eyed and desperate to get his words out, to say whatever it is he needs to say.

Hannah is only a couple of feet from him, still walking slowly, as she repeats herself. "I still can't hear you." She reaches a hand out to him, just out of reach. "It's okay, Dad. It's okay," she says, trying to calm him down.

Hannah woke up in a snap, sitting upright so fast she felt off kilter for a moment, her head feeling heavy like a bowling ball. As the reality of her dream settled in her thoughts, her hand instinctively found her lips as her stomach somersaulted. Diesel wiggled awake at her side, and her free hand found the soft fur under his chin, stroking it gently. Once her body relaxed again, Hannah peered at her cellphone to see it was barely even 3:30 A.M. She let out a heavy sigh and lay her head back on the pillow as Diesel crawled up from the bottom of the bed, nuzzling his head into the space between her chin and chest.

"Diesel, what is happening to me?" she whispered to him in the dark, wishing desperately that he could talk to her and explain everything.

After lying in bed for a few minutes more, just staring up at the white ceiling, Hannah decided to get out of bed slowly so as not to wake Jake and made her way into the kitchen for a soothing cup of coffee. She picked out her favorite Christmas mug, one that featured a Santa, but had seen better days with its faded glaze and chipped handle; she had stolen it from the garbage of the gift shop where she worked in Riverside Springs years ago. Hannah traced the edges of Santa's face with the tips of her fingers, lost in her thoughts that tried to make sense of her dream. In some way, she felt like her dad was trying to tell her something. But what? A shiver went through her, and Hannah shook her head to rid herself of such a ridiculous notion.

When her coffee had been made to her liking, Hannah brought it into the living room and turned on the Christmas tree lights and gas fireplace. She found solace in the soft glow each emitted into the dark room as she curled up under a blanket on the couch, cradling the warmth of the coffee in her hands. Her eyes slowly shifted to focus on the gifts under the tree, and a slight smile crept across her lips, pushing aside the shaky feeling still lingering in her body.

It was the day before Christmas Eve, which had always been *their* Christmas. Just her and Jake. They had a tradition of opening gifts over coffee and breakfast, which typically included cinnamon rolls, and then spent the day in their pajamas watching Christmas movies and playing board games. In the evening, they would open a bottle of wine and indulge in a special dinner, something they wouldn't usually have. Some years it was lobster, while other years it was an expensive cut of steak.

Hannah looked forward to this day each winter, but especially so this year. She needed this day to fill her heart again. They both did, really. For now, though, she could only hope Jake would wake up in a good mood. That maybe he would remind her more of the Jake she had fallen in love with all those years ago at a concert in Stonebridge, rather than the stranger she saw stalking about the house these days.

Diesel suddenly came bounding out of the bedroom, jumping right into her lap with a big yawn.

"Hey, you, my sleepy boy," she cooed as she stroked his back, causing him to melt into her lap.

Jake followed behind him, a hand covering his wide-mouthed yawn. Hannah's breath caught in her throat just then, waiting for him to speak first. He stopped and stared at her, and then smiled. "Merry Christmas, honey," he said groggily.

"Merry Christmas," Hannah replied. She noted how he used his pet name for her, taking it as a good sign, and let her shoulders relax. "Who woke up who?"

Jake lazily pointed at Diesel. "He just can't live without you."

Hannah giggled. "Well, there's a pot of coffee on."

"Thanks," Jake said and wandered into the kitchen, yawning again loudly.

Sounds of a typical morning in the DeLuca household poured out from the kitchen: the sound of kibble being chomped, water being lapped, coffee being poured, the refrigerator door opening and closing, a spoon tinkling against a porcelain mug.

When Jake reemerged, Hannah asked, "Did you sleep all right?"

He shrugged as he sat on the opposite end of the sofa. "Eh, not really. I woke up with some heartburn again around one o'clock, I think it was."

"Again?" Hannah asked. "I'm surprised I didn't hear you."

"I'm not—you were pretty beat last night. It wasn't anything a couple of antacids couldn't fix," he assured her.

Hannah frowned at him, but he wasn't looking at her to notice. "Do you think you should be having that coffee? Won't it aggravate your stomach?"

"It's fine," he said, waving her off with his free hand and sipping from his mug slowly before changing the subject. "Why don't we open some gifts?" he asked with a nod in the direction of their tree.

Hannah grinned excitedly. "Yes!"

She enthusiastically positioned herself on the floor in front of the tree and passed Jake his first gift to open. When it was her turn, Hannah was surprised by what Jake had given her this year, like he had put a lot more effort into it than any year before. The two of them belly laughed together as they helped Diesel open his presents, as he was simultaneously excited and terrified by the shreds of paper.

When all was said and done, Hannah leaned in to kiss Jake. "Thanks, love," she told him. "You put a lot of thought into this. It was just what I was wanting."

Jake smiled coyly at her. "You know, I do listen to you. *Sometimes,*" he said sweetly, but Hannah could hear a sort of sarcastic undertone in his words.

She forced herself to laugh a little, to keep things light. Underneath the fakeness, she grumbled at the way Jake would turn anything into some stupid joke, even the things that upset her. Like a laugh could somehow undo his words or actions. Jake leaned in to kiss her again, resting a hand on her cheek to hold her there in it.

When she was able to wiggle free, she asked, "What was that for?"

"I just love you, and I've missed you," he told her with his face mere inches from hers, holding her gaze so intensely.

"I've missed you, too," Hannah sheepishly said. She did miss him, but there was still something that left her unsettled about his sudden changes in attitude in just the last few days alone.

"Have you?" Jake asked, his eyes searching her face for the truth.

Hannah chuckled, feeling uncomfortable with his closeness all of a sudden. "Yeah, of course. I've been missing you a lot lately."

Before she knew it, the two of them were tangled up together in front of the fireplace. Jake was leaning on his elbows, hovering above her and staring into her eyes again with an endearing grin spread across his face. She couldn't remember the last time they had been together in that way, surprised that they had even found themselves there, given last night's events. As startled as she was by this show of affection from him, it felt right. Even with her own apprehension knocking at the back of her mind, reminding her it was still there. In this moment, lying here with Jake, she forced herself to forget about it, just for a little while.

Hannah spent most of the afternoon reading a new Christmas romance she had picked up on her Kindle, while Jake and Diesel both snored quietly on the couch as holiday music played through the speakers in the living room. With her eyes getting heavy, she decided to start on dinner before she, too, fell asleep, and they ordered a pizza instead.

Humming along with the music, she prepared a loaf of bread for the oven and then cut green beans for a side dish. Interrupting the afternoon, her cell phone buzzed in the pocket of her apron. Her hand instinctively reached for it, but she decided to ignore it in favor of the quiet. As it continued to buzz, though, her curiosity got the better of her and she took a quick peek to see who it was. Quickly, her thumb swiped to answer.

"Alan! Hey!" she exclaimed happily. "It's so good to hear from you!"

"Hannah! Merry Christmas!" Alan shouted into the phone; his beaming smile obvious even if she couldn't see his face.

"Merry Christmas," Hannah said with a giggle. "You're a couple of days early, though."

"I know. I wanted to give you a call today before the Christmas hurricane blows in," he acknowledged.

Hannah chuckled. "I can imagine with two kids it gets crazy."

"That, yeah, and all the extended family I have to contend with," he told her. "How are things with you?"

"Uh—" she hesitated. "Pretty good."

"You're sure?" he asked, sounding uncertain.

Hannah grabbed another handful of green beans from the plastic bag, continuing to cut off the ends. "Yeah, why wouldn't I be?" she asked, still glowing from her morning with Jake.

"I don't know," Alan said wearily. "You seemed a little off when we talked at Thanksgiving, and I haven't heard from you since—"

"I know. I'm sorry, Alan," Hannah told him sincerely, taking a momentary break from chopping. "Life's just been a little weird lately." She thought about her last session with Linda, where she was encouraged to open up to someone more, and who better than Alan? He had been like a brother to her all those years ago, her main confidant at that time. Aside from Jimmy, that is. The voice inside her mind pushed her toward him, but her heart resisted. It reminded her of the walls she'd so carefully built with bricks from friends who betrayed her confidence, who disappeared from her life without warning, and who tore her down with their words. It felt unwilling to surrender, reluctant to undo everything it worked so hard to create for her protection.

"How so?" Alan prodded.

Hannah picked up the knife again, hesitating to answer. Her mind churned, trying to decide quickly what she should say. "Just busy, I guess," she said casually. "The holidays are crazy with Jake's family, and it's been hard since my dad's not here this year, you know?"

"How are things with ol' Jakey boy?" he asked. "You guys figure things out? I don't need to come up there and set him straight, do I?"

Hannah laughed tensely. "Things have been a lot better, actually. He's been taking more time away from work, which has been nice," she told him with a hopeful smile.

The voice in her mind, though, questioned the validity of what she'd said. *Be honest,* it said. *Tell him about everything else, not just the good stuff.*

They talked for a while about Alan's daughters and the long wish lists they had both sent to Santa this year. As the conversation wound down, Hannah found a vulnerable moment to share with him the dreams she'd had about her dad. "Please don't think I'm a weirdo, but I've had these dreams that have felt so real," she said as she detailed each one. Alan listened attentively, mumbling something every so often to let her know he was listening. "I felt like I was standing there. Like—I could smell the house, feel the carpet under my feet. It lasted even after I woke up, too. That's the other thing—I woke up so wide awake even though it was only, like, three o'clock!"

Hannah could feel the hesitation on the other end of the phone. "Do you believe in visitation dreams, Hannah?" he inquired.

As she checked on the bread in the oven, Hannah asked, "Visitation dreams? I'm not sure I follow."

"Basically, that people who are gone can actually come visit us in our dreams," he explained.

Hannah cracked up. "You're not serious," she immediately said, even though she had questioned it being real herself. Tempering her tone and reaction, she told him, "I don't know. It's a nice thought, but there is a valid, scientific reason for our dreams. They are just our brain's way of working out our emotions, or events that have happened to us."

"You really don't think there's more after this?" Alan questioned.

Hannah paused before answering because she wasn't sure what she believed. "I mean—I don't know. I suppose I have wondered, and this has made me question it a bit, you know? I guess, in some way, I hope there is. Why? Do you?"

"I do believe there is more than just this," he confessed. "Maybe that's just the backwoods bayou in me, growing up believin' in haints and hollers and things, but existence is so much bigger than just us. There's gotta be more," he told her.

"Are you going all Agent Moulder on me? 'The truth is out there!'" she mocked. "In all seriousness, though, it's a romantic thought, but I think that's just all it is." Hannah wanted to tell him about the dream she had of Jimmy last spring that felt similar to these, but she didn't. The conversation was making her feel uncomfortable; it was begging her to open up her mind and heart, but she just closed up tight like a clam. "I should probably get going. I'm in the middle of getting dinner together here."

"Oh, sure," Alan said apprehensively. "I'm sorry if I said anything—"

"Don't be silly. I just need both my hands right now. That's all," Hannah said abruptly. "Wish the girls a Merry Christmas from me, okay?"

"I will. Merry Christmas, Hannah," Alan said again before hanging up.

Jake came into the kitchen just as Hannah was setting their plates on the table and about to pour the wine. Rubbing his stomach, he apologized for not helping her prepare everything. "Thanks for making all of this, honey," he said.

"You obviously needed some more rest after being up last night with that heartburn."

They toasted their wine glasses to each other, to better things to come, and dove into the meal.

Jake moaned happily. "This is all *so* good. You nailed it, honey."

As he shoveled another forkful into his mouth, Hannah offered, "Hey—I just wanted to say that I'm so happy to have this day with you. I know things have been a little weird between us, but I'm so happy to see you coming back to yourself. I feel like you're returning back to the Jake I know."

He lowered his eyes and nodded sullenly. "I know. I'm sorry I've been so distant, but I really do feel like things are only going to get better from here."

Hannah's lips formed a slight smile. She wanted to believe him, but the voice in her mind told her otherwise. It replayed for her each instance of his terrible behavior before today, when things seemed to be on the up and up, only to nosedive a short time later. Like all the other times in her life when she'd kept her hopes high about one thing or another, only to be let down.

Hoping to lighten the mood, she smiled and said, "Alan called before. He said to wish you a 'Merry Christmas.'"

Jake stared at her with his eyebrows raised. "Alan, huh?" he asked, not trying to be subtle about his annoyance. Hannah couldn't help but notice how the voice inside her mind had been right; she just hadn't thought the change would happen so quickly.

"Yeah, he called while you were asleep. He was going on and on about how excited the girls are for Santa." She giggled. "Apparently, Olivia asked for a pony, and Alan said he's dreading Christmas morning when there's not one in the yard for her." She looked up to see that Jake wasn't laughing, only staring at her stone-faced. "Well, I thought it was funny," she said facetiously.

Jake cracked a small smile, but Hannah could tell it wasn't authentic. "No, it is. It is funny," he replied flatly.

"What's wrong?"

Jake shook his head. "Nothing."

Hannah could feel her stomach clench. "No. What is it?"

"It's just that—it's weird, isn't it? That he always seems to call when I'm not around?"

Narrowing her gaze, Hannah asked, "Are you jealous or something?"

"No, of course not!" Jake blurted out, like he couldn't believe she would even suggest such a thing.

"So, then, what's weird about it? He's my friend," she insisted. "If you don't believe me, you can take a look at my phone. Read our messages. I don't care," she said, reaching for her phone.

Jake huffed and brushed her hand away from it. "No! Don't do that. I don't need to see anything. Just—forget it."

Without a thought, she said, "You know, Linda thinks we should consider marriage counseling."

"What does she know about what we need?"

Hannah looked up from her plate, her brow furrowed. "Well, I've talked to her about the problems we're having. This stupid bickering that comes out of nowhere. This jealousy. All of it."

Jake rolled his eyes, swigging the rest of the wine in his glass. "We're fine. This is just normal marriage stuff, Hannah. Besides—therapy is for people who don't have their shit together enough to figure it out themselves."

She laughed briefly. "Right. We're totally fine. That's why you got all uppity over my friend calling to wish us a happy holiday."

"I said to forget it," Jake told her coldly.

"I wish you would at least consider counseling for yourself, then. You're obviously struggling with—"

Jake scoffed, "I'm not struggling with anything! There is nothing wrong with me. Or us. I wish you would stop suggesting that there is. It's like you *want* something to be wrong!"

"I don't. That's the whole point," Hannah whispered as an uncomfortable silence settled over them. They busied themselves with eating and drinking, and Hannah wondered if he felt the urge to get up from the table and run as strongly as she did.

Then, as if nothing had happened, Jake spoke to her in an upbeat voice. "Did I mention how good this is? Babe, you did a phenomenal job on this meal. Really."

Hannah put on her best artificial smile, which felt like the only thing she knew how to do right these days. "Thanks," she said.

"Can you feel the potential in the air, Diesel? It's electric on days like today," Hannah dreamily whispered to him over her morning coffee. Jake remained asleep in bed, and the neighborhood was peaceful in the early morning hours.

It was New Year's Eve, one of Hannah's favorite days of the year since she was small. Without fail, she would become increasingly teary-eyed as midnight approached, as something much bigger than herself, than anyone, swelled inside of her. There was something so profoundly beautiful in the idea of new beginnings and blank slates, like every wildest dream she had could come true. As if, at the stroke of midnight, she would be reborn into someone entirely new.

Most of her friends made fun of her and blamed the over-indulgence of alcohol for her show of emotion during a night typically full of celebration. Hannah, though, unlike a lot of people she knew, had always felt everything in a big way—the good, the bad, and even the absence of either.

Curled up with Diesel, Hannah thought back to all of the years that had come before this one. When she was a kid, her parents made a big to-do about it, hosting parties for their friends with special snacks and drinks that were only for the adults. She had been allowed her share of food and sparkling grape juice in a fancy glass to make her feel like one of them. She had even been allowed to stay up until midnight, but often passed out on the couch long before then. As she grew up, the rules changed, and she was allowed to have a friend over for a sleepover and a glass of champagne at midnight to celebrate. In college, Hannah often found herself at friends' houses or local music clubs and bars. Life came full circle, as it often does, and she once again found enjoyment in just spending the night in with Jake. They would switch between all the television specials throughout the night, watching fireworks from around the world as the new year swept its way across the globe.

As soon as the stores opened, Hannah made her way around Bay Point running errands before the night's festivities. She visited the grocery store for some last-minute additions to their snacking spread, then headed toward the liquor store for champagne to toast with at midnight. She drove slowly along the back roads toward Bay Point Wine and Spirits, winding alongside the beach in town with an unobstructed view of Highgate City. The Tidewater Hellraisers played through the car's speakers, and she sang along while drumming her fingers on the steering wheel, a huge smile spread across her lips as she let the good mood of the day wash over her.

Walking the aisles of the small, dingy liquor store, Hannah thought back on the last year. She had been through a lot, and it was easy to get lost focusing on all of that, but there was also a lot of good that had come from it all, too. She had taken a big leap by taking a chance on herself to start her own business. Despite how rocky her relationship with Jake had been, things were feeling more and more like they had in the beginning. Since Christmas, he managed his work stress a lot better, which made being around him relatively painless. Except for this morning, when he had woken up in a cranky mood for the first time in weeks. She considered doing an intention setting exercise with him later on, thinking it might help to refocus him back to something positive, something to work toward.

It was only the other night when Jake uncharacteristically opened up to Hannah about his struggles with grief over the loss of her dad. They had been close from the start, having been more like natural father and son rather than in-laws, and part of her felt dumb for not realizing it would have affected him as much as it did her.

"I know he was *your* dad, but I loved him, too. He was so important to me, but no one seems to see that," he had cried to her. His tears had taken her by surprise, as Jake often struggled with letting himself show emotions like that. It was something she frequently observed in her practice with male clients, as if expressing themselves brought out weakness in them rather than strength.

Hannah could only stroke his hair as he talked, his head resting in her lap, and wipe the tears from her own eyes. Something changed after that, though, and Jake opened up to her more about how he was feeling. He even discussed what was happening at work and how it was affecting him. Hannah was happy to listen, feeling like she was seeing a side of her husband she had never seen before, and encouraged him to talk rather than bottling it up. It seemed to calm the bouts of heartburn and nausea, too, which made Jake finally see that maybe it was more related to stress than anything else. Besides that, Hannah knew the damage that keeping everything locked up tight could do to a person; her grief was a constant reminder of that.

She stood in front of the shelves of champagne trying to decide what to buy, when the air seemed to be completely sucked out of the room. She gulped like a fish out of water, desperate to breathe.

The thudding in her chest quickened to an intense pounding while the room began to spin, like she was standing on one of those zero-gravity Round Up rides at the county fair rather than the concrete floor of the liquor store.

Oh no, she thought. *Not another anxiety attack. Not here.*

She grabbed at the strap of the cotton sling bag that crossed over her chest, trying to lift the weight of it off her. She reached her free hand out for the shelf in front of her to steady herself.

Today is a good day. I was doing just fine. Please, calm down, she pleaded with herself.

Hannah grabbed the first bottle of champagne her eyes landed on in front of her and marched slowly and steadily toward the register, lifting each leg deliberately as if walking through wet cement. With shaky, sweaty hands, she paid for the bottle and stumbled through the door and toward her car. The cold December air was a shock to her system, and she struggled again to take in the frigid air as her lungs adjusted to the temperature.

Once behind the steering wheel, Hannah tore the bag off her body and tossed it onto the passenger seat. She laid the bottle of champagne on top of it and sat back, tilting her face into the sun shining through the windshield.

Hannah contemplated why this was happening to her now, since she was only thinking about everything she had to look forward to. Then she thought about the other proverbial shoe waiting to drop: how Jake's good mood would never last, and how there would inevitably be another knock-down, drag-out fight between them. It meant that she would unavoidably wake up just as unhappy as she had been the last few months, and how nothing would ever really change.

A shiver ran through her body, causing Hannah to start the car and turn the dial to the highest setting to warm up quickly. She laid her head back against the headrest, closing her eyes momentarily, to calm herself before driving home. The car's stereo kicked on, and The Tidewater Hellraisers started streaming loudly through the speakers again, but she turned it down to a faint whisper. Hannah pushed the button to retract the headliner in the roof of her car so the sun shone through the moonroof's glass onto her.

Watching the clouds pass overhead, she thought of Jimmy, who had been the first person she opened up to about her anxiety. He had taken it upon himself to learn how to help calm her in those moments. Hannah could almost feel Jimmy's hands on her shoulders now, strong and steadying. She closed her eyes again and practically heard the sound of his voice telling her to look him in the eyes as he told her about something totally random to distract her, usually something outlandish and funny. Jimmy had been be that rock for her countless times in the short years they were together. Even now, after all this time, Jimmy's calming presence lingered on in her life, outlasting his own.

Hannah opened her eyes and stared into the vastness of the sky above as if Jimmy were there looking back at her. Perhaps he was.

A little after eight o'clock that night, Hannah turned the television on to one of the cable channels to watch the New Year's

Eve celebrations from New York City. Jake had been out in the shed supposedly building a small table to be used in the laundry room. Hannah hadn't heard any power tools whirring all night, though, and figured he was hiding out there doomscrolling on his cell phone.

She busied herself in the kitchen, preparing snacks for their evening while she danced and sang to the musical pop act playing on one of the stages in Times Square. Jake finally returned to the house as Hannah started pulling some finger foods out of the oven.

As she plated the food onto platters, Hannah announced, "You're just in time. Everything is just about ready!"

"Oh, I, uh, didn't know we were doing this tonight," Jake replied, running a hand through his thick hair.

Hannah stood up straight as he sidled up next to her and popped a hot pretzel nugget into his mouth. "Well, yeah! What else would we be doing? Why did you think I went out before to get this stuff?" she asked, waving a hand at the plates of food and bottle of champagne waiting on ice.

"I didn't know that's what you were getting."

"I told you before I left the house, Jake," Hannah reminded him, her tone turning bitter.

He shrugged. "I guess I didn't hear you."

She turned back to the food in an attempt to hide the roll of her eyes and the anger flushing in her cheeks. "Well, it's almost ready," she said flatly.

"Eh, ya know—" Jake started, stumbling over his words, "I think I might just go to bed early tonight. I'm pretty beat."

Without looking at him, she suggested, "Why don't you just take a nap?"

"Nah, I'm pretty tired. I need more than a nap, I think. Besides, aren't we getting a little old for this, anyway?" Jake suggested condescendingly.

She could feel her chest begin to tighten with irritation, her hands bracing the edge of the counter. Hannah looked down at the floor. "Fine. Let me grab my pillow and a blanket. I'll just stay on the couch with Diesel tonight."

"You don't have to sleep on the couch—" Jake argued.

"No, I do," Hannah told him as she pushed past him and into their bedroom. She grabbed what she needed, her pillow and her favorite plush blanket with gnomes on it, and stalked back past him and into the living room without another glance in his direction.

"'Night," Jake whispered sheepishly.

"Goodnight. Happy New Year," she said coldly.

In the living room, Hannah pushed the ottoman against the couch to create a comfortable surface the size of a full bed where she could cuddle up with Diesel. She positioned her pillow against one of the arms of the couch and spread the blanket out before retrieving a small plate of snacks and a full glass of her favorite red wine.

After finally getting settled with Diesel, the reality of her night alone finally hit her, and a single tear fell from the corner of her eye. Hannah wiped it away quickly, not that anyone else was there to notice. The hollow ache in her core throbbed with loneliness, just enough to remind her it was there. This was the first New Year's Eve that she could remember being alone like this.

She missed Jimmy suddenly then, and how he used to make her feel like the most important person in any room. Despite the depth of his depression, she had always known he loved her truly and wholly, without question. She never wondered if Jimmy liked her for who she was underneath the fake exterior she put on for the rest of the world, because he showed her in big and small ways every chance he got. She had loved him just as much, and now that she was so many years outside of that last night together, she could see their walking away as their final act of love to one another.

Her memories of Jimmy were such a stark contrast to how things were with Jake now. He had slowly, and hardly without notice, become the man who *did* make her doubt if he could even stand to be in her presence most days. If he loved her like he once claimed to. It had driven her nearly mad these last few months, leading her to question her own worth.

Diesel shifted at her side and rolled himself over on his back, all four paws sticking straight into the air. Hannah giggled, watching one of his jowls flop open, revealing some of his teeth; he seemed always to be the goofiest when she needed it the most.

Rubbing his belly, Hannah whispered to him, "I don't know what this new year will hold, but I promise things will get better. One way or another. They have to." She only wished he could understand what she was telling him. That, although it might turn his little world upside down, they would be okay. As long as they had each other to look after, they would be okay.

Hannah was three or four glasses of wine deep by the time the last minutes of 2023 ticked away. At some point, her "I don't give a fuck" attitude took over and all she wanted to do was drink away the year. Or maybe it was just that she had let herself fall so far into the entanglement of her uncertainties. Either way, she stumbled into the kitchen, popped the cork of the bottle of champagne, and took a long swig.

"I'm not going to let him stop me from enjoying the New Year," she said, slurring each word.

With the bottle of bubbly in hand, Hannah plopped back down onto the couch next to Diesel. The official countdown began in Times Square, and a thick ball of emotion grew in her throat, making it hard to swallow. As she stroked Diesel's head slowly, Hannah finally allowed herself to cry.

"3… 2… 1… Happy *fucking* New Year," she said to Diesel, tipping the bottle in his direction before taking another long swallow.

Without warning, her cries turned to full, gut-wrenching sobs, which she tried to keep quiet to avoid waking Jake. Diesel nervously climbed into her lap and licked the saltiness from her cheeks. She planted a kiss on the tip of his nose and smiled sadly. "At least I still got a midnight kiss," she whispered to him as she continued to weep.

Her phone buzzed on the table beside her several times before she had even noticed. Without thinking to look at the Caller ID, Hannah swiped to answer.

"Hello?" she said, sniffling hard.

"Happy New Year!" Alan bellowed on the other end, cheers and pops of what were likely fireworks sounded off in the background.

Hannah chuckled between sobs. "Happy New Year, Alan," she said despondently.

"Hannah? What's wrong? What's happened?" he asked quickly, his tone changing from jovial to alarmed. She could hear a woman's voice in the background, likely Alan's wife, Phoebe, asking what was going on, but didn't hear him reply.

Hannah found herself unable to speak as the sadness had once again overtaken her. With her free hand, she cradled her face. She was too drunk to feel ashamed of her blatant vulnerability, so she just let herself cry.

"Hannah? Talk to me. What's going on?" Alan repeated.

With every ounce of strength she had left, Hannah picked herself up off the couch, wrapped the blanket around her shoulders, and stumbled out the back door onto the deck. With fireworks bursting overhead, she blurted out, "You were with me that day Jimmy ran off. You helped me through the worst day of my life then, and I know you'll help me through anything even though my head tells me not to trust you. I've been lying to you, Alan. I'm not happy. It's bad."

"Yeah, I can hear that. What's going on?"

"Everything is falling apart." Sitting on one of the cold metal patio chairs, she took a deep breath to steady herself. "Jake hates me, and I don't know where the fuck everything went wrong. Where did we go wrong? How did I get here, Alan?"

"What about Jake? What did he do?" Alan asked, trying to piece together the bits of information Hannah was feeding him.

"Pfft. Nothing. He's done nothing, and he's ruined everything by doing nothing," she answered drunkenly.

"Huh?"

"I thought things were getting better, but they're not. He totally blew me off tonight, and fell just short of calling me a stupid child. You know, he barely looks at me anymore, and forget about anything else. He's disgusted by me. I can see it in his eyes, Alan. I'm just married to myself at this point," she rambled on. "And don't get me started on the coffee!"

With concern peaking in his voice, Alan asked, "What about coffee? What? How long has this been going on?"

"For *months*. I wanted to tell you, but I couldn't. I don't know why because you're, like, the only friend I have left, Alan. You're the only one who cares about me. I just—I don't want to do this anymore."

"What are you saying? I can't lose you, too, Hannah. Not like that," Alan pleaded. "I will get on a plane tonight."

Hannah scoffed, "I don't mean like *that*, silly. I was thinking of our friend Jimmy tonight, though. I miss him so much, Alan. I want to be with someone who gets me like he did, ya know? I think I deserve that. Sometimes I find myself wishing I could go back to that time with him, just to feel that love again." Hannah folded herself over, her forehead resting on her knees.

Silence lingered in the 1,300 miles between them, as Alan let her cry. With a deep breath, he asked, "Listen—are you sure you're gonna be all right?"

Hannah nodded her head slightly, even though he couldn't see her. "I'll be okay. I just had an emotional day. And too much to drink." She giggled. "I just wanna go to bed and forget all about this night." She walked back into the warmth of the house, lying down on the couch again next to Diesel.

"I'll let you go then," he said. "Get some rest."

"Hey, Alan?"

"Yeah?"

"Do you think you could stay on the phone with me a little longer? Just until I fall asleep?" she asked drowsily.

"Of course. I'll stay here with you," he promised.

Hannah wedged the phone between her face and the pillow, wrapped her arm around Diesel, and closed her eyes. She could feel her hand rising and falling in time with Diesel's breaths. Before she knew it, sleep had consumed her. It was a fitful sleep, but when she woke up tomorrow, it would be a new day. A fresh start. Anything was possible.

January 3, 2024

Hannah is standing on the bottom step of the staircase that leads to her old bedroom in her childhood home. Her dad is sitting in his usual place in the living room, the same place he has been the last two times she has found herself here in this cosmic space with him. They are watching each other again, fully aware of the other's presence. She moves toward him faster than before, and the dream doesn't just end here. Not this time. She makes her way to the loveseat that sits adjacent to his, sitting on the corner closest to him. He's watching her and moving his lips, and this time, she hears words coming from his mouth. It's just her name, in a faint whisper, but it's more than the other times that they've been here.

"Dad, I can hear you!" she says, feeling the emotion flooding her eyes.

Her father's face softens and his eyes go wide as he asks, "You can?" His voice is a little louder but husky, like he hasn't uttered a word in months.

"Yes! I can hear you!" Hannah repeats.

Her dad reaches his hand out to her, which she takes in hers. She can feel the thickness of his fingers hugging the curve of her palm, the cracked roughness of his skin scraping against hers, the weight and warmth of it.

"Dad, I can feel you," she says in almost a whisper, unable to believe any of this.

"I can feel you, too, Hannah," he croaks.

They sit there for a few moments longer, holding hands, both with tears streaming down their cheeks. They don't say anything more because all that had been left unsaid between them is said now in the silence; words just aren't necessary now. Somehow, she just knows all that weighs on his heart in this moment. It's all the love he never expressed to her out loud. The goodbye that was stolen from them both. It's all there, laid bare between them.

Hannah's eyes opened slowly. She noticed her right arm extended out in front of her, with her hand curled slightly as if she were holding something. She blinked her eyes hard and sat up, staring at it still, not daring to move it. There was a warmth to it, while her other hand felt as cold as ice. She studied her empty hand, feeling a sensation there in her palm, as if something had once been there but was now gone. Hannah swallowed hard.

It wasn't real, the voice inside her mind immediately told her. *It was just a dream. That's all.*

Or was it? Hannah roughly shook her head, trying to loosen the grip of that idea from her mind. It was bad enough that she felt like she was losing whatever grip she had left on herself; she didn't need to add delusions to the mix, too. Her eyes landed back on her hand, still frozen in time, frozen in her dream.

But I felt him, she argued back with the voice. She took her other hand and gently grazed her palm with her fingertips, as if maybe her dad's hand was strangely still there. Like she could somehow feel it again, but her fingers only swiped at air and her own skin. She felt him. She knew it. Hannah kept tracing her palm with her fingers, remembering how rough his skin felt against hers, how her fingers had curled around his portly hand.

It was real, and he was here, she argued some more.

Hannah's stomach backflipped then, and she moved both hands to her lips. She could feel both palms starting to become slick with sweat as her chest heaved to draw in more oxygen. Panic was setting in. The perfect moment with her dad had gone, and she was left with only her anxiety.

You're really losing it now, the voice in her mind said. *You're going crazy.*

"No, no. I'm not. Don't let go," she whispered out loud, pleading with the voice to just let the moment linger a little longer. She knew, though, that she would never get it back. All she would have is the memory of it, and she desperately replayed every single detail so she would never forget it.

That dream represented everything she had wanted since her mother called to tell her that her father had quickly fallen ill. That day, she and Jake had been halfway across the state on a day trip, and she had been unable to get to the hospital before he died. As she cried into Jake's shoulder that afternoon, she shouted about wanting to have held her father's hand as he took his last breaths. Hannah carried that around ever since, this heavy anger. She wondered sometimes if it was really just guilt.

The voice of reason spoke up again, *That's it! That's why you had the dream! It's been on your mind, and, of course, your brain made up this story to make you feel better.*

"Maybe," she whispered. "Or maybe…"

As Jake stirred, Hannah pulled the sheets back and got out of bed in one fell swoop. Diesel lifted his head to watch her, deciding to follow her before she closed the door on him.

In the kitchen, Hannah propped herself up on her elbows in

front of the coffeepot. Her head rested on her forearms as she stared at her feet on the cold tile floor below. Her mind churned rapidly as her dream replayed in her mind, feeling it so viscerally all over again. All of the possibilities of what comes after this life intertwined with the memory of it, creating a tornado sweeping through the folds of her brain. She thought about her conversation with Alan about visitation dreams, and wondered if maybe the truth lie somewhere in the middle of fact and fiction. Somehow, that made her feel just a little better. A little more sane.

Hannah was still unsure of what she believed. There was a small part of her that had always thought there might be more than just this plane of existence, but there had never been any solid proof. Sometimes she blamed her occupation for making her too grounded in the human psyche to let go and embrace the unknown. Yet the more time went on, and the more loss she experienced in this life, the hope that there was something beyond this life only grew. That her dad could really reach out to her from beyond the grave.

She stood up straight, allowing her lungs the space to expand fully, and took deep breaths as she felt herself starting to relax again. Once the shakiness in her legs subsided, Hannah got busy feeding Diesel his breakfast and making coffee. She couldn't shake the freaked-out feeling still coursing through her, as she kept coming back to how real the sensation in her hand felt.

something is happening to my mind. i'm convinced i'm going crazy. really and legitimately crazy. i keep having these dreams about dad. 3 now. i'm always back home in harborvale, and it's just me and him in the livingroom. in each dream i got closer to him, and he went from barely seeing me to being able to touch my hand. when i've woken up from each one, it's like i've downed a case of red bull in my sleep or something, because i feel so wide awake. i can't shake this feeling of how utterly real it feels. the carpet, the way the floor creaks in all the usual places, the smell of murphy's oil soap from the last time mom cleaned all the wood paneling. everything is just so vivid. i keep telling myself it's just a dream, but i'm worried i'm hallucinating or something. i don't know if i should tell linda or not, mostly because i'm afraid she'll put me on a 72 hour hold. if it were schizophrenia or something, it would have presented itself years ago. i'm too old for a diagnosis like that now. maybe it's just a psychotic episode from the stress and grief? oh god...

i had a dream like that about jimmy maybe a week or two after i found out about his death. it was the same thing—it was so vivid and real. we were walking down the street in stonebridge going to meet our old friends from "the inkwell", the college newspaper we both worked on at SHU. we sat with them at the table and he asked me questions about jake, like he was making sure he was a good match for me. he put an arm around my shoulders and kissed the top of my head, just like he did hundreds of times in the years we were together. i always thought it was the sweetest thing. i put my head on his shoulder, and we just sat there, taking in the evening with our friends. i woke up then and i <u>swear</u> i could feel his arm around my shoulders, the weight of his lips on the very spot he kissed me in my dream. i could feel the weight and warmth of him against me, his head resting on top of mine. even the sound of his voice, it was like he was in the room with me. it freaked me out at the time, but i also felt so comforted. like he was telling me that he was still looking out for me somehow. that he'd never leave my side. it was like in real life, how messages can be communicated solely through expressions and gestures. it was like we had a whole side conversation. i just... knew.

now it's escalated to these dreams with dad, and all i feel is crazy. i feel desperation and sadness and heaviness. but this dream last night finally gave me that comfort, the closure i think i've been needing. i felt that same peace i had in that dream with jimmy. maybe my dad needed it, too. that final goodbye to his little girl.

i made the mistake of telling alan about the dreams a couple of weeks ago. he's all into ghosts and goblins, and he thinks i'm definitely having some otherworldly experience. i don't know what i believe, honestly. it sounds great, but can it really be? the reasonable, scientific side of me says no, that we know dreams are just a way for our brains to process our emotions and experiences. where does the line between reality and psychosis lie? and i know alan. i know he's a solid person, that he's not on the edge of mental illness by any means. so if i believe that about him, why can't i believe it about myself? honestly, i'd give anything for it all to be real. to be able to be in the same room with my dad again.

i think a lot about regret these days. like how i never got to say goodbye to my dad. how i never got to tell him all that he meant to me, or how i was proud to be his daughter. how i loved growing up and spending my days with him at the beach. i think about all the regret i have about jimmy. some days i wish i could take back the last 10 years and do it all over again. i wish i could've gotten over myself, moved past everything, and welcomed him back into my life as a friend. maybe then i could've been there for him. maybe it would have made a difference, or maybe it wouldn't have. at least he would've known how i felt. instead, i have to live the rest of my life haunted by what might have been. and, now, i guess i have to live through these dreams which are nothing but a reminder of all of that.

more than anything, i wish i could talk to jake about this, but he'd probably just laugh in my face. i remember when i could tell him anything, or ask him advice about anything. he used to speak to me in such a kind, non-judgmental way. he gave thoughtful, well-reasoned responses. now, he could care less about me or anything i might be going through. i miss my best friend.

January 5, 2024

In the days following Hannah's last dream about her dad, she hadn't been able to shake the feeling of his hand in hers. The sensation of it lingered through every part of her days. During sessions with her clients, she often found herself completely zoned out, staring at her hand lying in her lap. Whatever it was—a dream or some transcendent experience—it had shaken her entire belief system, launching her into a spiritual crisis. She was lost in what to believe, looking for some kind of anchor to grab on to.

Disoriented in the chaos of her thoughts, Hannah caved in the early morning hours and reached out to the one person she knew she could talk to about all of this.

> **Hannah:** *Hey, sorry for the early text. I had another weird dream the other night, and I can't shake it...*

Her phone buzzed with a response from Alan almost immediately as she brewed a fresh pot of coffee.

> **Alan:** *Don't be sorry. Been on the boat for half an hour already. Another dream? Your dad? What happened?*

Hannah: *This time, I was able to get to him, and he could talk. We held hands and cried together. It felt so real. I woke up as if I were still holding it, like I could really feel his dry skin.*

Hannah: *I'm scared that I'm losing my mind.*

Alan: *You're not. Obviously, it meant something to you. What do you think that is?*

Hannah: *I've been telling Jake this whole time how I just wanted to say goodbye to him. To hold his hand and tell him I loved him.*

Alan: *Well, it sounds like you got that. Maybe he needed that one last goodbye, too.*

A ball of emotion swelled in her throat as she read Alan's message that echoed the same sentiment that had crossed her own mind.

Hannah: *I hate to admit it, but I'm starting to believe you.*

Hannah: *I guess I really am losing my mind.*

Hannah: *No offense.*

Alan: *LOL. Well, I can't say my head has always been screwed on straight.*

Hannah: *I feel so fucked up right now, but also at peace?*

Alan: *I think that's the nature of closure. You feel comfort, but it doesn't always feel good at first.*

Hannah: *Can I tell you something else?*

Alan: *Shoot.*

Hannah: *I had a dream about Jimmy like this, too. A few months ago.*

Alan: *Really? Why didn't you tell me before?*

Hannah: *Because I thought it was just a dream, but now... I don't know if it was or not.*

Alan: *Well, what happened?*

Hannah: *We were with our college friends having dinner, and he was asking me about Jake. What he was like, if I was happy, stuff like that. We cuddled like we used to, and he kissed me on top of my head. I could feel that kiss long after I woke up.*

Alan: *Ya know, I've had visitations from Jimmy, too.*

Hannah: *Really?*

Alan: *A couple.*

Alan: *We're always playing guitar. Remember that painted acoustic one he had? He's always playing that one, never any of the others he had. We don't usually talk, we just play. It's always the same damn song, too, but I can't put a finger on what the hell it is. The only thing that changes is the setting. It's the park, my old apartment, the front porch at your old place. When I wake up, my fingers are still buzzing from picking at the strings.*

Alan: *It's the only time I play now. I haven't really picked up a guitar, or any other instrument, much since we moved. Definitely not since Jimmy died.*

Hannah felt a sudden and curious pang of jealousy that Alan's dreams had been much more active than her own, with visions of time spent with Jimmy. When he hitchhiked through a handful of states and crash landed in Riverside Springs back in 2009, Alan was the one who helped him get on his feet. He housed Jimmy, fed him, and even got him a job. Those two were as thick as thieves for years, way longer than she and Jimmy had been together. She let out a heavy sigh.

Oh my god. I can't believe I'm buying into this shit, she thought.

>**Hannah:** *Can I ask you something? After those dreams, how do you feel when you wake up?*
>**Alan:** *Happy, mostly. Then sad when reality hits.*
>**Hannah:** *I mean, your body. How does your body feel?*
>**Alan:** *Calm. Relaxed. Wide awake, though. For me, that's how I know it was a visitation and not just a dream. I feel different afterward.*
>**Hannah:** *That's how I feel! Like I've been running a marathon or something. And it's always around 3 am.*
>**Alan:** *I know you don't want to believe it, but I think our boy is trying to tell us something. What, I don't know.*

Deep down, Hannah hoped beyond belief that it could be true. They had missed out on the last ten years, but if it were possible to have a connection to Jimmy still, she'd hold onto it. If it meant that she had said goodbye to her dad, she'd believe anything. Another message from Alan interrupted her train of thought.

>**Alan:** *I hate to cut this short, but we just dropped anchor. Time to get to work! You can text or call me later this afternoon, like 4:00 or so.*
>**Hannah:** *Thanks. Have a good day!*

Hannah dumped several spoonfuls of sugar into one of her favorite mugs. It was a handmade one, painted in a deep shade of indigo. A palmetto tree was painted on either side in earthy greens and browns. She had found it on the shelves of the thrift store she worked at when she came home to Harborvale after that year in South Carolina. At the time, it felt like fate that this symbol of the home she had loved just randomly appeared there one day—this cosmic reminder of the one place where she felt most at peace.

With a shaky hand, she poured coffee from the pot over the sweet, milky mixture at the bottom, watching the colors swirl together until they formed a uniform, light caramel color. She took a long sip, letting the warm liquid cascade down her throat and into her stomach, warming her from the inside out. Hannah did feel better after talking with Alan.

Something within her changed with that last dream about her father, though. Maybe it was the closure she hoped would find her, or maybe it was her own acceptance of the experience she had. Whether it was real or not, it touched her in a way she would never forget. She finally understood that maybe some things just weren't meant to be figured out.

Jake wandered in to the kitchen with a yawn, making a beeline for the coffee pot. He shot Hannah a brief smile and a soft grunt in acknowledgment. She hesitantly returned the smile, then turned away and let out a heavy breath. She knew he didn't notice the anguish etched into the angles of her face, but she wasn't sure if what she felt was relief or disappointment.

"It's been a couple of weeks since we've seen each other," Linda started. "How were your holidays?"

"Eh, they could've been better. Christmas was all right. We have this tradition of disconnecting and doing our own thing a couple of days beforehand. It was nice until dinner. We spent Christmas Eve with Jake's family, and then Christmas Day with my mom. It's always fun to watch our nieces and nephews open their gifts." Hannah grinned at the memory.

"And what about your New Year? Did you do anything to celebrate?"

Hannah snorted. "New Year's was awful," she confessed, looking down at the carpet.

"Tell me more about what happened on Christmas and New Years'."

She let out a long breath. "Our Christmas was going well, until Alan called. We were having a good conversation, but then it took a weird turn. And then, Jake and I had a fight about it."

"Weird how?" Linda asked, cocking her head slightly to one side.

"I told him about these dreams I've had about my dad. I've been going crazy because they felt so real. Like, more than a dream. Anyway, I brought it up because I remembered what you said about opening up and leaning on my friends, and he started going on about 'visitation dreams.' He made it seem like it *was* real," Hannah explained.

"Well, what did you think?" Linda questioned.

Hannah shrugged. "I don't know what to believe. I mean, doing this job, it makes it hard to consider things like that. Doesn't it? Where is the line between psychosis and reality? Right?" She looked at Linda, genuinely wanting to know her opinion on the matter. She respected Linda and trusted her to be honest.

"I can see where you might feel that way, but I would also counter that there is still so much about the human brain, and the inner workings of our universe, that we *don't* know. I think the possibility is possible," Linda told her with a funny grin. "Tell me about the fight with Jake."

"I think he was weirdly jealous," she told Linda with a roll of her eyes. "He got all uptight that Alan called to wish us a 'Merry Christmas.'"

"Huh," Linda grunted. "And what happened on New Year's?"

"Jake and I have always had this tradition of staying up to watch the ball drop. We watch those programs on TV, have snacks, and champagne at midnight, you know? This year, I guess he was in a bad mood again and just went to bed early. We had a little argument about it. I wound up staying up with the dog, got a little drunk, and cried a whole lot. Alan called at midnight, and I was a complete mess."

Linda nodded slowly. "How so? What did you talk about?"

Hannah sighed. "When he called, I was crying so hard and I couldn't calm myself down. Everything I had been holding in just all came out. All the stuff between Jake and me. It's so embarrassing."

"Why was it embarrassing?"

"Because—he hasn't seen or heard me like that in a long time. Not since Jimmy ran off that last time before we broke up for good.

I feel ashamed in a way to admit we've got such big problems, Jake and I."

"How did you feel afterward, aside from embarrassed? Did you feel a little lighter, maybe?" Linda pressed her.

Reluctantly, she answered, "I did feel better, I guess. Lighter, like you said. It feels like Alan is reaching out more now, like he's afraid I'll do what Jimmy did. I promise you I'm not suicidal at all," she said quickly. "It's just like he's trying to make up for it somehow, texting me to just 'check in' on me and stuff."

"Why do you think that?"

Hannah shrugged again without giving her a verbal answer.

"Is it possible you think that because *you* feel that way about yourself? Like you need to make penance for not saving Jimmy?"

Hannah let her shoulders rise and fall again.

After a long pause, Linda decided to move on. "It may have been an admission made under the influence, but I'm proud of you for opening up to Alan. I think it's important that you have someone outside of this room whom you can talk to about these things. I wonder—who else has been there for you like Alan?"

"Recently? Not really anyone."

"Okay. Then, in the past?" Linda rebutted.

Hannah's mind turned through a carousel of faces from her past, picking out a few whom she had once considered her best friends. Her heart sank as she thought of them all now, how they had lost each other over the years.

"Jimmy, obviously. I've said it before, but he was the first person who saw me for who I really was. I could be myself with him, and I could talk to him about anything. He used to tell me that I was the only person in his life who *had* him, and the feeling was mutual," Hannah said. "I had this friend in college. Katie. She worked on the newspaper with me. We were in this clique with two other girls, but Katie and I were closer to each other than the others. She was kind of like my voice of reason for a while. She knew how to call me out on my bullshit." Hannah looked at the ceiling and chuckled, before the familiar ache in her core reminded her of how much she missed that time in her life.

"What happened between you and Katie?"

"It's a long story, but there was this other girl in our group, Whitney. She wasn't the nicest person—judgmental and kind of rude. She and I got into it when Jimmy had run away just before my graduation, and Katie just sat there and let her run her mouth. I was so mad at both of them. I needed them, and Whitney thought I shouldn't worry about him. Katie was too scared, I guess, to stand up for either of us. We were supposedly such great friends of hers. She did try to apologize a few times, but I just couldn't hear it at the time. We didn't speak again after that, and then I moved away."

Linda finished jotting some things down on the notepad in her lap. "I can hear the sadness when you talk about it."

"I think about her sometimes. I still feel sad and angry over the whole thing," Hannah admitted.

"Have you ever thought about reaching out to her?" Linda asked.

Hannah chuckled. "God, no," she said immediately. "Like Jimmy, I've looked her up on Facebook over the years just to see what she was up to. I don't know that I would ever reach out, though."

Linda nodded. "Is there anyone else you can think of?"

"There is someone else, but he hasn't crossed my mind in a long time: my old friend, Ray. Ray Donovan," Hannah said with a distracted grin, letting herself get lost in the memories.

"Tell me about Ray."

Hannah sputtered her lips. "Ray was Jimmy's boss when he worked at the record shop in Stonebridge. We actually went to high school together, Ray and I."

Linda raised her eyebrows slightly. "These people are pretty far back in your past. Is there no one more recently in your past that you can think of?"

With a shrug, she replied, "I don't know. I guess I've just been reflecting on the past so much, how it got me to this point. For better or worse. Ray was a big part of that." She paused before continuing. "We didn't have any friends in common back then, and I don't think we even had a single class together the whole time. I used to hang out in the store with Jimmy for hours, but Ray never seemed to care that I was there. When Jimmy ran away the first time, I would go by the store to just feel him. I was incredibly lost that summer, and Ray was almost like an anchor in the storm for me when I didn't have anyone else. He'd let me just stay there as long as I needed to, and we would talk about anything and everything. We eventually exchanged numbers and talked on the phone late into the night. We became good friends, and when I left for South Carolina, we stayed in touch, although not as frequently. Then, when I came back to Harborvale, we picked up where we left off, because I had started going by the store again pretty regularly. Partly because I missed Jimmy, and partly because of Ray. It just wasn't the same, though."

"How so?" Linda asked in the pause.

"Well, I was heartbroken the first time Jimmy left. He was my first real love, and it hurt to have him leave me. I was heartbroken when I came home from Riverside Springs, but it was a different kind of heartbreak. I can't explain it, but I was different. I was shattered, and it changed me. Not having Jimmy as a link between us anymore had made things weird, I guess." Hannah stopped talking for a moment, remembering the last time she had seen Ray. "Last I saw him, I was with Jake, actually. We had just started dating, and were walking around Stonebridge, popping in and out of the shops downtown. He wanted to go into the record store, and I kind of hemmed and hawed about it, but eventually went in with him. I had stopped coming around a while before that because I felt haunted by the memory of Jimmy and me. He came up to me when I was alone, trying to talk to me like the old days. The usual pleasantries, you know, but it was weird. I knew he wanted to ask about Jimmy, but when he saw Jake, I guess he changed his mind. I was thankful for that, but it still felt like a lingering, dark cloud between us. I never went back to the store, and we never talked again."

Linda grunted quietly, leaving room for Hannah to say more if she needed to.

Picking at her cuticles now, Hannah told her, "The store closed a few years ago and, last I heard through the town grapevine, Ray moved to Vegas or something and gambled his money away."

"We're nearly at time, but I do want to point out to you that, even though these friendships ended, there was always someone there for you to lean on. When one left, another appeared. Someone you *allowed* yourself to lean on. That you *let* yourself be supported by others, and I would encourage you to find that within yourself again. To let yourself go and feel the love that is around you. Especially from your friend, Alan. You told me a while ago how he tried for so long to find you, to give you the news about Jimmy. That means something, Hannah."

The afternoon sun shone bright, and the air had warmed into the high forties, bringing a surprisingly spring-like day to the dead of winter. Hannah put on a heavy hooded sweatshirt and went out for a walk along the bay. It was her favorite place to be, where she could do her best thinking. After today's therapy session, she needed the peace of that place to debrief from it.

As she walked along the path, Hannah bopped her head to the music streaming through her earbuds. The sun glittered off the gently lapping water below the walkway, but there weren't any boats going in or out of the harbor that afternoon despite the nice weather. She looked out at Highgate City, which was fully visible.

Hannah jumped a little as her cell phone's ringtone blared in her ears over the music. She took the phone out of her pocket to see who was calling. Shannon's name scrolled across the screen, and Hannah debated whether she should answer or not. She knew that if she didn't answer now, she would only be postponing the conversation for a later time.

"Hey Shan!" she said, putting on her best cheery voice.

"Hey Hannah! How are you?" Shannon asked.

"All right. I'm just out for a walk. It's so nice today!"

"Oh my gosh, I know! I can't wait for spring to really be here," she replied.

Hannah waited for Shannon to say more, but there was just silence. "So what's up?" she asked.

Shannon hesitated. "I just wanted to see how you were doing."

"Oh. Yeah, I'm okay. How are you?" she asked.

"Yeah, I'm good. I just wanted to check in with you. I felt like things were a little weird when you and Jake were here for dinner a couple of weeks ago," she told Hannah. "I wanted to say something sooner," she added quickly, "but I wasn't sure if I was just making things up, and I didn't want to upset you."

"Oh," Hannah choked out. She had figured Shannon had probably worked it out that night, but she hoped she would never bring it up. "We're okay. Just usual marriage stuff, you know?"

"Mm-hmm," Shannon acknowledged. "It's just that—you've seemed not yourself lately, Hannah. I know you're still processing everything that happened with your dad, but it feels like there's more than that. You never talk about Jake anymore, and when I bring him up, your voice changes. You just sound different."

"Well, yeah. We're both, apparently, still feeling out our grief over losing my dad. Jake finally opened up to me that he's been struggling, too, which surprised me, I guess. The holidays were so much harder than usual. Work has been stressful for both of us," Hannah explained. She could hear her voice becoming prickly, and made a note to tone it down.

"I know. I know it has. I didn't want to upset you. I'm just worried about you."

Hannah stopped to sit on a bench along the path, letting the cool breeze blow through her hair that she had neglected to tie back into a ponytail. She rubbed her fingertips along the bottom edge of the hair that was still wrapped around the front of her shoulder.

"Hannah? Did I lose you?"

"No, I'm still here," she said quietly. The thought of opening up to Shannon scared her, but she wasn't entirely sure why. What did she have to lose?

"Look—I'm sorry. I shouldn't have said anything—"

"No. You should have," Hannah proclaimed. "I wasn't totally honest. Jake and I—we haven't been okay for a while now. Like, for the last year or so, actually." She let out a quiet cough, trying to rid herself of emotion growing there in her throat.

"What? *A year?*" Shannon screeched. "What's going on with you guys? Why didn't you tell me?"

"I didn't want you to know. I didn't want anyone to know," Hannah said as tears fell down her cheeks, and the cold wind stung the wet parts of her face. "Work has been hard on him. I've told you that he's been working so many extra hours, and his boss is constantly riding him. He's pushing himself so hard for this promotion, but I'm not sure he's ever going to get it at this point. I'm honestly afraid he's going to have a heart attack or something. I mean—he's already having all of these stomach problems. What's next?"

"Can he take some time off or something?"

"Now that the holidays are over, yeah, but he doesn't want to," Hannah told her. "So, instead, he comes home angry every day. He's so mean and cold most of the time, and he doesn't ever want to do anything. We don't go out anymore. All we do is sit home and watch television, or he just zones out playing video games. I had to practically drag him out of the house to get him to dinner at your place that night," she admitted. "Nothing against you guys. It's just how he is lately."

"I mean, this *is* the same Jake I've known for the last how many years? I can't wrap my head around it. Hannah, why didn't you tell me all of this before?" Shannon asked again with an edge in her voice.

"Because, you know as well as I do that we don't air our dirty laundry," Hannah said, harkening back to the dozens of conversations they'd had about their upbringings. "I didn't want to impose on you either." She didn't have the nerve to tell Shannon that there was more, that she had trouble interjecting when Shannon was talking about herself.

"But that's what friendship is! It's inconvenient and messy," Shannon explained. "I want to be there for you, but I can't if you don't let me."

Hannah pushed out a heavy breath. "That's fair," she acknowledged. "But, yes, this is the same Jake. I have to remind myself of that often. I barely recognize him anymore."

"So, where are things with you guys now?"

"I have no idea. We'll have a good day here and there, and then it's back to being shitty. I never know when the tides are changing, or why."

"I'm worried for you two," Shannon admitted, her tone turning more serious.

"I'm just trying to still show him that I love him, that I'm here for him. Valentine's Day is in a couple of weeks, so I'll probably try to plan something special. To spark something, you know?"

"That's a great idea! Just keep at it, and he'll come around. I'm sure of it. I just don't want to see you guys split up or anything like that. You're so good for each other."

Hannah closed her eyes, steadying herself against Shannon's worries. She still had some fight left in her, and she hoped that Jake did, too. She was sure that he did on those days when things were good between them, when he wasn't afraid to touch her or at least acted like he wanted to be around her.

"I've thought about it, but I'm not there yet, Shan," Hannah reassured her.

"Yet? I don't like the sound of that. I don't want that for you, Hannah. Jake has been so good to you!" she exclaimed.

Oh my god! Is she even listening? Hannah asked herself, feeling the anger starting to bubble up in her. *How much more of this am I supposed to endure?*

Hannah ended their conversation abruptly, catching Shannon completely by surprise. She had to end it, or she knew she would say something she couldn't take back. That, and she just wanted to get lost in the music. Closing her eyes, she took a few deep breaths, feeling an anxiety attack lingering in the shadows of her nervous system. Hannah needed the quiet now to find peace within herself, whatever that felt like.

January 14, 2024

Hannah awoke in the morning with a fire in her belly that she couldn't explain. It had been a couple of months since Linda suggested she revisit some of the places from her past, locations that made her feel more at home with herself in an effort to reclaim some of the parts of herself she'd lost over the years. Perhaps it was the start of the new year that left her feeling hopeless again, making her yearn for a simpler time. In some way, Hannah felt like she was seeking something, being guided toward something, but she couldn't put her finger on what that was exactly.

She extended an invitation to Jake to take a ride with her, but he declined, citing the cold and the fact that it was only seven o'clock in the morning. Hannah felt the tension in her belly release because somewhere inside her, she knew she needed to do this alone. She bundled herself against the winter weather in her favorite fleece turtleneck sweater, pea coat, and a handmade scarf with matching gloves that had been gifted to her the previous Christmas, and left the house in a hurry.

Hannah followed her usual route to Highway 626, her arms navigating her vehicle with ease, as if from muscle memory, exiting at the sign that read "Sunset Cove." Without even realizing she had arrived, Hannah found herself frozen in place behind the steering wheel. Her eyes swept the familiar expansive parking lot with the campus laid out behind it, noticing three letters painted in dark blue on the sidewalk before her. "SHU."

A strange sense of pride swept over Hannah, a mix of both happiness and sadness. This feeling of admiration was new for her, because Safe Harbor University had been the butt of many jokes in the surrounding communities for a long time. "No clue, go to SHU," people would say with a laugh. Her mother had often repeated the sentiments with a harsh laugh. Hannah never really found it funny, no matter who it was coming from, even if she didn't particularly feel excited about being a SHU alumnus.

Everything felt so different this morning, though. Her years at SHU had been a special time in her life; it was the first place where she had truly come alive, and where some of her favorite memories were born. In some ways, this place felt like magic.

Bracing against the cold, Hannah slowly made her way around to the front of the university on the winding sidewalk. She would have usually taken the steep walkway that led behind the Student Center, but she wanted to see the face of her old friend first. To greet it properly. The campus was wondrously quiet, without a single soul in sight except for the squirrels scampering through the tree branches overhead. It was as if the campus had been evacuated ahead of her arrival, letting her stroll along with all the ghosts of who she used to be.

Standing on the sidewalk, front and center, Hannah marveled at how much this place had changed. She stared down the center walkway that cut the campus right in half; she remembered the dozens of times she stepped off the shuttle bus, having come from class on the secondary campus at this same spot, her feet carrying her into the heart of SHU. The buildings in front of her had received a facelift in the fifteen years since she'd last been there; they were all modern and new now. Hannah did a double-take, noticing the building on her right looked more like a spaceship from her vantage point.

Hannah steadily ambled up the walkway, coming to a stop in front of the Student Center. She tilted her head back to take in the four-story structure that had not changed in the least. She glanced around to see if anyone was watching her, but she was still entirely alone. Having made up her mind, she marched right up to the main door and gave the handle a little tug. Surprisingly, it opened. A somewhat devilish smile crossed her face as she took a hesitant but daring step into the building.

As the door closed silently behind her, Hannah glimpsed the expansive room before her. The reception desk was still as large as ever, standing a few feet from the main doors, and currently unmanned. The pod of lounge chairs was empty, and the offices that lined three sides of the building were completely dark. Her ears couldn't detect the sound of feet along the tiled corridors above her. It seemed the building was empty.

Hannah slowly climbed the staircase that zigzagged up the wall beyond the front desk. Her legs seemed to move on their own, carrying her in the direction of Room 202; she couldn't believe she remembered exactly where it was. That classroom had been the hub of *The Inkwell,* where most of their meetings had been held, where she met her three best college friends, and where she had melted into a puddle under her desk the first time she laid her eyes on Jimmy Taylor.

The classroom was dark, but had been left propped open by a rubber doorstop. Hannah poked her head into the room, finding the light switch just inside the doorway on the left side wall. The fluorescent lights buzzed on overhead, causing her to wince a little as her eyes adjusted to the brightness. Her gaze immediately fell on a group of desks that had been left in a circle at the center of the room. Things really hadn't changed here.

Hannah leaned against the threshold just as the room seemed to morph right before her eyes unexpectedly. The desks suddenly filled with bodies and faces she recognized, while indistinct chatter filled her ears. She could make out the front page of *The Inkwell* on a laptop screen left abandoned on the desk in front of her. Katie and Whitney hovered over Jenny's shoulders at a desk on the left side of the room, pointing at her computer screen. It seemed like they were having a heated conversation about something she couldn't quite make out. Hannah smirked remembering all of the fights the four of them had, but how quick they were to forgive one another. She missed those girls, having not been in the same room with any of them like this in so long. Those girls felt like home back then in the way they accepted Hannah as one of their own from the very start, and how they never tried to change her despite her quirks and shyness.

Joe and Chris, their fearless leaders, were standing off by the windows, whispering to one another. Brad was there, too, lying on his belly on the floor in the front right corner of the room. She got on her tiptoes to peer over his shoulder to see him biting his lower lip in concentration as he intently sketched out a comic strip about the university's president.

A breath escaped her lips as her eyes shifted left to find a chunky pair of black Airwalk sneakers, the laces untied, taking small steps back and forth in front of the whiteboard. Hannah's back stiffened as her eyes rose to take in the torn jeans and plain black hooded sweatshirt with the sleeves pushed up to the elbows. His hair was the same dirty blonde color as the sand down at the bay beach nearby, spiked out in every direction.

It was Jimmy, standing at the whiteboard in the front of the classroom, drawing something hilariously inappropriate in black dry-erase marker. He peeked over his shoulder to make sure Joe and Chris weren't paying any attention to him. As he reached up to add some accents to the top of his drawing, the overhead lights glinted off the studded belt wrapped around his waist.

A familiar voice called out from the opposite side of the room, "Thank god you're finally here, Hannah! We need your help with this!" It was Katie, smiling at her and motioning with a hand in the direction of the computer she was busy looking at.

Confused by the scene unfolding in front of her, Hannah parted her lips to speak, but her voice caught in her throat as she watched a younger version of herself seem to step out of the center of her chest and into the room. She noticed Jimmy, who had turned his head discreetly to watch Young Hannah join her girlfriends around Jenny's desk. She saw them make accidental eye contact with one another, their lips turning slightly into shy grins, and turned away quickly; Hannah's cheeks flushed, feeling like she had watched something that wasn't meant for anyone else to see.

Turning her attention back to Young Hannah and her friends, she watched as she lent her input to the group discussion with confidence, ultimately ending the debate among the three friends. The four girls smiled, chatted, and laughed with one another afterward, moving on to the next order of business, which surely had nothing to do with the newspaper. Hannah marveled at how easily her younger self fit in here, that she was really a part of something, even if she didn't realize it at the time. *The Inkwell* had been so much bigger than any of them could have ever known.

Just like that, this memory dissolved right before her eyes, and Hannah was left standing in the doorway of the empty classroom. She blinked her eyes hard several times, coming back into her own body in the present moment. The building seemed to be swaying around her, and Hannah gripped the doorway to get a hold of herself again.

The quiet ache of nostalgia that lived in her core gently pulsed.

What just happened? Am I hallucinating? she asked herself. *No, no. It was just a memory. It wasn't real. Don't be stupid.*

She blinked hard again as she slowly backed into the hallway, retracing her steps to the main floor. Hannah's knees felt weak, and she let herself flop down onto one of the lounge chairs in the alcove near the stairs. Her heart thumped heavily in her chest, while she struggled to take even breaths. The voice inside her mind kept prodding incessantly at her in an attempt to convince Hannah that her mental state had, in fact, deteriorated.

When she felt calmer after a few minutes, Hannah stood up and followed the long corridor down to the cafeteria in search of a bottle of water to quench her parched mouth. She peered through the small window in the door, noticing the lights were all on, but there didn't seem to be anyone there. Her hand found the long handle and pushed, lucky to find it unlocked. If anything, she would leave a couple of dollars near the register for the water she still planned to take.

This place had undergone significant changes, with more updated furniture and decorative elements on the walls. It was still painted in blue and white stripes, though, with school pride oozing out of every crack and crevice that had formed in the cinder block walls.

Just like before, the scene in the cafeteria changed right in front of her eyes. The room filled with students in shorts and T-shirts, holding their packaged graduation caps and gowns, as they eagerly talked with one another. A cacophony of noise rose as the scene came into full focus. Hannah spotted her younger self sitting with her two friends, Katie and Whitney, at a table in the farthest corner of the room. Even from this distance, she could tell that they were engaged in an argument.

"Oh no, not this day," she whispered to herself, trying to run from this memory, yet her feet seemed to be cemented in place. Her heart sank with the understanding that she was watching the last time she'd ever speak to the two of them. By then, Jenny had become a figment of their memories as she pulled away from her college life to help her family through a crisis with her sister. Hannah cautiously tiptoed closer to their table, but before she could get within earshot, the volume of her own voice rose above all the others and stopped her in her tracks. Everything in the room came to a screeching halt as everyone's attention turned to Young Hannah.

She looked back just in time to see Young Hannah stand hastily from her chair, nearly knocking it over behind her. "You can't see anything past your own nose, and *that* is pathetic!" she heard herself shout at Whitney. The younger version of herself then grabbed her backpack and slung it over her shoulder angrily, stomping through her on her way out the door. In shock at how their dispute appeared from this angle, she turned back to see what Katie and Whitney had done once she left, but the room dissolved back into the present day.

It was a day she never wanted to remember, but one that was burned into her DNA. It was the last day of finals before their graduation. It should have been a happy day but, instead, everything felt like it was falling apart. A couple of hours before that moment, Hannah found out that Jimmy had run away for the second time. This was the day Hannah was hurt and scared more so than ever before, and her two friends had completely let her down. Even with a heaviness in her chest, Hannah felt a certain respect for the strong young woman she had been. One who stood up for what was right, and wouldn't let anyone hassle her over that. Not even someone she considered a friend.

"Oh, we're not open for breakfast quite yet, Hon. Another thirty minutes or so, we will be," a warm, friendly voice called out to her. Hannah turned in the direction of it, to see an older, plump woman in a dark blue uniform smiling at her.

"Right, sorry," Hannah mumbled as she left the cafeteria, completely forgetting about the water she had come for.

She decided to take in some fresh, cold air to clear her mind and headed down the hallway to the end, where it exited onto a sidewalk at the back of the Student Center. Stepping outside, she shuddered against the chilly breeze and dipped the lower part of her face into her scarf. She looked to her left to see a steep sidewalk that led back to the parking lot where she'd left her car. Before she could turn in the opposite direction, Hannah's nose caught a familiar smell: patchouli and tobacco. Hannah's breath caught in her lungs as she turned her gaze to find Jimmy and Brad suddenly appearing on the sidewalk that ran along the back of the building. All morning, she felt like she was losing whatever grip on reality she had left, but this scene brought her a strange sense of ease.

Brad was riding a skateboard toward her, trying to perfect a heelflip while Jimmy offered up tips. He was leaning against the building, just on the other side of the doorframe, with one leg cocked behind him, his foot resting against the red brick wall. A cigarette was lightly gripped between the pointer and middle fingers of his left hand. Its smoke seemed to trail right into her nose. This time, Jimmy was wearing that ripped denim vest he used to love, the one covered in all kinds of patches and safety pins.

He turned to her then and grinned from only the corner of his mouth. Jimmy stared right at her, his glare as intense as she remembered. He took a long drag of nicotine and blew it out from the side of his mouth away from her. Moving his free hand in a small wave, he said, "Hey Harborvale."

Young Hannah stepped through her once again, taking a few steps in his direction with a hand on her hip. "I thought we had agreed you wouldn't call me that anymore," she retorted.

Jimmy chuckled. "My bad. As I remember it, we settled on Banana, right?"

She could feel a smile creeping across her mouth, remembering how he had started calling her "Banana" long before they ever became an item, and how she had secretly loved it all along, despite how she acted. Hannah turned to watch her younger self roll her eyes and smiled coyly at him, knowing she was trying so hard not to give him the satisfaction that she'd been won over.

"I think it was more you that settled on that."

"Tomato, tomahto," he told her with a curl of his lip.

"Don't you worry, Jimmy Taylor. I'll get you back one day. When you least expect it," Young Hannah promised before turning to leave down the steep sidewalk. "See you at the next meeting!" she shouted with a wave behind her.

"Ooh, I'm shaking, Banana!" Jimmy shouted back at her, his voice husky and cracking. In the next moment, he called out to her again, with something she could only now pick out as desperation in his voice, "Hey! Banana!" She watched herself turn back around, shielding her eyes from the sun to get a better look at him. "You comin' to my show?"

Young Hannah took a few steps back in his direction. "What show is that?" she inquired.

"My band, Cat Hair."

She cackled. "Cat Hair? You're joking."

Jimmy smirked again from the right side of his mouth. "What's wrong with it?"

The younger version of herself shrugged and shook her head, not trying to hide the fact that she thought the name of his band was ridiculous. "No, nothing. When is it?"

"Tonight. First Baptist Church basement in Cedar Cove," he told her before taking another drag of his cigarette.

Hannah watched as this version of herself crossed her arms over her chest, rubbing her chin as if she were deep in thought over it. "Hmm," she said with a grin breaking through her lips, "pretty sure I have something *way* better to do with my time tonight."

Jimmy choked on the stream of smoke he was exhaling, trying not to laugh. "Ouch, Banana. What could *possibly* be better than coming to see me play?" Catching himself, he quickly stammered, "Us, I mean. Brad, too. He's in the band with me."

As Young Hannah's mouth bobbed open a few times, the Hannah watching this scene unfold knows how quickly her mind is turning to find something clever to say. Anything to one-up him while also impressing him with her quick wit. She hated how Jimmy so easily tripped her up with what she, at the time, hoped was flirting.

With a knowing grin, Jimmy dropped the cigarette on the sidewalk and stamped it out with the toe of his sneaker. "I'll see you tonight then."

Young Hannah didn't say anything more, only shrugging and turning to continue back down the steep sidewalk. Once she was out of sight from him, she would pause behind a tree to send a text message to Katie begging her to go to the concert. She would agree, and spend the night poking fun at Hannah who was completely mesmerized as she watched Jimmy take command of a stage.

Hannah turned back to where Jimmy and Brad were on the sidewalk, knowing this part of the story only because she had stopped behind that tree without them noticing. She saw how Jimmy kept glancing down the path Young Hannah had disappeared down, as if hoping she would suddenly reappear. Brad laughed at his friend, punching him in the shoulder to snap Jimmy out of his daydream. "What about Kelly, dude?" she heard him ask.

Still without taking his eyes off the sidewalk where Young Hannah had disappeared, he replied only to ask for his skateboard back so he could take a turn brushing up on some skills.

Hannah watched them fade away right there in front of her as a feeling of sadness swept over her, as her mind clawed to hold onto it, wanting to just stay with them in the moment. If only she could have seen more of these moments of Jimmy's affection for her, which was unknown to her at the time. She felt silly for not seeing that exchange between Jimmy and Brad for what it was, a subtle admission that he felt the same as she did for him.

She stood there staring at the space behind the building, recalling all the times she and Jimmy had come out here during newspaper meetings to take a break. Sometimes, with Brad or others, but often just the two of them. They would sit on the sidewalk with their backs against the building, talking and bickering flirtatiously with one another; she definitely learned to hone her playfulness during those interactions with him.

Hannah remembered how he had worked so hard to teach her to simply balance on a moving skateboard. The muscles in her abdomen seemed to cramp from the memory of the laughter the two shared at her gracelessness. Jimmy never once complained about the death grip she held on his hands each time he got her back up on his skateboard.

Hannah followed the sidewalk back to the main walkway, past the library and some other new buildings she didn't recognize. As she rounded one corner, an old, brown brick facade appeared before her. She knew without having to look at the sign on the front door that it was the SHU police station. Walking closer to it, Hannah could make out the faint outline of a boy on a skateboard riding toward her, unsure if he was real or just a figment of her apparent psychosis.

As the figure approached, she could see it was Jimmy again. From a distant place behind her, she could hear her own voice call out, "What are you still doing here?"

Jimmy let his skateboard drift off into the grass as he walked toward Young Hannah with his focus solely on her. Hannah can clearly recall this day as if it were yesterday, the one where she was taken into custody on suspicion of making bomb threats against the university. She observed as Jimmy reached out to her younger self, trying so desperately to support her in that moment, and how she had rejected him over and over again. Really, it was more her insecurities that couldn't believe he cared about what might happen to her. Jimmy eventually pulled her into a tight hug, forcing her to be comforted. Hannah could swear she smelled the familiar blend of tobacco and patchouli again filling her nose.

Watching the replay of it now, Hannah could feel her heart swell as she saw herself give in, even just a little, to the kindness of another. To let herself be vulnerable enough to lean on someone, especially after the letdowns she had experienced with the campus police and her mother before this moment. Even when she still barely knew him.

As the ache in her core pulsed again, Hannah watched as the figures before her dissolved into nothingness. She was, once again, completely alone on this cold Sunday morning. Burying her hands into her coat pockets, she walked back to her car to find it was still the only one in the entire lot. Waiting for it to warm up, Hannah got lost in thought about the memories she had recalled today. She looked around, not quite ready to emotionally leave this place, so she decided to make a couple of other stops before heading home.

Pulling out of the main gates of SHU, Hannah headed east on Cypress Street. Her shoulders slumped when she saw that the University Diner had been bulldozed and rebuilt into additional dorms. Next to Room 202, the diner had been a popular meeting place for *The Inkwell* crew, who sometimes held meetings over plates of greasy hamburgers and French fries.

She soon pulled into the small parking lot of the Dunkin' Donuts near SHU, the one she used to frequent on her way to Chris's house. She and Jimmy, or she and the girls, often would walk there in the middle of the afternoon and evening hangouts. Inside, Hannah ordered a light and sweet medium-sized coffee. Closing her eyes, she took a long sip and could feel Young Hannah somewhere inside of her melt a little in the comfort of its recognizable creamy sweetness.

Hannah got back in her car and drove around the corner, through winding side streets, until she pulled up in front of Chris's family home. She had read through posts on Facebook that his family had moved out a few years ago, and she couldn't help but notice how much it had changed. The new owner had replaced the siding, the metal fencing around it, and repaved the driveway. It was entirely different, yet somehow still as she remembered it.

She parked her car across the street from the house, and suddenly could see her younger self and Jenny sitting out on the front steps. Hannah could hear their conversation, despite being inside her car with the windows closed, as Jenny cried into her shoulder. It was some time before Jenny had drifted apart from everyone when her life had become too hectic to keep up with *The Inkwell*. Jenny had disclosed her feelings for a female friend who didn't reciprocate them; the friend in question wasn't interested in girls, and wasn't open to exploring anything more than a friendship with her. She had been gutted, her first real heartbreak, and Hannah had felt so sad for her friend.

Sipping her coffee, she watched as her younger self hugged Jenny even tighter. "You will find love one day, Jenny," she could hear herself saying, "and it will be better than anything you've ever imagined. Trust me. If it can exist for me, it will for you, too."

Hannah wiped away a tear as she listened to the encouragement she offered to her friend, urging her to keep following her path, because good things would come to her if she did. What she really saw was the makings of a therapist, the rock her friends would come to for advice or just an ear to talk to. It reminded her why she had chosen this life, even if it sometimes felt like a burden.

When the images faded from the front stoop, Hannah shifted the car back into drive and pulled away from the curb. She decided to take the long way back home to Bay Point, through Stonebridge, and then Harborvale. It was the route she usually took home from SHU or Chris's house. She had a destination in mind, but when she saw a familiar sign post of the side of the road, she hastily pulled into the parking lot where it stood.

Hannah stopped the car and leaned forward, peering out of the windshield at the dilapidated building before her. It was the old music club in Stonebridge called The Junction. A frown formed on her lips as she thought about all the hours she spent inside those doors. Her lips upturned a little as she remembered dancing with Whitney, Katie, and Jenny while listening to their various friends play in crappy rock bands. Hannah closed her eyes, envisioning the night that Jimmy's band, Cat Hair, finally got their debut on an actual stage there. Poetically, it had been their last performance as a band.

Then, she recalled how she bumped into a tall, handsome stranger by the bar and how she would go on to marry him only two years later. Hannah let out a deep breath and took a sip of her coffee, wondering where everything between her and Jake had gone wrong. Her eyes traced the sharp edges of the collapsing roof, and the torn canvas awnings swaying in the winter wind. She couldn't help but think that if her marriage were a physical thing, it would look just as battered as this place that once had been filled with happy people.

Hannah shifted the car back into drive and continued on her way, taking a short detour off the main road to South Liberty Avenue. She pulled off onto the side of the road in front of a two-story house marked as number two hundred three. She stared at the navy blue home with a brick staircase that led to the front door and the expertly manicured front lawn. It was the Taylor family home, where Jimmy had lived during their time at SHU. Hannah had practically lived in that house herself during those years, having spent so many long weekends housesitting while Jimmy's parents were off on yet another vacation. Hannah could feel a rock form in her stomach, thinking of how she stood on that brick staircase all those years ago hearing his mother tell her that Jimmy had run away and no one knew where he was headed. In that moment, it had felt like her entire world was caving in around her.

Something caught her eye, though. A small garden flag staked into the lawn near the stairs read, "The Patels." Her heart sank again; the Taylors no longer lived there. Not that she was going to ring the bell in anticipation of a warm welcome from Jimmy's mom, Bonnie, or anything; Hannah was always pretty sure Bonnie despised her for getting close to her son.

All of that meant, though, that the bedroom there on the right side of the second floor would no longer be painted in that soft blue color that was mostly covered by posters of obscure British punk bands, and that the smell of the patchouli incense that had seeped into every fiber of the gray carpeting had long since been scrubbed away. Closing her eyes, she could transport herself back into that room again. Back to those long nights in Jimmy's bed, holding him close as his body shuddered from sobs as he felt completely out of control of his own mind. She could again feel all of the worry she carried back then as she tried to love him back to the Jimmy she knew so completely.

She wasn't sure if she expected his family to have stayed in Stonebridge or not. Hannah wondered when they had left and where they had even gone. Out west to be near Jimmy's brother, Jasper, was most likely. He was their prized child, anyway.

This stop, more than the others, made her truly realize how much the world had changed. It hit her hard how all of those people had moved on from their past lives, but here she was trying to relive hers all over again.

Hannah's Journal
Sunday, January 14, 2024

i went to SHU today on a whim, and found myself reliving some of my memories from back then. at first i thought i really was going crazy this time, because i couldn't talk myself out of it like before. it almost felt like i was watching a movie of my life or something, as an observer from some other time and place. it was the strangest thing, and i'm still not convinced that i wasn't hallucinating the whole time. grief, depression, and anxiety can do so much to the human mind, after all. i keep reciting the diagnostic criteria for things like schizophrenia and bipolar disorder to convince myself that i _am_ of sound mind and body. most days it helps, and i can find the strength to keep moving forward. other days, i start researching psychiatrists in my area and medications they would likely prescribe. if i take a moment to take a deep breath, i know i don't meet the criteria. it doesn't add up, and i think i _know_ i am okay. it's just this nagging voice in my head...

i have to admit that some of those memories i had long forgotten about because they just weren't happy ones. like that fight with whitney and katie, or the day i was harassed by the police because they thought i made bomb threats.

maybe it's because i'm so many years out from those events now that i can see how even the worst of them showed me the best in myself. like how i stood up for myself, even if it meant going against people i loved. how i was born to be a helper. that i am worthy of a space in people's lives, that i was all along.

it's also so much more than that. i've been feeling lonely for so long now, pining away for my old friends and my old life. i've felt my heart literally ache with missing them. but i realized today that they're all still a part of me. i think back on all of those memories, those people, and i can see the very ways they left an imprint on my life. whether it was showing me the strength i carried in myself, teaching me to be more outgoing or funny, showing me what real love and care looked like, or just making me feel like i was part of something. i guess, in a way, i'm made up of all of their loose parts. that i've been created, like some frankenstein monster, of these pieces of all the people i have loved. i'm more like a patchwork quilt, or a tiled mosaic art piece. i am glued together with light and sweet coffees, constellations, guitar chords, conversations around a beach bonfire, whispered secrets in a friend's ear, crappy lunches in the SHU cafeteria, rock band battles, long walks around the mall, a caring hand reaching out for comfort, late night drives, concerts at rundown bars and church basements. it's what makes me, me. it's the clever comebacks, the philosophical conversations, the types of books i read, and how i feel about the current state of our government.

tonight i'm finding more comfort than sadness in this fact. that i haven't <u>really</u> lost anyone because for as long as i'm here, they always will be part of me. i guess i can only hope that fragments of me still remain with them, too. that i'll never really be forgotten so long as they're still around. my thoughts come back to the passion i once had for writing, and this idea that i could keep us alive on the pages of a book or in the lines of a poem. if only i felt like i could do it all justice, but i've never been that good.

i'm sitting here now thinking back on it all, and i can feel this same stirring in me that i felt this morning walking around campus. i couldn't figure out what it was, exactly, but i think it's something like love. love for the hannah that was stuck in that weird in-between of not being a kid anymore, and not quite being an adult yet. she thought she was so broken back then. unlovable and unworthy. yet, i watched her today in her element, with her people, and my god how that girl shined. i wish i could go back and tell her she is lovable. that she is worthy. that she is perfect the way she is. to own it. sure, she had jimmy to tell her those things time and again. he'd tell her how beautiful she was and that he only had eyes for her. how smart, creative, caring, and personable she was. he'd find ways to weave it into conversation or leave little notes for her around the house with affirmations on them. anything to build that girl up. i wonder what would have become of her had she actually listened to all of that, rather than all of the negative voices of her past. maybe it's too late for it to make a difference now but, to the twenty-year old version of myself that i feel waking up inside of me, i love you. i am proud of you. you can do the hard things. you are so worthy and deserving of love and good things.

it's pretty fucked up how it takes someone dying to make you take stock of your own life. both jimmy and my dad died too young. what if that happens to me? i've carried these wounds around for a long time, but somehow the people who caused them have all faded from my life and memory. it feels like such a waste of my time and energy to keep shouldering it all. life is too short, and now that's all coming back into view. i wonder if i could find a way to put it down, if i'd be a better partner to jake, or a better friend to alan and shannon. it's just so sad that it takes something so heavy to make you open your eyes.

"I took your advice and went for a walk around the SHU campus last weekend," Hannah blurted out as soon as she walked through the door to Linda's office.

Linda's eyebrows raised in surprise. "Really? I'd forgotten all about that. How did it go?"

"It was enlightening," Hannah told her with a little chuckle. "It brought up a lot of memories for me. Good and bad, but it made me feel so grateful for the time I had there. For the person I was then, too. I never gave her enough credit. I don't think I was expecting all of that."

"That does sound enlightening!" Linda exclaimed, as her voice showed more emotion than usual. "What were you expecting?"

Hannah's eyes went wide as she tried to think back. "I'm not sure, but I don't think I was expecting *that.*"

"Tell me more."

Blowing out a lungful of air, Hannah explained the specific moments she relived that morning as if she were watching a movie of her life. "I hope you don't think I've completely lost it. I think it myself more and more with the dreams and now these visions I had on campus," she said with a nervous laugh.

Linda laughed with her briefly. "I don't think you're crazy about any of it. I'd say your experience at SHU was more like a flashback, which we typically associate with a post-traumatic experience. I don't believe that's the case for you, but I do think that your mind was reliving these significant moments in your life for a reason. It's quite beautiful that you had that experience." There was a long pause as the two women sat, looking at one another. Eventually, Linda asked, "So what is front of mind to talk about this week?"

Hannah shrugged. "I don't know. I guess I'm just worried about my mental fitness. I'm genuinely worried there is something wrong with me, Linda. It's caused my anxiety attacks to start up again."

"What do you mean 'again'?" Linda questioned with narrowed eyes as she jotted something down on her notepad.

Hannah explained to her that she had been having anxiety attacks since high school, and promptly apologized for not mentioning it sooner. She detailed her concern that they were happening frequently after many years of not having any, and how she had always been able to identify her triggers when they did happen. Until recently, that is. Though, as she rattled on, she began to see a pattern in their appearances. The anxiety seemed to grow when she considered what life could look like if she were happy, because the reality of the state of her marriage and other relationships always seemed to be hiding in the shadows at the back of her mind. The resentment and anger she felt would flair, and then it would begin.

"Well, there has been a heavy weight on your shoulders, Hannah. I'm not entirely surprised that they're cropping back up now," Linda told her.

Hannah shrugged. "I guess. It's just frustrating after all this time, you know?"

"I can imagine. Do you feel like you can manage them? I can write a referral for a psychiatrist friend of mine, if you feel like you need some help getting over the hump."

Hannah shook her head adamantly. "No, no. I'm managing okay."

"Let me know if you change your mind," Linda encouraged her. "You mentioned before you opened up to Shannon about some of your marital concerns. How did that feel?"

Hannah grunted. "Not great. I felt like she wasn't really hearing me. She was more concerned with the thought that I was going to divorce Jake, and she didn't want that for me, but didn't bother to ask if that's what I wanted."

Linda paused a moment. "So then let me ask: Is that what you want?"

She didn't know what she wanted. The idea had popped into her mind before, but she hadn't taken the time to weigh it all out. Stuttering, she answered, "I'm not sure. I mean, I still love him, but I also know that sometimes love isn't enough. I think my time back at SHU reminded me that I deserve more, but I'm still trying to figure out how long I'm supposed to wait for Jake to give me that. These last few months have shown me that anything can happen in the blink of an eye, and I don't want to waste my life waiting for him to love me right."

"You don't have to have all the answers right now," Linda gently replied. "It's just important that you know your options and know that each one is completely valid."

With a slight shake of her head, Hannah picked her hands up from her lap briefly and said, "I feel like I can't distinguish if I really feel that way, though, or if this is me just trying to leave before he has a chance to, you know? There have been so many times in our relationship, more so earlier on, that I seemed to be just waiting for him to leave me. Like everyone else. How do I know the difference?"

Linda pursed her lips. "That's a good question, and I think one that deserves the proper space and time to be answered. It's okay that you're questioning it, because you still care. Follow your heart, Hannah. I don't think it's led you astray yet."

Hannah snorted and picked at her cuticles.

After a beat, Linda continued. "I noticed a parallel between Jake and Jimmy, and I'm curious if you see it, too? You've mentioned that Jake's mood seems to be very up and down, like how Jimmy's was. We do know he had a diagnosis of Bipolar II, which explains that. Jake's, though, are different. They seem to be more due to circumstance."

Hannah nodded in understanding. "Right."

"I'm curious if it's bringing back some of those old feelings you had when you and Jimmy were together? Like repeating a cycle, in a way?" Linda wondered out loud.

"No," Hannah said flatly. She considered the question again briefly before definitively saying, "No, because it *is* very different."

"How so?"

"You said it yourself. It wasn't Jimmy's fault. It was his diagnosis. What was happening inside of him was largely beyond his control. Whether it was a chemical imbalance, or maybe it was never Bipolar, but an actual brain injury from all the falls he took over the years. I don't know that we'll ever really know which it was, but that's besides the point," she explained with a long exhale lingering on the last words. "I know that Jake is limited by his lack of knowledge on how to navigate his emotions. I understand that, but you know, Jimmy was never mean to me. Short sometimes, yeah. Even a little cold. He never took it out on me, though, or blamed me for whatever was happening to him internally. He never made it personal.

Jake does. He takes everything out on me, like I'm this horrible person. He makes it personal just to hurt me, I think."

Linda's mouth moved into a slight smile. "I see. So you feel like Jake is taking his anger and stress out on you and, essentially, blaming you for his feelings?"

"No," Hannah said sharply. "Not that I *feel*. That I *know*! I know because he has told me. He's outwardly blamed me for the money stuff, his bad moods, and these stupid ideas about how Diesel loves me more than him. He's outwardly made mean comments right to my face, sometimes disguising them in snide, sarcastic jokes. How I'm an emotional dumpster fire, or how he used to find me more attractive when we first started dating. No amount of backpedaling could fix that one."

A wave of frustration washed over Hannah. She felt misunderstood and unheard, a feeling she had grown accustomed to throughout most of her life. She also felt blindsided by the shift in conversation from something positive to focusing on the other end of the spectrum. All the pent-up rage of the last few months came rushing forward and took aim at Linda.

I know this is a significant point in my process here, but is now really the right time to be pushing back so hard? Why is she doing this now? Hannah wondered.

Linda looked down at her notepad and back at Hannah. "You're right. This is your lived experience, not mine. I'm sorry if it came off like I was trying to tell you how to feel. I do want to ask, though—have you considered that Jake's moods are something he can't control?"

Her tongue still lashing sharply, she replied, "I have, but I just keep coming back to the fact that he doesn't have to be such an asshole. He doesn't have to hurt me, but he chooses to.

He chooses to push my buttons, to twist the knife deeper into me."

"Okay, and I understand why you feel that way. Let's focus on what you can control in this situation. We can brainstorm constructive ways to tell him how it makes you feel when he makes comments like that," Linda suggested.

The urge to get up and run was overwhelming; the desire to be anywhere but here in this room with Linda coursed through her veins. Heat rose from her chest and up her neck, as the irritation she felt became unbearable to sit with. She turned to glance at the clock on Linda's desk to see that there were only about fifteen minutes left.

Just a little longer, she told herself.

Linda persisted. "One word keeps coming to mind in all the weeks we've been talking. I keep coming back to the idea of safety, from growing up to where you are in your life now. It seems to me that you've been constantly seeking a safe place to put down roots. Would you agree?"

"Yeah," Hannah reluctantly admitted. "I put a lot of trust into other people time after time, only to be disappointed. Friends, my parents. The amount of times my leash was slackened only for it to be tightened again without a warning or even a reason because their trust in me had been revoked, or how my sadness or sickness was met with annoyance rather than comfort. It was always easier to just stay silent, but if I can speak freely, I'm feeling pretty disappointed. You keep telling me to be empathetic to Jake, but I feel like you're not hearing how much this whole situation is breaking me down." She paused and chuckled, but not in a funny way. "You know—if he were physically abusing me, you'd be telling me to leave, right? You would be making calls to shelters or whatever, to find me a place to stay that was away from him. You wouldn't let me stay in that situation for one more day. I don't think that you see I'm sitting here with these invisible scars because I don't think you'd be telling me that I need to learn to be more empathetic, or temper my reactions." She glared at Linda, her lungs working double-time as she worked to calm the beast inside of her.

Linda looked at her wide-eyed for a long moment, letting the air settle between them, before saying, "It was always my intention to make this office a safe space for you, and myself a safe person for you." She then asked, "Who's made you feel safe?"

Hannah answered immediately, "Jimmy was always so loving and caring toward me. Toward *everyone*, really. He was supportive of everything I wanted to do, and I could trust him wholeheartedly. I'm starting to realize now that Alan is also someone I feel safe with. That last time Jimmy ran off, he was the first person I thought to call because I knew he would keep a level head and be there with me in the mud of it. He's making me see what true friendship is again, and I'm questioning my relationships with other people in my life because I don't have that with them."

"Curiously, you don't consider Jimmy's leaving a betrayal of your trust?"

Hannah shook her head, repeating the same sentiments she had earlier. She knew what she was getting into ever since the first time he disappeared from her life, when he had come clean to her about his illness and the shame he felt about it. She watched him fight a constant uphill battle against himself for years, and she watched how exhausted it made him. She also understood this more than most, due to her own struggles.

"Has Jake ever made you feel safe?"

"He used to," Hannah said with her demeanor turning cold again. "Not anymore, though."

Linda cocked her head to one side a little as she jotted down some more notes. "I wonder if your difficulty processing the grief over Jimmy's death is tied to that feeling of safety? That living in those memories, rereading your journals over and over again, is a way to keep him alive and hold on to that safe place he provided you with? What do you think?"

Hannah braced her hands tightly on the armrests of the chair, her knuckles turning white. "You're probably right. The times when I'm able to disappear into my memories of Jimmy and Alan, that life we all shared, have been the only comfort I've had in a long time. All of this stuff with Jake has made me question what's in my own heart. I think I'm so stuck on Jimmy these days because he was the first safe person I ever knew. When I've needed courage in social settings, I've always thought of him and what he would do. When I've needed to find calm amidst the shitstorm of anxious thoughts in my mind, I'd sometimes imagine him there with me. There was a time when Jake had been that person for me, but he's since given that up. So what else can I do?"

It all made sense suddenly. The desire for her past, especially her life with Jimmy. He used to be her refuge from the rest of the world. Her peace. In those years with him, things didn't seem as bad as they had been before him. Maybe Linda was right. Perhaps she was just looking for some kind of proof that there were people out there who wouldn't disappoint or hurt her. Or maybe, more realistically, it was just to open those old wounds. To keep feeling this devastating pain, because pain was the oldest emotion she knew. It felt familiar, like an old friend she had grown comfortable with. That's what happens with prolonged exposure, though: you learn to dance with your demons, rather than fight them.

Hannah gritted her teeth, bearing down on the arms of

the chair a little harder. "I can't do this anymore today," she announced. She picked her bag up from the floor, gripping its long strap in her fist, and stormed out of the office. She was tired of people trying to convince her that Jake was somehow justified in his behavior and that she was solely the problem. That this yearning in her heart for something more, something better than this, was the reason that everything was falling apart. Not the result of it.

As she walked out to her car, Hannah wasn't sure where she should go from here. She and Jake had once created a home where she felt the most at ease, the most secure, but it hadn't felt that way in months. With all the fighting and tension between them, home felt more like a battleground where her nerves were always on edge, ready for anything. It was only in the pages of her journals that Hannah could escape into the past to be surrounded by love and support. She had no choice but to walk back in that door, though, and try to make something from her unfulfilling life.

Hannah's Journal
Monday, January 22, 2024

~~AAAAHHHH~~!!!!!!

that's the scream i want to scream in the worst
way if it wouldn't raise eyebrows or cause the
police to be called out to my house. i've moved
beyond the status quo anger to blinding rage. i
wouldn't be surprised if i crack a tooth with how
hard i'm grinding my teeth all the time. i'm
honestly afraid for the walls of my house and my
fists that want to see what they look like on
the inside. i seriously feel like a teenager again
with this pent-up frustration, and i just want to
take it out on something. i'm desperately fighting
to urge to throw the glass jar on the bookcase
next to me. just to see it shatter. to see it break
in the way that i feel broken. i keep reminding
myself to drop my shoulders away from my ears,
but i just can't seem to relax.

i opened up to shannon about everything with jake,
and that felt like a giant mistake. she just
disregarded everything i said, like it was more
important for us to stay together. give him
more time! try harder!

what more can i do if he won't talk to me? if
he won't also try? i fucking hate that this is
somehow my responsibility to fix. and then on

the opposite side of things is nicole who's been telling me to just leave jake. i don't need them to tell me what to do and i sure as hell don't want their opinions. i just wanted someone to listen to me, to understand where i'm coming from. now i just feel more confused about what it is i want, like i can't separate their voices from my own. how can i stop from feeling like i'm going to rip in half with the tug-of-war they're playing? i want to shut them up, the voices of my friends who have become these constant echoes between my ears. each of them represents a side of myself, this internal argument that's playing on a loop in my mind. leave jake, or stay and fight. at times, i want to leave him, and then i don't at others. i just want to silence my thoughts for even a few minutes.

and linda! every time i think about my last session with her, i just get angry all over again and start looking up other therapists in my area. i usually enjoy our sessions, and i've found her really helpful and honest, but i felt like she was picking sides, too. and that's on the side of jake. she made it sound like like i'm not giving him enough empathy or benefit of the doubt. what about me? don't i deserve some compassion for what i've been going through? what i am still going through? i literally walked out of the appointment because i was afraid i was going to take all of my aggression out on the arm of that chair. part of me doesn't want to go back. it felt like something broke between us in that room, and i don't know if we can fix it. i guess it was trust in her that she would lead me to the challenging bits in a safe, respectable way. that will take time to rebuild, but is it worth it? maybe i just need some time to cool off.

all anyone wants me to do is to keep giving more of myself to jake. give, give, give. as if i haven't given enough. i've faded so far into the background of my own life that i've totally lost any identity i had as hannah. i'm just jake's wife. people don't call me by my name anymore, either. that is my identity now, like i'm some fucking stepford wife. how long do i keep giving? how do i even move into a new space of being hannah _and_ jake's wife? it has to be possible for both to be true, but it seems like every woman i know has sacrificed parts of herself for the sake of her marriage. i wonder if they feel the way i do about it, though? do they even notice? why does it have to be this way?

i think my visit back to SHU really helped to spur this clashing inside of myself. ever since i've been on this journey to rediscover me. it's like this confidence i've long since lost is starting to grow again, but it doesn't seem like jake knows quite how to process the change. now i'm someone who is pushing back, and not just accepting his bad moods and mean words. it's the second big shift i've gone through in the last year (depression and now self-discovery), so i get that it's jarring. he never really knew that version of me, the one who stuck up for herself. he's only known this broken one that was badly sewn back together. i want to give him the time to get to know me all over again, but i don't know if he wants to.

i wish i could just be a total, uncontrolled bitch. to linda. shannon. nicole. jake, most of all. for as damaged as i am, i'd never be able to be that person. that will likely be my undoing: not being mean enough when i have every right to be.

Hannah pulled up to the house after work to find that Jake's car was still missing from the driveway; he should've been home almost an hour ago. She checked her phone but found no messages from him saying he would be home late. The last message she sent to him, saying precisely the same, had gone unread. She wasn't entirely surprised since Jake's mood swings often meant he turned quieter and considered Hannah even less. She lingered there behind the steering wheel, her head resting back on the seat, letting the heaviness of the day sit on her shoulders. Lucy had made an appearance in the office today after several weeks of no-shows and seemed to be a complete shell of the girl Hannah had seen last. She had bawled for the short time she was there over how alone she felt having lost friends so easily. Like how someone misplaces their car keys or wallet; there was a nonchalantness to their disappearance from her life. For Hannah, all she could think of were the old friends she, herself, had lost to time and circumstance. Some bitterly, others in the same apathetic manner than Lucy described.

Once inside the house, she hung up her coat, slipped her feet out of the ballet flats she'd been wearing, and tossed her laptop bag onto the chair in her office. Diesel was practically bouncing on his tail with excitement to see her, much like the character of Tigger in those old "Winnie the Pooh" movies she used to love as a kid. Hannah fed him dinner first before changing out of her work clothes. Otherwise, she would've been tripping over him the entire time.

Hannah heated some leftovers in the microwave and poured a glass of wine; she was more interested in the drink than the food, but attempted to eat anyway. She sat on the floor of her office with the Tupperware container and pulled out the box of old photographs she started organizing a few weeks ago. It was the only thing she could think to do to slow the thoughts racing in her mind after Lucy's session today.

The first pictures she came to were from a college party at the school where her ex-boyfriend, Manny, and a couple of her high school friends had been enrolled. Metropolitan University was similar to Safe Harbor University, but more expensive and farther away from Harborvale. She laughed into her wine glass before taking another sip, her eyes remaining fixed on the drunken faces in the photos. Hannah looked at one particular image of her and Melissa sitting together on a cracked leather couch, their cheeks pink from the kind of vodka that comes in a plastic gallon jug. The two girls had their arms wrapped around each other in a tight hug, both smiling from ear to ear. It was back when there was nothing but love between them, after Amanda had left the two of them behind.

Hannah could feel the emotion rising in her throat and took another sip of wine to drown it, to push it back down, as memories of their falling out resurfaced. The two met through Amanda, but didn't become close friends until sometime in their senior year of high school. In hindsight, it was probably because Amanda had moved away, and so they decided to cling to one another in her absence. Melissa and Hannah kept in touch through college via text and instant message conversations at all hours of the day and night, getting together mostly when Melissa came home for breaks or when Hannah visited her at her dorm. It had been possible, after all, for Hannah to maintain this friendship and step into her new life at SHU. She sniffled, thinking about how that had been out of the question with Amanda.

"Screw her," she whispered.

In her third year of college, though, Melissa changed. It began with partying not just on weekends, but also on weeknights. Then, over time, Hannah noticed how Melissa slurred her words more often when they talked on the phone, and how her eyes always seemed glazed over when she saw her during school breaks. So when Melissa complained of chronic pain that seemed to move from one place to the next, Hannah worried that her friend's body was fighting back against the constant flow of alcohol and other party drugs she eventually admitted to using. She wanted nothing more than to believe her friend, that there was something wrong with her, but it became more apparent over time that she was merely chasing ways to numb herself.

Melissa's condition continued to worsen over the next year until it culminated in a big fight between the friends during Spring Break of their final year of college. Hannah recalled being woken up by a phone call from Melissa at 2:00 A.M. She was in tears because of the immense pain she was in and wanted Hannah to meet her at a hospital about two hours away. When she questioned why she was going so far, Melissa confirmed that the doctors at the hospitals nearest to school and Harborvale would no longer treat her due to their suspicions that she was only drug-seeking; even her family had refused to meet her, so she needed Hannah's support.

Jimmy had rolled over in bed then and groggily asked Hannah if everything was all right. As she remembered it, Jimmy had just lost his job at a magazine in Highgate City and they were spending some much-needed time together housesitting while his parents were away for a few days. Hannah had bent over to gently kiss his forehead, whispering for him not to worry before tiptoeing downstairs to talk to Melissa. She could still see the way his lips curled ever so slightly before he promptly drifted back off to sleep.

Hannah could feel the guilt even now, remembering how she wasn't able to meet Melissa at the hospital at that late hour; she had a full day of work the following morning that she wasn't able to miss. When Melissa fought back, Hannah attempted to explain that it was too late for her to call out and, besides, she needed the money to pay off the textbooks she had put on her credit card that semester. She could recall the worry she had felt over missing her last payment, and feared missing yet another one. It didn't matter what Hannah said, though, because Melissa was only going to be satisfied with her friend sitting in the chair next to her hospital bed. Hannah tried to offer other options, but Melissa didn't want her to just stay on the phone with her, nor did she want Hannah to talk her brother or roommate in to being there with her. Eventually, Melissa broke out in a never-ending stream of vitriol, accusing Hannah of being selfish, claiming she had never been a good friend to her, and expressing the hope that one day Hannah would understand what it meant to feel such immense pain. Even now, the memories of those words stung.

She did her best to calm Melissa down and tell her she didn't mean those things. She even yelled back, defending herself by listing off all the times she'd answered the phone in the middle of the night to listen to her cry, picked her up in all kinds of shady places because she was too wasted to get home, or all of the other times she had visited Melissa in the hospital with magazines, puzzle books, and face masks in-hand. It made no difference, and Hannah eventually just hung up the phone.

Through the small-town grapevine, Hannah heard that Melissa had wound up in a rehab program a short time after that. She never did hear anything more about it, but she hoped Melissa managed to stay sober and healthy. Hannah sometimes wondered about her still, but with no trace on social media, she'd likely never know unless an obituary appeared online one day.

Despite the lingering regret and sadness, Hannah couldn't say she regretted what she had done, or hadn't done, depending on how she looked at it. She tried to be a friend to Melissa, but eventually, she had to come to terms with the fact that she was being taken advantage of. That, and the fact that it's impossible to help someone who doesn't want to help themselves. Jimmy had seen it long before Hannah did, and often tagged along with her on those late-night drives to pick Melissa up from whatever bar or frat house she'd found herself in; he was just worried for Hannah's safety, and she loved him for that. He had grown tired of Melissa's behavior long before Hannah did, too, but he had been a good sport about it all. When she crawled back into bed that night, tears streaming down her face, Jimmy enveloped her in his arms and listened as her heart broke over another dead friendship.

How she wished to be held like that now, to be squeezed so tight that her broken pieces could fit back together once again. A warm, wet sensation on her face snapped Hannah out of her daydream. It was Diesel licking the salty tears from her cheeks. She didn't even realize she was crying, or that she had wrapped her own arms around her body for comfort. Hannah tossed the photos back into the box, having lost all motivation to organize them, and pushed it back under her desk. The front door swung open with a thud suddenly, and the sound of Jake's loafers clomping along the floor echoed through the quiet house.

He used to hold her in such a way that she swore it made pretty every ugly part of her. She longed for it now, but knew she couldn't have it. That realization hurt, causing the ache in her stomach to pulse. She took a deep breath, preparing herself for the worst of him, but still hopelessly praying for the best.

Hannah reached into the warm oven and pulled out the lemon meringue pie she had carefully crafted for dessert tonight. She held the pie up at eye level, inspecting the crust and the lightly browned meringue peaks.

It looks okay, she thought before taking a couple of sniffs. *Smells good.*

Usually, she would still have been in the office seeing clients, but Lucy had canceled for the second week in a row after resurfacing for one, very short, session at the end of January. Her excuse this time was a stomach bug that was flying around the school where she taught. The week before, it was the common cold. Hannah wasn't entirely buying her excuses, but there was only so much she could do; at least Lucy was canceling instead of just not showing up.

Then, Brian, the client she usually saw after Lucy, had also canceled because he had planned a romantic date night complete with dinner and a movie in Highgate City with his partner. They ended up having a brief phone session, which was essentially her client bragging about how he managed to secure a reservation at a trendy new restaurant. There had been a twinge of jealousy since Jake hadn't planned anything like that for her in years. Still, all the Valentine's Day advertisements gave her hope that she could turn this thing around. That if she made the nice dinner and wore the sexy lingerie and the flowery perfume, she could make Jake fall in love with her again. She never thought she would miss sex as much as she did but, in recent years, there had been a steady drop-off in the intimacy department. Especially this last year when it really took a nosedive. With her newfound free time, Hannah left the office early to start on her next attempt to revive the love between them.

Lemon meringue pie didn't exactly scream romance, nor did it feel appropriate for the middle of the winter, but it was Jake's favorite dessert. Desperate times called for desperate measures, and things between them had certainly reached that level; she would do anything just to see him smile again. To make herself smile again, because the more time went on, the more the idea of divorce pushed itself into her mind. A knot tied itself in her stomach at the thought. On one hand, the concept itself was liberating. On the other hand, though, she saw the biggest failure of her life to date. There would be no way she could face her friends or her mom if it came to that.

A little groan from underneath her brought Hannah back to the present. She looked down to see Diesel at her feet, looking expectantly at the chicken sitting before her on the counter. Hannah glanced at the clock as she slid the bird into the oven, not needing to set a timer since it would be done at precisely the time Jake would be walking in the door from work.

She rechecked the time just to be sure; her nerves were weirdly getting the best of her, like she was getting ready to go on a first date rather than a dinner at home with the man she'd been married to for ten years. Hannah poured herself a splash of wine, just enough to help ease her worries. Things were timing out perfectly. Too perfectly, but she tried not to think about the other figurative shoe waiting to drop.

After tidying up the kitchen, Hannah changed out of her work clothes and began digging around her closet for something a little more casual to wear. What really mattered was what she was going to wear underneath everything; that would be anything *but* casual. Diesel trotted into the room and made himself comfortable on top of the bed, watching her as she slipped on the black lacy push-up bra and thong she bought at the mall the week before.

"Your thoughts?" she asked him with a silly laugh.

She turned to pull out a pair of dark denim jeans that she knew Jake loved to see her in, along with a flowy black top featuring lacy, fluttering sleeves. Hannah fixed up her hair and makeup in the bathroom mirror before doing a quick spin for Diesel, who just lay there and wagged his tail like the best boy.

"Hopefully this will grab his attention," Hannah told her reflection in the mirror with a heavy sigh, and marched back into the kitchen to check on the food. She put the finishing touches on the mashed potatoes and heated the corn on the stove top.

With still some time to spare until Jake got home, she decided to send him a quick, flirty text message.

> **Hannah:** *Can't wait to see you soon, babe. I've got a few surprises for you.*

It was a few minutes before her phone chimed with a new message from Jake, making her throat instantly tighten.

> **Jake:** *Working late.*
> **Hannah:** *Seriously? I told you to be home on time tonight. I've been planning this dinner for a week.*

Jake: *I'm doing my best, Hannah. I'll be there when I can. Just eat without me if you're hungry.*

Hannah grumbled low, leaning her back against the countertop. She nearly knocked the phone from her hands as her thumbs moved with intensity across the keyboard.

Hannah: *That's not the point!*

Jake didn't reply after that, which did nothing to quell the anxiety and anger growing inside her. She paced the kitchen for several minutes before pouring more wine into her glass. She wished she had someone to talk to who wasn't a dog, but she knew her friends would all be busy with their significant others, who actually wanted to spend this day of love with them.

When the time on the clock ticked to 5:15 P.M., she pulled the chicken from the oven and put the sides into two serving dishes.

"I should've known it was all going too perfectly," she said to Diesel, who sat at her feet, still begging for some chicken scraps. With a roll of her eyes, Hannah gave in. "Fine," she whispered, as she dropped a few chunks of meat onto the floor for him to enjoy.

As she took the last sip of her wine, the front door swung open with a force as Jake walked into the house. Hannah was shocked to see him standing there, figuring she would be left to enjoy this meal on her own. "You're here!" she gasped.

Jake smiled weakly. "I'll have to go in early tomorrow since I didn't finish everything today, but I'm here," he told her.

Hannah returned the smile, a meager glimmer of hope shone then, that he had made the effort to be at home with her tonight. There was still some tension in the air, but Jake was actually home.

"Well, dinner's ready, so whenever you are…" she said in her most cheerful voice.

Jake followed her into the kitchen. "I'm surprised you're not in sweats," he told her with a raised eyebrow.

"I wanted to look nice for you, and there's more than meets the eye," she said flirtatiously.

Jake remained silent as he eyeballed the pie cooling on the counter. "You made this?" he asked with an air of disbelief in his tone.

"I did!" Hannah proudly proclaimed.

"It doesn't look half bad."

She walked over to him and threw her arms around his neck. "If you clear your plate, you might even have your *choice* of dessert tonight," she told him in a breathy voice.

Jake's hands hesitantly found her waist, but he looked everywhere but at her. "I see," he said simply. "Well, I'm starving. Let's just eat." With a pat on her hip, Jake released Hannah and took a seat at the kitchen table.

Hannah stood frozen in place, her arms hanging loosely at her sides. Dazed, she found her feet underneath her after a few beats and walked over to the table to join him.

Did he even notice I was trying to flirt with him? she wondered.

Jake seemed to be feeling down, and Hannah tried extra hard to be funny and silly, hoping to bring some levity to their meal. It worked a couple of times, but he mostly remained flat.

"So—did your boyfriend call today?" Jake asked after a long period of silence.

She looked up at him, confused. "What are you talking about?"

"Alan?"

Hannah cracked up. "No, why would he?"

Jake snickered. "It's Valentine's Day."

"Okay? And I'm sure he's busy having a nice night with Phoebe and the girls."

A soft grunt left Jake's throat.

"What?" Hannah asked.

"Nothing."

"No," she snapped, shaking her head. "No, don't do that. Don't start something, and then pretend like you didn't."

Jake's eyes met hers, and she could feel the coldness in them. "Fine. It just seems like there's something between you two."

Hannah's eyes went wide, and her jaw fell open. "You've gotta be kidding me."

"Do I look like I'm kidding, Hannah?"

"Why would you even think that?"

Jake let out a loud puff of air. "Please. All the secret phone calls behind my back?"

"What? There's nothing secret about my conversations with Alan. I've always mentioned when I talk to him—"

"That's a lie," Jake said curtly. "New Year's? I heard you talking to him from the bedroom. Staying on the phone together until you fall asleep? How cute."

Hannah looked at him, blinking fast. She couldn't believe what Jake was accusing her of. "Okay, so one time I didn't mention it. It was nothing."

"Why not mention it if it was nothing?"

She shrugged slightly. "Because I knew you'd react like this. Why would I light the fuse to that bomb? I had a private conversation with a friend about the current state of my marriage. I fell to pieces that night, and I just needed someone who would be there for me. I needed to feel less alone." Jake's cheeks flushed, but Hannah couldn't tell if it was out of anger or embarrassment that she had spoken to someone else about his behavior. "He's just a friend, Jake. I promise," Hannah assured him, reaching her hand out to cover his.

He looked up from the mashed potatoes he had been pushing around his plate, meeting her eyes again, and moved his hand out from under hers. "I just feel like I'm losing you to him now."

"What do you mean?" she asked, keeping her hand extended out toward him.

"First Jimmy, now Alan," he explained.

Hannah pulled her hand back then. "Jimmy? How were you losing me to Jimmy?"

"You've just been so wrapped up in him lately."

Her mouth opened and then closed quickly as she tried to think of something to say in her defense, but Jake wasn't necessarily wrong. Hannah had been consumed by grief over Jimmy's death, but she had been reaching out for Jake all along. Surely he had seen that. Hannah felt her cheeks flush. "This is ridiculous. I thought we were over this," she said. "Jimmy's dead. Let me repeat it so it sinks in: *he's dead*! He can't steal me away from you!"

"I just didn't think you'd be pining over him still!" he shouted.

"I'm not *pining* over him—"

Jake interrupted her, "Yeah, okay. The Tidewater Hellraisers? Care to explain that?"

Caught by surprise, Hannah asked, "What about them?"

"You didn't think I would look them up, did you? I kind of liked that song that came on when we left Shannon's that night, so I searched for them online. I guess I shouldn't have been surprised to see Jimmy-fucking-Taylor listed as the lead guitarist and singer," Jake shouted, his face turning a bright red.

Hannah crossed her arms over her chest. "Okay. And? What are you trying to prove here?"

"That you *are* pining over him! That you're in love with him still!"

With a roll of her eyes, Hannah spat, "Oh, please! I was there when a lot of it was being made. I watched him perform those songs for years. Hell, I even helped him write some of them. I was pretty proud of that. They're important to me not just because they were Jimmy's, but because they're a part of me too. I've been trying to find that part of me again, and that music helps. Besides, if anything, I'm pining over *you*! I've been trying to get you to notice me for months now! I was practically throwing myself at you when you walked in the door, and you couldn't even look me in the eye!" Her rage was poking at the surface, begging for her to lash out and punch something. Hannah inhaled sharply, fighting to maintain her composure.

Jake hung his head. "I'm just not in the mood," he said quietly.

Hannah snorted. "You're never in the mood anymore."

"It's like—now that I've heard his voice and saw his face, all I can think about is you with him," Jake humbly admitted. "He was a good looking guy with a lot of talent, and I'm sorry I can't be that for you."

"Jake—"

"Anyway, thanks for making dinner, but I'm gonna head off to bed since I have to be up and out at dawn tomorrow to make up for leaving early for this." He stood from the table and walked out of the room.

"Jake, wait—"

He didn't even turn around to look at her one last time, which Hannah was thankful for because he would have seen the tears welling up in her eyes; she couldn't bring herself to be vulnerable in front of him anymore. She found herself locked up tight around him lately, and the only emotion able to seep through the gaps in her walls was her fury. Deep down, she wished she could let him into her world more, that he would give her that safe place to land that she was so desperately seeking.

Before she realized what she was doing, Hannah was on her feet and marching into the bedroom after Jake. He stood there in only his boxer briefs, looking at her with his plaid pajama pants hanging loosely in his left hand. Jake watched as Hannah undressed, her movements quick and jerky. In only her bra and underwear, she turned to face him.

"If I'm so hung up on Jimmy, if I'm cheating on you with Alan, why the *fuck* did I go out and buy this stupid shit for tonight? Why am I trying so damn hard just to get you to look at me?" she huffed and put a hand on her hip, waiting for an answer.

Jake continued to stare at her, not saying a word. Hannah angrily grabbed a T-shirt, sweatpants, and a more comfortable pair of underwear from the dresser and stalked off to the bathroom. With a slam of the door, she threw her clothes to the floor and turned the shower on to the hottest setting. All the words she wanted to scream, but couldn't, reverberated throughout her body, bouncing off her bones and organs. Her body visibly shook from it. Stepping into the hot water, Hannah instantly sank to the floor of the shower stall as her shoulders shuddered with silent sobs.

Hannah's Journal
Wednesday, February 14, 2024

it's late and i should be asleep, but even the melatonin can't calm me down enough tonight.

i tried. i made jake's favorite dinner and dessert. i bought the fancy lingerie like shannon suggested i do. stupidly, i went along with it because i guess i thought if i couldn't win him back with everything else i've been doing than i might as well try with my body. ugh, what a disgusting thought. i'm so mad for reducing myself to that. i feel so ashamed of myself for trying to find love and connection through sex. i feel much like the twenty-something year old version of myself all over again. the one who crawled in and out of beds looking for the same kind of love she got from jimmy. i still struggle with that piece of my past, to forgive her for doing what she could to survive. at least this time it's with my husband, though it does little to make me feel better. all of this effort for what? for him to just tell me he's going to be home late. for him to just blow me off. like it was nothing. and now i'm spending the night on the couch because i just can't even stand the thought of being near him right now.

i really feel like i'm at the end of my rope, and i don't know if i can keep forgiving his shitty behavior. like how he keeps throwing everything in my face. when we were at shannon and rob's a few weeks ago, he made some stupid comment about people getting over the things they loved in college, an obvious reference to jimmy. he keeps bringing him up, too. like tonight, he admitted that he's been mad at me because i didn't tell him i was listening to jimmy's music. i don't know why i would have to. it's not like he'd be mad at me if i suddenly started listening to metallica without running it by him first. i think back to watching jimmy play, and it was always something really special to witness. it was as if the guitar was an extension of his arm, of his heart. besides, it's the legacy he's left behind. it's a piece of him that can never die, and i think that's really beautiful. all it takes is the push of a button, and for 3 minutes, jimmy isn't dead.

jake accused me of still "pining" for jimmy, which is absolutely not the case. when i first really told jake everything about jimmy and me, after i had found out he died, he nearly turned green with envy. jake let it get to him and accused me of never really loving him in the first place. like i was only with him because he was the next best thing. i thought he had moved past that, but i guess that was a lie because he brought it up again tonight how he felt like he was losing me to jimmy. it just doesn't make sense! jimmy is six feet under. it's like he wants me to choose between him or jimmy. but there is no choice to make here. i guess he just needs to feel like he's won or something, but i don't know how else i can show him that i choose him. i've been choosing him for 10+ years.

or maybe the decision i have to make isn't between jake and jimmy. maybe it's between jake and i. why do i feel like life is repeating itself again? the deja vu just smacked me upside the head. it's like me and jimmy all over again. i had to make a choice back then, and i chose to leave jimmy for the sake of my own sanity. i couldn't live with the constant worry he put me through, how he never really took care of himself as he should have. so i chose me, and i can see that it's going to come down to me making a choice on who to save. is it me or is it jake? i don't even know that i have the strength to make that decision again. look where it got me last time.

jake even went so far as to call alan my "boyfriend" tonight. he says he feels like he's losing me to alan now, too. we've always been <u>just</u> friends. well, we were more like brother and sister back in the day. we were both without siblings, and we leaned on each other to fill that void. when we met, i was happily with jimmy, and i never once looked twice at alan in any other way. not even for a fleeting moment. it always annoyed me, both of us, really, that most people can't even fathom a man and a woman being best friends. like there always has to be more than that. i guess jake is falling into that way of thinking.

in hindsight, i wish i brought up the fact that he has so many female friends at work. i've never been worried about them, because i trust him.

what a double standard, right? i've only met one of them, but the others i have no clue about other than what he tells me. the way he acts about alan, i wonder if i <u>should</u> be more worried about the other women in his life. what's that saying? blame is just a confession in disguise? makes me wonder. i'll keep that one in my back pocket for another day, another fight, because i just know this is bound to come up again.

honestly, if i were jake, i'd be more worried about other men who are within my reach. like the UPS driver at work, drew. it would be so easy for me to step over that line. i think he's waiting for me to make the first move. some days i feel so sure my resolve is going to give, but i keep reminding myself that i'm not that person. in some weird way i almost <u>want</u> to cross the line with drew because then jake's suspicions would actually be true, and he would have a real reason to be mad at me. i may have lost so much of myself back there, but i haven't lost my morals. i can't possibly start now.

despite all of that, i'll be damned if i let jake come in the middle of my friendship with alan. he's just going to have to learn to deal. i'm honestly so thankful for alan. i feel like he's been the only rock i've had in all of this. at first i wasn't sure i could really open up to him about it. unlike everyone else, he's truly just listened to me as i vented and worked things out in my head. i had really looked to my girlfriends to be that for me, because i thought they could maybe relate with the men in their lives. i should've been looking at alan all along. he's always been good at keeping his footing in high-stress situations, and was never one to pick sides. we talk often, but i hope we can meet face-to-face soon. it's just not the same as when we lived in riverside springs. back then, he'd always be at the house on campbell street with me and jimmy, or we'd see him at the park/skatepark/coffee shop/anywhere else around town, or we'd be at his apartment. i know it'll be hard, but i hope we can make this long distance friendship into something like what we used to have.

i keep thinking about my conversation with nicole, and her questioning why i wouldn't leave jake. at the time, i told her it was because i knew that the person he is now is not the real jake. that when we're good, we're great. both of those things are true, but there is more to it. i have so much regret for leaving jimmy standing on that front porch on campbell street all those years ago. he loved me so deeply, and he was struggling so hard, and i left him. i know, it was the best thing i could do for me at the time, but i do wonder what would've happened to us had i stayed. when i look at jake, i also see someone who loves me deeply, but is struggling. i don't want to repeat the same mistakes with him. i don't want to find myself ten years down the line wondering "what if." so i keep finding the strength in me to keep trying. even though my mind and my heart are so very tired. i just have to keep forcing my body out of bed every morning, and putting one foot in front of the other. it doesn't sound like hard work, but it is, and hard work eventually gets rewarded. at least that's what all these years of people-pleasing has taught me. in a roundabout way.

Hannah left for work a lot earlier than necessary, even though Jake had left long before the sun was up. She just had to get out of that house where the silence hung heavy in the air like a thick fog, and the walls seemed to buzz with the overlapping sounds of every argument they'd ever had. It felt less like home with each passing day.

When she got into her office, Hannah locked the door behind her, not bothering to turn the overheard fluorescent lights on as they had been grating at her nerves for weeks. There were a couple of hours before her first client of the day, so there was no rush to get the space ready. Besides, the dark just felt better; the darkness allowed her to hide in the hollowness she felt within.

She sat at her desk to eat breakfast and watched a video on YouTube of one of Jimmy's last musical performances. Every time she watched it, Hannah looked for some subtle sign of what was to come. She knew him better than anybody, probably even still, because he let her see the sides of his heart he never showed anyone. Not even his mom who he had always been close to. Hannah noticed the slight hesitation in his body before he took the mic, and how he seemed stiffer than usual through a couple of songs at the beginning of their set. By the end of the show, though, he was goofing off with the drummer and cracking jokes for the crowd between songs; he was magically back to his usual, smiling self and it didn't seem like an act or a mask he put on to hide his depression, either. So it was hard for her to believe that Jimmy would kill himself only six weeks later.

Her cellphone buzzed with an incoming call from Alan just then. Before picking up, she made sure to pause the video. "Hey! Everything okay?" she asked immediately, knowing he should have been nearly halfway through his workday on the fishing boat, floating somewhere off the shores of Louisiana with limited cell service.

"Yeah, yeah. I'm just untangling some old nets right now, but I happened to have some service, so I thought I'd give you a call," Alan told her.

Hannah swiveled her chair so she was facing the window. "Oh, okay. What's up then?"

"I just had this bug in my ear that I need to check on you," he admitted.

"Me? I'm doing fine," she lied. Immediately, she regretted it; she knew Alan would pick up on it in her tone, too.

"You wanna play that game with me, girl? I know you too well, and it doesn't sound like you're bein' truthful with me."

She sighed. "Fine," she admitted. "I could be better. Is that why you called? How did you know?"

Alan cursed under his breath at the unforgiving rope he was trying to separate from itself. "I had this dream about you last night, and I knew I had to call you. So, tell me what's going on."

"A dream? About me? What about?" she asked in rapid-fire succession. "No, wait! Was it a weird, sexy dream because I don't think I want to know if it was," she teased before collapsing into giggles.

Alan facetiously sighed. "No, it wasn't. Thank the good lord. You weren't actually in it. You know me and my thoughts on dreams, and I just had this feeling you needed help. I couldn't shake it, so I'm callin' ya. Now—tell me what's goin' on."

Hannah felt like there was more to Alan's dream than what he was telling her, but was afraid to ask. She told her friend all about the disastrous dinner plans she had made and how Jake had rebuked her physical advances.

"Every man knows that when a woman buys fancy shit like that, it's not for her," Alan joked.

"I didn't even tell you the best part," Hannah quipped. "He thinks you and I are having an affair."

Alan whooped with laughter. "What?"

"I know!" she shouted, a hearty laugh erupting from her belly. Hannah rolled her eyes and continued, "He said he feels like he's losing me to you. Oh, and to Jimmy, too."

There was a pause as Alan considered this. "Jimmy? How so?"

"Beats me. He was upset that I was listening to The Tidewater Hellraisers. It's a long story, but one of their songs came on when we were in my car, and he apparently looked them up and found out that it was Jimmy's band."

"It's just great music. Who cares who's playing it?" he asked rhetorically. "That's crazy, Hannah. Phoebe knows we talk, but she isn't all bent out of shape about it. I know she'd love to meet ya one day, and she cares about you because I do. Don't be mad at me for saying this, but I almost feel sorry for the dude. I mean, he must think pretty low of himself, huh?"

"Well, I think that's just it. I'm pretty sure he doesn't feel good about himself at all. Especially lately. Not that he would ever say it, though."

"I hope you told him I was nothin' to worry about. We're how many hundreds of miles apart?" Alan asked with a laugh.

"I think it's more like *thousands* of miles," Hannah corrected him. "I did tell him that he doesn't have anything to worry about with you, but I don't think it made a difference. It's so ridiculous."

"I say this with a lot of love, I just want you to know that. You, my friend, are a beautiful person. Inside and out. Could I ever look at you as more than a friend, or a sister-type? Hell no."

"No offense taken, because I feel the same way about you."

"Aw, shucks. You think of me as the sister-type, too?" he asked in a voice attempting to be a lot softer and high-pitched than usual. "Maybe we can do a dress swap whenever we see each other next!"

Hannah giggled. "You're so weird."

"In all seriousness, though," Alan began, changing the subject, "how are you holding up? I can't imagine it's been easy."

"It's not. Frankly, I'm tired of all the bullshit," she admitted. "I feel like I am always having to convince him that I love him, and I want to be with him. It's exhausting. He's just going to keep believing what he wants to, even if it's not the truth."

Alan thought a moment. "To him, it is the truth."

"I guess."

"Now, I'm not trying to push you one way or another, but have you thought about getting away for a little bit?"

"What do you mean?" she asked. "Like a vacation?"

Alan chuckled. "More like a separation period."

This time, Hannah hesitated to respond. It was a viable option, and landed somewhere in the middle of divorce and just sucking it up. "To be honest, Alan," she mumbled, "I've been thinking of more than that. Like, actually leaving him."

"Really?" he blurted out. Hannah could hear the surprise in his voice.

"Yeah," she breathed. "I'm just also confused. I don't know that I *can* leave him even if I wanted to."

"Why is that?"

"I don't know that I'm strong enough," she acknowledged. "I've never been on my own before. Like, lived on my own."

Alan grunted in disbelief. "Hannah, you're probably one of the strongest people I know. If you're that unhappy, don't let fear stop you. If you want to stay and work it out, then you should, but because you want to. Not because you're scared." He paused for a brief moment before continuing, "I just want you to be happy. You don't need to make any decisions today, so just take some time to figure out what you need. Okay?"

Hannah faltered, feeling tears well up in her eyes. "You know, I think you're the only one who thinks that."

"And, hey, if you want to just get away for a weekend or longer, the door is always open here. Listen, though, I gotta run. Looks like we're pulling up a little early today. Call me if you need anything, ya hear?"

"I hear," she replied before hearing the familiar disconnecting beep in her ear.

Hannah pressed play on the video once again. For now, it was enough just to get lost in the music for a while because he was right. She didn't need to think about it all right now, and she didn't need to have all the answers just yet.

With her sessions for the day done, Hannah sat at her computer, staring blankly at the screen. The room was hauntingly quiet without the sound of the overhead lights buzzing or soft music that she would usually be playing. She should be busy typing out progress notes, but she had once again gotten stuck in her own thoughts after coming to Lucy's file. In her appointment earlier in the day, Lucy discussed losing many of her friends after getting married because she was living a life so different from the rest of the crowd. With each session, Hannah found it harder to separate her own experiences from Lucy's, and she worried about her ability to really help given how open her own wounds still were. She thought often about referring Lucy to another therapist, but she just couldn't accept that failure. Maybe the thought that she could help Lucy heal meant that there could still be hope for herself.

Hannah closed out of the online electronic health record program she was using and navigated to her Facebook page. She clicked into the album of wedding photos she had gotten back from their photographer, as well as friends and family, about a month after she and Jake had wed on the bay beach by SHU. She clicked through them, but instead of feeling joyful, she felt a heavy sadness in her heart. She and Jake had been so happy and in love, but in the present tense, they had barely talked since the Valentine's Day disaster. She examined the look in his eyes in those pictures, and how he gazed so lovingly at her.

Where did it all go? she wondered. *When did we go from soulmates to roommates?*

The following picture she clicked on was of her and Jake with their bridal party. Each of them had chosen only three friends each, mainly because Hannah just didn't have many friends back then. She chalked it up to never being popular enough or interesting enough; all those years of bullying and whispers behind her back had made that much clear. Or the fact that it was she who had been the cancer in all of her friendships. Even now, Hannah found it hard not to blame herself for every single failure, including the shortcomings in her marriage. Perhaps it was because she was the only one who took responsibility in those situations, but it was somehow easier to believe that she was just not a good person. Almost on cue, a chorus of her old friends' voices rang in her ears, and all the cruel things they had once told her bled into one.

Forwarding to another picture, she was face-to-face with herself and her three bridesmaids: Shannon, Wendy, and Brooke. The girls had worn coral chiffon dresses, perfect for a beach wedding in the heart of the summer, while Hannah wore a simple white dress. She felt a particular remorse as she examined their faces, feeling sorry that of the three of them, she only still had a relationship with Shannon. She turned her gaze away from the picture to stare out at the bare branches of the tree just outside her window that were swaying in the harsh wind of the winter storm that was starting to blow in.

Wendy had walked into Hannah's life after Riverside Springs; she was her first friend back home once the dust had settled, and Hannah found the courage to start over again. At that time, it seemed as though her existence was one continuous transition with very little peace at all, and Wendy had been that steady something she needed back then.

The two friends had met at the thrift store where Hannah had worked through high school and college. Wendy was so outgoing and loud, never caring what anyone else thought about her. Well, that was the persona she liked to portray, but Hannah had always been able to see the nervous, soft, and sensitive person underneath all of that. Wendy was a couple of years younger and, when they met, she was in her final year at SHU. She left that job, though, when she graduated with her degree in business.

Wendy was the one who had pulled Hannah out of the pit of heartbreak she had fallen into on the drive home to New Jersey that summer. She had a way of needling Hannah to go out with their coworkers when the store closed at night that eventually made her oblige; Wendy was also the one driving Hannah home every time she drank to excess to drown Jimmy's face from her memory. She was even with Hannah the night she met Jake at a concert at The Junction in Stonebridge. The three of them turned out to be great friends, until they weren't anymore.

When Hannah married Jake, Wendy became unexpectedly avoidant; she suddenly refused to hang out with them at all. Hannah knew she had been dealing with some family things, as her father and mother had both fallen ill. She tried to be there for Wendy, checking in with phone calls and texts. Hannah would even visit her at the store where she worked in Cedar Cove, where she held a managerial position. No matter how tightly Hannah tried to hang on, she just continued to drift away.

Through a series of twists and turns, the two reconnected through Facebook a few years later and picked up right where they left off. At first, anyway. When they eventually met for lunch at a new restaurant in Cedar Cove, Wendy felt like she was a million miles away, even though she sat across the table from Hannah. Their friendship was never the same, but Hannah put blinders on to all the red flags that kept cropping up until Wendy went back to blowing her off entirely. She left messages for Wendy, trying to figure out what had gone wrong. She never called back, and the two never spoke again.

As for Brooke, Hannah remembered meeting her through mutual friends sometime in college. She was certain it was at a college fraternity party, but the details were hazy. What was amusing was that the two girls didn't seem to like each other at first. After some time, Brooke admitted to Hannah that she thought Hannah hated her for the longest time. Through fits of giggles, Hannah told her she had the same thoughts about Brooke. It was enough to cement their friendship right then and there.

Brooke and her boyfriend moved into an apartment near Hannah and Jake, and the four friends got together often for dinners and video game nights, swapping hosting responsibilities regularly. Brooke helped Hannah with putting together favors for the wedding, and she returned the favor when it was Brooke's turn to walk down the aisle. Hannah was even there at the birth of her first child, and assumed babysitting duties to help them out as they found their footing as new parents.

When Brooke's marriage seemed to dissolve in the blink of an eye, she became an entirely different person that Hannah failed to recognize. She had become angry and bitter, taking it out on anyone who crossed her path. Hannah was no exception.

She received a text from Brooke one morning with threats of violence against Hannah and Jake for harboring her soon-to-be ex-husband, as if he were a fugitive. It made no sense to Hannah, who knew he was staying with his brother over an hour away from Bay Point.

Hannah never told anyone, but she spent several sleepless nights peering through the blinds, afraid Brooke would show up at her house to follow through on her threats. Jake slept soundly through it all, of course. Once the worry passed, she blocked Brooke's phone number and deleted her from all her social media accounts. Hannah had been working at the local county clinic at the time, and one day, a referral for therapy services came in with Brooke's name on it from a local hospital. For obvious reasons, Hannah passed it along to a co-worker but was happy that her old friend was at least getting help for whatever had happened to her emotionally throughout her divorce.

It was clear now how she had a tendency of choosing friends the way an animal rehabber picks up injured creatures off the side of the road; the damaged ones pulled her to them. On the outside, Wendy didn't appear to be a broken person, but Hannah saw her more as a dog with a broken leg who was pretending to be healthy and tough. The truth was, she had been heavily impacted by bullying at a young age like Hannah, even if she didn't want to admit it. Brooke came from a broken home where she witnessed domestic violence on a regular basis. It was no wonder she cracked in the way she did within her own marriage. Everyone carries some baggage, but Hannah just wished she could make a friend who was well adjusted despite it.

With her shoulders heavy from the invisible weight of Wendy and Brooke that she had never seemed to shake, Hannah turned back to her computer and closed out of Facebook entirely. For once, she found writing those progress notes to be the distraction she needed from the heartbreak she had brought on herself.

Hannah's Journal
Friday, February 23, 2024

i thought of two people today that i haven't thought of in a few years. brooke and wendy. i blame it on my session with L this week. she brought up something about this tik tok trend about naming the people who would carry your casket when you die. the internet has really become a weird place. it made me think, though, about my past friendships. i used to have a tribe, as L put it. at SHU it was me, katie, whitney, and jenny. everyone else from "the inkwell," too, i guess - chris, joe, brad, jimmy, and all the others. then in riverside springs, i had that whole gang. in both places, i finally found people who accepted me for who i was. i felt comfortable. safe. now i just have a couple of friends, spread all over the place, that have never even met each other! how crazy is that? i wonder who would carry my casket if i died tomorrow? jake would out of obligation, because how would it look if the husband of the deceased didn't? maybe a family member or two on his side, but it would be more for jake than me. i can see him blocking alan from participating because he'd be unable to look past his own feelings. shannon and rob? maybe. nicole would likely make up some excuse why she couldn't fly out for the funeral. end of list.

the trend of the "tribe" is so interesting to me because that's how humans used to be. we lived in intentional communities, leaning on our neighbors for goods and services on top of social interaction. now, so many of those things are brought into the community rather than created there. even our means of socialization is wired into our homes through the internet. yet, these kids online are using the term "tribe" when it feels like anything but. it's just funny to me. honestly, i'd love to live somewhere that still felt like that. maybe then i would feel like i was part of something. riverside springs used to feel like that for me, between the group of friends i had and the family-owned shops in town. i wonder if it still would?

i miss those old days when life just wasn't so complex. most of the time i blame that complexity for the difficulty i've had making and keeping friends. anything is better than blaming myself, even though i still always do. i think my adolescence really fucked me up in that regard. everything i did was nitpicked by my mom or my peers. my interests, what i wore, how i spoke, or how my body chose to grow and mature. i wasn't allowed to exist as myself until i went to SHU. by then, i think it was too late. fitting the mold had always been more about survival than really wanting to fit in or change. when you're told over and over again how much you suck at this thing or that, you just start to believe it. i think back to those afternoons when the newspaper crew used to hang out at chris's house for hours, into the wee hours of the morning. and all those nights in the backyard on campbell street, where jimmy and i lived in riverside springs. we'd host these barbecues and dozens of people would show up, some of them we knew and some we didn't. it didn't matter, though, because we had an open door policy at campbell street. everyone was welcome. there was no fear of strangers back then, just curiosity and respect. i miss that house. i miss all that it meant: love, friendship, softness.

i remember a small handful of times when i would just sit there on those nights and look around at everyone, feeling this aching in my soul for the joy and love that was there between us all. in those times i knew that by the time i got home, or when everyone had left, that i would be missing it already. that i would long for it still, looking forward to the next opportunity to feel it again. i remember telling alan about that through happy tears one night during one of those parties. he smiled and hugged me, then told me, "don't you ever change, o'malley." i don't think that part of me could ever change, the one that feels everything so much deeper than the average person. as much as i wish it would some days. it's sad because i haven't felt that way in a long time. most of the people i surround myself with these days do more to drain my cup than fill it. back then, i don't think i ever knew what it felt like to live with a perpetually empty cup. now, it's my every day. i'm pretty sure i could sit here and cry for hours just thinking about it. those people. that love. the aching. why don't we ever see how special a time, a place, or a person is until it's too late? i kick myself for taking it all for granted, but it will never be enough of a penance.

February 25, 2024

On Sunday morning, Hannah woke up feeling like she'd been run over by a bus at least a half a dozen times during the night. It was seven o'clock in the morning, though, which was the latest she had slept in weeks. She rolled over to find the rest of the bed was empty. Not that she was surprised, since Jake had taken to sleeping on the couch for the last week and a half. Hannah knew he was just avoiding her, but he made a show of rattling off the same excuse every morning of how he crashed out on the couch watching a movie the night before.

Hannah sat up and grabbed her cell phone from the nightstand, but her hands lost their grip on it when her eye caught today's date—February 25th.

A breath escaped her lips. "Fuck. A whole year," she whispered to the empty room. Reaching for the spare blanket at the bottom of the bed, Hannah hugged it close to her and let her head fall heavy on the pillow again.

It had been one year since Jimmy took his life. The thought of it sat like a rock in her stomach, where the familiar ache and emptiness pulsated. That feeling had become something like a friend to her now. It was expected, and oddly comforting because it meant she still felt a connection to him. That Jimmy would always be alive as long as she remembered him.

Hannah could hear Jake and Diesel moving around the house, but she wasn't quite ready to get out of bed and face him yet. She needed time to practice her best neutral face and tone so she wouldn't have to explain to him why she was in a mood, because she knew Jake would never remember the significance of this date. Hannah didn't want to have to tell him, either, and see his eyes roll at the mention of Jimmy's name.

She reached a hand to her side, feeling around in the sheets for the cell phone she had dropped. She was sure Alan would have been awake for hours, and he was the one person she wanted to talk to right now. He would understand.

> **Hannah:** *Good morning, my friend. Not even out of bed yet, but today sucks.*
>
> **Alan:** *I can't believe it's been a year. I miss that dude something fierce.*
>
> **Hannah:** *Me too. It still feels weird to say that. Wrong.*
>
> **Alan:** *It shouldn't. You have every right to say that—more than most.*

Hannah grinned slightly, thankful for the affirmation. When she first read the news, she felt as though she had no right to mourn Jimmy. Not when there had been so many people long after her who had loved and cared for him, and all she had done was walk away without looking back. Except that wasn't true because, for the better part of a decade, she did look back every so often. Sometimes, for longer than just a glance.

> **Alan:** *You holding up OK?*
>
> **Hannah:** *Meh. I guess. What about you?*

Alan: *Heavy. I just feel so damn heavy today.*

Hannah: *I hear that. It still doesn't feel fair, does it? Why did it have to be him?*

Alan: *Lord knows.*

Hannah: *You know how I feel? Angry.*

Hannah: *I feel so fucking angry at him some days. We both went through a lot. We both had our fair share of demons, but we were both supposed to survive all of that. I really believe that, and I'm so mad that he gave up. That he let go while I'm still, even now, trying so hard every day to put one foot in front of the other and keep going.*

Alan: *I know it. It pisses me off my girls will only have his memory to cling to now. They loved him so much. We all did.*

Alan: *Olivia came into our room this morning, asking for Uncle Jimmy. Today of all days. I broke down.*

Hannah: *It's nice she still remembers him at least.*

Alan: *They both do, but Olivia does more than Charlotte.*

Alan: *Olivia said Jimmy came to play with her last night. They played with her dolls, and then he told her a story so she could go back to sleep.*

Hannah: *Oh, okay...*

Alan: *I didn't want to ask what story he told her.*

Hannah: *Probably better that way. Knowing Jimmy, it was something scary and weird, and questionably age-appropriate.*

Alan: *Well, she didn't have any nightmares, so it couldn't have been that bad!*

Alan: *I laughed, because she said that Jimmy farted on her nose.*

Hannah: *Please tell me you don't mean an actual fart?*

Alan: *No, but that'd be funny as hell!*

Alan: *He used to do this thing with them where he'd tap their nose and blow a raspberry at the same time. It was something he did since the day they were born, and it made them laugh so hard. I miss that. No one can make them laugh like their Uncle Jimmy could.*

Hannah: *Aw, that's actually really sweet.*

Alan: *Wait a second! We're talking about Jimmy coming to visit Olivia, and you haven't thrown your psychology in my face. Don't tell me you're coming around to all of this?*

Hannah: *I am now of the attitude that the possibility is possible.*

Alan: 👀 🤫

Hannah: *Yeah, yeah.*

Hannah: *So, are you going to do anything special today to remember him?*

Alan: *I'll probably head out to the docks later with two chairs and a couple of beers. Spend some time out there with him. Raise a toast. I do that a lot.*

Hannah: *That sounds nice. I forgot it's warm where you are. It's been so cold here, otherwise I'd do the same. Maybe I still will. We'll see. I feel like I should do something, anyway.*

Hannah: *Well, I should get up and take a shower. Have some coffee, at least.*

Alan: *I'm on my 3rd cup. Get on my level, girl.*

Hannah: *Thanks for being my friend, by the way. I'm happy we reconnected. I don't know what I'd do without you today.*

Alan: *Ditto.*

That momentary show of emotion toward Alan surprised her and left her a little embarrassed; she had never really been comfortable telling other people what they meant to her, but losing Jimmy had reminded her of how important that was. That ache inside her throbbed again, harder and more painful now, as her regrets lingered over how it was too late to let Jimmy know. To tell him she still cared about him, even after all those years. Even though she thought it less often now, Hannah had sometimes wondered if that information would have changed the outcome of the February 25th of last year.

It was natural after experiencing a suicide for someone to question what they could have done to save their person. Hindsight is always twenty-twenty, as they say, and it's in the aftermath that they see the possibilities of choices that they could have (should have?) made instead. She knew a Jimmy that no one else did and, in her heart, she just felt like some nugget of information she carried about him, his life, could have held the key to his survival. Realistically, with the way things were between them, there was no way for her to know. Hannah knew all of that, but it didn't help to soften the edges of his loss.

She pulled back the sheets that felt like they weighed at least one hundred pounds, picked out some fresh clothes for the day, and headed straight for the bathroom without acknowledging Jake or Diesel. Hannah turned the shower on to the hottest setting and stepped in. As soon as the water hit her skin, she leaned her head against the wall and broke down in quiet sobs. It had been a matter of time until those floodgates opened today, but she was at least thankful it happened here in the privacy of the shower.

Just before noon, Hannah emerged from her home office, where she had been holed up with the door closed. She grabbed her car keys from the hook by the front door and told Jake, "I'm going out for a while."

He responded simply, "'kay."

She was glad he didn't ask where she was going or offer to tag along, because she knew it would just be another fight if he knew she was going out to celebrate Jimmy's life; Jake had a hard time not reacting with anger or annoyance if the topic came up, or when she even mentioned Alan or Riverside Springs because it meant Jimmy would always be lurking on the background of every story.

The marina that connected her side of town to the business district was eerily empty, with boats shrink-wrapped against the winter weather and pieces of dock stacked high throughout the parking lot. She slowed down on the peak of the bridge to glimpse the bright February sun shining off in the distance. This place was truly beautiful, but something felt off about it today. It hit her suddenly as her car crested the top and picked up speed, that this town didn't feel like home anymore. She felt sort of like a stranger here, as well as in her own life.

Will I ever find a place that feels like home again? she wondered.

Navigating through the small side streets of Bay Point, she managed to find a parking spot not far from her destination. The Salty Pelican was one of her favorite restaurants in town, owned by a chef who was a transplant from Charleston, South

Carolina. Hannah loved to eat there when she felt particularly homesick for Riverside Springs, allowing herself to indulge in the Lowcountry cuisine they served.

The restaurant was still relatively quiet with only a few patrons trickling in for an early lunch that Sunday. Hannah asked for a table by the back windows that overlooked the bay and ate her way through a plate of crab cakes, accompanied by a side of rice and beans and a sweet tea. She reminisced about her first night in Riverside Springs, and that first meal she shared with Jimmy at The Sweet Grass Grill. They had been separated for months by then, in the wake of Jimmy's mental breakdown which caused him to leave town in the middle of the night. It hadn't taken much for him to convince Hannah to come be with him in Riverside Springs; she had loved Jimmy so deeply, and had been ready for a big change in her life. The view from where she sat now was far from the one she looked out at that night, but if she closed her eyes, Hannah could swear she felt the thick, Southern evening haze enveloping her.

With a full belly, she walked down the block to the corner liquor store. She wasn't exactly sure what she was looking for until she saw it there in the fridge—a forty-ounce bottle of Olde English. The cashier looked at her funny as he rung her up, but she brushed aside her timidness. Olde English had been something their friends in Riverside Springs would often drink because it was cheap, and they were all broke most of the time. She slipped the bottle into her bag slung across her chest and walked down to the docks at the end of the street. This place was typically deserted this time of year, with no boats coming or going and no one out for a leisurely stroll along the beach. Hannah was glad for the sharpness of the silence.

At the very end of the pier, she pulled her coat tighter around her as she sat down, her feet dangling over the edge. As she leaned forward to see the sloshing water and ice a few feet below her, she wondered if Alan was on a dock somewhere near his home in Louisiana doing this very same thing. Before today, they hadn't talked all that much about Jimmy, or their shared loss, and she was curious whether he cried at random times like she did or if Jimmy crept into his thoughts sporadically through each day. Did Alan listen to his music in the car, or watch videos of him playing guitar on his cell phone? If he didn't do any of those things, what did it say about her? About her willingness to move on?

Hannah pulled the bottle out of her bag, unscrewed the top, and took a long swig. She grimaced at the taste, and swallowed hard.

Gross. How did we ever drink this stuff? she asked herself with a chuckle.

Hannah sat for a long time, just staring out at the horizon and how the water seemed like it could stretch on forever. She imagined that somewhere in the vast distance laid out before her, where the water and the sky blended into one, was where Heaven met Earth. A slight smile formed on her quivering lips as she poured some of the liquor out into the water for her former sweetheart. There was so much she wanted to say to Jimmy, and it all came flooding forward at once.

"I've missed you so much, you stupid bastard," she said as she managed a laugh through the tears that flowed effortlessly. "I know we were as good as strangers, but I never forgot about you. I don't know how I ever could have, but I never stopped caring about you, Jimmy. I need you to know how much it broke my heart to hear what happened to you. I'm sorry I—I'm just—"

Hannah shifted her body so that she now sat cross-legged with her head bowed, letting the tears fall from her cheeks onto the legs of her jeans. Maybe she was silly for talking to someone who wasn't there, but she somehow knew he was still listening to her.

"I'll always wonder if I could've saved you somehow, but what I do know is that I'll always love you. You were the greatest friend of my life," she whispered into the breeze, wiping her cheeks dry with the back of her sleeve. Hannah stood up, taking one last look at that spot where the sky and bay blended into one, and walked back to the warmth of her car.

February 27, 2024

The throaty cackle of Jimmy's laugh causes Hannah to grin big and giggle in response. She's always loved his laugh, how it is always so deep and genuine. Jimmy's head is cocked backward, but she can still see the tremendous smile on his face, even from this angle. His Adam's apple bobs in his throat as his breath moves out from his lungs in intermittent spurts. She watches Jimmy as his hands cup an off-white porcelain mug, as if he were warming them with the hot coffee it holds. With his shoulders still shaking, Jimmy snaps his head back to its normal position and meets Hannah's eyes. They sit with their eyes locked on one another for a while, letting their laughter naturally die down.

They had just been talking about this show Hannah had seen on television. It was one of those shows that highlight viewer-submitted videos of stunts gone wrong, and she was telling Jimmy about one in particular that she had found funny.

She looks around the room, taking in the forest green decor and natural wood accents. The booth she and Jimmy are sitting in is dark green with a pale pink and white floral pattern splashed all over the vinyl cushions. Behind his head is a wall of mirrors that runs the length of the room, which her gaze follows until she spots a large U-shaped booth at the very back of the dining room. She recognizes this place as the University Diner, which Hannah knows no longer exists in her plane of reality. Yet, here they are in this place that they used to visit a few times a week for dates, hangouts with their friends, or newspaper meetings.

She looks back at Jimmy and takes in the creases framing his mouth like parentheses, a physical reminder that he used to be happy. That he used to smile and laugh so freely. Jimmy runs a hand through his hair, which isn't dirty blonde anymore. Instead, it's darkened to a more golden brown color and is cut neatly so that it shows off his natural curls. He looks different from how she remembers. More mature. She realizes that this is the Jimmy she never got to know in life. This is the thirty-something version of him, yet it's still her Jimmy.

He starts talking again, but his words are muted. Hannah grins again, understanding every bit of what he is saying despite the silence. She listens intently and sips from her coffee cup, careful not to burn her mouth. Neither one of them is letting this moment go to waste, taking in the time they have together over this unknown space and time. Hannah can't ignore how whole she feels sitting there with him, a feeling she hasn't had for some time.

Hannah's eyes opened softly to the flickering glow of the television in her bedroom. She groans, listening to the voice of the *Forensic Files* narrator drone on about DNA and mass spectrometry. She tapped the screen on her cell phone to see that it was barely three o'clock in the morning. Despite the early hour, Hannah felt wide awake.

Not that Hannah could focus on the episode, though, with her dream replaying over in her mind. It felt as real as the dreams she had with her dad, like she had really been sitting in that diner with him. It reminded her of the dream she had of Jimmy a few months before. Hannah could feel herself spiraling as her brain made connections between all her dreams and the way she argued with herself over the legitimacy of what she had just experienced. She wished it were all real, and that she could really find a way back to that booth. She thought wistfully about those little moments, those days and nights that revolved around coffee runs and Jimmy's cigarette breaks, talking endlessly about anything.

She reached a hand up to wipe the wetness from her cheeks. These were not the violent sobs she had expelled only two days before, but rather a quiet and gentle sadness. The aching in her core fluttered awake then in his absence. From her loneliness. From her desire to turn back the hands of time.

When she reached Linda's office for her weekly therapy session, Hannah had managed to gather herself enough from the complete meltdown she had at home. That ache inside her had grown to full stomach pains and nausea; she hadn't eaten anything yet today, nor was she able to choke down her morning coffee. Her head ached from the lack of caffeine and the thoughts that spun a million miles a minute, it seemed.

As soon as Linda opened the door to her office to welcome Hannah in, she could see the alarm on her face and asked, "What's wrong?"

Falling into the plush armchair, Hannah covered her face with her hands to hide the ugly pain escaping from her body. She imagined a dam bursting behind her eyes again, allowing for the tears to flow without hesitation or warning. Linda nudged Hannah's arm with a tissue box, which she gladly accepted. It was several minutes before she could speak, and when she did, she recounted to Linda her dream about Jimmy in great detail.

"It felt so real. Like the ones I had about my dad. I woke up feeling so comforted in his presence, but then reality sank in, and all I felt was a heavy emptiness. I feel it right here," she said, massaging her hand over the place where her ribs branched out from each other.

Linda nodded slowly, a slight frown on her face. "Empty is an interesting word to use."

"These dreams are like taunts of what I so desperately want and can't have. It's unfair!" she shrieked.

"I see. Tell me more about this emptiness."

She replied with an unwarranted irritation coating her words like a heavy syrup, "It sits here, right in my stomach. It's been there since Jimmy died, and it hasn't left. It's not bad some days, but other days, it hurts so fucking much. Like today. I know I haven't been able to adequately describe what all of this feels like. Lord knows I've tried, but it never makes sense to anyone. It barely makes sense to me! They just look at the time we had apart, as if that should determine how long and hard I grieve. They don't consider the time we actually had together." She took a deep breath. "I was thinking about it this morning, and I imagine it's something like losing a limb. You know how people lose a leg or an arm, but still feel it there? The whole phantom limb thing? Jimmy is like my phantom limb. I cut it off when I left that day to come back to Harborvale, but he was always still with me. I have always felt this connection to him. I can't quite explain that part, but I believe now that it might have been something cosmic. Fate or destiny, I don't know. It's unexplainable how two young people could be that tightly linked to one another. Sometimes, for a year or more, it was dormant, and I barely noticed it. Other times, there would just be this buzzing inside of me, like it was calling out for him. Or vice versa. When I would feel that tingle, I would have to look him up online for it to settle at the sight of him happy in pictures. Or what I thought was happiness, anyway. Now, the phantom limb phenomenon is gone, too, and I just feel this cavernous emptiness. I don't know—I'm just talking nonsense now."

"I think I understand what you're trying to say. It's clear you two had a profound connection," Linda affirmed.

Hannah nodded quickly. "Ya know, all I wanted was to just say 'goodbye' to my dad. I got that, but in a dream. Now, here I am, having this dream where I'm just talking to Jimmy, when I have so desperately wanted that very thing. I've spent the last year wishing I could rewind time to go back and find a way to stay in each other's lives as friends. It's almost like my wishes are coming true, but then I wake up to realize they never did."

"I can imagine that must be very hard. What are you going to do today to care for yourself?"

Hannah shook her head. "I have no idea what I'm going to do with my time. I feel like I need to keep myself busy somehow. Maybe I'll go through some of my old journals and pictures again for the reminder. The comfort."

Linda's lips formed a tight smile. "Is it comfort or punishment?"

She wasn't sure, so she only shrugged.

"As much as you want to, Hannah, we can't go back in time. We can't undo what's already been done, especially things like death."

With a click of her tongue, Hannah told her, "I *know* I can't undo the past or change the course of history. I *know* that. I think it's more about me just wanting to feel seen and understood. That's why I've been clinging to my memories of Jimmy so hard, because he was that safe place for me, the one who never failed to see or understand me. I want that again."

Linda pondered this notion. "It seems to me that you have that in Alan, no? To continue with the idea of the possibility being possible, maybe Jimmy is working through him somehow?"

Hannah's jaw fell open as something seemed to click into place in her mind. The day after Valentine's Day, Alan told her he had a dream about needing to call her. He never did tell her about the dream itself, other than to say she hadn't actually been in it.

Could it be? she wondered.

"I think it's important for you to engage in something that will ground you in the present," Linda continued. "Maybe take a walk, get some fresh air, and feel the sun on your face. What do you think?"

Hannah contemplated how empty the house felt even when Jake was home. Maybe it was just more a reflection on how she felt on the inside of her mind and heart: hollow and alone.

"I guess. It's better than being in that house, even though Jake will probably work late again, because that's all he ever does these days. Not that we're really talking right now, anyway. Home just doesn't feel like a place I want to be anymore," she admitted.

"What does home mean to you, Hannah?"

After a few beats she answered, "It's funny because I always thought of home as the place where my loved ones were. My parents, when I was young. Then I used to think anywhere Jake and Diesel were, that was my home. Like they were my own heart living outside of my body, so wherever they were, so was I. Now I look at it more as a place again, but where I can feel safe and accepted and loved. I want a place like that again."

"That's profound. You've shifted the focus from home being about other people to being about you. That's interesting, don't you think?" Linda posed.

Hannah pursed her lips together in thought. "Yeah, I guess it did. You know, I've been considering myself more, how I feel about certain things and what I want out of life."

Linda nodded. Changing the focus, she asked, "I wonder if you have anything coming up that you're looking forward to?"

Hannah looked up at the ceiling, thinking over her schedule for the next few weeks. All she pictured in her mind's eye were blank spaces on a calendar. "Not really," she said. "The only thing I can think of is that Shannon is having her baby soon. She's due in a couple of weeks. I guess that?"

"Okay, that's something positive. A new baby is always exciting, and it might give you a fresh sense of purpose to be there for your friend in this time of transition. I wonder if you might want to make a plan for something to look forward to. Something for you. Like, a trip or something."

Hannah considered Linda's suggestion, but the thought of going anywhere with Jake right now made her stomach churn, and the idea of taking a solo vacation was even more depressing.

"Alan's offered to have me come visit with them for a while if I needed to get away. That could be nice," Hannah dreamily replied, getting lost in the thought before reality came crashing down. "Well, not really. Jake wouldn't be okay with that plan. He'd just think I was going to consummate the affair he thinks I'm having."

"It's just something to think about," Linda said with a polite smile. "We are at time for this week, though."

Hannah spent her Monday afternoon at home, having canceled her appointment with Linda a couple of days ago. Given how irritated she'd become during the last couple of sessions, she thought a break was necessary; she truthfully needed some time to deliberate on finding a new therapist or sticking it out with Linda since she already knew Hannah's backstory. In the morning, she drove over to the local craft store to buy some supplies and settled herself onto the couch to teach herself how to crochet. Hannah had come across an article a couple of weeks ago about its benefits for calming the nervous system. She figured it would take a small miracle to calm her own nervous system down enough to make a difference, but she also knew any small steps toward some kind of healing was a good place to start. After watching hours of instructional videos on YouTube, though, she had only managed to amass a giant knot.

So much for that, she thought, feeling more annoyed than relaxed.

Hannah frowned, hearing her cell phone ring from its spot on the desk in her office. With a groan, she peeled herself off the cushions and rushed to see who was calling her. When she saw Shannon's name, she considered letting it go to voicemail, unsure if she was in the mood for a two-hour conversation today.

"Hey, Shannon," Hannah said, trying to sound upbeat.

"Sheesh," Shannon replied. "You could at least pretend to be happy to talk to me."

Hannah apologized. "I was, like, half asleep on the couch. What's up? How's baby watch?"

Shannon laughed loudly. "Nothing yet, but it's still a little early. I'm ready, though. I feel like a houseboat."

"Aw, I'm sorry, Shan. Soon enough," Hannah told her encouragingly.

"Yeah, but I was just bored and thought I'd give you a call," she said nonchalantly. "How are things with you and Jake?"

"Ah, so you were bored and thought to check in on your friend's crumbling marriage for some hot gossip? Nice," Hannah joked.

Shannon giggled. "Don't be a bitch. You know what I meant."

"Things are still status quo craptacular," she replied.

Shannon whined. "Still? I just can't believe this is the same Jake. He needs help, Hannah. You need to get him to see someone."

She clicked her tongue and snapped, "Don't you think I've tried? He feels like therapy isn't for people like him, people who are strong enough to pick themselves up by their bootstraps. He walks around and says that nothing is bothering him and that we're just fine. What else can I do?"

"Just tell me you're not getting divorced."

"Would a divorce really be the worst thing at this point?" Hannah pointedly asked.

"You *have* to give it more time. You have to give him another chance to work on it, more space."

Choking back another laugh, she questioned, "How many more chances do I give him, Shan? How much more time? We've been at this for, like, a year now."

"*That* long?"

"Yes, Shannon," Hannah said exasperatedly, "*that* long. Pretty sure I told you that, though."

"What about Valentine's Day? You never told me how that turned out. Surely, that had to have done something, no?" Shannon questioned.

"It was a disaster. I don't even want to talk about it, but we haven't really talked since."

"Ugh," Shannon croaked. "Well, mine was pretty shitty, too. Wait 'til you hear what happened…." Her friend went on to describe in detail the dinner that Rob had tried, and failed, to make her. It resulted in her trying to stomach it for his sake, but she wound up with her head in the toilet for the rest of the evening. The two of them snacked on chips and pretzels instead.

It pained Hannah to listen to her complaining. She wanted to tell her that, at least, her husband had tried. That he had *cared* enough to try. There was a lot she wanted to say, but she forced herself to stay quiet despite the angry words bubbling up in her throat. Instead, she gritted her teeth, occasionally placing a few grunts and filler responses into the mix.

The more she sat there listening to the sound of her friend's voice, the more cross she became with herself for letting herself believe Shannon might have some genuine interest in what was going on in Hannah's life.

Suddenly, Shannon said, "You know, you could have at least pretended to have been interested in my story."

Hannah wasn't sure if she was joking or not, but before she could decode her friend's tone, she snarled back at Shannon. "Oh, I'm sorry. *You* were the one who called to check on *me*. So silly of me to think this wouldn't just be another episode of 'The Shannon Show.'"

Shannon's voice sputtered on the other end, "Wh—what? Hannah, what are you talking about?"

She held back an angry laugh. "What I'm saying is, you are so full of shit, Shannon. You don't care at all what happens to me and Jake, as long as it's some solid story to tell everyone about, making you center-stage of the conversation."

Her friend let out a shallow breath. "That's not true, Hannah. I *do* care about what happens to you two. You guys are my friends, and I love you both so much. Where is this all coming from?"

"It's coming from years of having you just talk over me, of not giving me the chance to speak to you, my best friend, about the heavy shit going on in my life. I'm drowning here, Shannon, and you don't even care!" Hannah shouted into the phone.

"I see it, and I do care, Hannah. I do." Shannon's voice turned tearful. "I'm—I'm sorry."

Hannah ran a hand through her hair as a mixture of relief and shame swirled around her mind. She didn't know what else to say. What could she say, really?

Shannon sniffled. "I'm here to listen if you want to tell me more. I promi—"

She ended the call, not wanting her friend's empty guarantees of her time and attention. Hannah stood at the back door and looked out over the yard, her arms crossed over her chest. The sun glinted off the light layer of snow still covering the grass from the storm they had a few days ago. Gloom hung heavy on her shoulders like a weighted blanket as she questioned if anyone would ever really care about her. Would anyone ever really listen? Hannah knew that Alan would, but she didn't want to keep bogging him down with all of her problems; she knew all too well what it felt like to be taken advantage of like that.

Hannah steps up to meet Jimmy on the sidewalk of a strip mall in Harborvale, in front of the only pizzeria in town. A big grin crosses both of their faces. She leans in to hug him around the shoulders. His arms are strong and warm as they wrap around her waist. When they pull back, Jimmy puts his hands in the front pockets of the brown pair of Dickies pants he is wearing. Hannah slips her right arm through the crook of his left and, together, they walk into the pizzeria.

She let's go as Jimmy walks up to the counter, speaking to an employee in a white T-shirt stained with tomato sauce, while Hannah grabs a seat at a small, square table. Jimmy joins her with two pint glasses of beer, one for each of them. While they wait for their food, they talk. The conversation flows naturally and endlessly. Their laughter comes easily.

When their pizza arrives, Hannah and Jimmy each eat slice after slice until their bellies are full. All along, they continue to talk. At one point, Hannah says something funny enough to make him laugh hard. She watches as he tilts his head back, eyes squinted, cackling from a place so deep in his stomach. Hannah hunches over in her seat, a hand over her mouth to stifle the laughter that is erupting from her. The two of them share in this moment of pure joy, and it is enough.

Once the pizza has been devoured, and their beer glasses are empty, Hannah and Jimmy walk out of the pizzeria and back down the sidewalk to the parking lot. Her arm is linked through his again.

They smile at each other before Hannah lets go of his arm and walks off in the opposite direction.

Hannah's eyes flew open, taking in the bedroom walls around her in the dark. She looked to her left to find Jake's side of the bed empty again. She'd grown so used to being alone that his absence in their bed didn't feel that big anymore. Reality hit all at once that she'd just had another dream, and that Jimmy was really dead. Tears fell unchecked as sadness swept over her like a tsunami wave.

This was the second time in the span of a month that he had come to visit her in her dreams. Though she'd probably never admit it out loud, she did believe now that he was coming through to her, even if she couldn't explain how that could be possible. It didn't matter anymore, frankly, because these visits meant so much to her. Like there were no hard feelings on either side, and that their connection was as strong as ever. Being a creature of habit and pattern, Hannah easily picked up on how these visits were more vivid than any dream she had ever had before, how she could remember even the tiniest of details, and how she always woke up feeling energized.

"What does it all mean? What are you trying to tell me?" she whispered to the dark room, as if he were there with her, listening.

Rolling over, Hannah felt the familiar ache in her core. This morning, it served as a poignant reminder that she missed him more than she ever thought she would. She tapped the screen of her cell phone to see it was only 3:31 A.M. She turned back over onto her left side, pulling Diesel close to her for a cuddle. She let herself cry into the soft fur of his neck, knowing she wouldn't be going back to sleep anytime soon.

Hannah's Journal
Sunday, March 17, 2024

dreams. what do they mean? what purpose do they serve? it's all i can think about these days. i spend every spare second i can trying to dissect the meaning of it all, but i'm coming up short.

i had yet another dream about jimmy. it was like the others where i woke up around 3am but felt like i had just downed a case of red bulls or something. i felt every touch, heard the sound of his voice so clearly, and smelled that familiar nicotine and incense on his clothes all so vividly. the last two i've had, we're just hanging out like we used to, having coffee or pizza, and we're talking about nothing in particular. not like that first dream i had months ago. we're happy and we laugh a lot. it's nothing special, but it's everything. it's enough that we're just together.

i'm really starting to believe alan. that there is more out there. i can't believe i just admitted that on paper. i've been doing so much googling lately about different ideas of the afterlife, if it's possible to have these "visitation dreams." i went so far as to go to the bookstore and pick up some reading material that was recommended. books about other paranormal and near-death experiences. that kind of thing. i read through one, and just started another. i find the near-death experiences to be the most fascinating. the details of meeting deceased loved ones and life reviews are really compelling, and remind me of my dreams with my dad and jimmy. of course, there are hypotheses out there that they can be explained due to a burst of neuro-chemicals flooding the brain but there is an emotional depth that is described in these stories that i can definitely relate to. i just started reading another book by a hospice nurse who recounts her thirty years of working with the dying, and their experiences as they near the end of their lives. there, again, seems to be a commonality in their deceased loved ones visiting in the days and weeks before their deaths. some people even talk to their loved ones and reach out for them. it's hard to call it a coincidence when you read the same stories over and over again.

but... if i were to believe alan, and these books, that these dreams are more than just dreams, and jimmy and i are actually hanging out together, i have to wonder why? i've been thinking about this for a couple of weeks, and i wonder if it's for the sake of healing. hear me out. i've spent the last 10 months regretting that i hadn't spoken to jimmy since we parted ways. that we just let each other go so easily and left so much unsaid. so maybe this is some weird way of healing that hurt in me. to give me that time i've been needing. and maybe... maybe for him it's healing, too. i remember the days when i was younger, so deep in my own depression, and how lonely i felt in that pit. how it felt like no one loved me, or even <u>thought</u> about me. i imagine he probably felt the same way, and maybe these visits are a way to heal that hurt in his soul. to show him that he was still loved, and cared for, thought of fondly and often. even despite everything. maybe it's the type of closure we both need to move on.

in thinking about the dreams of my dad, i think there might be something to that healing idea. i haven't had a dream about him since the last one, where we finally were able to talk and hold hands. our final goodbye, really. i somehow know i'm not going to be seeing him in my dreams again. in a way, it makes me sad, but also happy because i feel like his soul got what it needed to find peace at last. in the end, isn't that what we all want? i feel a lot less sad about his loss these days, too. of course i still find myself missing him and wishing i could tell him about this cool thing i saw or did, but it's different now. it's not so... heavy.

i had this realization the other day that i'd rather believe jimmy and i are helping each other heal somehow, instead of fighting against it. like we had done for each other when we were young. how we were able to be our most authentic selves when it was just the two of us, and how we were able to create this beautifully safe space that meant everything. i just think it's a beautiful thought and, right now, i need that more than logic. maybe that's just okay for now.

aside from all of that, things with jake and i are feeling more grave since the botched valentine's day dinner. there are more nights than not that he sleeps on the couch, and i can't remember the last time we talked about anything meaningful. i was talking to my online therapist friends about some of it during one of our video chats, and one of the girls suggested i plan a special getaway with jake for a change of scenery, to really reconnect. she even suggested going cell phone free to limit distractions. i liked the idea of it, in theory. it just depends if jake can separate himself from his phone that long, or from work for that matter. can i even stand to have him be my only source of social output/input?

honestly, some days i'm not sure how much i really want to keep trying. i'm just so tired. i don't necessarily want to leave him, but i don't want to keep doing this, either. i just know something has got to give. i don't know what my limits are, but i sense i am getting close. like the finish line is cloaked in the smoke from a damp fire pit; it exists, but where exactly?

April 8, 2024

Hannah jolted awake to the shrill ringing of her cell phone. She guessed it was still pretty early in the morning, given how disoriented she felt, like she'd only been asleep for a couple of hours. It figured that the one night she was sleeping deeply, there would be something so jarring to pull her out of it. Her hand fell heavily onto the side table, groping for her phone. She opened her eyes just enough to see the outline of the buttons on the screen and slid her thumb along the bar to answer.

"H'lo?" she croaked.

"She's heeeere!" A voice sang loudly, especially for the early morning hour.

"Who is—Shannon? What time is it?" Hannah asked, rubbing the sleep from her eyes.

"It's… uh. Oh, sorry, it's a little after four o'clock. I just couldn't wait to call you!" Shannon cried.

"What's happened?" she questioned, still trying to get her bearings. Hannah hadn't heard from Shannon since their fight a month ago. Not that she had tried to reach out to her, either. She needed space and, honestly, she didn't know quite how to apologize for blowing up at her friend like she did. What she said had been the truth, but she had said it in such an ugly way.

"Hannah, wake up!" Shannon laughed, seemingly like she had forgotten all about their dispute. "Hazel Mae has arrived!"

As her brain finally processed the words her friend was saying, Hannah's eyes went wide. "Oh! Oh my gosh!" she whispered loudly, causing Jake to stir again. "How exciting! How is she? How are *you*?"

Shannon giggled. "She's absolutely perfect, and I'm doing fine. I won't give you the gory details of labor, but I don't ever want to do that again."

Jake turned over and murmured, "What's going on?"

Hannah pulled the phone from her ear to tell him about the baby as she turned back the covers to get out of bed. For a change, it was nice to have him nearby to hear the good news. Jake's iciness had been slowly melting away in the last couple of weeks, but Hannah kept her imaginary sweater on, waiting for the weather to change at any moment again.

"Tell them I said 'congrats,'" Jake said before rolling back over.

Hannah nodded at him in the dark as she closed the door behind her to let him get back to sleep. "Jake sends his well wishes," she told her friend.

"How are things on the Jake front, anyway?" Shannon asked cautiously.

Ignoring the question, Hannah exclaimed, "I'm awake now, so tell me more about the little princess!"

Shannon listed off the baby's stats and the minute-by-minute play-by-play of the delivery, even though she said she wouldn't, while Hannah brewed a pot of coffee.

"When are your families coming to meet her? I don't wanna step on toes," she asked when Shannon finally ran out of air.

"My parents aren't flying in until tomorrow, and Rob's parents have that appointment for his dad that they've been waiting forever for this morning. They won't be here until around noon, I think they said. So come this morning! Visiting hours start at eight o'clock, I think. Bring Jake along, too."

Hannah glanced at the clock, noting the hours she had to get herself together before heading out. "I'll be there, but he has to work this morning. I'll bring him by to see you at home once you get settled so he can have a chance to meet her." Hannah thought that, even though things had been pretty neutral between them lately, it would still be a lot nicer to have this time to herself today.

Hannah stopped just outside of Room 330, taking a deep inhale to steel herself for this visit with Rob and Shannon. It was a happy occasion, and so she did her best to push aside her feelings about Shannon. She strode into the sterile, white hospital room to find her friend looking lovingly at Rob, who cradled their new baby in his arms. Shannon's face lit up when she entered the room, arms outstretched to her friend. Hannah squinted, noticing the brightness of the lights, having grown so fond of the dark.

"Come here and meet your new niece!" she said enthusiastically.

Hannah robotically leaned down to hug her, wondering how Shannon was so good at ignoring the awkwardness. Rob delicately passed Hannah the baby girl swaddled in a blue and pink striped blanket from the hospital. Hazel's eyes were closed as she slowly wiggled around in Hannah's arms. She smiled at the little one, speaking softly as she remarked on how beautiful she was.

After a few minutes of basking in the glow of this happy morning, Rob spoke up to ask, "Are you going to stay for a little while? We realized last night that we forgot a couple of things at the house, so I wanted to run back real quick."

"I could just go for you. I'm sure you're exhausted, too."

Rob shook his head and laughed. "Honestly, I'm the most awake I've ever been. I guess the shock that this is real hasn't sunk in yet. I know where everything is, anyway, and you three can have some much-needed girl time without me over your shoulders."

"Okay, sure." Hannah smiled at him politely, feeling embarrassed that, of course, he knew about their argument.

Hannah sat on the edge of the hospital bed with Hazel still in her arms and pivoted to face her friend. "So you're doing okay? You don't mind me staying while Rob is gone?"

"I could totally use a nap, but I just don't want to take my eyes off her for a second," Shannon told her dreamily as she moved the edge of the blanket that was blocking her view of the baby's face.

"Do you want her back?"

"No, no. Let her be with her Aunt Hannah for a while." Shannon and Hannah exchanged smiles. "She might not be your blood, but you're her mama's bestest friend. That counts for something."

The two friends sat in silence for a few beats, their eyes fixed on Hazel as if afraid to make eye contact with each other. Hannah felt uncomfortable in the quiet, like there was something her friend wanted to say but wasn't. She quickly tried to find something to talk about, but kept coming up short.

Breaking the silence, Shannon pointedly said, "You ignored my question earlier." She looked at Hannah, who raised an eyebrow in question. "How are things with you and Jake?"

"We don't need to talk about him," she replied, trying to steer the conversation away from any topics they might clash over. "This is a big, special day! We should be talking about this little cutie!"

"Hannah, stop. I want to talk with you about this. You were right about what you said, how I tend to bulldoze right over the conversation. I want to make sure my best friend is okay, but I'm just not sure how to even ask at this point."

She sighed, fighting the urge to roll her eyes. "Well, he's been sleeping in our room for a couple of weeks now, but he's still so hot and cold."

"You know—I was thinking about what might help you two, and I think you should try to do something special for your anniversary this year."

"I don't know, Shan. I don't feel much like celebrating our love, or what's left of it, this year. I doubt Jake does, either."

"Hear me out," she demanded. "You guys didn't even get to celebrate your ten-year anniversary because of everything with your dad. It just got glossed over, and it was such a big milestone. Maybe a little romantic getaway would be what you both need to spark the match again."

Hannah took in Shannon's suggestion, her eyes scanning every bit of Hazel's face. She cleared her throat, having let herself get caught up in the idea of new beginnings and hope. "You're not the first person to suggest it, actually. I've been thinking about it. It *could* help, but I just feel like I keep putting the effort in while he doesn't care enough to try. I honestly can't remember the last time he did something for me, to make me feel special. I've been fighting like hell for us, but all I do is fail. I'm tired of it!"

"So don't let it fail this time," Shannon said.

Hannah scoffed, "If only it were that simple! I can put the effort in. I can control myself, how I act and react, but I can't control him. I can't *make* him put the time in."

Shannon considered that. "That's fair, but isn't it still worth a shot? I mean, this whole thing is just so silly—"

"Silly?" Hannah snapped. "If only you knew, Shannon, you wouldn't call it 'silly.'"

"So *tell me*, Hannah. Tell me so I understand and don't say stupid things to make you mad at me," Shannon begged. "You've just been together so long. Don't give up now. I just don't want to see you guys split up."

"I know, you've made that abundantly clear," Hannah growled. "Sometimes love just isn't meant to last forever. Sometimes it's only meant to get you so far. Maybe we've just reached the end of the line." Hannah shrugged her shoulders, letting her voice trail off.

"Point taken," Shannon said sheepishly. Another awkward silence fell over the friends who busied themselves with watching the baby sleep soundly in Hannah's arms. "So, what do you think it is that's bothering him?" she hesitantly asked.

"Pfft. Work, for one thing. He's back to doing a ton of overtime again. Some of it is mandatory, but a lot of it is him just volunteering. He's all uptight about our finances. Starting a therapy practice is expensive, but he's been spending as if nothing has changed." Hannah shook her head slightly, lost in thought. "It's been so long since we've—*you know*—"

"Had sex? Hannah, I just had a baby," Shannon giggled. "Just say it."

"I guess it's been so long that I don't even remember what it's called," Hannah responded sarcastically to lighten the mood, which caused the two friends to laugh. "But, seriously, it's been months. Since Christmas."

"Yikes," Shannon grimaced.

"Yeah, and now he's suddenly jealous of my friend, Alan. Would you believe he accused me of having an affair with him?"

Shannon's eyes went wide. "What? Wait, who is Alan?"

"Oh, he's a friend of mine from South Carolina."

"South Carolina?" Shannon asked, cocking her head to one side.

Hannah shrugged. "Yeah. When I lived in Riverside Springs? With Jimmy?"

"Right, right. You did tell me about him, I think. Why does he think that? Are you seeing him a lot or something?"

She laughed. "I haven't seen him at all! That's the thing! He lives in Bum-Fuck, Louisiana. I just think Jake sees Alan as an extension of Jimmy, or something. Which, don't even get me started on *that* whole thing—"

"What whole thing? Jimmy?"

She nodded slightly. "When I really told him about my relationship with Jimmy, how close we were and all of that stuff, he became really jealous. He said he felt like he was losing me to another man."

"But you told me you hadn't been in contact with him in years, so what is there for Jake to be worried about? It's not like he was some major love of your life or anything."

Hannah inhaled sharply. "He might not be *the* love of my life, but we did love each other deeply."

"Yeah, but you were only kids," Shannon countered.

Hannah scoffed again. "Does it matter how old we were? Besides, we weren't in high school. We dated through our twenties. We were old enough to go to bars and rent an apartment together. Even if we were kids, it doesn't change what we had. He was the most important person in my life at one time, and I've never had a friend like him since."

Shannon's eyes fell to her fingers pinching at the flimsy sheet on her hospital bed. "You're right. I'm sorry," she whispered.

To keep the conversation moving forward, Hannah continued, "So, yeah. I guess Jake felt like I was still in love with Jimmy or something. He thought I didn't love him anymore, or want to be with him," she told her.

Shannon's face tensed. "Are you still in love with him? Jimmy, I mean."

"No!" Hannah shrieked, causing the baby to stir. "No," she repeated in a more hushed tone this time. "It's not like that."

"To play devil's advocate, I could see how he might feel that way, though. The way you talk about him—"

"Well, I didn't ask you to play devil's advocate, Shannon," she retorted.

Shannon bobbed her chin. "I know, but the way you're grieving for someone you didn't even know anymore—"

"You mean grieving for someone who played a huge role in shaping my life?" Hannah shook her head. "You know, you're just like everyone else. I haven't asked for your opinions or your advice."

"I just don't understand why you care so much about him still—"

Standing up abruptly, Hannah gently placed Hazel back into Shannon's arms and collected her bag from a chair by the windows. "This is supposed to be a happy day for you guys, and I am obviously ruining that, so I'm going to see myself out."

"Hannah—"

"And, for the record," she said, cutting off her friend, "it doesn't matter if you understand any of it. I'm your friend, and I'm hurting. I need you. That's what should matter."

She gnawed on her bottom lip, standing on the spot for what felt like several minutes, but was only a few seconds, before she turned to leave. Stalking down the hallway, Hannah nearly plowed into Rob as she rounded the corner toward the elevators.

"Whoa, hey!" Rob shouted in surprise. "Where are you headed in a rush? Everything okay?"

Hannah blinked several times, her hands raised in front of her to keep a barrier between her and Rob. They had known each other for years, but had never been close despite her relationship with Shannon. He talked more to Jake when they were all together, but it was basic guy banter; really, she barely knew anything about him outside of what Shannon told her.

Hannah fought back tears, not wanting him to see her cry. "Sorry," she said with a shake of her head. "I just have to go. It was good to see you." She quickly shuffled around him and rushed for the elevator a few feet away that was starting to close.

"Hannah, wait!" Rob called out to her, but she managed to squeeze through the doors before it was too late, catching a glimpse of the confused look on his face.

On the first floor, she walked so fast toward the main doors that she was nearly at a jogging pace, her breath heaving in her chest. By the time she found her car in the parking lot, she was barely holding back the anxiety attack and tears. Scrambling into the driver's seat, she rested her head back and finally let herself break down. The end of their friendship was growing ever closer. She could just feel it.

Brace for impact, she told herself. *This one is gonna hurt.*

shannon had her baby girl on the 7th at 11:32pm. i got to meet my new niece, hazel mae, yesterday morning. she's a long, lean string bean at 7.2lbs and 21" long. she's such a doll with a full head of hair and chubby cherub cheeks. i wonder who she'll take after? shannon's more fair, eastern european side or rob's dark, brooding italian side? shannon was doing great, and it was nice to see her so happy and vibrant, even if labor was tough on her.

for some reason, she wanted to talk about jake and me. i wanted to just keep it light, and keep the focus on that gorgeous little baby of hers. but, no. i let my anger slip out again, which i feel bad about. i just snapped. i mean, in my defense, i told her that i didn't want to talk about it, but she pushed the issue. she kept offering her thoughts on everything, and trying to tell me what to do to save my marriage. it's frustrating because i don't think she's getting how bad it is, how hurt and broken down that i am. she wants me to give her all of the juicy details, but i don't think i should have to for her to believe me. i tried to tell her some things, but it felt like she was just trying to argue with me. i know she has seen what a shell of myself i've been. she's told me so. it's disheartening that my best friend is turning her back on me. how good of a friend is she really?

i think i'm just too good of an actor, you know? too good at pretending all is well, so when it's not, people downplay it. it's my gift and my curse. it was always just easier to suck it up than deal with the disappointment of being misunderstood over and over again. it's exactly what i'm doing in my friendship with shannon. how do i break the pattern? how do i walk away and be okay with crossing another name off my list of friends? there won't be anyone left soon...

shannon suggested that jake and i take a trip to celebrate our 10 year wedding anniversary since we didn't get to when it rolled around last year. we always made it a point to do something special on our anniversary. whether we took a vacation, went on a little day trip, or even just had a nice dinner out. we used to have a love worth celebrating, though. the day is also kind of tainted with the memory of the grim reaper coming to collect. a trip isn't the worst idea. i keep flip-flopping about it because i have my doubts that it will make anything better, but then i think that it's maybe worth a try. maybe year 11 is a good time for a restart? maybe?

despite my indecision, i did some googling for ideas on where we might want to go. i thought about tennessee, which was where we were supposed to go last year, but then i thought it might bring up too many bad memories.

i found this quaint little town in rhode island called castlerock harbor. it seriously looks like something out of "gilmore girls." it just seems like the idyllic place to slow down, reconnect, and spark some romance. there are some really cute restaurants right on the water, and i found a waterfront bed and breakfast that would be perfect for us. i asked jake what his thoughts were and, surprisingly, he didn't fight me at all. he wasn't super excited about it, but his reaction was better than i anticipated. it's sad that i can't just be happy about it. instead, i am wondering <u>why</u> he agreed. does he want to change things between us? is he finally seeing we're in trouble? or is he finally acknowledging that he's burned out from work and needs a break? either way, i'll take it. i have everything booked for may 2 to 6.

and, before i go any further, i am putting this in writing for myself. so i remember to think of myself in all of this. i've decided that this is going to be my last effort to turn this thing around. i know it's largely out of my hands because it comes down to jake making some changes, but i can at least set the stage for it to happen. i want us to be able to talk like adults, openly and honestly, about where we stand and where we want to be. whether that's together or separately. apologies would be nice, but at this point, it's just empty words. i want to see changed behavior. i want attention and affection. i just want him back. i just can't take much more of the let downs, the silent treatment, the snippy comments, or the self-deprecation that turns into accusations against me. i'm practically living my life as if i were single at this point anyway. so either this will make us or it will break us. those are the only options we have left.

don't get me wrong, divorce still isn't something i want. but i also don't want this. i've been able to choose myself before, with jimmy, and i know i can again if i need to. it was at a heavy cost. i had to burn down my life in riverside springs and start over back home in harborvale. i have to remember that i can't let my light go out just to make sure someone else can shine. i've been doing it my whole life, and i just can't keep it up any longer. so if i need to make a choice, i will choose me. i will make my younger self proud of me again. she deserves that much, for someone to finally choose her again. that person should be me.

Between sessions in the late afternoon, Hannah made it a point to call Alan to wish him a happy birthday. Something she had always admired about Alan was how excited he would get for birthdays, whether it was a friend's special day or his own. He used to say that people weren't celebrated nearly as much as they ought to be, and a birthday was the perfect excuse to do so. His birthday was easy to remember since he and Jimmy had been born only a couple of days apart in the same year.

When he answered after two rings, Hannah crooned, "Happy Birthday to you! Happy Birthday to you! Happy Birthday, dear Alan! Happy Birthday to you!"

He roared with laughter throughout her dreadful rendition. "Oh my word, Hannah! I can't breathe!" he croaked.

She couldn't help but crack up as he coughed from laughing so hard. "I hope you're not implying my singing was bad? My voice only cracked once!" she joked.

"Of course not! I thought you'd hired a dang chorus of angels to serenade me." He chuckled again. "Thank you, though. I'm surprised you remembered!"

"How could I have forgotten? You're only four days ahead of Jimmy, and how could I forget that joint birthday party you guys had for your 25th?"

Alan winced out loud. "I think I'm still hungover from that night."

"I might be, too, honestly," she giggled. "Speaking of ragers, what do the girls have planned for you tonight?"

"I'm not entirely sure. I haven't seen them yet, but I did have two handmade cards in my lunchbox today. Phoebe usually does a crawfish boil or somethin' every year, so probably that. The girls love it, but they think it's gross when Pheebs and I suck the heads."

Hannah mockingly gagged. "Because it *is* gross!"

"Bah. You just haven't had a proper boil."

She laughed. "*Anyway,* how come you're not home yet? Isn't it kind of late?" she asked, glancing at the clock. Alan would've normally been home and showered by now. "I can let you go if you need to focus on driving."

"You're keeping me awake, so no. I'm so beat. It was a fucking day. The boat had some engine trouble, so it was all hands trying to get us back up and runnin'. But that's why I'm late gettin' home today," he managed to tell her before yawning loudly. "Sorry. Ugh, I can't wait to put my feet up and crack open a cold beer."

"How far away are you?" Hannah asked.

"Only a few minutes. Tell me what's new with you."

Hannah told him all about her new niece and her vacation plans with Jake.

"Wow, and Jake was on board with the plan? How're you feeling about it?" he questioned.

"Okay, I guess," she said after a moment of hesitation. "I'm looking forward to the trip itself. I've never been to Rhode Island before, so that will be a fun experience, at least. I do have some qualms, but I guess I'm trying to stay hopeful that he can manage to be decent for a few days."

Alan grunted. "I hope so, too. For your sake. You deserve a break."

"Funny you should say that," Hannah began, "I, um—I told myself that this would be my final push."

"What do you mean?"

"That if nothing changes after this trip, I'm leaving him," Hannah explained, her voice cracking.

"I see."

"I just can't keep doing this. I can't keep pouring everything into him if he's not going to reciprocate. I have *no* idea what that means for my future, but I guess I'll cross that bridge if I get to it." There was silence on the other end of the phone, and Hannah wasn't sure how to interpret it.

"You know I'll support whatever decision you make," Alan finally told her. "And, if you need a place to go, you're always more than welcome here. Don't even ask, just get here."

Hannah chuckled. While she knew he had good intentions, she couldn't help but wonder how his wife would feel about Hannah staying with them for an extended period of time. She couldn't help be feel like she'd be a bother, getting in the middle of the two of them trying to raise their little girls. "It's all so uncertain at this point. Who knows?"

"I'm serious."

She cleared her throat before responding. "I know you are, and I appreciate that. You know, I can't tell you how wonderful it is to have someone like you to talk to. When I try to talk to my other friends, it's a whole lot of my repeating the same shit I've said twenty times before, and what I should or shouldn't do. So, thanks for just letting me talk and supporting me through this mess."

The comfortable silence they'd always known briefly settled itself into the space between their words before Alan said, "Hannah,

I know you. You're more than capable, and I know you've got this. You don't need me, or anyone else, to tell you otherwise. I'm just worried about you, that you'll be okay with whichever way this goes. I don't want to see you break yourself into a million little pieces again. It was hard watching you shatter when Jimmy left that night, and I can only imagine how much it broke you to leave him, and everything else, behind. I wish I could've been there for ya then, but I know you had to make it a clean break, ya know? I got it, but I'm glad I get to be here now."

Hannah sucked in a shallow breath. "If experience has taught me anything, it's that I know I'll be okay. Even if it hurts a whole lot at first." She could hear the door of Alan's truck close. "Are you home?"

"Mm-hmm. Finally."

"Hey, uh, anything on your front porch?" she asked, grinning so big she was sure he could hear it through the phone.

Alan paused. "Yeah, there is. How did you—what did you do?"

Hannah's eye caught the time on the clock, sending her heart fluttering into a panic because her next client would be there any minute and she hadn't bothered to prepare. "You'll have to open it and see, but I have to run for another session. Let me know when you open it! Happy Birthday, my friend!" she squealed before hanging up.

A few minutes later, Alan texted her a selfie with the open box. She had overnighted a gift of New Jersey specialties for him to enjoy, including her favorite staples: a log of Taylor Pork Roll, a six-pack of beer from her favorite brewery in Bay Point, and a box of saltwater taffy. Hannah stared at the picture for a few moments, just taking in his toothy grin, a smear of dirt across his forehead, and his platinum blonde hair that was cut into a short buzzcut.

Seeing his face again brought all of those nostalgic feels back to the surface, the quiet sadness of missing those simpler times.

Her phone pinged with another text message from Alan.

> **Alan:** *Thanks for this! I'm cracking open one of these beers now. The dry ice kept them nice and cold! You'll have to teach me how to make this pork roll. What is it? A log of meat? Don't tell the girls, but I'm hiding the taffy from them so they don't eat it all. Pheobe included.*

Hannah's Journal
Wednesday, May 1, 2024

we leave for our trip early tomorrow morning. the closer it gets, the more i'm looking forward it. i'm nervous, too, though. i don't know what to expect. it's been so long since we've even been on a vacation, but i'm trying to focus on the fun of the adventure ahead more than anything else. i think jake is looking forward to it, too. he seems to be in better spirits the last couple of weeks, which is positive. maybe he really is starting to see that a break from work would do him some good. i caught him looking at the hotel's website last night, and he said he really wanted to spend some time relaxing in the hot tub. i like the sound of that!

apparently, jake's job will be making decisions about promotions in the next week or so. i know a promotion would make him happier, but i worry that the workload would just get worse. the happiness of having "made it" would only last so long before he's back to being a miserable lump. on the other hand, maybe things really <u>would</u> get better if he were out from under his boss. his stress might actually be less, which would mean less of an emotional rollercoaster and less sleepless nights for both of us. and fewer days of overtime would mean more time at home with me. i don't want to get my hopes up here, though. they probably won't make any decisions, anyway. i mean, they've been talking about creating that new position for over a year now. what's a little more time?

another bright spot in my day today was my session with L. she started using the journal i gave her almost every day. she even wrote a letter to her friend with all she had wanted to say, but couldn't. she read it to me, and i had a hard time not crying. she was so incredibly brave and vulnerable in her letter. i'm really impressed with how far she's come. it's days like this that make me happy to be doing what i'm doing. it reminds my <u>why</u> i wanted to do this, and that maybe i'm not so awful at it after all. curious, too, how we are both traveling down mirroring paths. ever since the beginning, i have seen so much of myself in her, and with each session that seems to become more apparent.

it did make me think, though, that i really should try to write that letter to jimmy. i just don't feel like i'm ready still. i wonder if i ever will be? L was brave enough to confront her demons head on and, if we really are that similar, i should be too. except i'm not. goodbye just feels too permanent, like i would be killing him all over again. i'm just not ready to embrace that kind of forever yet.

jake is in the shower right now, so i figured i'd have a few minutes of solitude to recap our first night. i don't want him to know i brought this along, in case he gets any ideas to go snooping. it wouldn't be the first time my privacy was invaded like that, whether it was my so-called friends stealing my journal and blabbing my secrets to the whole school, or my mom reading through it whenever i wasn't around. i know she did because i'd get into trouble for what i wrote in it, even if i was only just writing the truth of my experiences and feelings. i just don't want my journaling to be the thing that causes a fight this weekend. i don't want to be walking on eggshells while we're here, but i am delicately tip-toeing so i don't rock the boat.

anyway, we drove up to castlerock harbor yesterday afternoon and got into our hotel room around 4:00 in the afternoon. my stomach was in knots the whole way because i was so nervous being stuck in a car with jake for longer than a few minutes. by the time we got in, i was exhausted even though the drive only took about 4 hours. i guess it was partly because of the anxiety dump i had when we finally parked. i wound up taking a 2 hour nap. at least i woke up in time for dinner. we walked into town across this long footbridge, and jake even held my hand. this place is so picturesque, with the sun setting over the sound and all the sailboats bobbing in the gentle waters. i'm pretty sure i saw a seal or an otter or something (do they even live in rhode island?). we ate dinner at this brewery at the marina, and managed to snag a table at the edge of the dock. jake was much more engaged with me. it was nice to feel like i was talking to him and not a brick wall for a change. after dinner, we took a little walk around town but we didn't see much because it was pretty dark by that time. i guess the nap didn't do much to refresh me, because i wound up sleeping so heavily last night. that, or i just felt so relaxed.

i was surprised by jake this morning. i was the first thing he reached for when he woke up. i can't remember the last time we cuddled like that. it was so nice to just rest my head on his chest, and listen to the beat of his heart while he stroked my arm with his fingertips. i felt whole again, being there in his arms. like i could almost forget all the bullshit between us. it gave me hope.

sounds like we're going to head into town for breakfast, and then walk around to get a lay of the land. it should be a nice, easy day. this trip is really shaping up to be what i wanted, so why won't the nagging voice in the back of my mind shut up? i'm choosing to ignore it, and jump in with both feet. i really do love this man.

S leep had not come easily for Hannah like the night before, and she had woken up for the day at 3:37 A.M. Jake did not sleep well, either, having tossed and turned all through the night. She glanced over at him now in the darkness of their hotel room, glimpsing the sheets wrapped around his body like an expertly wrapped burrito. Something was off with Jake again, but Hannah couldn't quite pinpoint what it was.

As she plodded quietly into the bathroom, she thought back on the previous day. They ate breakfast at a greasy spoon kind of diner in the heart of Castlerock Harbor's downtown. Jake had been all smiles and talkative, even reaching for Hannah's hand over the table. Then they had walked with hands clasped through the sloping downtown streets, wandering in and out of the mom-and-pop shops that lined both sides of the road. Lunch had been great, and, in the early afternoon, they stopped off in their hotel room where they sloppily and clumsily fell into bed together. It was the first time since Christmas.

Hannah tiptoed out of the bathroom, and sat in one of the armchairs by the window. She opened the curtains gently, letting just a tiny bit of light into the room, enough so she could watch the sun rise over the sound through the misty morning. She backtracked again through the day before, stopping to think how Jake had changed sometime in the late afternoon. It was just before dinner, and he had been on his cell phone. She couldn't tell what he was reading, but whatever it was must have been the reason for his mood shift. Over dinner, Jake's face appeared tense with a wrinkle between his eyebrows that never seemed to relax. He didn't talk much, and he barely made eye contact with her, letting his eyes wander all around the restaurant the entire time. Back in their hotel room, Jake had simply tucked himself in bed, angling his body in such a way that Hannah couldn't snuggle up against him if she tried. He watched television until he drifted off to sleep.

So what changed? She worried it was something work related because he would have told her if it were something about his family or a friend. All Hannah knew was that she felt grumpy watching Jake sleep so peacefully while she was still so tired. She watched him in bed, his muscles twitching ever so slightly as snores rumbled out of his open mouth. He'd never been much of a snorer except for restless nights or when the heartburn had become particularly bad. She wondered which it was this time.

"Hey," Jake suddenly whispered to Hannah in the dark. "How long have you been awake?"

She eyed the time on the digital clock on the nightstand nearest to her. "About an hour."

He peered at the time, too. "Couldn't sleep?"

"No!" she snapped. "You were flopping around like a fish all night. You kept stealing the blankets, and you were snoring so damn loud."

"Oh," he said. "Sorry. I did have some heartburn last night."

"Again? Did you take anything for it?"

Jake sat up and stretched his arms out in front of him. "Yeah, I found some Tums in the toiletry bag. I felt better, but I guess it didn't help with the snoring, huh?"

Hannah shook her head. "It definitely didn't. How often are you still having heartburn?"

Jake rolled his eyes up, pursing his lips in thought. "I don't know—it comes and goes. A couple times a week, maybe?"

"That's way too much. Why have you been hiding it from me?"

"I'm not hiding anything, Hannah. I just didn't think I needed to tell you every time it happened. Besides, I probably just overate last night. It's fine," Jake rebutted. "So, what did you want to do today?"

"Are you sure it's not stress? You seemed off last night at dinner," Hannah remarked.

He blew out a sharp breath. "I'm not stressed. It was just something I ate. Now, are you going to tell me what you want to do today or are we just going to sit here?"

"I don't know," she replied, shifting herself to look out the window again. "What do you feel up for? I don't want you to push it—"

"I feel fine, Hannah," Jake said with an edge of annoyance still in his voice. He cleared his throat and tried for a more upbeat tone. "Maybe a hike?"

"Should we try Harborlight State Park?" she suggested, pushing her worry aside; if Jake was going to try to be more positive, then she could too.

He nodded without another word and abruptly got up to change.

Hannah and Jake settled on breakfast at the diner again before making the drive to the park. Their conversation over breakfast seemed forced and unnatural, with the tension between them having grown into a third traveling passenger. Hannah tried again asking what was wrong, but Jake denied anything was bothering him. She didn't believe him, but dropped it; she knew better than to push by now.

Jake drove through the winding, barren roadways while Hannah pulled up maps of hiking trails to pick from. They chose a trail that wound its way around part of the coastline inside the park. To their dismay, it was already crowded with other hikers, despite being early in the season; the trees were just beginning to turn green once again and the daffodils bloomed only about a week ago. She had hoped for some breathing room from the rest of the world on this hike, but instead, they kept running into the same family with two very rambunctious children.

When they reached the beach area, Hannah and Jake diverged from the trail to take a walk along the sandy shores. It was still cold at that time of the morning, but Hannah didn't care. She stopped to sit on the edge of the grass to remove her sneakers and socks. With her toes in the sand, she stood tall and took a deep breath of the cool, salty breeze blowing gently in her face. There had always been something in her that came alive at the edge of the ocean. Like it could wake up the little girl that still lived inside her heart, skipping along and giggling as the gentle waves nipped at her toes.

The ocean served as the backdrop for some of Hannah's favorite memories: afternoons spent building sandcastles while her dad fished at the shoreline, splashing about in the waves with her high school friends, those endless bonfire nights in college, skipping stones with Jimmy at the bay, and her wedding to Jake.

She felt a kind of kindred spirit with the ocean; something calm that could turn destructive in a moment, always churning. There was a certain mystery in its vastness, much like the never-ending depths of her own mind.

Letting the icy water wash over her feet, Hannah realized Jake was not anywhere near her. Her head spun in either direction, looking for him amongst the other people on the beach, only to spot him sitting on the grass with his face buried in his cell phone.

"Seriously?" she whispered to no one, stomping through the sand back to where he sat. When she reached him, she asked, "What are you doing?"

Jake looked up at her with a flustered look on his face. "What?" he asked.

"You were the one who wanted to go for a hike, and you're just sitting here on your phone? Are you kidding me?" she asked through gritted teeth, her voice low to avoid attracting the attention of a family walking the trail nearby.

"Oh," he mumbled, putting his cellphone in the front pocket of the hooded sweatshirt he'd put on that morning. "I needed to sit down for a minute because my stomach felt uneasy, and I took my phone out to just read an article to calm down."

Hannah sighed. "The ocean waves weren't calming enough?"

"Oh my god," Jake quietly growled as he rolled his eyes at her.

"Do you want to just head back to the car?" she asked, crossing her arms over her chest.

"Yeah, I think I do," he softly replied.

Hannah sat back down on the grass without another word to put her socks and sneakers back on, then stalked off up the trail. Jake followed behind her at a distance, his hands stuffed into his pockets. At least he couldn't hear how Hannah cursed him under her breath the whole way back to the parking lot as she avoided making eye contact with other hikers on the trail who looked at her curiously, as if her anger were painted vibrantly across her face.

Back at the hotel, he took a hot shower and got into bed, drifting off to sleep quickly. Hannah, on the other hand, couldn't rest. Her gut shook with the anger sitting heavy there. Her muscles felt restless, like the only way to calm them was to punch something, or scream, or maybe run until her legs and lungs gave out.

She opted for a walk down to the beach to watch the water gently lap against the rocky shore. A feeling slowly crept into her heart, then spread throughout her body in every direction. It was a deep, undeniable understanding that this had all been a colossal mistake, because she knew deep down that their life would simply return to normal once they were back home in Bay Point. When she thought about it, a simple phone check had been enough to ruin two days of progress, for it to all revert back to how things had been at home for the last year. The only thing that had changed now, was the scenery.

Jake is never going to change. Not for himself, and certainly not for me, she reflected.

The thought sank into her stomach, tying into a tight knot. Hannah stood up and searched the beach for flat stones, filling her left hand with them. She slid out of her flip-flops and walked out into the water until it reached the middle of her shins. It was cold, numbingly so, but that's all she wanted then. To feel nothing. She tried to skip one of the stones but threw it too hard, causing it to sink. Hannah tried again, but the same thing happened. She grabbed another stone and, this time, lobbed it as hard as she could into the water. Then another. And another. And another. She threw them all, hard, finding momentum in her anger. Her arm eventually became sore, and her cheeks were soaked with salty tears.

Hannah took a deep breath, looking up toward the sky, where the sun shone brightly through the passing, pillowy clouds. Through her tears, she asked her dad, Jimmy, or whoever to help her find the strength she needed for whatever was to come.

May 5, 2024

The next morning felt like Groundhog Day. Hannah woke up somewhere around 3:30 A.M. again, after having been restless most of the night because of Jake's snoring and flailing about. The night before, at dinner, she had practically begged him to go easy on the greasy food and alcohol. As usual, he had brushed off her suggestions and done as he pleased, but it seemed like Hannah was the only one paying the price for it.

When he eventually woke up, she questioned whether he was feeling okay.

"Yeah, I'm fine," Jake said, his tone obviously aggravated. "Why?"

"You sure? Because you snored like a chainsaw all night, and look at the bed sheets! They're all over the place," she pointed out.

Jake raised his eyebrows and plastered on the fakest smile she'd ever seen. "Yeah, totally, honey," he told her in a cheery voice, a complete one-eighty from just a second ago.

They walked into town for a pastry and coffee from a cafe they had passed on their travels. On the way, Hannah reached for Jake's hand to hold, but he brushed it aside and stuck his hands inside the front pocket of his hooded sweatshirt; he made some excuse about his hands being cold in the crisp morning air, but Hannah knew better. She, too, shoved her hands into the pockets of the light denim jacket she wore; she couldn't help but feel completely put off by his phoniness, anyway.

Over coffee, they discussed their plans for the day. Hannah wanted to visit the nearby town of Brush Harbor, known for its thriving community of artists. Jake seemed indifferent to the idea, telling her, "It's not really my thing, but if you wanna go, I guess we'll go." She figured he was just trying to make up for cutting their hike short the day before.

Brush Harbor was nearly identical to Castlerock Harbor but with a more eclectic and artsy feel. Dozens of people walked up and down the sidewalks, poking their heads in and out of each of the studios that lined the small maze of winding roads. Hannah marveled at the walkways, crafted from cobblestones that had been hand-painted in a myriad of colors and designs. It made her miss the afternoons she used to spend in the city with Amanda, walking through the halls of art museums, big and small.

Jake, on the other hand, trailed behind her with his eyes glued to his cell phone. Hannah just kept moving forward, letting him linger in the background of the day. He did go into some of the studios with her, but then would stand there while she browsed and talked to the artists and other patrons. Most of the time, though, Jake stayed out on the sidewalk typing messages furiously on his phone.

Watching him through the window of a glassblowing shop, she thought to herself, *Why can't he just fake it for me? Just once?*

Hannah thought back to the dozens of times over the years that she had put her feelings aside to participate in something that mattered to him. Like how she endured hours of Anime movies because it was what Jake wanted to watch, or the times she played those complex board games he loved with several card decks, dozens of miniatures, and multiple sets of six-sided dice. That's what you did in relationships, though. Sometimes, you just had to take one for the team to make your partner happy. On their team, she was clearly the MVP. Without the trophy, anyway.

When she met him outside, she asked, "So what do you wanna do? Are you hungry or something?"

Jake, who had been tapping his toes against the sidewalk, answered flatly, "Not really."

"You okay?" she questioned again, for the probably fifth time since they'd gotten out of bed.

"Hannah, I'm fine," he said, his tone more stern this time. "All of this just isn't my thing. That's all."

Her shoulders slumped. "Do you wanna just leave?"

"I mean—if you're ready to…" his voice trailed off.

They ambled lazily along the sidewalk in silence for a few steps as Hannah mulled over her choices. "I guess we can," she said solemnly.

"If you're not ready—"

"Look—You're *very* obviously not having a good time," she said, stopping in the middle of the sidewalk to look at him. "Let's just go."

"I'm going to find a place to sit outside and read for a little bit," Hannah told Jake when they returned to their room at the inn.

"Okay," he responded as he got comfortable on the bed and clicked on the television.

Hannah rolled her eyes as she opened the patio door of their room, her Kindle and cell phone in hand. The sun shone brightly on her face as she walked down the back lawn toward the small strip of beach where a couple of Adirondack chairs were set up. She chose one that was partially shaded by a white birch tree, tucking her legs underneath her and leaning heavily against one of its arms.

She was able to read a couple of chapters before her cell phone buzzed on the opposite arm of the chair. Glancing at it, Hannah saw a text notification from Alan.

> **Alan:** *Haven't heard from you. How's the trip?*
> **Hannah:** *Could be better. Started out strong, but something is up with Jake. I don't know what, though.*
> **Alan:** *When do you go home?*
> **Hannah:** *We drive back tomorrow morning.*
> **Alan:** *Give me a call when you get home, ok?*
> **Hannah:** *Everything okay with you?*
> **Alan:** *Yeah. I just figured you'd want to vent or something.*
> **Hannah:** *Oh. LOL. I will.*
> **Alan:** *Safe drive tomorrow, ok?*
> **Hannah:** *Thanks.*

Hannah could hear footsteps in the grass behind her as she put the phone down on the arm of the chair. Jake stepped into her periphery, stopping in front of her with his brow furrowed.

"Who was that?" he asked stiffly.

"Just Alan," she responded nonchalantly.

Jake snickered loudly as he moved toward the chair next to hers, plopping heavily into it.

"What now?" Hannah asked.

"I dunno. You're all pissy with me that I've been on my phone a little, but then you run out here to spend time on your phone talking to him?"

"I didn't run out here to talk to him. I was reading my book, and he texted to see how our trip was going," Hannah said curtly, feeling utterly tired of this narrative he was so desperately trying to create. "And don't downplay the amount you've been on your phone. I feel like I'm practically on this trip by myself."

"I don't trust him," Jake said plainly, ignoring that last bit. Probably because he knew Hannah was right.

"You don't even know him. How can you have an opinion like that?"

"It's just weird, Hannah. He shows up out of the blue, and now you're best friends?"

"We were the best of friends before, and we've been able to pick up where we left off. I think it's a beautiful thing, personally," she said with a click of her tongue. "You know—you have all these female friends at work, and I don't say shit to you about it. God forbid I have one guy friend. It's not about whether I trust those other women or not. It's about trusting you, which I do. I guess it doesn't go both ways here, though."

"Maybe it doesn't," he said coldly.

Hannah lost her cool, her voice rising in anger. "You can't be serious? What reason have I *ever* given you not to trust me?"

Jake stared out at the water, indifferent. "It's just—I don't even know you anymore, Hannah. You're dressing different and suddenly you're into this heavy punk music. You spend so much time at home behind the door of your office with your nose in your journals. I felt blindsided with all of these secrets about Jimmy, and now you've got this new friend who isn't new at all. He's just a link to a part of you that I don't know. I don't even recognize that person, but *he* does. Next, you'll tell me Hannah isn't your real name or something."

"Don't be ridiculous, Jake. I *knew* you were jealous of Alan."

"I'm not jealous!" he yelled, drawing the attention of a couple walking alone the shoreline.

Hannah winced, wishing Jake would keep his voice down. Shaking her head, she turned away to avoid their eyes as they disappeared up a trail leading back to the hotel grounds. "So this is what's bothering you? Is this why you've been so distant and weird the last couple of days?" From the corner of her eye, Hannah could see Jake's hands squeeze the armrests of his chair.

"I didn't get the promotion," he finally admitted quietly.

Hannah's head jerked back in his direction. "When did you find that out?"

"Friday. They sent out an email that Ben fucking got it."

"Ben?" Hannah questioned, unfamiliar with that name.

"The new guy that got hired only, like, three months ago. I had seniority. I put the time in, and for what? So some *kid* can take what I worked so hard for? It's fucking bullshit!" Jake slammed his fist down on the arm of the chair, causing Hannah, to jump in her seat. "I *told* you Gabrielle had something against me. Nothing I do is good enough for her."

"So, you knew about this since Friday, and you didn't say anything? You just let it eat at you? You let it make you sick and keep us both up at night?" she asked, her voice rising again. "Who's keeping secrets now? When were you going to tell me?"

"It's not like that. I was going to wait until we got home to say anything because I didn't want to ruin the trip."

Hannah burst out into cackling laughter.

Jake looked at her at last, his hands upturned in question. "What's so fucking funny?" he asked.

"You didn't say anything because you didn't want to ruin the trip, so instead, you ruin the trip by being an absolute grump. Makes perfect sense."

"I was trying, but without the pay raise now, I was worried about how much you were spending. This inn couldn't have been cheap, and then this morning you were talking about wanting to buy some art pieces to bring home."

"So when it's something I want, you decide to hold the purse strings tight. If *you* want a new video game system or something, that's fine, though. I get it now. I understand completely," Hannah said, her words heavy with sarcasm.

"That's not—it's not like that," he stammered, his voice wavering. "So what? Do you just hate me now? Because I think you should just say it if you do."

Hannah laughed again quietly. "I don't *hate* you. I love you, but I don't think I *like* you very much right now. I think that much should be obvious. I have loved you enough to keep trying to make this work. Like planning special date nights, and this long weekend away, because I'm trying to build back what we had." She turned to him with a pleading look. "I've been working so hard on myself to overcome the grief and this depression. I've been seeing Linda for months now. I've been doing the hard inner work in her office and in the pages of my journals. I've been excavating all of this shit that weighs me down, that's been weighing us down. I've been trying so desperately to get back to the person you once loved. I *know* she's still in there."

"I never stopped loving you, Hannah. It's you that doesn't love me. I don't care what you say. You just wish I were more like Jimmy. More creative and cool. Better looking, even. I dunno," he babbled.

"I wish no such thing! Jake—how many times do I have to tell you that I'm not in love with Jimmy? I love you. I'm in love with you."

He shrugged. "It's just not the same anymore."

"You're right. It's not, but because we're different people now. It happens."

"How am I different?" he asked defensively.

"You're not the same guy you were when we met. You haven't been for a long time, Jake. You're not the funny, happy–go-lucky guy I used to know. You're just so angry and moody all the time, and you've turned mean. You don't pay any attention to anything that isn't work or video game-related. I might as well be a ghost. It's been tearing us apart, but you don't even seem to notice. Or you're just not bothered by it, I guess." Jake cleared his throat to say something, but Hannah continued talking. "Apparently, you don't trust me anymore. I shouldn't be surprised since you've been slinging these cheating accusations at me. I keep trying all these different ways to show you that I love you and that I want to be with you. I'm putting so much effort into fixing this, but you clearly don't want that."

"That's not true at all. I do want to fix this," he told her.

She scoffed, "Oh, so now you'll admit that there is something broken between us? I've been trying to tell you for months, but you kept brushing me off. Now it's too big. It's too late." Hannah's eyes welled up with emotion as she felt her heart starting to crack a little bit more with every word. "I can't do this anymore, Jake. I deserve more than this."

She turned to look at him. His eyes were still fixed on the water, and his fingers were picking at a splintered piece of wood on his chair. She waited in the tense silence between them, willing him to say something. Anything.

When he didn't, the words she'd been holding back from saying spilled out from her lips. "I want a divorce."

To anyone other than Hannah her confession would seem impulsive, yet it was anything but. She had agonized over this decision for months and, in this moment, the answer had come to her so clearly and plainly. Each muscle in her body relaxed, and the cloudiness that lingered over every thought evaporated; it felt right.

That got his attention. Jake turned to her, his lips pressed into a thin line. "This isn't the end, Hannah. Don't be like that. We can still fix this."

She let out a loud exhale, intensely holding his stare. Hannah lurched out of her chair suddenly, wiping the wetness from her nose and cheeks with the backs of her hands. Gathering her Kindle and phone, she stomped through the grass toward their hotel room without another word.

<h1 style="text-align:center">Hannah's Journal
Monday, May 6, 2024</h1>

i said it. the "d" word. i don't think jake took me seriously. he thinks we can fix it. at least that's what he said, but it just made my blood boil. we wound up having this same fight we've had so many times before, and it just clicked for me. i knew what i needed to do, and it was the most peace i've felt in a long time. jake watched me move around the hotel room the rest of the night, but i could barely even look at him. it seemed like he wanted to talk more, but what was there left to say? i eventually just got into bed and stared at the wall until i finally fell asleep. i've got nothing left to give, not even another tear.

we're home now, by the way. we got in a couple of hours ago. the drive was quiet and weird. we wound up checking out way earlier than we initially planned because there was no point in staying any longer than we needed to. i picked diesel up from the dogsitter while jake just stayed home and hid in the shed. typical. when things get hard, he retreats into himself like this. i don't know if it's that he's trying to escape into his little dream world where everything is fine and wonderful, or if he's trying to sort it all out. honestly, i'm not sure if he would recognize an emotion if it jumped up and bit him. i unpacked everything, ran the laundry, and made some food for later while he's still out there. i know we have a lot more to talk about, but i don't know where to start. i don't know what's going through his mind, which is unsettling.

for as certain as i am about this, i'm fucking terrified. i've never been on my own, and i don't know what that will look like for me. my other concern is how i'm going to manage this financially. i've never been great with numbers, and putting together a budget feels super overwhelming. i don't even know where to begin, but i do know i need to figure it out sooner than later because everything else kind of hinges on that. it just hit me that i might not be able to keep my practice open. i'm barely breaking even right now with the overhead and the slow growth of my caseload.

i didn't regret leaving the clinic until this very moment. at least it would've been stable income without the additional expenses. i wonder if they would take me back? that is, if i even want to stay in the therapy world. if i'm honest with myself, i'm super burned out trying to help everyone else fix their lives. i've barely had the time to fix my own. what would i do, though? my practice has been everything to me. it's what i worked so hard for, and went into so much debt for. it's who i am. the one who listens. the one who gives it to you straight, who has good advice, and asks the hard questions. i got into this career because i was good at it, and i wanted to make a difference in the lives of others. i don't know that i've really done that and, if i have, at what expense? if i were 18 again, i think i'd have that "the world is my oyster" feeling. at this age, it just feels something like a mix of failure and free-falling into nothing.

i keep hearing how expensive divorce can be, but i really don't want to fight with jake over anything. if he wants whatever, he can just have it. except diesel. i will fight to keep him, and i have a feeling that i am in for it. i just want to this all to go as smoothly as possible. i hope that jake can at least give me that much. after everything, that's all i really want. i deserve that much.

i doubt i can afford this house on my own. i'm not sure where jake stands, but he's probably in the same boat as me. it makes me sad to think we'll probably have to sell it. i do love this house, despite everything. we've had so many good times here, and poured ourselves into making it ours. there are bits of both of us in every corner. the question is: where will i go? i don't know that i'd get a mortgage on my own with the way my credit is, and i don't really have anyone to lean on like that until i could get back on my feet. there's little room for me between spouses and kids. i mean, alan offered me a space with him, phoebe, and the girls, but i couldn't do that to them. besides, he's halfway across the country. though, if i don't keep my practice, would the distance from bay point really be an issue? i guess i'll just look for an apartment. the question of where still remains. i would look close to bay point and harborvale but, again, if i don't keep my practice, i could go anywhere. then i think about how much i can afford, which i don't know yet. yeah, i better get on that budget...

why does it feel like i just burned down my whole life? i know this is the right thing for me to do, but suddenly staying in one place just feels a whole lot easier. maybe burning it all down isn't the worst thing, though. i can <u>really</u> start over in a brand new life. maybe even in a brand new place. i could be whoever i want to be since i won't just be "jake's wife" anymore. the possibilities are exciting, but frightening. i chose this, and i know i can rise from the ashes. i did it years ago when i walked out on jimmy. this time, i'm not leaving with a mountain of heartbreak. just hope... and a little overwhelm.

the last piece of this is telling people. shannon is going to flip a lid. nicole probably won't even care even though she thought i should leave. alan will understand. but, oh god—my mom! i can only imagine what she'll say, and the million ways she'll blame me for all of this without knowing the backstory.

well, i said i didn't have another tear left, but here i am crying again. my tears aren't for jake, or even for our marriage. they're for me, and this giant hill i still have to climb. i wish i knew that actually making the decision would be the easiest part of all of this. i just feel so swamped by these contradicting emotions, this combination of utter worry and serene calmness. i guess it's true what they say, that the right thing doesn't always feel like it at first.

May 7, 2024

Hannah slept to her five o'clock alarm the morning after their return from Rhode Island. Not that she had to be up for work today since she'd taken an extra day off, but it felt good to keep her routine intact. The rest of the bed was empty, which she was thankful for; Hannah wasn't quite ready to face Jake just yet. She lay in bed just staring at the wall, her mind spinning with everything she needed to do.

A while later, Hannah padded into the kitchen to find Jake cooking enough eggs and home fries for two, and a whole pot of coffee already brewed.

"Good morning!" he said in a cheerful tone.

"Um, g'morning," Hannah hesitantly replied. "What is all of this?"

Jake shrugged. "I just thought you deserved a nice breakfast this morning."

"Okay…"

"What? I can't do something special for my beautiful wife?" he asked as he walked over and kissed her cheek.

Hannah pulled back from him. "You can't just erase everything with hugs and kisses and breakfast. We can't just pretend the last couple of days didn't happen—"

"I know I can't. I just wanted to start on a better foot now that we're back home. To make up for our trip," he told her, his voice dripping with sincerity.

It did nothing to change her mind. "Jake—"

"I can't lose you, Hannah. I can't. I love you too much to just let you walk away. I'll do the therapy. I'll do whatever you think I should do. I promise."

"Jake!" she shouted. "Therapy would've been helpful *months* ago. It's too late now. I've made my decision, and you have no one to blame but yourself. I hope that one day you can see that it's been in your hands this entire time. What's more likely is that you'll just keep blaming everyone else, dead or alive."

He shook his head, walking back toward her. Jake moved his face right in front of hers, their noses nearly touching, and wrapped his arms around her waist. "It's not too late, Hannah. Don't say that. We're supposed to be together—you and me. Forever. You said it yourself just the other day that you still love me. As long as we've got love, we'll be okay. Love will be the thing that keeps us going."

Hannah wriggled out of his grasp, taking a couple of steps back from him, her hands outstretched to block him from advancing again. With her voice rising with annoyance, she repeated, "It *is* too late. Besides, I know better than anyone that love isn't enough. If it were, I'd still be living in that tiny house on Campbell Street with a gum wrapper tied around my ring finger. You and I wouldn't even be here right now! But it isn't enough. There comes a point where there's gotta be some fight, some commitment, to keep choosing each other. I've been making the choice to be with you, but I just can't anymore." She paused to lean herself against the counter, exhaling loudly. "You know, you do this all the time…"

Jake shook his head slightly as if to shake off a surprise right hook to the face. "Do what?"

"You'll be such an absolute asshole, and then you'll get all sweet again. You'll do all the things I've been begging you to do, but then it will all go to shit again in, like, two weeks. It happens every time, and I've been so fucking stupid to deal with it for so long. I said what I said, and I meant it. You may have ignored it, but I haven't been happy for a while, Jake. It's not just grief, either. It's everything, and I'm just so fucking tired of it all."

Hannah stared at him, her eyes still dry. Perhaps that well had finally dried up. In a way, she felt uneasy about how at peace she felt, rather than being a sobbing, angry mess. Jake stood in front of the stove, a spatula in hand, looking down at the floor. In the silence, the seconds that ticked by felt more like hours.

"I'm gonna take a walk. I'll see you back here tonight for dinner. Take something out for me to make, will you?" she asked as she walked out of the room.

Hannah changed into a pair of athletic leggings, a sports bra, and a tank top with a witty fitness pun across the chest. After she laced up her sneakers, she popped her AirPods into her ears and left the house. She followed her usual route down to the bay and called Alan.

"Hannah, hey," he answered breathlessly. "You didn't call yesterday."

"I know, I'm sorry. Is it a bad time?" she asked.

"No, I'm just sittin' here watchin' the lines. I guess you're home?"

Hannah bobbed her chin up and down. "Yeah, we got home early yesterday. I'm out for a walk right now. Jake and I just got into it, and I needed some space."

"Ah, shit. What happened?" Alan carefully asked.

Hannah spent the next several minutes recounting their argument at the inn, how she'd blurted out that she wanted a divorce, and how delusional Jake was acting this morning.

"Damn, girl. You're sure about this now?"

She answered immediately, not needing to give it another thought. "I am. I feel so calm right now about all of this, which is weird because I feel like I should be a mess. I mean, I'm worried and a little stressed about next steps, but it's like a weight's been lifted, you know?" She took stock of her body, how her shoulders were at ease and her thoughts were slow and deliberate now. It felt odd after all the months of teeth grinding and living with this knot in her upper back that just never went away. Until now, anyway.

"Like a two-hundred-something pound weight?" he joked.

Hannah laughed loudly. "Exactly."

"Sorry," he apologized. "I don't want to talk poorly about the guy, but it's good to hear you laugh like that. So what's next for you?"

She sputtered her lips as all of the items on her mental to-do list scrolled through her mind. "Pfft. That's the big question, but I have no freaking clue. I can't afford to keep the house, and, to be honest, I don't even know that I can afford to stay here in New Jersey. I haven't looked at anything yet, but I've been hearing that rent has really gone up since we left our last apartment. Plus, all the expenses to maintain my practice really add up."

"You've got a place here if you need it," Alan reminded her.

"I appreciate that, but I wish you weren't so far away. I have so much here to take care of right now."

"That's fair, but the offer is there if you need it," he repeated.

"I know, thanks. The part that feels overwhelming is figuring out how to *actually* get divorced. That, and I have to find a way to tell my friends. And my mom."

"You don't have to go holding any press conferences just yet. Maybe it's just better to figure out the other stuff first," he suggested.

Hannah considered what he said, scrunching her face in thought as she walked. "You're right. Maybe it's just wishful thinking, but hopefully it'll curb the unsolicited advice."

"I doubt that," Alan said with a faint laugh.

"Again, you're probably right," she said with weighted breath.

They chatted for a while longer as Hannah took her time walking through the park along the waterfront. She eventually stopped to lean on the railing, watching all kinds of boats coming in and out of the harbor. In the back of her mind, though, she was really just killing time until she knew Jake would have left for work. When Alan had to go to take care of some equipment, Hannah followed the path back out of the park and headed home.

Dinner was plated and waiting on the kitchen table by the time Jake arrived home from work that night. Hearing the door close lightly, Hannah called out a pleasant greeting and was met with a neutral tone. It was more than the malcontent grunt she expected to hear in return, which had been enough to ease the knot in her stomach. She wasn't under any illusions that this would be easy, but she wanted to maintain some level of civility while they were still stuck together.

Jake joined Hannah at the kitchen table to eat once he changed out of his work clothes. "How was your day?" he asked.

"Good," she said, caught off guard by his interest. "How about you? How was work?"

"It was fine. Managed to congratulate Ben without punching him in the face, so that was a positive thing," Jake told her with a low chuckle.

"That's something," she said with a light smile. After a momentary pause, she said, "So, um, I was hoping we could talk more about our plans."

Jake looked up from his plate. "All right. Let's just get this over with."

She averted her eyes from him, feeling sorry now for what she was doing to him. It was evident from the pain visible there that this was the last thing he wanted. Hannah pushed the feeling aside, recalling all the times he had disregarded her pain in the past.

"I did some research this afternoon about our options for filing. We can do this with the help of lawyers, or we can do it on our own. It's obviously cheaper to handle it ourselves, but for it to work, it has to be uncontested. So we would need to be on the same page with everything," she explained cautiously.

Jake hesitated, pushing a piece of zucchini around on his plate. "I don't want this—"

"Jake—" Hannah grunted.

"Let me finish," he interrupted, putting a hand up to stop her. "I don't want this. I don't want to lose you." Jake stopped to take a deep breath, and Hannah could see the tears welling up in his eyes. "I know I haven't been the best husband or friend to you lately. I'm sorry for that. I haven't been able to look much past my own shit, and I see now how much that has hurt you. I can't go back and change it, as much as I wish I could, but I'm not going to fight you on this. I'm not going to stop you from leaving, if that's what you want."

Hannah didn't know what to say, so the two of them just stared at one another with silent tears streaking down both of their faces. As angry as she'd been with Jake, and for as much as he'd broken her, she never wanted to do the same to him. More than anything, she thought he might feel relieved that she wanted to split up so he didn't have to be the one to initiate their ending; she was so sure he was just as unhappy in this thing as she was, but he didn't want to play the part of the bad guy.

Clearing the emotion from her throat, Hannah said, "Then I think we should talk about how to split everything up."

Jake shook his head. "I want the stuff from the shed, whatever's rightfully mine. You can have everything else."

"Well, no. Let's split it up because I don't know what I'm going to do, and if I'll really have the room for anything. The stuff in my office, I'll take. What about the furniture?"

"You can have it or toss it. It doesn't really matter to me."

"Jake, come on," Hannah groaned. "What about the kitchen stuff?"

"I just want the barbecue stuff," he answered bluntly.

"What if we split the silverware and plates down the middle?" she suggested.

Jake shrugged. "Fine."

Hannah rested her hands heavily on the table and pleaded with him, "Jake, I need you to take this seriously. Please."

He exhaled a deep breath. "I know, and I am. I really don't want anything else."

A heavy silence fell between them. Hannah took a long drink of water and said, "The house—I calculated everything, but I can't afford to buy you out. If you think you can—"

He interrupted her again, "I don't know, and I don't care. I wouldn't be able to stay here without you. You're in every nook and cranny of this house."

"Okay," Hannah whispered. "Well, I can call Sue to come by so we can talk about what we need to do to list it. The only other big thing is Diesel." She looked down at him, her good boy, as he sat at her heels enthusiastically waiting for a bit of her dinner.

"That's not even a question," Jake said promptly. "I love him so much, but I don't think he could live without you, and I wouldn't want to take him away from you. I'll miss the shit out of him, but he should go with you."

Hannah's shoulders fell away from her ears with relief. "Are you sure?" she asked.

Jake looked down at Diesel, who was still staring at Hannah intently. "Look at him. He knows who he wants to be with."

They both smiled at one another sadly and ate the rest of their dinner in silence. Somehow, the ending of their marriage felt like the weird, awkward moments at the beginning of any relationship. It was in the not knowing what to say to each other, and the clumsy glances across the table. A deep love that exists between two people that neither want to acknowledge. It's funny how life comes full circle like that.

As they moved around the kitchen, clearing the table and putting leftovers into Tupperware containers, Hannah told him, "We'll need to have a plan to divide everything in order to file without lawyers. There's some form we need to fill out. I think that's the best thing for us. The cheaper option, anyway. If we can just work together on this."

"All right. Give me the night to think about it. I just need some time," Jake replied, then offered, "I can sleep on the couch for a while, until we figure out what to do with this place."

Hannah's eyebrows raised in surprise. "You sure? We could always switch on and off or something," she suggested.

Jake shook his head. "No, you should have the bed. I'll be fine," he said as he went to the bedroom to collect his belongings from the nightstand on his side of the bed.

i'm glad that, so far, this divorce stuff is going relatively smooth. between sessions today i paid the fees for the documents and filled out my half. jake filled out his parts tonight and we even put together the property settlement agreement. he was true to his word in that he took the night to think things over and was ready to talk with me about how to divide our things in the morning. i was surprised. i was wondering if this wasn't some stalling tactic to figure out how to convince me to stay. also, i can't believe he had to sign something that gave me permission to revert back to my maiden name if i wanted to. it's crazy that we're in 2024 and that's still a thing. i'm not really sure what i'll want to do about my name. i know it would be easy to just stay hannah deluca, but i miss being hannah o'malley. that's what a large part of this healing journey has been, anyway. finding <u>her</u> again. it feels fitting to walk into the future with the name i was born with. for now, it's at the bottom of my to-do list and there is <u>a lot</u> to do.

i'm happy that jake isn't fighting anything, and that we've been able to talk this all out. i'm going to put the paperwork in the mail tomorrow. the state website said it could take up to 6 weeks to finalize, which is fine. it's better than some of the nightmares i hear about it dragging on for a year, or more. in the meantime, we both agreed to stay in the house until it sells. jake will just stay on the couch, and i'll use the bedroom. things feel a little weird right now, which is to be expected. we've both been trying to keep a good amount of physical distance between us so there's no confusing normal daily activities for attempts at affection. it's manageable for now, but we obviously can't do this long-term. not that we plan to.

i called our realtor, sue. we were both able to meet her on our lunch breaks today to talk everything through. it's all moving so fast, which i hadn't expected. not that i'm complaining. the sooner the better, i think, so we can both move on and start rebuilding. sue is going to send over some paperwork tonight for us to sign, and then she'll be by in the next day or two to put a for sale sign out front and take pictures of the property.

i feel really anxious that the house will sell fast like sue said. i'll need a place to land if it happens, and i feel like my mom is my only likely option. i haven't even told her about the divorce yet. i can't imagine being under the same roof with her again. we never got along that well. she was always up my ass about something, nagging me about how i looked or what i was doing with my time. even the friends i hung out with, or the guys i chose to date. nothing was ever good enough for her. i could never talk to her about the problems i was having growing up, because she was so judgmental and would just yell at me for feeling hurt or sad or angry about the situation. i think i'll be over it before i can unpack my clothes. maybe i should stay at a hotel or something until i can get an apartment. it just feels like a waste of money, though.

i called shannon and told her everything. she actually cried. i knew she'd be upset, but i didn't expect her to be <u>that</u> upset. she knew this was a possibility, so i don't know why she's taking it so hard. it's probably just post-partum hormones. anyway, by the end of our conversation, she did say she understood why i was doing it. she said she was worried for me, for what i'm going to do moving forward. she doesn't want me to be alone, or feel lonely, in my new single life. i found that funny, because i'm looking at is like an emancipation more than anything. besides, i think it would serve me well to have some time for just me. i appreciate her concern, but i don't want to just jump into a relationship or anything. it felt nice, though, that she was worried. it means she does care, which means a lot. we haven't exactly been on the best of terms but we have started talking here and there. until this announcement, we've just avoided discussing any of the big stuff.

i called nicole today, too. she didn't answer, though, which was no surprise. i texted her about the divorce, and got an immediate response. again, no surprise. she's always in it for the drama but she was surprisingly dismissive. i thought she'd be singing my praises, but she told me that she didn't think i'd ever leave him. that i wasn't strong enough to go through with it and be on my own. i just stopped responding after that. first of all, she was being really rude and, second of all, she apparently doesn't know me at all. it has never been so obvious to me than it is now that nicole's friendship has run its course. she was never the greatest friend to begin with. i think i always knew that deep down, but now i've hit the end of my patience. no, not patience. it's healing. i've finally begun to heal that part of me that rolled over and accepted substandard behavior and care from other people in the name of being loved and having friends. it was never love or friendship, though. i know that now. since i'm starting my life over again, it doesn't hurt to re-evaluate my friendships, too. this one, i'm crossing off my list and i feel okay about that.

i managed to see linda today. she had a cancelation in the afternoon so she was able to squeeze me in. i told her everything from our trip to my decision to leave jake. she questioned me a lot about it, not wanting me to make any hasty decisions. i thought if anyone wouldn't think it was hasty, it would be her. i mean, this has been on my mind for months now, and we've talked about it in so many sessions. this was anything <u>but</u> hasty. i really just need to re-think my therapeutic future with her. i keep coming back to this question, and i feel like that alone should tell me what i need to do.

i ran into drew in the hallway today while i was in the office. the temptation was strong, but i forced myself to just keep it professional. it felt weird, and i think he picked up on it, too. the whole conversation was awkward, to the point that he asked if i was okay. i guess i'm not really hiding the stress of this pending divorce well. i didn't mention it to him. the divorce, i mean. i didn't want to give him false hope or mixed signals. if i'm being honest, i know i'd never like him past the sexual tension. i've thought a lot about those months after i came back to harborvale when jimmy and i broke up, and how i was just looking for love in the arms of all kinds of men. it felt good initially, but that feeling never lasted. i know anything with drew would just be the same. i wasn't built for casual love, anyway. i was made to love with a devotion so deep that it consumes me, even if it breaks me. drew is a nice guy, but we'd never have that kind of love. he was really just a catalyst to me realizing all that i was missing from jake. he helped me to see that i wasn't being loved in the way i needed. for that, i am thankful, but it's time to move on from the fantasy.

i've thought a lot about jimmy this year in the wake of everything. especially the ending of our relationship. all of the regrets and what-ifs i've carried. i think that his greatest show of love for me was letting me go that day, and <u>not</u> fighting for me to stay. it's like he let me go so i could have a chance for something more, because he knew i'd never be all the way happy and secure with him. it's weird for me to say, because i never wanted us to end, but i get it now. i can see it so clearly now that i'm here letting jake go so both of us can have a chance of being happy again because, in reality, neither of us has been happy together for a while now. i'm showing myself love for the first time in what feels like forever. i'm choosing me, and leaving this life behind for something more. whatever that looks like.

May 9, 2024

Hannah stood in front of the mailbox at the entrance to the park by the bay, a thick envelope of legal papers in her hand. It was early morning, with the sun just starting to rise over the water. The park was quiet except for the high-pitched calls of a flock of seagulls flying over the water. She breathed deep the heavy salt air that held a pungent fishy smell on this humid morning.

This was it. With a shaking hand and another deep breath, she dropped the envelope through the slit at the top of the mailbox. The heavy packet landed on a pillow of paper inside with a dull thud. Hannah placed both hands on top of the mailbox and stared down at it. Despite her fears about the future, and the great big unknown laid out in front of her, there were no regrets or second thoughts. All that existed in this moment was a sense of finality.

She followed the path from the parking lot down along the bay, stopping about halfway to take in the beauty of the morning. The early sunshine glittered off the water, and the sky was painted in bright hues of orange and pink. Some stars were still visible overhead, but they'd soon be gone as the sun outshone them. Hannah leaned against the railing, staring up at them. She thought of Jimmy then, how he had loved to teach her all about the stars and planets. When she was outside on a clear night, she would always look for Orion's Belt and sometimes wonder if he was looking up at it, too. Orion's Belt was the easiest constellation to find, the first one he taught her about. Hannah looked for it now, but couldn't seem to find it. She vaguely recalled Jimmy once telling her that it was only visible from late fall to early spring; it was too late in the season to see it now. She frowned slightly about that; she often let herself dream that Jimmy now lived among the stars that made up Orion's Belt, that his soul had become a star like he always hoped would happen upon his death.

Turning back to look out at Highgate City, Hannah realized that it had been almost a year to the day since she read Jimmy's obituary while looking out at this very skyline. All of these memories with Jimmy seemed to flood her mind now, especially his music for some reason. That familiar ache in her core pulsed a little to let her know it was still there, even if it seemed more dull and infrequent than it did before.

On the walk back home, Hannah decided to call Alan to tell him the news. "It's official. The paperwork is in the mail," she declared.

"Wow! That was fast!" Alan remarked. "How do you feel?"

"It was fast, but I think we both needed it to be. I feel a lot better now that it's out of my hands, you know? Now I can really focus on making some plans for my future."

"Any ideas?"

Hannah laughed. "Not really. My mom said I could stay with her for a little while after the house sells. Begrudgingly, but she did say 'yes.' After that, I have no idea."

"You'll figure it out, I know you will," Alan assured her. "I'm happy for you, Hannah. Not that this all happened, but that you put yourself first."

"Thanks. I'm happy for me, too," she told him with a smile beaming across her face. It was true. Despite all the heartache of having to make this decision, she felt uplifted and hopeful for the first time in a long time. The possibility of a life all her own was exciting. "I don't know what I would have done without you this year. I'm so glad you kept looking for me."

"Aw, c'mon now. You're going to make a grown man cry," Alan told her with a laugh.

She laughed back and joked, "I've been known to make a grown man or two cry before."

That made him laugh from his belly. "I'm glad you never lost your sense of humor."

"Well, it's coming back," she told him. "But, seriously, I've realized this year that the people I've surrounded myself with have just not been my people. They've never really understood me, and my joys and pains go largely unnoticed. Not with you, though."

"Ya know, I miss those good ol' days in Riverside Springs. We were such a tight-knit little family back then," Alan said wistfully.

Hannah grinned, losing herself in more memories. "Hey, what was that toast we always used to say? About friends? It was so simple—"

"To friends like these?" Alan offered.

"Yes!" Hannah hollered. "That was it! I loved that, being able to honor our friend group with only a few words. Our family. It was the best time, wasn't it?"

"Yeah, it was a special time," he agreed thoughtfully.

"Ugh, I just want to feel that again," she admitted. "I want to feel completely whole with a group of people. Completely myself."

He let out a short breath, "Me too. When I left Louisiana after my parents died, it didn't feel like home anymore. Riverside

Springs and those people gave me back that feeling. It feels better being back here now with Phoebe and the girls, but I still do miss South Carolina a whole lot."

"You think you'll ever go back seeing that Phoebe's parents are still there?" Hannah asked.

Alan's lips sputtered. "Maybe one day."

As Hannah rounded the corner of her street, the house she had once loved so much came into view. A white wooden sign had appeared in the time she'd been gone. *For sale*, it read in big, red letters. She hesitated a step at the sight of it there, but then a slight grin crept across her lips. It wasn't just a realtor's sign, it was more like a finish line she needed to cross to enter into this next phase of her life.

Hannah's Journal
Saturday, May 11, 2024

as of 2 days ago, the divorce papers are in the mail and the for sale sign is posted on the lawn. there have been a lot of cars driving slowly past the house, which is a little creepy. i've been doing a good job of avoiding the neighbors as i've come and gone from the house. it's been hard enough talking to our friends and family about the divorce, and i don't feel much like talking about it more often than i have to. it's none of their business, anyway.

speaking of—i called my mom a couple of days ago and told her everything. it was just as i expected, complete with the squawking "what?" when i initially told her about the divorce, to the line of questioning about what i had done to save my marriage. even after i told her it was my decision, she made it seem like _he_ was leaving _me_. i shouldn't be surprised, and i didn't bother to argue. she's reluctantly going to let me stay with her whenever the house sells. i promised it wouldn't be for long, only until i can get back on my feet. it's better that way. for both of us.

i've paused my client sessions for right now. i've referred a good bit of them to other therapists, the ones that really don't have anything serious going on. as i've been reviewing files, i can see just how much progress my clients have made with me between the clinic and my private practice. it made me feel good to see that because for a long time i've been feeling so ineffective and like i was floundering in my career. if i do find a way to make it work, then there will be other people looking for help, and i'll rebuild. i'm down to less than half my caseload right now, which feels more manageable. i anticipate L leaving my services soon, too, since she's really just thriving. it's not helping my financial situation, but it's just temporary. i'll have a good chunk of change from the sale of our house. from what i calculated, i'll be able to pay back the rest of what i owe on my student loans, maybe my car, and still have money to live on. that's life-changing, not to have to worry about money like that. i'll be able to secure a place to live with that money, so i can then just focus on everything else i need to figure out. i just have this gut feeling i won't be keeping my practice open. so it makes sense then to start lightening the load.

i've been online looking at apartments, and everything out there is so expensive. i want the money i'm coming into to last. i don't have any single friends that would want to get a place with me. i've been researching cities outside of nj to live. new orleans popped into my mind. i've always been curious about it, and i could see it being a fun place to live with all the live music, art, and parties. plus, i have a therapist friend there, so i wouldn't be totally alone. and alan is only about an hour outside of the city. it would be awesome to live nearby him again, and to be able to get to know his wife and kids. i just have to keep my head out of the clouds right now and come back down to reality. i need to be smart about this.

when i mailed the divorce papers, i wound up spending a good amount of time just walking along the path. i stopped to watch the boats and look at the city coming to life. the stars were still kind of out, and i was thinking a lot about jimmy, about myself, and who i used to be. how far away from that person i found myself, but how i'm getting a little closer every day to her. something clicked in me while i was standing there. a poem. i started writing it in my head, and i've been repeating it to myself all day. it felt so good to be inspired like that again. to be able to express myself creatively in that way. i can't remember the last time i sat down to write anything—a newspaper article, a poem, a short story. i came home and scribbled it down on a scrap piece of paper, but i figured i'd copy it here to have a safe place to keep it.

i think of you most
during the in-between times of the day.
in the early morning when the sun glitters off the
bay with the promise of a fresh start.
oh, the possibility and the adventure
of what lies ahead.
and when the sky is painted in
bright oranges and pinks

in the quiet evening hours.
unapologetic in their fluorescent existence.
the highlight reel of the day.
the way a person could fall in love
at the mere sight of it.
those in-between hours are when
you're most alive to me now,
but you were never my in-between.
you were always my mid-afternoon,
when the sun was at its brightest,
the time of day where all the action was
the vibrancy of our youth.

i had two more dreams about jimmy. one two nights ago, and the other just last night. in the first dream, i was trying desperately to call him, but he either never answered or picked up but wouldn't talk. sometimes he called me but never said a word. in the last part of it, he sat on the edge of my bed just looking at me with such sad eyes. he didn't reach out to me or talk to me. he just sat there. and then in the dream i had last night, he was playing a gig in some bar while i was sitting on a stool watching. he and his bandmates wore facemasks, like the surgical kind doctors wear. at one point, he took his mask off, but his face wasn't his. instead, he looked like something out of tim burton movie. it was freaky!

i think the weirdest thing is that i woke up each time just kind of knowing what he's trying to tell me through these dreams, which is different than the others because i was always left questioning their meaning or what he was trying to communicate to me. if anything at all. but the dreams have evolved now. i can't explain it. it was like, even if we had stayed close, he would've never told me how bad he was getting again, because he wouldn't have wanted me to worry about him. nor would i have recognized the person he'd become. we all change eventually. that's life. jimmy and i always knew each other on a level that others still can't comprehend.

i would've always recognized you, jimmy, even if i were blind and deaf because there are parts of you that will continue to live on in me. and vice versa - parts of me will continue to live on in the memory of your life. we are forever entwined because of the love we shared. that kind of connection is hard to forget. you'll always be one of the main characters in some of the best chapters of my life's story.

maybe that's a good place to start my letter...

Hannah and Jake's house sold quickly to a cash buyer; they couldn't have asked for an easier transaction, but it had all happened way faster than either of them had anticipated. Jake wound up moving to Cedar Cove and into his parents' home. To Hannah, it seemed like a minor miracle she hadn't run into him in her journeys through the area. They hadn't spoken much since the closing date, exchanging only a couple of text messages that were usually about Diesel. Not that there hadn't been attempts by Jake to reach out to her; he kept texting her to see how she was doing, and sometimes to see if she wanted to grab a bite to eat. Hannah left a good number of messages unanswered; they were divorcing for a reason, after all.

Jake made it a point to tell her shortly after they moved out of Bay Point that he had quit his job without having anything to fall back on. He explained to Hannah that he had finally had enough with the demanding hours and the complete lack of recognition. That, and he blamed the job for the dissolution of their marriage. Hannah had mixed feelings about the whole thing. On one hand, she was happy that he had gotten out of there, but she was angry that he still didn't take responsibility for his part in their divorce.

She was upset, too, that it had taken him so long to leave that job when she had been practically begging him to quit for an entire year.

Hannah was living back home in Harborvale with her mom. Her practice was still open, but she was barely seeing clients. A lot of her time was spent apartment hunting. She had looked into every possible apartment complex in New Jersey, but rentals were so expensive. There was money in the bank for her to fall back on now that the house had been sold for way over asking. She paid off all of her debts, and still had a sizable amount left. Hannah wanted to be conservative with that money, though, and not just waste it on rent. She was hopeful that she could find a small home to buy, and use that money as a down payment. That could take a while, and she was in a time crunch.

Since she was certain she would be closing her therapy practice, Hannah eventually expanded her search beyond New Jersey. She had gone into the office just two weeks ago to find a letter from her landlord under the door, letting her know that the rent would nearly double at the end of her lease term, which was only a month away. Hannah researched states up and down the East Coast, because she knew she wanted to be by the water. She, regretfully, hadn't done much traveling to know the kind of place that would make her feel happy and free, so she found it hard to pinpoint a location that might feel like home.

Rubbing the sleep from her eyes, Hannah walked down the stairs from her childhood bedroom. Her nose had followed the scent of coffee into the kitchen, where her mother sat at the table.

"I was wondering how late you were going to sleep!" her mother grumbled as she glared at Hannah from over the newspaper she was reading. "You look like hell."

Hannah stared at the outer pages of the newspaper, stunned but also not surprised that those were the first words of her mother's mouth this morning. Her eyes found the time on the microwave. "It's only 5:30, Mom," she said flatly as she poured a heavy dose of sugar and milk into a mug, followed by coffee.

Her mom grunted. "I took Diesel out for you. He was practically dancing on his tail to get out to pee while you were still sleeping."

Diesel sat at her feet as Hannah took a seat at the table across from her mom. "Right. Thanks," she simply replied. It was best to keep her responses short when her mother was in this kind of mood, as it would minimize any additional criticisms she'd throw her way.

"So what's your plan for today?" her mom asked.

Hannah shrugged. "I'm not sure," she said wearily. This had been the conversation every morning since she'd moved in. She figured her mother just wanted her space back, and she couldn't blame her. Hannah, herself, wanted out in the worst way. "I'll probably send out emails to my clients that I'll be closing the practice down. Find some referrals to send them."

"What a shame. You barely made it a year," her mom clucked.

Hannah sighed. "I know, Mom. It's out of my hands, though."

"Have you found an apartment yet?"

"Not yet, but I can always go stay at the Holiday Inn out on the highway if it's a problem," she replied with a roll of her eyes that her mother missed behind the newspaper.

"Hannah, don't be so dramatic. Please. I'm not in the mood for it today," her mom told her curtly.

Hannah quietly got up from the table, taking her coffee upstairs to start crafting a farewell email to the few clients she had left. Despite how ready she felt to do it, when she sat at her computer, the words just didn't come. She picked up her cell phone and scrolled through her messages, looking for a distraction. When she came to Alan's name, a slight frown formed on her lips; it had been a couple of weeks since they had last spoken to one another. Even then, it had been a quick life update over a text message.

Life had become chaotic not just for Hannah, but also for Alan. His mother-in-law had suffered a heart attack at the end of May. That had prompted Phoebe to take a leave of absence from her job to go to South Carolina to care for her while she recovered from emergency bypass surgery. While she was away, Alan took on the parenting duties in addition to his strenuous work schedule, leaving him utterly exhausted. He told her just the other night that Phoebe was back home in Louisiana, but that he was still the primary parent as she was busy studying for her last few final exams of a master's program she was enrolled in; she would be graduating in August if all went to plan. Hannah admired how Alan and Phoebe worked so well together as a cohesive team, thinking back to when that had been her and Jake.

Knowing how rundown Alan was, she had pulled back from leaning on him so much throughout the sale of their home and the divorce process. She tried to be a support for him, but what he needed more than anything was a babysitter for his girls, not just an ear to talk to. That was all she could offer, being so far away. It was probably for the best that they both focused on their own lives for a little bit, but she couldn't deny that she missed her friend. Hannah frowned again, making a mental note to check in with him later even if it were just a text to say hello. For now, though, she needed to focus on writing this email already. She didn't feel sad like she thought she would, or should. That, more than anything, worried her because being a therapist had been her identity for so long. For right now, that chapter was over. It should be a big moment, but it was more like a quiet letting go.

Hannah is strolling down a stone sidewalk, her eyes fixed on the marbled pattern the sun is making as it shines through the vegetation overhead. She knows this place well because she used to spend hours on end here with Jimmy and her friends. She picks up her eyes and marvels at the empty walkway in front of her. Lush green shrubs line either side of it, while oak trees form an umbrella of shade over the entire expanse of the path. She meanders to the end of it, where she sees a large water fountain. The whole way there, Hannah can feel someone walking beside her. They had been close enough to touch, yet she couldn't for some reason. Nor could she see their face, but she somehow just knew it was Jimmy there with her.

Standing in front of the fountain, she turns to her right, toward the water. There is a long pier jutting out over the bay, with long benches lining each side of it. She looks down again at her feet, suddenly feeling a hand brush lightly against her cheek as it sweeps the hair out of her eyes and behind her ear. Hannah quickly turns to see who had done that, but there is no one there. She feels the presence sweep behind her to her left side, so she snaps her head in that direction to see him standing there.

It is Jimmy. He just stands there in a gray T-shirt with the name of a band on it that she can't quite make out, a black pair of Dickies pants, and worn Airwalk sneakers on his feet. His hands are shoved into his front pockets, his shoulders slightly slumped. Hannah meets his eyes, and he smiles at her crookedly from the corner of his mouth.

Hannah snapped awake in an instant, sitting up fast, her heart pounding in her chest. It took a moment for her to ground herself in the surroundings of her childhood bedroom. When she had calmed down enough, she lay back on her pillow and stared at the ceiling. With the shock having worn off, Hannah quickly fell back asleep.

Hannah is staring down at an envelope lying in her open hands. There is no address or name on it. She turns it over, feeling the thickness and the weight of it. Before her is a gravestone made of light gray granite. She reads the inscription:

James "Jimmy" Taylor
April 22, 1985 – February 25, 2023

She notices an engraving of an acoustic guitar on the right side of the stone, much like the one he used to play. Hannah can feel Jimmy's presence there, just over her shoulder, as she stands in front of his final resting place. When she turns around, though, she doesn't see him there. He can only be felt in this place. She understands now that he brought her here to see this place, just like the park.

Hannah turns back toward the headstone, and her eyes find a familiar face. It's Bonnie, Jimmy's mom. She just stands there watching Hannah curiously, but she doesn't speak to her. For once, there doesn't seem to be any animosity lingering behind her eyes. Hannah reaches out then, putting the envelope into Bonnie's hands. She looks down at it, then back at Hannah, and the two women simply smile at one another.

For the second time that night, Hannah woke up without warning. Tears came to her eyes instantly as she replayed this new dream over again. Somehow, she knew she was holding a letter for Jimmy in her hands. The goodbye letter she had been trying to write for the last year. In her dreams, at least, she had found a way to actually get her words out. She considered why she gave the letter to Bonnie of all people, or why she was being so friendly toward Hannah.

She turned to her other side, contemplating what it meant to have Bonnie in her dream, and why it left her feeling so unsettled to see her in that way. She closed her eyes tight and forced herself to fall back asleep.

Hannah walks through the hallway from a room at the very back of a house. It feels familiar to her, like she's been here before. Like she could close her eyes and still navigate its layout with ease. She has the feeling that someone is following her, but when she turns around, no one is there. As she walks, she peers into a bathroom on her right. Her eyes immediately fix on a beautiful stained glass window at the top of the far wall, featuring simple square panels in rows of varying colors. Bright oranges, blues, greens, and reds. Across the hall is another room, a smaller bedroom than the one she had emerged from. As she plods along the cool hardwood floor, Hannah crosses through the kitchen and then the living room with a brick fireplace along the wall to her right. She can hear music coming from outside somewhere. It sounds like the simple strumming of a guitar. She opens the front door, stepping out onto the wide, white-painted front porch. To her right are two rocking chairs with a table between them. The music is still playing, but Hannah can't find the source of it, so she decides to just sit in one of the chairs and listen. Looking out beyond the porch, her gaze drifts to a bright pink duplex diagonally across the street. It was a house she used to sit and stare at for hours, its vibrant color drawing her in like a moth to the sun.

Hannah's eyes shot open. Air filled her lungs, but it felt heavy like water and made it hard to breathe. She sat up hastily, grabbing at her bedsheets and gulping oxygen. Her hands found the soft fur of Diesel's back and lightly stroked him as her breathing returned to normal. She slowly reacquainted herself with the room around her, despite it being a shell of what it used to be. Hannah looked across the room to see her suitcases still packed, catching her exhausted reflection in the mirror she had propped up on an old bookcase.

Her mind replayed each dream over again, and suddenly, Hannah knew what Jimmy was trying to tell her. He was pointing her in the direction she needed to go now, where she could start her life over again. A place she could heal and find herself all at once. Hannah needed to follow her True North back to the place she had once called home. Back to Riverside Springs.